PASSION AWAKENED

He drew her to him. His body was damp from the heat. Its unanticipated contact shocked her. . . . Tenderly, seekingly, his mouth touched hers. And she was distracted. The skin of his lips was as tender as a new spring leaf, she mused. Who would have thought that? They moved across her mouth. A quiver she had never felt before snaked into her stomach. A little alarmed, she pulled away and heard him groan.

"There." His soft, sweet tone was musical, the voice she had always admired, and his face so very close that she saw only shadowed planes and golden angles lit by the setting sun. "Say my name."

"Jacob," she whispered obediently.

"Good," he whispered back. His mouth covered hers, wet and urgent. She closed her eyes. He was too, too close. Too pressing. A pressing heat, heat like the brutal summer's day that lay thickly over the room, enveloped her body.

He pulled at her lower lip, released it, then parted her mouth with his tongue. Its tip touched her teeth, then probed around them and searched above them and between them. He touched her tongue. She gasped.

She had seen people kiss, a little, but hadn't imagined it would feel like this. Nor had she thought that a kiss would taste—that a man would taste—so good.

WILD INDIGO

JUDITH STANTON

HarperPaperbacks
A Division of HarperCollins*Publishers*

HarperPaperbacks
A Division of HarperCollins*Publishers*
10 East 53rd Street, New York, NY 10022-5299

ISBN 0-06-108707-6

First printing: October 1998

Printed in the United States of America

❖ 10 9 8 7 6 5 4 3 2 1

To my parents, Clyde and Betty Jane Phillips,
sixth and seventh generation descendants
of Moravians, and oral storytellers
of the first order.

ACKNOWLEDGMENTS

With grateful thanks to Virginia Kantra Ritchey and Kit Stewart, who shepherded me through this story from its very beginnings, and to my agent, Pamela Ahearn, who steered it in the right direction. Many have contributed factual material and insights: retired Salem College history professor and guide at Salem, Inc., Dr. A. Hewson Michie; psychologist Dr. Judith Brill; pediatrics nurse Winoka Plummer; architect Josh Gurlitz; biologist Robin Gurlitz; and librarian Kathleen Thompson. The wonderfully trained guides at Old Salem tirelessly answered my questions about buildings, clothing, food, lighting, and the myriad of other authentic details of daily life available at this restored site. Most thanks of all go to my husband, Peter Harkins, for supporting this latest dream and for giving me the best line in the book.

WILD INDIGO

Salem, North Carolina, June 1780

The lot said *nein*. No.

Not again, Jacob Blum thought in disbelief, palming the slender wooden reed that held the decisive slip of paper.

Casting the lot had already denied him two possible brides—the one his fellow leaders in the Moravian community had recommended and another he had thought might benefit his children. With this third draw, the lot denied him even the opportunity to travel to Pennsylvania to seek a helpmate there.

Expressionless, he handed the paper across the table to Elder Frederick Marshall.

The senior Moravian's face fell as he confirmed Jacob's third rejection. "Perhaps we have failed again to ask the proper question, Brother Blum."

Sister Elisabeth Marshall, sitting beside her husband, discreetly cleared her throat. " 'Tis not as if you were a Single Brother who could marry at his leisure. You have three children."

Jacob buried his head in his hands and laughed. His four fellow Elders shuffled in their seats, obviously uncomfortable with his outburst. Or perhaps with his awkward situation. Who among them had last sought a wife in vain?

And who had ever needed one more?

Jacob tried to muffle his laughter as Brother Marshall tapped the reed on the table and Sister Marshall coughed. Single Brother Philip Schopp paged noisily through his precious papers. Across the table, Single Sister Rosina Krause set her round face in disapproval.

"I cannot think laughter seemly in this matter, Brother Blum," she said in her soft German.

"No, of course not."

But better to laugh than to rail against the lot. If this test of his faith or endurance continued, it would drive him mad.

Two months ago, Jacob and his fellow Elders had first cast the lot in the hope of finding him a new wife. For the last hundred years, Moravians had cast lots to seek God's will in important matters. Jacob had not yet been born when the lot ordained that they embark from Germany for Pennsylvania. He had been a lad when the lot granted them permission to seek a new settlement in the North Carolina wilderness. He had been a young husband and father when the lot approved his move to the new community of Salem.

Once Salem was settled, Moravians continued to rely on the lot to decide where to build a house or store, whether to start a new school, whom to join in marriage. In a simple religious ceremony, an Elder would draw a reed containing a slip of paper marked *ja* or *nein* or left blank. The blank slip instructed them to ask the question later or frame it in a different way.

Jacob had witnessed this ceremony many times—too many times of late, he thought. So far, divine wisdom had not guided him to the wife he sorely needed.

The Elders had first put forward Eva Reuter, the comely Single Sister who taught in the fledgling school for girls. She knew something of children. The lot came up *nein*.

Last month the Elders had begged him to propose someone himself.

The widowed Sister Baumgarten, he had said.

"That would put seven children all together under one roof, Jacob." Marshall had raised his objection evenly.

"You seem to think that seven under her care would be worse than my three alone with me," Jacob had said. "At least hers mind."

Her ability with children had never been put to the test, for the lot said *nein* again.

So on this hot June afternoon, the Elders had asked whether he should go to the Moravian settlement in Pennsylvania. There were suitable prospects there.

Now the lot had squelched even that thin hope.

"Brother Marshall, my children must have a mother."

The two women Elders nodded sagely. Frederick Marshall returned the reed to the deep wooden lot bowl that sat on the hand-rubbed oak table.

"True enough," Single Brother Philip Schopp spoke up. "After what Nicholas did last week, I may have to ask you to take him from our new school for boys."

Jacob stiffened in his older son's defense. "What has he done?"

The schoolmaster sniffed. "Nicholas has been . . . difficult."

Jacob met that accusation head-on. "Difficult! How?"

"Your offspring denounced the little Tatum brothers as Tories and then formed an alliance with the other boys to shun them."

Jacob felt the tension in his neck. But the hothead had done worse. "Is that all?"

"No. He did on one occasion pelt some other boys with pumpkin seeds launched from a spoon."

"Not smaller boys!" Jacob said, half wanting to thrash his son, but also amused by his antics.

"No. Only boys big enough to fight back," Schopp answered, his tone sardonic. "I recovered the spoon and told him to take it home."

Jacob could not hide a grin. So that was what had happened to their spoons. No doubt Nicholas had subjected his victims to more than one assault. Jacob would have to confront his mischief maker. It would be hard. His older son was much as he had been at twelve, smart and bored and full of beans. Jacob himself had never been made to mind, and he no longer knew how to control the boy, short of trussing him up and stuffing him in the loft.

Jacob needed a wife's advice. His son needed a mother's softer influence.

"Moreover," Marshall interjected, "Brother Bonn says your second son is too thin. Is he sickly?"

"Not sick," Jacob said. "But yes, Matthias is thin.

That is why I suggested Sister Baumgarten, who cooks for all those children."

Rosina Krause gave Jacob a self-conscious look over her imported spectacles. "There is one other problem."

Jacob shook his head, only too aware of what was coming next. "My daughter."

Sister Krause lowered her voice. "Anna Johanna—" Almost involuntarily, she held her hand up to her face. "She—"

"I know. She stinks."

Again the four Elders nodded as one.

Jacob rubbed his neck uneasily. His sons posed problems, he'd admit it. But his four-year-old daughter's peculiarity had defeated him. He did not understand it. He knew for a fact that the only adversity in her charmed life was the loss of her mother. Was that adversity enough to explain her fear?

"She will not let me bathe her. I cannot even get her out of that dress. When I try, she screams." The men grimaced, but the women muttered as if they understood. They couldn't, Jacob thought. "No, I mean screams, then holds her breath till she turns blue."

Sister Krause leaned forward. "So what does Brother Bonn—"

"Our esteemed doctor says naught. Or rather, he suggests naught. He says that in time she will recover from the death of her mother. He says in time she will grow out of it. At this rate, she'll outgrow that dress first. Meanwhile . . ." Jacob shrugged.

"Meanwhile, Brother Blum, you need a wife." Frederick Marshall resumed control of the meeting.

"Very well. We will consult the lot again next meeting."

"Next meeting!" Jacob exploded. "Two months have passed since we last cast the lot. We lost Christina a year ago."

"And you should be in mourning." Marshall pursed his lips in admonition.

"Believe me," Jacob said sharply, "I'm in mourning every day." Thinking of his sweet wife, his friend from childhood, he softened his tone. His flare of temper sullied her memory. This haste to marry did, too. But without her gentle guidance, his family had gone awry. "My children need a mother. I need the lot cast again—now."

"We never rush the lot," Marshall reminded him.

"We haven't rushed it. We—I—have been very patient with the lot. All three lots. I will abide by its decision. But my children's needs are foremost now."

Marshall whispered to his wife and then to Philip Schopp.

"Brother Blum, 'tis unprecedented." Marshall spoke in the voice reserved for Sunday service. "To seek the lot too often questions the Savior's will. Waiting may be to a purpose. But if you will stand outside, we will consider your request."

"Very well." Jacob knew what that meant. Elders had to stand outside whenever the Board pondered a matter that bore on them. He buttoned his coat and left the *Gemein Haus*, where the Elders had their meeting room and the Single Sisters also lived.

Stepping into the afternoon heat in Salem Square, Jacob let out a frustrated breath. He could no more stand and wait than raise his hand and part the sea. Passing Brother Schopp's modest house where the new school for boys was held, he smiled at the thought of Nicholas launching pumpkin-seed artillery. Inventive boy, like his father.

Who should be a more sober father. Christina had kept them all in hand. He repressed pangs of loss and need. He missed her, and had little hope of replacing her sweet company and tender affections with this new bride.

He passed the new cistern, which he had finished just last month. A farmer drew water for placid red oxen, perhaps safe now from the war. A British soldier filled a bucket for his sweat-streaked horse. His small detachment had arrived just this forenoon, part of the ceaseless flow of soldiers from both sides that alternately flooded the town, all but occupying it at times.

Jacob's hard work had paid off. The town's water system—his design, his labor—was working. For all concerned, it seemed.

He strode on, across the town's spacious central Square, past a small structure that doubled as market stand and firehouse. His firehouse. An engine, ordered from England, had been delayed by the war, and he had designed an interim firewagon too.

"Guten Tag," an older neighbor addressed him in German.

"Good afternoon," said a younger Married Brother, one of the few men besides himself who had learned much English. At least now some in Salem could mingle with backcountry settlers and not stand out as foreign.

"Jacob," Samuel Ernst called out, bearing down

on him from his little one-room leather shop. "Are not the Elders meeting?"

"Yes, Samuel. At this very moment."

"You are not with them." Samuel backed him up against the split-rail fence that surrounded the Square.

"The lot," Jacob said in a private voice. "They're discussing whether to cast the lot for me."

"Ah. Again? Mine was answered first time." Samuel, who had married Eva Reuter just last week, gave him a comradely punch in the arm.

Jacob grunted obligingly.

Samuel settled his short, compact body against the fence.

"I still need a house for the night watch."

"We know that," Jacob said, careful not to promise what he could not deliver.

"Now more than ever." Samuel furtively inclined his head toward two Redcoats walking up from the Tavern, spurs clicking on the plank walk. Jacob had seen them earlier. Their British detachment had fled a losing action near the South Carolina border and stopped here to replenish supplies. Their presence for days on end, and that of other soldiers, had led the unarmed Moravian community to increase the number of guards posted at night. The new guards needed a place to meet and organize. Alerting two hundred people to danger was no small task.

Although Jacob understood his friend's concern, he had to caution him. "That house is more a matter for my Supervisory Committee, which meets next week."

As town planner and builder, Jacob ran the

Supervisory Committee and represented it to the Elders. To his thinking, the Elders represented the soul of their communally run society, and the supervisors its pulse. All business matters, including pricing goods and building structures, came to his supervisors first.

Five years ago, when the town was new, he had relished his duties as leader, builder, dreamer. Now with familiarity and the war, he shouldered them.

"All the more reason for you to press for it."

Jacob's gaze followed the soldiers. "I will build you your watch house, Samuel."

"A simple log hut will do."

Jacob barely heard his friend. The soldiers had, very inappropriately, fallen in step with a young, pretty Single Sister, burdened with linens from the tavern.

The woman gracefully acknowledged the men, her white collar and apron banners of purity against her modest rose-colored dress. Jacob saw the stouter man take her by the arm. She jerked away.

"Samuel," Jacob barked. "Come!"

In ten strides, he blocked the two men's way. Samuel caught up and stood behind him.

"We will help our Sister, thank you," Jacob said sternly.

He wasn't about to reveal a Sister's name, although this one's escaped him in the tension of the moment. He braced himself to protect her.

Quickly the soldiers stepped back, hands down and palms facing outward. Sometimes he forgot how large a man he was. His anger waned as fast as it had risen. Up close, these men were young, their tired faces drained of color. Their red coats, which looked crisp and ominous from afar, betrayed their recent battle with a ragged rip, a dangling button, a torn epaulet.

"We were just adding this." Stepping up smartly, the young corporal held out a wadded-up garment stained with blood. "From our lieutenant."

"Very well," Jacob said, and took it without looking. It had the feel of fine clothing, finer than he was wont to wear.

The soldiers clicked back down the plank walk. Jacob watched for a moment, then glanced at the young woman, sure he saw alarm flash across her face. As suddenly, she hid it and favored him with gleaming amber eyes. Wild eyes. Wolf's eyes. They danced, untamed, amused, and his heart pumped an extra beat.

He looked away for modesty's sake, and looked back for courtesy. Her eyes matched, he noted soberly, an errant wisp of amber hair that strayed from under the crisp white *Haube* that capped her head.

Then he realized that noticing her hair was not a sober thought. He tried to suppress it, but his gaze swept her bright, framed face. He fought for control. Each and every Sister had to wear the *Haube*, he reminded himself.

But few wore it to such effect.

"I thank you, Brother Blum." Her arresting, throaty voice contradicted her dancing eyes. "But they meant no harm."

"They had no right to threaten you, Sister Mary—" Jacob, caught off guard by his wayward thoughts, cast about for the rest of her name.

Magdalena, perhaps. But Mary was all he could remember.

"Margaretha," Samuel prodded.

Of course, Jacob thought. Mary Margaretha, the foundling. She had no last name. He remembered the fiery night when he had rescued her, a wild white child in a deerskin Indian shift, hoarding dried pumpkin and sweet potatoes in a stolen sack.

Rescued or, some might say, captured. That night she had struggled wordlessly, clawing him and kicking her heels into his shins. He and his wife had calmed her down. Later the community had taken her in, giving her a home and a Christian name. But no surname. To this day, no one knew who she was, apart from the obvious fact that she was white. Not even she could say.

Well. His little thief had grown into a woman.

". . . and neither do you, Brother Blum," he heard her saying sweetly as his attention snapped back to the here and now.

"Neither do I?"

Her bold gaze trapped him, then dropped to her arm where his free hand gripped her sleeve. Her elbow. He let it go as if it were a stick that turned out to be a snake.

"Forgive me, Sister Mary," he muttered hastily. Single Brothers and Sisters lived separately—were kept separate—for a reason. To say nothing of overwhelmed Widowers. "I meant no—"

"Everyone calls me Retha," she said lightly, snatching the stained shirt from his hands and spinning on her heel, linens scooped up to her breast.

Samuel Ernst bolted after her, opening the separate door to the part of the *Gemein Haus* where the Single Sisters lived. She disappeared inside, the herringboned wooden door banging behind her.

Jacob stood, thunderstruck, in the middle of the Square in the hot June sun. The little wildcat! She had been here all along, through his long wait, through every lot that had been cast. A Single Sister, and available. He should have thought of her himself, but hadn't because she had lived so quietly among them. Because, to him, she was still that lost child. And because Sister Krause had never mentioned her. She had even denied there were any suitable single women.

He could see for himself that was not so.

How old would Sister Mary—Sister Retha—be by now? They had never been sure of her age. As a child, she had neither known nor said. She had spoken little in those days, struggling to learn German. In time, she told of years spent with the Cherokee, the tribe that found her and took her in when she was too young to keep an account of her age. Today she could be seventeen, nineteen, twenty. Of an age to marry, surely.

Still, what did she know of children? Until her recent marriage, Sister Eva Reuter had taught the girls. Perhaps the Sisters had kept Retha away from children on purpose. Rumors of trouble had stalked her from the first. Rumors that she couldn't speak, started fires, had been raised by wolves.

Nonsense to all of that, he thought. Especially to the fires. As the town's planner and builder, he had organized all fire protection after a rash of minor fires. If a chimney so much as clogged, he knew of it.

And clearly, Sister Retha had learned to speak German—with his older son's spirit and his little daughter's sass. Jacob had the feeling Retha was either's equal on their worst day.

The equal of his children! It was a dangerous, powerful thought. He let it rumble around in his head, like thunder from a distant storm. Dangerous. He could fight fire with fire. Powerful. He could manage unruly children with a woman who had lived more wildly than anything in their wildest dreams.

"Jacob," Samuel called. "They want you back."

Lost in thought, Jacob scowled at his friend's amused face.

"Your Board. The Elders." Samuel pointed to Philip Schopp waving from the door of Unity House. "They want you."

Resolutely Jacob crossed the plank walk, for once barely noticing how well his crew had built something. In the meeting room inside *Gemein Haus*, the Elders arranged themselves along both sides of the long, narrow table. He hung up his flat-brimmed hat and sat among them.

"Brother Blum, we have consulted the lot," Marshall began. He turned the wooden bowl reverently in his hands. "We must meet at the earliest time next week. You may ask then about a wife."

Beside him, Elisabeth Marshall looked glum. "We recommend no one, however. We have come to the end of our tether. The only other widow is too old to take on children."

Jacob felt her unspoken words: *children such as yours.*

"And Sister Reuter, whom the lot denied you, truly was our only candidate," Rosina Krause added, her round face firm. Jacob all but snorted. He knew better. What was the woman trying to hide? "The marriageable among us are spoken for or already married. We have always had more men."

Frederick Marshall scanned the Elders' faces and stopped at Jacob's face. "We can ask at the farm settlements."

"Unless you have a better idea," Sister Krause added.

He did. Jacob closed his eyes. Amber eyes dared him, amber hair curled. A slim crooked elbow filled his hand.

"There is one other," he said, smiling with relief.

That night, Retha strained to hear the young wolf's cry. In the dark, close heat of her attic dormitory, she held her breath and listened. Nothing yet. Around her, half a dozen girls rustled under light sheets as they settled down to sleep. Someone whispered, someone answered, but she couldn't make out their words. Gossip, no doubt. It used to be about her. Someone shushed them, and the attic door shut softly.

Pale moonlight shafted through a deep-set dormer window, but Retha needed little light. She rolled out of bed and crawled to the door, the hem of her simple gown bunched in one hand. The door opened quietly, and she praised her own foresight. Bear grease on hinges had done the trick.

Two flights of steep stairs led to the kitchen in

the basement. On the first-floor landing, she paused. Only the sound of someone snoring drifted down the stairs. Old Sarah Holder, already asleep. How many times had Sister Sarah failed to stop her from excursions in the night?

This time, Retha thought, she had good reason to go. She listened again for the wolf. No sound, but she felt its call.

Downstairs, the kitchen's clay tiles cooled her feet. She could smell supper's cabbage and burnt ashes from spent fires. Moonlight seeped through high windows, lighting neat rows of tables set for morning. But the great hearth's black maw revealed nothing. The larder's door was black too. She knew its contents well. She opened it and took a little bear grease, a knob of forcemeat, a small marrow bone.

She hadn't taken a thing in years, she thought, justifying herself. And tonight her cause was a good one. Half-healed, her young wolf was far from independent. Its wild golden eyes, trusting and wary all at once, stirred her soul. One day on a woodland search for dyes, she had seen a flash in the corner of her vision. A gray shape had dived into the dark recesses of a nearby cave. She had followed, coaxing it to her with a small piece of salt bacon she had brought for a meal.

Tonight she wrapped its food in a length of muslin, knotted the cloth around her wrist, and left the house. The air was hot, heavy with rain that would not fall. She slipped across the Square, crouching along the fence line, one eye out for watchman Samuel Ernst. Sure enough, he turned the corner, a great conch shell in one hand. Off and on all spring, soldiers being everywhere, he would sound it to alert the town. But never because he sighted her. Unafraid, she knelt behind a newly planted linden tree.

She watched Brother Ernst peer down a narrow alley between two half-timbered homes before looking straight at the little tree that hid her. Or at her. She stilled herself. For the longest time, he stared, then started toward her. She gripped her package tighter. A raucous burst of voices stopped him in midstride. He hurried toward the Tavern.

Safe again. Her fingers eased their grip, and she scooted across the dusty street, flattening herself against the rough brick-and-timber wall of one of the homes.

Brother Blum's home, she thought, with unaccustomed pleasure. He had been odd today, a great golden bear rushing to her rescue when she needed none. How his square-jawed handsome face had flushed when she pointed to his hand holding her arm fast.

Samuel Ernst disappeared into the Tavern. She slipped past Brother Blum's house and onto the sloping field that led to Tanner's Run, the creek that fed the Red Tannery. She passed the bark sheds, the scouring building, and the vats.

Tonight at *Singstunde*, the evening song service, Brother Blum had made up for his earlier awkwardness. As his rich baritone lofted through the oak-beamed ceilings of the *Saal*, his gaze had riveted her to her bench. Why look at her now? she wondered. Always before, he gazed off into the air when he sang, rapt, enraptured. For years she had watched him, listening with hushed admiration, wishing she could learn German faster, wishing she could sing like that.

Wishing a man like him would take her from the Single Sisters into a home of her own.

Not Brother Blum himself, of course. Until just last year, he had had that plump, happy wife, the first Moravian woman to soothe her fears. The one who died in the smallpox epidemic, leaving him in sole charge of their dreadful children. Everyone was talking about Jacob Blum's problems with them. Carefully, because he was an Elder. Even kindly, because he was well liked. But talking all the same.

Barefoot, she welcomed the creek's lukewarm water as she crossed it. A dwindling flow glinted in the moonlight. Whimpers greeted her as the young wolf propped on its front legs and dragged itself toward her.

Cautious, it slurped bear grease off her palm. When she teased it with the forcemeat, it growled.

"You're getting stronger, girl," she said, pleased with its show of spirit. One hugely swollen hind leg grazing the ground, it lurched onto three rangy legs, struggling to wag its tail and balance on three huge feet all at once.

So brave, she thought, with a catch in her throat. And like her, a foundling.

Downstream, she had come across its pack, mangled by some farmer scared of wolves, and left for buzzard bait. The cruelty and waste tore at her heart.

Still wary, the young wolf let her stroke its plush fur.

Leaving it to gnaw a marrow bone, she lifted her gown to clear the creek. She was so glad to be outside. Down here the air was almost cool. She had never understood why white men slept in houses. On hot nights the Cherokee would lift bark flaps to the evening breeze. They had been her family, and she missed them, even though she had never truly been one of them.

Life had been simple, and she had been free, before the soldiers had massacred the clan that had adopted her.

Where the meadow leveled out and the grass had been grazed short, she spun in place. She hadn't been old enough to join the ball-play dance of the Indians who had raised her. Perhaps they wouldn't have taught it to her, a white child. But they had let her watch. She remembered its stately rhythm, their hypnotic chants, all day and through the night. And tonight she danced as women danced, advancing toward men who weren't there for her, and whirling and dancing away.

In her mind she heard the tribe's soft, insistent drum and their gourd shakers' happy rattle. Her body moved to memory.

"Sister Mary Margaretha!"

Rosina Krause's harsh whisper stunned Retha to a stop.

"Not only have you no permission to be out—" Rosina continued.

"—but there are soldiers everywhere, dear." Sarah Holder shakily took her arm. "Redcoats, Tories, deserters."

"Their persuasion wouldn't matter a jot if they laid their hands on a pretty young thing like you," Rosina scolded.

Retha's joy from the dance curdled. What if the Sisters had seen her wolf? She stole a glance at the creek. No sign of it now. Breathing in little gasps, she lowered her head.

On her shoulder, she felt Sarah Holder's trembly hand. Old age, Retha thought, hoping she had not frightened that sweet old woman and wishing she had been more discreet.

"I didn't mean to alarm you." She had not meant to anger them either. But she would leave the house again for her wolf. She willed it to hide, be safe, be well until she could come back with more morsels from the pantry.

Slowly, deferring to Sister Sarah's arthritic tread, she walked up the field toward Brother Blum's house.

"You have gone too far this time, Mary Margaretha," Rosina Krause said softly. "What were we thinking to let you roam the woods for dyes?" The measured scolding raked Retha's nerves.

"Even that is far too dangerous now," Sarah added solemnly.

Retha bit back words. It was not dangerous for her. They could never know how safe she was, her feet silent on secret paths as Singing Stones had taught her.

"My thought exactly," Rosina said, brisk with authority. "You have worried me all spring. You take too many chances, Mary Margaretha. Traugott Bagge's store has no need of so many dyes."

"And the rest of us, we can do without," Sarah added.

Sarah's hand on her shoulder, Retha plodded up the slope.

"Out in the backcountry, people have been killed while sitting at their own hearths," Rosina said ominously. "We are fortunate neither side has occupied our town. It may yet come to that."

Sarah nodded her nervous agreement. " 'Twill be safer for you here, dear, and we will feel so much better."

Rosina went on, ignoring Sarah's concern. "I will not even ask what you were doing out at this late hour!"

Good, Retha thought. Because she had no intention of telling. But her mind raced. How would she care for her wolf?

As they squeezed through the alley, a door slammed shut. Sarah shrieked, Rosina jumped, and Retha's heart pounded.

Caught, and caught again.

"I came to help," a deep melodic baritone sounded around the corner. Jacob Blum's voice! His large body loomed over Retha and her keepers. Her eyes well adjusted to the night, Retha peered at the massive shape to make sure it was him.

It was. Inspecting the alley, he held up his torch. The older women moved into its light, closing ranks in front of Retha.

"Sisters," he began, with a note of surprise on seeing women out after dark. "Is aught the matter?" He identified them one by one. "Sister Krause. Sister Holder. And Sister—?"

He lifted his torch higher but obviously couldn't see past them to her. Retha didn't want him to. Lowering her head to hide her face, she saw a waterfall of white. Her shift. It shone in the torch's light. Brother Blum would think her brazen as a nanny goat. This afternoon she had taken a certain delight in embarrassing him. He didn't look embarrassed now.

She was in a fine pickle. Best to own up.

She lifted her eyes to his. "I fear 'tis I, Brother Blum."

Jacob suppressed a laugh with difficulty. His prospective bride sounded contrite, but her eyes weren't.

"Sister Retha," he nodded courteously, marshaling his amusement as the Sisters tried to hide her thin summer shift behind their outspread skirts. Too little and too late. He had glimpsed her dancing, and the sight had propelled him into the night. For her safety, he told himself. "I trust that you are quite all right."

"I am very well, thank you."

"Ah. I was thinking of the soldiers this afternoon."

"What soldiers?" the older women asked in unison.

Jacob noticed Retha move from one bare foot to the other. "Two soldiers blocked Sister Retha's way across the Square this afternoon and I—"

"No, they didn't." Retha cut him off. "I was safe as safe could be. They only brought more laundry—"

"—and I sent them on their way," Jacob concluded.

The two older women stepped aside with her, and all three whispered violently. Jacob couldn't make out their words, but he knew trouble when he saw it, Retha's—and his.

Lantern light gilded her hair, which flowed unbound over her shoulders and down her back. Lush, beautiful hair. It was a sight for her husband and no one else. He looked away, but not soon enough. How it had fanned in the moonlight as she danced. His insides twisted with longing to touch it.

A man should have a woman. He needed one. This one.

He had no idea why Sister Retha would have crossed the creek, but he had seen it all, wakeful and restless, thinking about the complaints made against his children at his meeting with the Elders. Moonlight washed the night, but they slept soundly. Even Anna Johanna, whose sad little dress he had just hung up to dry.

The three women returned, grimly silent. He hadn't caught a whispered word but recognized the tone. Chastisement. Retha was in trouble. Somehow his presence made it worse.

Of course. Sister Krause knew that he had asked for Retha by the lot. Now she found Retha outside at night, half-dressed.

And he had the great misfortune just then to step out of his house. What was Sister Krause thinking?

For that matter, what should *he* think?

He tried to catch Retha's gaze, but she studied the plank walk. Defiantly, he thought. When the

Sisters nudged her to leave, Jacob offered to escort them all across the Square.

"Thank you," said Sister Krause, firmly placing herself between him and Retha.

Jacob recognized the tactic. The Single Sisters were formidable in defense of their own. At the low stoop of the Sisters House, Jacob pleasantly said his goodnights in order of seniority. "Good night, Sister Holder. Good night, Sister Krause." Then he glanced down.

An enticingly slender, outrageously bare foot paused at the threshold.

What *could* he think?

"Good night, Sister Retha," he mustered.

She looked at him with daring, questioning eyes darkened by the night. Intimate eyes.

His heart leaped. She wanted something from him, but what?

"Good night, Brother Blum," she whispered, and disappeared from him for the second time that day.

Her unasked question kept him awake till moonset.

Retha had thought she could bear blood.

Against the hot afternoon light flooding the scullery of *Gemein Haus,* she held up the lieutenant's dripping linen shirt and shuddered. Blood stained one shoulder down to the narrow tucks that marched across its breast. The brown stain reminded her queasily of the blood oozing from her wolf's injured leg.

Shaking her head to dispel a fear she couldn't name, she drenched the shirt in the waist-high wooden washtub. Better to think about her present predicament than allow that nameless fear to gnaw at her. To think about the Single Sisters catching her last night, about facing the consequences this morning in Rosina Krause's immaculate office, about losing freedoms she had worked for all these years.

Sister Sarah Holder had broken the news. "You know we have only your best interests at heart."

"We need help in the laundry anyway," Rosina Krause added.

"But my dyes—"

"Your dyes and whatever else you were up to last night have gotten you into a great deal of trouble."

"Trouble! The town depends on my dyes. I make money for us." Retha ground her teeth. She knew more about dyes than anyone in Salem. After the town's appointed dyer had been dismissed, she had supplied Traugott Bagge's store.

"That's not the trouble I meant," Sister Rosina said.

Her tone sparked rebellion in Retha's heart. For a moment she considered the stoic forbearance she had learned from the Cherokee. She had done no wrong.

"Besides, there really is a lot of laundry since Sister Eva has left us to become Sister Ernst," old Sarah added cheerfully.

After a childhood wearing practical deerskins, Retha despised doing laundry. Being cooped up in the dank scullery with strangers' sweaty clothes, harsh lye, and dirty water was an unjust punishment.

"I have done no wrong," she protested.

"Don't mock us, Sister Retha," Rosina Krause said mildly.

"I'm not mocking you. I wouldn't. But what have I done?"

"We don't know what you do, where you go, or why. But we know it is not safe. You're safe here, and needed here."

"Besides, Sister, everyone knows you're of an age—" Sarah's wrinkled face turned crimson.

"Of an age!"

"Of an age where we've found it wise to help the younger of our Single Sisters stay on the path," Sarah had concluded decorously.

Water from the washtub slopping around her,

Retha realized at last what they suspected. An offense so serious they hadn't even named it in the dark. They thought that she had gone out to meet a man. She hadn't. She wouldn't. No man would ask her. Samuel Ernst hadn't, nor had a host of Single Brothers before him.

Not that she had wanted the men who hadn't asked. If it hadn't been for Brother Blum's celestial singing, she would hardly have noticed a man in the town. No, she wanted freedom to do her work. And now for the first time, she wanted urgently to escape the crowded *Gemein Haus* into a house of her own.

And she wanted what her friend Eva had found—love.

Plunging the lieutenant's shirt under soapy water, she scrubbed its stains against the built-in washboard. Let its ridges bark her knuckles raw. How she loathed the rusty sight, the coppery smell of blood. She closed her eyes on an older, darker memory of a blood-stiffened deerskin dress. But only for a moment would she let that memory drag her spirits down.

She ran the soppy mess through creaking wooden wringers, dunked it, scrubbed it, wrung it out. Over and over. Laundry had been one of Eva Reuter's chores. Now she was Married Sister Eva Ernst. Last month the lot had permitted stocky Samuel Ernst to seek Eva's hand in marriage. Pink-cheeked, plump, and fluttering, she accepted. After that Sunday service, they were formally betrothed, and the next week, married.

Samuel had wanted Eva, and Eva had wanted him, Retha thought dreamily, escaping for a moment the burden of her chore. For the hundredth time, she wondered if romance would ever come her way. Not likely, not among these Moravians. They had taken her in and raised her. But then, they baptized slaves. Like the slaves they bought, baptized, and ultimately freed, she would stay an outsider, tainted by her years among the Cherokee.

She held the white shirt up to the window. It was clean, almost as good as new, but the work left her unsatisfied. She preferred messy dyebaths and all those beautiful colors—rose, amber, indigo. She hated laundry. A sense of futility swamped her. But she would not give in to it. She never had. She lifted her chin, hung the shirt out to dry, and washed for supper.

By the time Retha slipped into the *Saal* for *Singstunde*, a low red sun still parched the streets of town. Not even the room's thick brick and timber walls warded off the long day's heat.

Fanning herself with her hand, Rosina Krause scowled as Retha squeezed beside her on the bench. "You are late."

"I had to put my wash back on the line."

Rosina's lips made a small O of disapproval in her round face. "You should have pegged it properly."

Behind a cupped hand, Retha whispered, "I did. But Sister Baumgarten's cow didn't notice that when she charged through."

Rosina shushed her as the choir burst into song, flute and oboe voices weaving melody around the day's concerns. Heat rose from the benches, from the floor. Retha bowed her head.

What a day. What a couple of days. Sister Rosina

would think she prayed. Perhaps, Retha thought, she did. Perhaps these songs were prayers, as Cherokee chants had once seemed to her. Tonight Brother Blum's perfect baritone grounded the choir's evening offering. Song sharpened the angles of his jaw, lightened his wide, serious brow, softened his generous mouth. She had heard him a thousand, thousand times, his voice rich and full as water under rocks, as powerful and secret.

Surely he would help her.

Jacob joined the singers at the front of the *Saal.* He welcomed *Singstunde,* the hour of song before time for bed, would have welcomed it more if the close, hot room hadn't been crowded with Redcoats. These latest troops would no doubt lodge in Salem for a time before marching on. Far from repelling either these British or the Continentals, the Moravians' neutrality seemed to draw troops to the town—as an oasis, as a trading center, almost as a place to rest. Inevitably, they brought rumor and suspicion.

He was sick of intrigue, wariness, news of battle, and he would rather have no reminders of them during services. Although, on second thought, better the soldiers come here than occupy the town or plunder its stores. Only recently they had done both in Bethabara, the nearest Moravian village, making the threat implicit in their uniforms seem ever more imminent.

Gladly he turned a well-trained ear to the band as its members tuned their instruments. Music was his mainstay. When the small band began a familiar

Bach chorale, he felt its winding richness freeing his soul from daily cares.

He had plenty, too many. Three of them sat along the front bench between Brother and Sister Ernst: Nicholas and Anna Johanna red-faced and restless in the heat, Matthias with his head lowered in his perpetual pious reflection.

Jacob's fourth, newest care had not arrived. For a moment he scanned the room, trying not to think of Retha's daring or her silent dance. The Single Sisters had in all likelihood confined her to *Gemein Haus.*

Halfway through the choir's first piece, movement caught his eye. Retha tried to sneak along the back wall, but she was too strikingly tall to go unnoticed. The bodice of her rose dress tapered to a plain flounce that danced about her trim waist. It was not so modest a dress as he had thought. He searched for his place in the songbook.

The chorale ended, and he looked up. Retha had taken a seat on Sister Krause's bench. The older Single Sister appeared to be scolding her, but he couldn't hear a word. Retha whispered something back and lowered her head, her starched white *Haube* rigorously taming what he remembered as a mass of amber hair.

Such restraint was more than he could manage. Suddenly, acutely, he wanted to see Retha's glorious hair as it had been the night before. He wanted to free it himself, comb his fingers through it, drape it over the backs of his hands. For a moment he lost all sense of the service, of the close, hot room. He was imagining a waterfall of golden hair over creamy shoulders when the choir started its next chorale.

Without him.

Discreetly, tenor Brother Schopp poked his ribs. Feeling chastised, Jacob picked up his part. Surely the man couldn't read his thoughts. He fixed his mind on the bass line. At his solo, his concentration lapsed again. She hadn't moved except to raise her head. Midnote, he caught her gaze and held it.

Amber eyes, golden smile. He almost lost his way.

Mercifully, the song service ended, and Brother Marshall said a final prayer. Jacob joined the worshipers spilling onto the main street. Outside it was barely cooler, but he was thankful for any respite from the heat. From his own heat.

What had come over him tonight?

"A word with you, Brother Blum." Philip Schopp tapped his shoulder.

Jacob looked up, puzzled to see Schopp frowning, until he followed his line of sight.

"Nicholas does not appear to have learned his lesson," Schopp added.

Jacob's twelve-year-old son streaked into the open lot, gathering schoolmates around him. Jacob sighed heavily and started to pursue his son across the Square. But he thought better of his paternal impulse. After he had rated Nicholas in private, man to man, the boy had asked for another chance. Jacob fully intended to allow him that.

"I talked to him about not inciting trouble," Jacob said stiffly. "He understands."

"He had better," the stern schoolmaster answered. "We have little enough room for the boys at my house, and none for agitators."

Jacob raised a brow at the young schoolmaster's indictment of his son.

"Now, that one is another story." Schopp pointed to Matthias, hands clasped behind his back as he slowly tracked his brother. "Would that more boys were so serious."

"*Ach,*" Jacob said, "that one is too serious."

Schopp gave him an incredulous look and stalked off.

Jacob hadn't addressed this son's problems, and scarcely knew which he dreaded more—his older son's sins or his younger one's relentless piety. Both had worsened since their mother's death. Or did piety improve? Not when interlaced with zeal. Thin and solemn, Matthias would be quick to tell tales against his brother—as well as his sister.

Jacob looked up. From across the dusty street, Sister Ernst came up, almost clucking, her skirts ruffling around his daughter like a plump guinea hen's. As soon as Anna Johanna arrived, she grabbed a fistful of his breeches at the knee—the one touch she would tolerate, the one that she initiated. He dropped his hand instinctively to comfort her but snapped it back.

His heart knotted. He couldn't touch her. No one could. He had racked his brain for an explanation. She had been a bold, happy child up until the day her mother died. Deep down, he knew Anna Johanna's aversion to touch was no simple, physical matter. His somber little girl had not recovered from her loss. She needed . . . he no longer knew what. Not attention or love or distraction. He had exhausted himself on all counts.

She navigated from front to side to back, shrinking from the milling crowd, his friends, her brothers.

"You must be Anna Johanna." A throaty feminine voice came from behind him.

Jacob twisted his head around to see the white-capped head of a woman kneeling. Retha addressed his daughter.

But why? And why so close to him? He clamped his teeth against a renegade wave of desire.

"How d'you know that?" His daughter sounded mystified.

He was too, for reasons of his own. To date, the child had repulsed the nearest neighbors. Her speaking to anyone outside their family was a bold step.

"Because you're with your father, and I want to talk to him in a minute," Retha said matter-of-factly.

"Me first?" Anna Johanna asked tremulously.

"You first."

Cautiously Jacob turned his body. Retha was smiling warmly at Anna Johanna, who reclaimed her hold on him. She started plucking at the knot that tied his breeches below his left knee. He had a worrisome vision of his wool-threaded stockings, freed by her nimble fingers, sagging down to buckled shoes and exposing his calves to all the congregation.

"Who are you?" Anna Johanna asked.

"I'm Retha, and I like your pretty red ribbons."

Anna Johanna let go of his breeches to touch the simple ribbons tied under her chin. All Little Girls wore red ones, Married Sisters blue ones, and Widows white.

"Yours are pink," his daughter said.

"Yours will be too when you're older," Retha assured her.

"How older?" Anna Johanna asked intensely.

Jacob forgot the threat to his socks.

"Oh, old enough to be a Single Sister. When you turn seventeen."

"My mama's were blue," Anna Johanna volunteered. Jacob marveled. His grim little daughter was talking with a virtual stranger. And of her own accord, she had introduced her mother into the conversation.

"That's because she was a Married Sister," Retha said gently, then glanced up at Jacob, as if to ask whether he objected.

Not in the least. He gestured for her to go on.

"My mama's dead," Anna Johanna said, blunt as only a child could be.

"I know that," Retha said soothingly. "I'm sorry. You must miss her very much."

Anna Johanna took a step back, onto Jacob's buckled shoes. She teetered. He frowned. Retha had gone too far. He reached for Anna Johanna's shoulders but stopped. Never touch her. A screaming fit was bad enough behind the thick walls of their home.

"How d'you know that?" Anna's searching whisper hurt his heart.

"My mama died, too. I miss her."

"Oh." In the long silence that followed, Jacob could hear men's and women's voices in the crowd around them, and a wood thrush from far away. He could almost hear his daughter thinking.

"But you're a big girl."

"I was little then. Just about your size."

Anna Johanna began to wring her skirt, always a bad sign. Jacob readied himself to run her home, kicking and screaming, if he had to, before she got to the worst.

But Retha continued. "I was sad for a very long time."

"Me too," Anna Johanna said softly.

Jacob held his breath, hardly daring to move. What wild magic was Retha using on his little girl? Then he saw Retha reach for Anna Johanna's hand. Stop, he thought. She couldn't know the danger. He had a powerful urge to scoop his daughter up and run, to protect them both, protect them all from another fit.

Too late. Retha squeezed the small hand, and he waited for the scream. It never came.

"Now," Retha said, releasing Anna Johanna's hand and shaking out her skirt as she stood up, "I need to speak to your father."

"All right," Anna Johanna said solemnly, grabbing at his knees.

Retha's eyes came to his chin. "She's a sweet girl."

He didn't know whether to nod agreement or shake his head. What was this encounter about? Retha couldn't know he planned to ask for her in the lot. But what was he supposed to say? He knew he couldn't put together two words in a row to thank her for the miracle she had wrought.

She tilted her head at him. By tonight's abundant torchlight, she was even more temptingly pretty than his lone flare had revealed last night. Her face was wide and open, her gaze direct, every last wisp of her hair properly tucked away. A knot of desire tightened his groin.

"Can you keep a secret?" she asked.

He wondered which one. The soldiers, her dancing, her shift—or the way he was looking at her lush lips?

"Of course," he said, remembering his position. People confided in Elders about all sorts of things. Single Sisters, however, did not confide in any man, Single, Married, or Widowed. Sister Krause was Retha's proper channel.

"I need your help."

She must really be in trouble.

"I do regret last night," he offered promptly. "My untimely—the Sisters must have thought that I . . . that we . . ."

How awkward, he thought, kneading the back of his neck.

But Retha laughed. "They did! Of course they did. But you and I know better. I hope you're not in trouble over me."

"Not at all."

"I am. But not because of you. Because they found me outside in the first place."

She paused, and her bright demeanor dimmed.

At last a sign of doubt. "Which was why?" he prodded.

"I was feeding my wolf," she said in a rush.

"Ah. Your wolf," he echoed, taken aback by her unexpected statement and struck by a flash of insight. Mary Margaretha must suffer from an excess of fancy. He had heard of that in women. Perhaps that was why Sister Krause hadn't named her as a marriage prospect. After all, half a childhood spent with Indians had to have affected her in some strange ways.

"So you need help," he prompted.

"No, not me, my wolf," she whispered.

Jacob knotted his brow, suddenly understanding last night's misadventure. "You were in the meadow feeding an animal?"

She nodded gravely. "Twice a day since I found her by the stream. She's hurt. She's improving, but she can't hunt. So I need your help. I can't get away in the day for a while." Her hand made an impatient gesture. "Because of my new work in the laundry and new—" she paused "—restrictions."

"I'm sorry to hear that," Jacob said. He was not sorry about the injured animal but about her punishment. He stepped back to reflect on her revelations.

Her moonlight dance had been no aberration. Knowing she shouldn't, she had gone out after dark. From the start, she had been a wild child, but such a deviation from proper conduct was serious. Unfortunately, he had already proposed to the Elders that he take her to wife. Women could change their minds, but men didn't. For him to step down would spoil her reputation. Now Sister Krause's silence made more sense.

His own impulse made less.

"Will you feed her for a few days? She's out past the Red Tannery, beyond the creek. She hides in a hollow log. But she needs meat, day and night."

"You want me to feed a wolf—day and night?"

"Oh, no." She lowered her voice conspiratorially. "I can still slip out at night. I'll just go nearer to morning."

Dismayed, Jacob searched her face. It was guileless. Her plea was not. She disregarded the community's standards as readily as she dismissed the danger of being out alone. He cleared his throat. "I cannot allow that," he said, as Elder, as example to his children, as her groom to be.

Her eyes blazed briefly. "You're the only one I can ask."

"Sister Retha," he said patiently, feeling the weight of his position. "I am an Elder. I cannot let you do this. 'Tis neither safe nor right."

"It cannot be wrong." She lifted her chin, as once before, he noted, irresistibly. But this was a sensitive negotiation. He had to answer with reason and deliberation.

"Perhaps it is," he said. "Back home, in Germany, we controlled the wolves. We trapped—"

"The Cherokee taught me to honor the wolf," she interrupted eagerly. "Not to help her would have been a sin."

A sin, he thought. Her conviction touched him. She would not want to hear the whole truth. In Germany they had slaughtered all the wolves long before his time. He dragged his hand across his face, buying time to shape a responsible answer.

He should turn her down. He was a builder, a planner, an Elder, not *this.* Conspirator. Wolf tamer.

Still, the beast had not hurt her. Wolves, though rumored to be about, had never attacked this community or raided its stores. He let his eyes range over her determined, pretty face.

"I need your help."

Her sweet plea cascaded over him. He rubbed his neck and reconsidered. It mattered to her enough to risk her reputation. "Very well, then. I will care for it."

"In the day?" she asked cautiously.

"Day and night." He gave her a stern look. "You're not to go out. What does it need?"

"Food, scraps, meat. But don't try to touch her. Not until she's eaten. She's very shy." Her gaze strayed toward his daughter. "Like someone else we know." Retha whirled to go, then whipped back. Clasping his forearm with surprisingly strong fingers, she whispered, "You'll go, you'll really do it?"

He shook his head even as he said yes, even as the imprint of her hand burned through his linen work shirt, through the coat he wore to the service. He swallowed hard.

Her amber eyes were lively again. "The larder's out of marrow bones, but she loves marrow bones."

And Retha was gone. Jacob felt as he had one day with a team of runaway horses, graceless and exhilarated. As effortlessly as she had touched his little girl, Retha had spun him off his ordered path. A man in his position had no business meeting a woman in the moonlight and then pledging to undertake wild missions for her by day and by night.

It was madness on his part. On hers, simple need.

No, trust. She had turned to him, he realized. She had selected him as the only man that she could trust.

A band of hope squeezed his heart.

She was wilder, bolder, and, strangely, kinder than he had imagined. For months the town's wives and mothers and teachers had struggled to help his children, to no avail. Kneeling, she made friends with his daughter in a trice. Just as, no doubt, she befriended that beast of hers.

Intrigued in spite of himself and feeling not a little reckless, he hoped some earnest prayers would turn his luck with the lot.

Rushed, dusty, and late, Jacob came to the Elders' weekly meeting straight from his work at Steiner's Mill. He knew he and his fellow Elders had a full agenda, for with the war, worldly matters had spilled over into the group's spiritual concerns. He also knew that Brother Marshall eschewed delay.

"You have had a busy week, Brother Blum." Marshall neither rose nor looked up from his notes. "Our meeting has commenced without you. We have confirmed the addition of three townsmen to the night watch in response to rumors of a raid. If you have no objection."

Brother Marshall would not countenance objection, but Jacob had one. He crossed the room, raising a cloud of dust as he swatted his breeches.

"Three is excessive. Our community has barely seventy brothers. With both armies demanding our trade, our duties have stretched every man to his limit."

Marshall held his stern expression, and Brother Schopp mirrored it. Sisters Elisabeth Marshall and Rosina Krause looked on with mild concern.

Taking a moment to formulate a more diplomatic answer, Jacob stroked the back of his chair, its beeswax finish soft as skin. Woman's skin. He curled his fingers into a fist. He had to get to the business at hand.

But a woman, he thought wryly, was the business at hand.

"The four of you have voted on this, I take it."

"We have." Marshall raised one drooped eyebrow, as if Jacob's comment constituted a rebellion.

"I support the Board's decision," Jacob said at last. "So long as every man consents to the burden he will incur."

"They do," Marshall said brusquely, referring again to his notes. "Before you arrived, Brother Schopp reported on the raid on Bethabara. Colonel Williams's regular army took a wagon, supplies, and one hundred twenty gallons of their good brandy."

Some in Salem were in spasms of fear that they too would be raided, Jacob knew, despite his negotiations in these last difficult months to forestall such a raid by either army.

"They were in retreat. They could have done more harm than that," Jacob said flatly, finally seating himself.

His fellow Elders, men and women alike, seemed tense. They could not be so tense as he, waiting for this meeting to address the subject that mattered most to him.

"I fear they will do worse, Brother Blum, and closer to home," Sister Marshall said anxiously.

"I have not found Continental leaders averse to

reason," Jacob reassured her, his gaze falling on the wooden lot bowl at her elbow. His stomach knotted.

He wanted this drawing of the lot to be over and done.

At the same time, he did not. All week he had seen Retha only during evening service. There he had not been able to penetrate her bright resolve. It kept her sitting, arrow-straight and primly regulated, amidst the Single Sisters, through the singing of chorales.

All week too, the task of feeding her wolf filled him with ever greater misgivings. Was he keeping her from going astray or leading her into deeper disobedience? Soon, however, the beast would be well, making her disobedience as well as his contribution to it moot. He had tried to see her disregard for rules as a one-time, well-meant effort to rescue a poor suffering beast. He held to a hope that she would transfer her concern for one wild thing to his unruly children.

Brother Marshall tapped his quill pen. Its feather fluttered like a nervous bird. "We await your reports on the Friedlanders, the watch house, and Steiner's Mill."

Jacob fixed his gaze on his packet of reports and tried to think. His vision blurred. One reed in that lot bowl could change his life, his family's life. Almost objectively, he noted that his heartbeat sped up at the thought.

He wanted this bride with a desire he had not felt when the three previous lots were drawn.

"Report, Brother Blum," Marshall said.

Jacob lifted his gaze from the lot bowl.

Marshall smiled slightly. "We shall not forget your solemnities."

Blood heated Jacob's face. He paged through his ledger to conceal his thoughts and prepare for the rest of the meeting. He had only to report decisions that his committee had already made.

"The, um, watch house . . ." He found a sheet of calculations. " 'Tis complete, but the balance is not yet paid to Gottlieb Vogler."

"How much is owing still?" Philip Schopp asked officiously. He always opposed dealing with Vogler, a disassociated Moravian but a respectable man.

"Half the cost of Vogler's logs. But the amount is not the question," Jacob said firmly. "Rather, the manner of payment."

"He scorned currency?"

Jacob prayed for patience. With the war, the new Continental government's currency was unstable. "Vogler should not accept currency, nor should we expect him to. We should pay in hides, salt, or harvest stores—"

Marshall and Schopp fell to a heated discussion of which would be less burdensome to the town and more fair to its vendor. Hides were everywhere in good supply, but salt was hard to come by, and harvest was some weeks away.

Jacob halted their discussion. "He is willing to take payment after harvest."

"I presume you did not promise that," Marshall said.

"We discussed it."

"Why bring the matter before us?" Schopp asked.

Jacob slowed his answer. "As head of the Supervisory Committee, negotiating price is my prerogative. But the Board of Elders approves the manner of payment. Hides or salt or after harvest. Which one we accept is up to us."

"Not if you have given him expectations," Schopp said.

"If the drought does not destroy our crops, I should think Brother Vogler and his bride would prefer the food," Rosina Krause interrupted mildly.

"He is no longer Brother Vogler," Schopp argued.

"To some of us he is," she said.

" 'Tis settled then," Jacob said. "Food, after harvest. As to the Continental Army's drafting of the Friedlanders, I have urged them to apply to Bishop Graff for certificates of exemption."

"They should have paid the exemption tax," Schopp said.

Sister Krause harrumphed. "A threefold tax is a stiff penalty for farmers to pay during a war, Brother Schopp."

"Having failed to do so, they should fight," he persisted.

"Would you really have them fight, when it is an article of our faith not to bear arms for any government?" she asked.

Jacob ended the familiar, fruitless argument with a decisive change of subject. "As to the mill-race, I have added two men to work on it."

"More deserters?" Schopp asked sharply.

"We think so." Jacob withheld his belief that they were British. If so, they sought concealment desperately and would work all the harder. The British might hold Charleston, and Cornwallis's Redcoats might be poised at the North Carolina border, but in skirmishes throughout the state, Whigs were overwhelming superior forces of Tories.

"Even with them, how much longer will repairs take?" Marshall asked.

"Yes, Brother Blum, how long? You know the Continental troops grow restless for their grain," Elisabeth Marshall added.

Jacob had no simple answer for the Elders, none of whom participated in the heavy and dangerous communal work. " 'Twill take time. The damage from spring flooding was complete. The stream must be dammed and diverted, the waterway allowed to dry, all old timbers removed, new ones seated—"

"But when do you see the end?" Marshall prodded.

Jacob stifled his frustration. He saw an end to work at the mill, but not to this interminable meeting. He forced himself to sound patient, practical, knowledgeable, all of which he was, most days. "Another month, at best."

Rosina Krause broke the stranglehold of pressing subjects by reaching across the table for the lot bowl. As head of the Single Sisters, the drawing of the marriage lot was her affair.

" 'Tis time, Brother Marshall," she said, pushing the bowl to the center of the table to make her point. "We have tormented Brother Blum long enough this afternoon."

The women shared knowing glances. Abruptly the tone of the meeting changed. Marshall put away his notes, and Schopp's pinched face softened.

Tensions eased. A faint, hot breeze made its way through an open window, ruffling a sheet of Jacob's neglected ledger. He closed the book and self-consciously straightened the damp stock that choked his neck.

He had waited all afternoon for this moment. All week, in fact. Sweat poured off his body, but not from the heat. When the lot had been cast for Christina, he had been too brash to understand its power and far too young to imagine either the permanence or the poignancy of union.

Now he did. If the lot said yes, his fate, his family's fate was sealed. A pleasant fate, he thought, if satisfying his desire were his only object. But misgivings reared up, more potent than desire. Could Retha, the foundling, friend of Indians, rescuer of lame wolves, be the right woman to mother his children?

Brother Marshall bowed his head. "Guide us, Savior, in the matter of Brother Blum's proposal to Sister Retha. May all here present bear witness this time-honored expression of Thy will and cheerfully carry out Thy commands."

Elisabeth Marshall retrieved the small, deep bowl and placed it in front of her husband. He closed his eyes. With a light click of wood on wood, she rearranged the reeds, turned the bowl, and guided his hand to its blunt rim.

Brother Marshall's lips moved in silent prayer as his fingers found the ends of the three reeds. For the fourth time, he selected a reed for Jacob, pulled it apart, and gave the slip of paper to his wife. Holding it up to the light, she squinted worriedly. Then a grin spread across her face.

"*Ja*, Brother Blum, yes," she said, barely containing her feminine excitement. "Sister Krause may propose to Sister Mary Margaretha on your behalf. The lot says yes."

Lowering his head, Jacob thought of a flash of white shift, a flare of gilded hair, a bold dance of slender feet. A surge of triumph flooded him. A triumph of desire.

But what had he done to his family?

More to the point, what would Sister Retha do to them?

"You think about it, Sister Retha. And you think long and hard about those children," Rosina Krause said later that day in her immaculate office, moments after giving Retha the astounding news.

The lot granted Jacob Blum permission to ask for her hand in marriage.

Retha's head spun. Marry Brother Blum! Be a mother to his children! A week had passed since Jacob Blum took on the care of her wolf. His proposal, properly made for him by the senior Single Sister, left Retha speechless.

"And you make up your mind as quickly as you can. Don't you change back and forth as Sister Grimm did last winter," Rosina scolded.

"I'll try," Retha said feebly.

"Those children cannot be expected to wait on girlish indecision." Rosina's words followed Retha as the enormity of Jacob Blum's proposal drove her blindly from the little office.

She was a girl no more.

Throughout the night and the next day, Retha did think long and hard about the children and their father, even into the afternoon while she stood folding the Tavern's fresh linens into a willow basket.

Jacob Blum had gone and gotten permission to marry her.

Dizzy at the thought, she pressed a hand against her forehead. She hadn't decided to agree to it. There was so very much to consider. Accepting him meant accepting them.

Jacob Blum, Rosina Krause, and the whole community, when it came right down to it, would expect her to marry him now that the lot had said yes. Would expect her to put her work behind her, even her life as a Single Sister, such as it was, even her wolf. Would expect her to join his household and care for his children.

What did she know of children? Especially boys.

Worse, what did she know of men?

She wished her thoughts would fold as neatly into place as these sheets and pillowslips. In her heart of hearts she knew that her wolf was the least important thing, yet at first it was the hardest to let go. The wolf had come to her, wild and free and needy, reminding her of everything she once loved of her woodland life with the Cherokee. In saving its life, she had won back a piece of that past. She would be trading its wildness for the mysterious misery of Jacob Blum's strange daughter, a misery so like her own after her own mother's death that she wasn't sure she could face it.

The prospect of any child needing her to be her mother daunted her. Let alone one who had fits. She had heard Anna Johanna screaming once in the streets of town, had seen her clinging to that dress. Retha sympathized. She herself had suffered terribly, having lost both parents at once. But how would she manage the child? It was one thing to talk to her for a few moments, quite another to have the care of her for life.

What if the little girl hated her?

And what of those half-grown sons?

She couldn't even talk to Brother Blum about the marriage. Yesterday he had left town, committing his children to the care of Samuel and Eva Ernst. He hadn't said a word to her, either about his proposal or about tending her wolf.

Retha slapped the last pillowslips in place just as the haunting sound of Samuel Ernst's conch announced the afternoon's market on the Square. Well, she thought, tucking her load inside the basket's rim, the market won't be crowded, the weather being what it was. Outside, the afternoon was muggy, the sky dark with scudding clouds, like her thoughts. Sometimes in this dry, hot summer, clouds like that brought rain, but not often lately.

What had Brother Blum been thinking, to ask for her hand in marriage?

She swung the heavy basket to her shoulder and headed up the street.

He must be desperate. She tried to ignore gossip, truly she did, having too often been its subject. Even so, everyone knew he had had trouble with the lot. Twice, some said three times, his proposals had been denied. Surely that was why Sister Rosina urged her to decide.

Retha regretted asking him to feed her wolf. Now that she was actually doing the laundry, it was clear she could have managed feeding it herself. Since she asked Brother Blum to do it, he had spoken to her only once. She stopped in midstride.

Only once. The day *after* the Elders' meeting. The day after the lot had been cast.

She balanced her load and put her thoughts together. He had known then. Even while he had been talking to her about her wolf, he planned his proposal. And said not one word of his intentions. Never mind that Rosina Krause was supposed to tell her first. Such secrecy made her mad enough to turn him down. She had the right to do so.

And she owed him nothing. Not much, she amended.

That day, they had met accidentally in the Square.

"I have yet to see your wolf," he had said, his voice rough, almost grumpy.

"You have fed her though, thank you very much."

"How do you know?"

"I see her."

"That wasn't our agreement." Although he scowled in the bright afternoon sun, his lake-blue eyes were drilling hers.

She tried to placate him. " 'Tis naught. I stop by the creek before I come back with the laundry."

"We agreed that's too risky for you," he said sternly.

We didn't, and it isn't, she thought. Alone outdoors, she was smarter than she had ever been. More slippery, more careful.

Brother Blum grunted, gathered up his children, and left. As if he hadn't known the first thing about his pending proposal. As if he had no feelings for her at all.

Loaded with laundry now, she slipped around to the Tavern's back door, angry just thinking about his silence, his indifference. She would tend the wolf herself.

Brisk and genial, Jeremiah Meyer lifted her basket over the bottom half of the door.

"You wait," he said, retrieving a mound of linens from a corner of the room and piling dirty bedclothes high on her basket. "Here are more. The British lieutenant and his detachment rode out before noon."

At the sight and smell of a blood-soiled sheet, she sniffed fresh air and made a face. " 'Tis a foul task I do for you, Brother Meyer," she teased, hoping her manner would mask the queasiness that flooded her.

Brother Meyer laughed. "The Lord loves a cheerful heart."

Retha swept the basket to her other shoulder, then climbed the hard-packed, dusty street, dodging ruts. She wouldn't think about laundry now. She would think about her wolf. It needed food, but she had best avoid the larder.

She neared the Square, her destination straight across it, through the crowd. She searched the vendors, hoping her friend Alice would be here with husband Gottlieb Vogler. Some years ago on market day, Retha had met the exiled couple, and they had become fast friends when Retha spoke to Alice in her native language. A full-blooded Cherokee who naturally shunned settlers, Alice sometimes didn't come for weeks.

The marketplace bustled with traders. With little regard to rich or poor or Whig or Tory, Moravians in neat, plain dress set up their wares alongside ragged settlers and backcountry trappers in buckskins. Two-wheeled carts and heavy wagons displayed smoked meats, tanned hides, a smattering of early summer beans and corn. One woman offered flowering herbs. On any other day, Retha would have bought some to try for dyes. A shabby man at a rickety cart hawked small game. The wolf would love a squirrel, but its price was beyond her means.

She stopped at a spotted cow tied behind a wagon. A tired-faced woman with an infant at her breast urged her closer to the cow. "She didn't freshen again this year so she weren't worth naught but for butchering."

Retha peered over the wagon's side to see what else they had brought. One poorly made quilt, whether for themselves or for sale, she couldn't tell. Her nose wrinkled at the pungent smell of cow. The Cherokee she lived with had survived on game, had hated stinking cattle. For her, learning to eat beef had been no easy task.

"I need marrow bones," she said anyway.

"Got no marrer bones. Kept 'em at home. Don't make no money," the woman's husband said.

Retha understood. They were so poor they probably lived off bone soup. She backed away, but her legs struck what felt like a log. She collapsed, spilling her load of greasy tablecloths and smelly bed sheets on top of her. Shoving them off her face, she pushed herself up and braced on the heels of her hands. A giant man extricated his legs from her load and crawled out from under his wagon.

"Oh, Gottlieb," she gasped. "I am sorry."

Gottlieb Vogler stood and gave her a hand up. He was bigger even than Jacob Blum, his hands ham-sized and facial features big out of all proportion. So was his gentle welcome.

"Alice will be glad to see you," he said heartily.

"She came?" Retha looked but saw no sign of her friend's flowing black hair. "Where is she?"

"T'other side of the wagon, handing me my tools. The wheels almost came off since the Continentals requisitioned it last winter. I guess we were lucky to get it back."

Retha streaked around the wagon and found her only Cherokee friend in the world standing by a cumbersome toolbox, her Indian face beautiful even where smallpox had etched it. Alice greeted her in the broken German she had striven so hard to learn. The minute Retha explained about the wolf, they switched to speaking Cherokee, consciously hushing its loud tones so as not to draw attention to themselves.

"Marrow bones?" Alice laughed. "Of course you can have marrow bones. And for a wolf."

Retha heard approval in her tone. Alice would have proudly saved such a noble animal herself. She skirted the wagon and helped Retha restack her linens. Her friend showed a lot of courage, Retha thought, to come here with her husband and risk facing crowds of white men who hated her kind. Locals and Continentals had obliterated Alice's clan that terrible spring seven years ago when Retha's own adoptive Indian family had been killed. Only Alice's ravaging smallpox had repelled the soldiers and saved her life.

At the market, Retha chatted as Alice listened, wrapping two marrow bones in pillowslips and stuffing them between dirty sheets. It took a while to explain why the Single Sisters had grounded her to *Gemein Haus.* She was about to tell her friend about Jacob Blum's amazing proposal when the buzz of the market died out.

"Redcoats!" a voice cried out.

Retha heard horses pounding up the road.

"Continentals!" another shouted.

A churning cloud of dust brought neither. Five local militia, wearing a hodgepodge of buckskin and scavenged uniforms, slowed their horses to a trot on the dusty street. Retha tensed. Unruly, half-regulated Liberty Men, who sought out Tories, Redcoats, and Cherokees with unremitting fervor in so-called support of the efforts of the Continental Army.

Alice ducked under the wagon.

"I thought they left her alone these days," Retha muttered to Gottlieb, who stood on alert.

"Now they think she's a spy," he grated softly.

"A spy? For whom?"

He wagged his great head in disgust but did not answer.

Slowly Retha comprehended. After Colonials had slaughtered them, the Cherokee were allied with the British. "Alice a spy for the Redcoats? But you're Moravian. You're neutral. We all are."

"No longer, Sister Retha." She heard regret in his voice for a faith he still honored. "I went against the lot, marrying outside our faith. And a Cherokee woman to boot. Perhaps you were too young to note the scandal."

Retha patted his hand sympathetically and smiled. "Oh, no. Your romantic sacrifice was all the talk among the Single Sisters."

The huge man actually blushed.

"But what can we do for Alice now?"

"Let her hide. 'Tis best if they don't see her. Until I see who it is." His big hands clenched and his gentle eyes blazed as the small band drew up in front of the market.

Retha had a shock herself.

Jacob Blum rode into the Square with the small band of Liberty Men. Sliding off his mount, the troop's red-haired captain barked orders at his men. Jacob swung off his overworked tavern hack and confronted the captain. He answered angrily, chopping the air with the blade of his hand. With a final gesture, the captain stalked over to the spotted cow.

Jacob marched after him, plunging into the argument as the captain haggled with the poor settler and his wife. Retha steadied herself on her friend's strong arm, listening to the worn woman defend her price.

Jacob resolutely took up the woman's cause.

Retha gawked. Neutral, she reminded herself without being reassured. Jacob was supposed to be neutral.

But he looked militant. She studied the object of

his anger. She couldn't see the captain's face, but red hair bristled under the battered brim of his tricorn. A chill crept over her. She hated redheaded men.

Jacob jerked off his hat and swatted road dust from his breeches. Sim Scaife had wrecked his day. As usual. The thick-skulled, rabble-rousing Liberty Man had hounded Jacob for years, convinced that any Moravian who spoke English was a British spy. As if Jacob didn't have enough problems balancing the Moravians' precarious relations with both the British and the Continentals.

"Don't dicker with the woman, Baker," Scaife was shouting to his sergeant who'd gone to purchase the spotted cow.

Hearing the woman's feeble protest, Jacob plowed toward the fray. And checked himself. A flag of red-gold hair captured his attention. Amongst the shoppers in the crowded Square stood his intended bride—with Gottlieb Vogler. It only needed this. He had been but a day away, and she was compromised again. But he could not well put her in a box.

"We can take the blamed cow outright," Scaife threatened.

Alerted, Jacob bit down on frustration. At this moment he couldn't even notice Retha. Not when Scaife's malice demanded his attention.

With a yellow grin, Scaife dug into a shoulder pouch, pulled out a handful of Continental bills, and shoved them in the husband's face. "But we got money."

The farmer snorted. "That paper ain't worth a

hoot. I come here for barter."

Jacob wedged in between captain and sergeant. The farmer was right. Paper was worthless, a hundred bills on any given day worth what one had been the day before.

"The town will trade you in salt, Finney," he said in his formal English. Most of his fellow Moravians would not understand a word he said.

The woman furtively shook her head at her husband. "We need wheat."

"We have only salt," Jacob went on, "unless you can take something from the store." He knew the woman needed staples. Everyone did. The summer was already hot and dry. The wheat crop had suffered, and corn was looking bad.

The woman shook her head.

Scaife's lips thinned into a mocking grin. "You've naught to bargain with, woman. But we'll be glad to take it off yer hands for free."

Jacob turned on him, aware of the crowd clearing a circle around them. "You can have what you came for, free food and rooms at the Tavern. Let the woman trade her cow." Then he spoke to the woman. "But we cannot trade wheat, Mrs. Finney."

"We ain't got any—" she began.

"We have no wheat either, not to sell or trade," he explained. "The army requisitioned it. 'Tis theirs as soon as they round up wagons to transport it."

"So you say," Scaife growled back in Jacob's face.

"I showed you the papers," Jacob answered edgily. Scaife's men tried to break through the circle of townsmen and settlers, but Scaife waved them back.

Jacob prepared for the worst. The hotheaded

captain was unpredictable. This morning, holding a pistol to his head, Scaife had read Jacob's requisitions from the Continental Army for grain, but had still taken him for a spy. Then he ordered Jacob to translate his German documents, minutes of church business for the Bethabara settlement, dull with convincing detail. Scaife chose not to believe him.

"I ain't a fool, Blum." The man's face flushed to match his carroty hair. "Your tavernkeeper let that English lieutenant stay five days, and the day he left heading east, we catch you going south with a packet of sealed documents."

"I translated them for you."

"They were in German."

"All church business is in German."

"They could have said aught. I may not know German, but some Englishman would." He spit on the ground. "Everybody knows you're a bunch of Tories."

Jacob hid his annoyance behind a shrug. Whigs thought Moravians were Tories, and Tories thought they were Whigs. They were neither. When the British ruled, Moravians paid them their due. Now that the Colonies had independence, Moravians paid taxes to the government in power. Threefold taxes, so they wouldn't have to bear arms for the state. Some were drafted anyway.

Some even fought. Jacob was sorely tempted to. Partly because he knew he would do a better job than Sim Scaife and his ilk, and the brutal war would end sooner. But more because of how he had come to love the promised freedom of this land.

His blood raged to fight for it. Nicholas was not

unlike him in that. Guilt trickled through him. What if his own secret relish for battle had somehow found expression in his older son's intemperate nature. He dared not by word or deed set an example that would feed his son's belligerent leanings.

Besides, Jacob reminded himself, he did not have the choice of bearing arms. Every ounce of duty, faith, and honor in his soul bound him to stand by his community. The best that he could do was keep men like Scaife from destroying it.

And Scaife would try. Jacob wished the man had stuck with his hardscrabble life of hunting and trapping on that precious property he had finagled out of some poor settler. The wilderness life took the edge off his spite. War honed it.

"I will trade for Finney's cow, Scaife."

"I'm here to say you won't," Scaife said, bracing his legs to fight, three of his men outside the circle.

Jacob assessed him. He outweighed the Liberty Man by a good three stones, but Scaife's meanness could make up the difference. Scaife hoisted his musket off his shoulder and feigned a move to hand it to his sergeant. Instead, he tossed it in the air, grabbed it by the bore, and swung it low like a scythe.

Jacob saw the blow coming and stepped over the weapon. With a growl, he tackled the man, toppling him over into the dust. Scaife's bony hands scrabbled up, his dirty broken fingernails digging into Jacob's throat. Jacob wrestled the man's hands to the ground and pinned them over Scaife's head.

"'Twould not be a fair fight, Captain." He shifted, letting the thin man beneath him feel his weight. Around them, the circle tightened, a wall of

Moravian men cutting off Scaife's men from rescue or reprisal.

Scaife's narrow gaze darted up to the pressing crowd, as if noticing it for the first time. Jacob knew what he would see alongside his townsmen. A few Whig farmers and trappers who depended on the town for trade. A couple of suspected Loyalists, driven by need, who had taken a chance on coming to market. Whig or Tory, they had all dodged fire from every side. No one would go out of his way for Sim Scaife.

"Yeah. You got reinforcements." His accusation was loud enough to provoke the crowd. No doubt, he hoped to stir them up.

"I fight my own fights. Save yours for the British."

"You gave them rooms."

"They took the rooms. Your army gets all our wheat."

"You gave them horses."

"They took our horses. They took everyone's." Jacob lowered his voice, striving to come up with something to convince Scaife that Salem was truly neutral. "They didn't find the best ones."

Scaife barked a nasty laugh. "Well, I'll be," he said, as if he would never have thought the neutral Moravians had wits enough to hide a horse. He squirmed under Jacob's weight. "I give."

"Give what?" Jacob blinked, uncomprehending.

"Give up!" Scaife snarled impatiently.

"What is 'give up'?"

"Yield, man. I yield, Blum, I'll let you be. Let me up."

Shaking his head, Jacob released the man's hands and raised himself off his body. The circle of townsmen melted, but Jacob watched cautiously. Scaife shrugged inside his sweat-stained buckskins, grabbed his musket from the sergeant, then looked up.

"If I catch you out spying . . ." Scaife bared his yellow teeth in a half-hearted attempt to placate the man who had defeated him.

"We are not enemies," Jacob said to him quietly. "Go. Brother Meyer will serve your supper."

Scaife collected his men, who followed him down the street with their ragged horses. Breathing a sigh that mingled anger and relief, Jacob surveyed the crowd milling in the Square. A disgusted hunter packed up pelts and deerskins to leave. A farmer spread out meats and vegetables hastily stowed from harm. In this lean summer, trading his stores meant he was desperate. Mrs. Finney took her baby out from under her wagon's seat.

All was well, Jacob thought. He had forestalled another ugly incident. Relieved, he looked around for Retha.

She was standing in the circle of Gottlieb Vogler's arms.

What else would the woman dare to do? he wondered angrily. His gut filled with an unfamiliar, powerful emotion.

She was his. His. He clenched his jaw. He could not be jealous. Not of Gottlieb Vogler, of all men. Still, she looked far too secure in Vogler's arms, too trusting of him.

She should have come to Jacob. Marching up to them, he could see her pale face damp with tears.

"Are you hurt?" he rasped, not in enough control to ask what he needed most to know.

Are you safe? Are you mine?

Breaking away from Gottlieb awkwardly, she lifted her eyes to Jacob's. Then her gaze traveled nervously down his soiled shirtfront, down his dusty breeches. Impatient, unsettled, he endured her inspection, then gently touched a hand under her chin.

"Who hurt you?"

She averted her eyes. "No one. 'Twas naught."

CHAPTER 3

"Do you understand my question?" Retha felt Jacob Blum's massive presence, his breathing still ragged from his fight. "Are you hurt?"

Yes. No. She shook her head. She wasn't hurt. She wanted him to go away. If he hadn't come after her looking like a thundercloud, she might have stilled her trembling. She might have ignored the bile that had risen in her throat while he grappled with the redheaded captain.

Whoever that man was. He was vile, she knew it without knowing how she knew. When he had raised his hand, gesturing rudely in the air, then swung his musket at Brother Blum, she had flown into Vogler's arms, her wits as scrambled as if the captain had swung at her.

Now Jacob took her elbow protectively, as he had that day with the soldiers, and drew her to the edge of the crowd onto a crackling span of drought-dried grass.

"Can you answer me? Are you hurt?" Jacob repeated huskily. Though he sounded riled, to her his soft German had the silkiness of song.

"No, not hurt." She shook her head, eyes closed

against a confusing sweep of tenderness. The man who wanted to marry her was safe, he was holding her elbow tight. She had decided to accept his proposal the minute she had seen him ride into town, tall and stalwart and in charge. Yet as the argument escalated, fear overwhelmed her until he took his quarry down. It was as if he had been fighting for her, as if she had thrown her heart into the fight with him. She would have died if he'd been hurt.

"Look at me, Sister Retha." His voice sounded gentle, but she opened her eyes to a darkly troubled gaze. "Something troubles you."

"I . . ." What could she say? That the sight of the redheaded man had made her skin crawl? That the prospect of Jacob being hurt had torn at her heart? "Fighting upsets me."

"Humph," he grunted. He didn't sound convinced. "Fighting upsets a lot of people, but no one else cried."

She felt her cheek and found it wet. " 'Tis only perspiration, Brother Blum. From the heat."

He leaned in to inspect her face, possessively, as if he had a right. He smelled of dirt and horse and manly endeavor, and she felt her face flush. "Heat doesn't damp your lashes," he said firmly, trailing a finger just beneath her eye for proof. Her breath caught at his tender touch. "I know a dirty, tearstained face when I see one. I have a great deal of experience."

"So you do," she said, his confession reminding her of his troublesome daughter. "But I never cry."

"Anna Johanna says much the same." A corner of his mouth crooked up, but he controlled it.

"Never," she repeated, even as she felt the tears herself. Tears were only tears, she told herself, scrubbing away evidence with a corner of her apron. It wasn't crying until you sobbed.

"So." He drew away from her, his countenance turning decidedly sober. "Tell me what you were doing in Gottlieb Vogler's arms."

"Because of the fight," she offered, loosening her grip on her apron and letting it fall back down.

His eyes followed her gesture, but his voice softened dangerously. "In his arms," he repeated slowly.

"The Voglers were protecting me." She carefully cited the couple, not the man. In fact, she had flung herself away from Jacob's fight, a scream lodged in her throat, heedless of impropriety.

Jacob arched an eyebrow.

"Alice and Gottlieb are my friends," she explained.

"Your friends." Jacob's eyes narrowed. "Sister Retha, what am I supposed to think—what is the town supposed to think—to see you in the arms of a man like that?"

She didn't like his commanding tone and almost said so. "You should think naught of it. I was scared."

"A man who, apparently without regret, disassociated from us by his own choice."

"He has regrets," she said impulsively, and bit her tongue. Jacob Blum wouldn't like knowing the Voglers confided in her about such private matters.

"How would you know of his regrets?" He guided her by the arm farther from the edge of the crowd and stopped in the middle of the Square. "Tell me the truth, Sister Retha."

He probably ordered his children around like this. By all reports, it hadn't worked with them either. Her irritation rose.

"The truth? The Voglers are my friends. I needed them, and they comforted me. 'Tis none of your affair."

"Perhaps not," he said flatly. "Not yet." But the muscle in his square jaw rippled with tension.

"Not at all."

An odd look crossed his face, and he shifted his weight from one large leg to the other. "Surely Sister Krause has spoken to you." Exasperation laced his voice.

And suddenly she understood everything, his touch, his concern, his anger, every word he'd said since he stomped over. He was thinking of her as his betrothed before he'd even asked.

Her heart raged. She was fairly sure that Brother Ernst hadn't prefaced his proposal to her friend Sister Eva in this blunt, unfeeling way. "Oh. Your proposal. 'Tis hardly the time or place."

A rueful smile creased his face. "At least we agree on that. So she spoke to you."

"She did." And it hadn't been pleasant. Retha gave him as frank a look as she could manage. "Sister Rosina told me to think long and hard about marrying you and your children."

He dropped her arm and stalked off, describing a tight circle before returning to loom over her. He was so big, so rugged, racked with anger, and yet, as his flushed face told her, so embarrassed.

"She said that?" He paced a slightly larger circle and loomed before her again. "That doesn't leave me with much to say then," he added darkly.

She couldn't guess what that meant.

Yes, she could. *He* was going to turn *her* down. She had just squashed any chance of having a home of her own.

Instead, he ran his hand over his blond hair and kneaded the back of his neck. "Um. Sister Retha." With his words, his anger seemed to dissipate, and for the first time he looked awkward, boyish. Retha's stomach took a wild and unaccustomed dip. "My proposal . . . 'tis not as I intended."

He made a clumsy gesture toward her. "Walk with me. Away from this."

He led her to the far side of the Square and leaned against the split-rail fence, burly arms folded across his chest. "Let me put it to you this way. I know Gottlieb Vogler. For trading, he's as reliable as an oak. But I was an Elder when we disassociated him. He flaunted the lot. He put what he called love for that Cherokee woman over its clear direction not to marry her. And never looked back."

Retha thought Jacob sounded somewhat sorry about his role in the dismissal, but knew he couldn't understand the whole of it. She would give her life for devotion as strong and true as that which she had seen between Gottlieb and Alice.

"He does love her," Retha said.

"That may be. Nevertheless, because he's no longer one of us, 'tis not seemly for a Single Sister to associate with him. With them. Even if they have been your friends."

His tone grew milder, and he was almost relaxed leaning against the split-rail fence. She would give him the truth he asked for: she wasn't ashamed of knowing them and had nothing to hide. "Gottlieb Vogler rescued me one winter. Out past the waterfall. I was looking for dyes and found their cabin after it started to rain. He brought me home."

Glancing up, she saw Jacob scowling, and quickly corrected herself. "He and Alice brought me home. They said they needed supplies from Traugott Bagge's store."

"You were fortunate, then," he said noncommittally. "Nevertheless, 'tis not safe for you to associate with Gottlieb Vogler. The country is at war. And his wife is Cherokee."

This was going too far. She cut him a look. "His wife is my friend too. My only Cherokee friend. Cherokees found me and adopted me into their tribe. I passed my childhood years with them. Or have you forgotten?"

"No one has forgotten, Sister Retha. Which is why you need take especial care."

"Take care! About Alice?" Puzzled, Retha had an urge to pace out a circle of her own. Then she recalled Gottlieb's words about Alice's danger. "You too believe her to be a spy."

Jacob nodded with slow, infuriating certainty. "More to the point, Scaife does."

"That man? That redheaded Liberty Man? Perhaps she *should* spy against him. It was Liberty Men—locals—that wiped out her clan. If she hadn't had a ravaging case of the smallpox, they would have killed her too."

"Small wonder she would want to spy against—"

"Brother Blum," Retha interrupted, defending

herself as well as her friend, "do you think I would knowingly consort with a British spy?"

"I think you might unknowingly consort with a British spy, someone you admired for some other reason."

She bridled at his calm, patronizing voice. "I do admire the Cherokee. They saved my life."

Jacob made a noise of frustration and muttered, mostly in English, "*Ach*, stubborn woman, in the name of all that's good and merciful!"

Retha understood every word. "Perhaps we don't always know who the good and merciful are," she replied in her own halting but unaccented English.

His eyebrows snapped together, then recognition dawned. "Of course. I had forgotten. You speak English."

"Not often anymore."

"All the more reason for you to choose your friends with care."

"What do you mean by that?"

With an impatient grumble, he drew himself up to his full, formidable height. "Sister Mary Margaretha, are you altogether unaware of the war that is going on around us?"

She shrugged irritably. "Of course, I'm aware of—"

"That each side suspects us of spying for the other? Scaife plagues me because I, a German, speak English. He thinks I'm our town's liaison to the British. And now you speak English, too. Suppose he found you outside town with your friend."

"I would never let myself fall into that man's hands." Retha wrapped her arms around herself to hide a shudder at the thought. No one, no one could track her in the woods. Singing Stones had taught her well to bend but not break twigs, to conceal her tracks in streams, to step carefully around the greenery that lined the forest floor.

"Listen to me. If he caught you out there, you would have to explain yourself in English. You couldn't defend yourself otherwise. One sentence of your good English, and he would clap you in the garrison brigade before you could blink."

"He would not catch me," she insisted.

Jacob gave no weight to her remark. "I want you to stay away from Alice Vogler."

Retha merely nodded, unable to promise that, but telling herself her nod was not a lie. She didn't see her friend that often.

"And don't speak English. Coming from a Moravian Sister, people will mistake you—as they have mistaken me."

He had a point. Even the Moravians had mistaken her, and she'd been wrong for them. She always would be. She propped herself against the fence, thoroughly out of sorts. A young linden tree screened them from the bustle of the market. He leaned against the fence next to her, his shadowed face inscrutable as she searched it, unsure what to say until the words left her lips.

"Everything is wrong between us now, isn't it?" she muttered. Jacob Blum had briefly offered her a precious dream, and she had planned to say yes. Now all her difference would drive him away.

"I hope not, Sister Retha. I only want to keep you safe until you are fully under my protection."

He cupped her small hands in his large ones as though protecting her already. An unaccustomed feeling of belonging stole into her guarded heart.

"I am bound to the lot," he went on, "and we drew an affirmative. I cannot back down. Nor do I wish to. We need you, every one of us."

He wanted her for his children.

Her brief sense of belonging skidded away. Her face burned with mortification. Upright, stalwart, handsome Jacob Blum needed her to tend his children, and nothing more. She thought with longing of Brother Ernst's obvious pride in his new bride and of Gottlieb Vogler's deep, abiding love for his wife.

Neither, it seemed, was to be her fate. Marrying Jacob Blum's whole family was a high price to pay to escape life as a Single Sister and gain a home of her own. And for her, that home would come without the tender love that she envied in her friend's match.

"Sister Retha?" His hands clasped hers warmly. "My home will be yours. Our home. There is no higher calling than to be a Married Sister."

She could not bring herself to look at him. She looked across the Square at his neat half-timbered house. A home, which she had always wanted. She looked beyond the Square, beyond carts, wagons, settlers, and townspeople, to her meadow. It shimmered in the searing afternoon sun. She knew its every rock and stone and tree and twist of creek, day or night, heat or frost. The meadow called to her, and beyond it, the forest, the freedom of the wilderness beckoned to the part of her heart that would always be Cherokee.

When her gaze returned to him, doubt clouded his lake-blue eyes.

"What more can I offer you?" he asked.

Love, she thought.

"Your offer is a good one," she said, her heart thudding dully against the inevitable. Marriage by the drawing of the lot. The groom requested. The Elders advised. The lot gave permission, sanction. At least Jacob would abide by the lot that he had sought. Who else would ever ask for her—the way Samuel had asked for Eva, the way Gottlieb had given up his world for Alice? And who was she, a foundling, to hope for love?

"And so yes, Brother Blum. I will marry you."

"Jacob. In private, I want you to call me Jacob," he said, giving her a quick smile as he squeezed her hand. She allowed herself to savor his sure touch.

"I will be a good husband to you," he added.

Because he needed her, she reminded herself. Still, she'd heard nothing but good of Jacob Blum. His tone held so much modest pride and yet entreaty that she had an urge to touch him. She stifled that urge. He said he needed her. It occurred to her that need was a kind of wanting. She wondered if it could become a kind of love.

Jacob led his tavern hack to the town's large barn, heart thumping in his chest. It wasn't from the fight. He sloughed off the concerns of Brothers Samuel Ernst and Frederick Marshall, both of whom had seen the altercation. The watchman approved, the Elder did not. Jacob didn't care what either thought.

As always, he had done his part for his town. No, what plagued him was something else.

He had bungled it with Sister Retha. Rosina Krause hadn't helped, of course, by introducing his proposal to his elected bride in such crass terms. He couldn't control what his fellow Elder said. He clenched his jaw in sudden anger. Between the war and his wife's death, he had little enough control over his life anyway. On top of that, he had lost his sense of humor.

Scaife had riled him. Perhaps if the fight hadn't sent Jacob's blood boiling with the sheer joy of action, he would have kept his wits about him and proposed to Sister Retha like a man. She had accepted his half-witted offer with a look of resignation. It cut him to the quick. He never wanted a reluctant bride.

Inside the barn, he mopped his brow. Compared to the stifling heat, the barn was cool. He welcomed its dark recesses. She was beautiful, yes, but he liked everything about her, even the way she had stood up to him. She had countered every one of his meddling questions.

No, he told himself, he wasn't meddling. He was exercising his rights as her Elder and her bridegroom.

He smiled a little at the thought of Retha's determined but ill-advised loyalty to the Voglers. He admired that in her, actually. Not that her loyalty was altogether misplaced. When Vogler had stood up against the community to marry the woman he loved, he had lost all but her. Jacob had loved his own wife in a quieter, easier way. Part of him envied Vogler such conviction, such passion, even while

Jacob had exacted Retha's pledge to stay far, far away from the man and his Cherokee wife.

Despite the hounding possessiveness that made Jacob bristle to see his bride in another man's arms, Jacob believed her innocent. Her tremors and her tearstained face convinced him that the fight had terrified her. The fight, or something about it.

He wished she had been willing to say what. He could not brush away his nagging feeling that she had secrets.

For it seemed that she did. And those unacknowledged secrets—not the likelihood that her friend was a spy nor the danger Retha could face if caught speaking English—disturbed him now.

The horse gave itself a hard shake when Jacob lifted the saddle from its back. In fact, he thought Gottlieb as fortunate in Alice's devotion as he himself had been in Christina's. Sadness nudged him strangely. What would *she* think, his original bride, the adoring mother of his children? Would she wish only for Retha to be good to those children? Or would she also wish Jacob happiness, affection such as they had known together? A brief image of her quiet smile flickered in his memory and vanished. Was it approval, or portent?

He sighed heavily. Few enough people found true affection in marriage, whether by lot or by random human choice that some would ascribe to love. With Christina, he had been fortunate that circumstance, proximity, and childhood ties had combined to bring together two like-minded, companionable people. Jacob was not without hope for himself, even this second time.

If he could but clear up one bothersome question. He handed the horse to the tavern's slave and prepared for an assault on the Single Sisters' silence about one of their own.

"What is the matter with Sister Retha? Surely there was a reason you never proposed her for the lot," Jacob said impatiently to Rosina Krause an hour later in her office at the *Gemein Haus.* At eye level, a rack of lightweight leather buckets, essential for the fire protection brigade, hung along the wall. He sat ignominiously under them, kindling a conflagration of his own.

Sister Krause's chin dimpled in hesitation. "There is naught the matter with her. Naught that could prevent her from being a suitable—"

"Then why did you not recommend her in the first place? You said there was no one suitable." He couldn't keep an accusing tone out of his voice.

Sister Krause shot a question back at him. "Are you the reason she was out that night we found her in the meadow?"

"Of course not," he said, indignant. What kind of Elder did she think he was? But then, he could understand why she might ask. What if he had stepped out that night for a rendezvous with Retha? Illicit trysts were not unheard of among courting couples, and his fellow Moravians were not intolerant of ordinary human passions. If he had been with her, the Sisters might well have dealt with her more lightly, not virtually locked her up.

"But you were there," Rosina observed dryly, giving him his first view of how she held sway over a bevy of older girls and women.

"At the end, yes."

Sister Krause leaned forward, a commanding movement he recognized from Elders' meetings. "Do you know what she was doing there?"

Jacob wouldn't lie, but he wouldn't betray Retha's confidence either. "I do now," he said carefully.

Instead of questioning him further, his fellow Elder pushed her ample body away from her desk and stood gazing out the window. Jacob knew the Square was virtually empty, the market done for the day, and anyone left driven inside by the blaze of heat. He had to admire the way the Sister dangled him, puppetlike, for her own purposes. He was a negotiator himself.

After a long moment, she closed the shutter with a snap. "Then perhaps you know why Sister Retha has slipped out of the house night after night since the day we took her in."

"Every night?" Jacob was dumbfounded. He had no idea.

"We don't know if she went out every night."

Her simple answer couched a bleak confession of failure. Jacob understood at once. One of the first women to arrive in Salem, Sister Krause had a keen sense of duty and responsibility. She would not take failure lightly.

"Surely Samuel Ernst would have detected her," Jacob said, struggling to sound calm and logical as new and sharper doubts assailed him.

"No, not Brother Ernst. He never did. She has

always been elusive. We tried to keep her . . . absences to ourselves, but Sister Holder and I could never be sure—"

"Sister Holder knows?" Jacob asked, all too aware of how knowledge traveled in a town that did not yet number two hundred citizens, counting children and infants.

The Elder's round face softened with unexpected sympathy. "Sister Holder knows, Brother Blum, and I know. No one else, save you."

He let out his breath. His family did not need to be objects of further gossip. "Good. That is good, I think. But how did Sister Retha get away with it?"

"How did she slip out? I have often wondered. We simply could not watch her every night." Rosina Krause cleared her throat nervously. "If you can keep a secret . . ."

Jacob nodded reluctantly. He didn't need another secret.

"Myself, I sleep through thunderstorms, and Sister Holder snores."

Jacob laughed, and suddenly felt less out of place in this pristine office. Losing control of his life frustrated him, but the Sister's life was hardly all in order. He sobered himself. "I beg pardon, Sister Krause."

"Oh, no. 'Twould be comical if it were not so serious."

It was serious. Jacob worked his hand into his neck, thinking. His bride-to-be had to have a reason for being out at night. "Do you know why? Have you any idea?" he pressed.

Rosina Krause shook her head. "We have none.

We don't know why or how often or even where she was going."

"Do you think she was up to . . ." he trailed off. She had been feeding her wolf only a short time. That was not her reason. She had denied consorting with spies so forthrightly, he couldn't imagine that either. And as for another man . . . no, no. He couldn't think she would. She was innocent to her core, he felt it in her shy response to his touch.

It was a moment before he realized that Rosina was waiting for him to continue. "She couldn't have . . ."

"No, Brother Blum. Apart from the deception, we cannot say that she has done aught wrong. In fact, when she was very young, we assumed she was sleepwalking. I can only tell you that she has done it from the beginning of her life with us. Oh, and that the night you came upon us, we found her, ah, dancing."

Like a sylph, Jacob thought, but said nothing. Rosina Krause need not know he had seen Retha, too.

"Do you think she's sleepwalking now?"

"No," the Sister said decisively. "She was wide awake the other night."

Liebe Gott, Jacob swore to himself. Or prayed. His bride-to-be had wandered the night for years. He would never know why, when, or where she had gone, and not even the Sisters could say how often she had stolen away. He could not know if she would continue, or quit.

If only he could foresee what Retha's irregularities would mean for his children. If only he could foresee what they would mean for him. His impulsive decision to ask for her hand was looking reckless and irresponsible for all concerned.

Sister Krause was so forthcoming, he should not ask for more. Still, he sought reassurance.

"Surely you have an opinion about what should be done."

"Brother Jacob, the lot said yes. 'Tis our faith to abide by the Savior's will as He reveals it through the lot," she said with simple faith.

Sometimes simple faith left him grinding his teeth. "But knowing what you know, you could have forestalled my request."

She looked torn. "I could not. 'Twould have put Sister Retha in a bad light—when, as far as we know, she has done no grievous wrong."

Without even thinking what he was doing, Jacob began to stalk around the small office. The Sister stopped him with a firm hand on his forearm.

"Brother Blum, our lot is the Lord's will. He has proven it so time and again. You may be the bedrock of her happiness. She may be the wellspring of yours."

Jacob studied the woman's round, earnest face. She cared for the girl more than she let on. He would care for Retha, too. Whatever folly his neglected senses had driven him to commit, his rational mind would deal with the consequences.

Hot afternoon sun streamed in through the tall, paned windows of the *Gemein Haus* meeting room. The assembled crowd sweltered in the heat. Retha stood beside her bridegroom, dazed. The thick, humid air made it hard to breathe. She tugged at the peplum of her new linen dress, a wedding gift from the older Single Sisters. Already damp with perspiration, its fabric still scratched where it touched tender skin. Sister Rosina, for once aflutter with excitement, had laced her up too tightly.

Retha swallowed against the narrow ribbon under her chin. It tied her clean, starched *Haube* around her just-washed flyaway hair. The ribbon was still pink. She was still single.

Her hands shook, her knees trembled. It was her wedding day. She thought she might explode.

Jacob's children looked explosive too. Brother and Sister Ernst, who were keeping them for a couple of days after the wedding, herded them to Jacob's side. The thin son shuffled, the large one giggled. Retha scarcely knew as yet which boy was which. Brother Samuel reached out an arm to still the giggler. When Sister Eva shushed the daughter and leaned over to whisper to her, Retha swallowed against a lump of confusing emotion that lodged in her throat.

In minutes, she would be mother to them all.

Jacob intervened with a snap of his fingers. The children went quiet. Retha stole a sideways glance at him and shivered in the heat. Her bridegroom. She scarcely knew what marriage meant.

He seemed larger here, confined to whitewashed walls. Taller, meeting her on the even ground of the wide planked floor. Wider, suited in his dark Sunday coat, its buttons marching down its front almost to his knees. More dignified. Even more commanding than when he had questioned her on market day.

Five days ago. So long ago. And now they were being married. So soon.

He caught her glance and gave her a quick, sure smile. As he had done all day, all week since they last met. Last argued. She wasn't at all clear where they stood with each other, except that he felt bound to marry her and she had bound herself to marry him.

That agreement reached, they had not been allowed to be alone together since.

He had communicated with her nonetheless with a smile across the Square, an intent gaze from his nightly station in the choir. Less encouragement from him, and she would not be here, her resolve wilting in the heat. His strength, his will, his distant warmth had held her to their purpose. All week she had thought of flight, digging her fingernails into her palms.

What had she been thinking to say yes to him, to his children?

She barely heard Brother Marshall's formal German liturgy. She did not, in fact, know all of the educated words he used. She longed for her old simpler life with the Cherokee, for wilderness, where wolves trotted free and indigo grew wild, where deer marked trails from high meadows to cool ponds, and she knew them all—plants and paths and creatures of the wild.

Not this. House, husband, children. They were not for her. She feared—she knew—she was not for them.

"I will," she heard Jacob say, his baritone voice mellow and firm. *Love her, honor her, care for her.*

Then Brother Marshall called her name, and she

put her mind to what he said. Her vow was not the same as Jacob's. *Love him, honor him, be subject unto him.*

How could she promise Jacob that? In the heat, a prickle of anxiety stole down her back where perspiration dampened it. She already had so promised him.

"I will." Her voice cracked, and she felt her soul split too. She had been free, compared to this. Hard as she had tried to fit in with the Single Sisters, she didn't know how to be subject to him or anyone.

And what of love?

Her heart shrank. He had yet to say a word of it.

Jacob took her hand and held it while Brother Marshall brought the service to an end. During those long moments, she was aware of nothing but a warm pulsing between them from his hand to hers.

Then Jacob turned her to face him, his blue eyes darkening to indigo as he drew her hand to his mouth and kissed her fingers with his lips. She thought she heard a stirring in the crowd, a rustling of assent.

He moved closer still and bent his tawny head toward hers.

"*Liebling,* sweetheart," he whispered for her alone, and brushed her lips with his, a caress as tender as the first spring fern. Her heart moved in her chest. Toward him. No one had ever said that, done that. No one ever before.

"Where are they taking Sister Retha?" Anna Johanna's voice quavered at the ceremony's end.

Her little hands tugged at the ties on Jacob's black Sunday breeches, jarring him back from a taste of heaven to the here and now of fatherhood.

Moments before, a full dozen heartbeats before Jacob was remotely willing to release his new bride, Sister Ernst had pulled her into the small anteroom off the large chamber. With an unpleasant shock at losing the sight of Retha so soon, Jacob watched the women disappear.

"Yes, pumpkin," he said absently. "She'll be right back."

"Is she our new mother now?" Anna Johanna asked, twisting the tie harder.

With a jolt, Jacob realized that his daughter had indeed understood his explanation last night. He searched her face for evidence that she was thinking of Christina. It was all innocence. Momentarily he surveyed his own heart, reminding himself of the promise he had made before Christina died: her children would not go motherless. So he had pursued the lot.

Whatever niggling doubts spiked up between his hope and his desire, this marriage was his first wife's wish. It was the Savior's will.

"Yes, pumpkin, she is your new mother. And she'll be waiting for you when you come home from your visit." Now he only hoped that Anna Johanna wouldn't destroy the double knot he had specially tied at his knees to withstand her tenacious fingers.

Her grip tightened trustingly, and he was glad he had insisted on his children being at the ceremony, especially Anna Johanna. She was safe with him.

"Does that make you our new father?" Nicholas

asked, smirking, unable to contain his delight over making such a clever joke on a solemn occasion.

"No, it does not," Matthias said in his precise, scholarly way. "It makes him our very old father still." The boy's rare laughter bubbled up. Jacob looked down at his middle child, hands piously folded while he grinned wickedly, and joined in the boys' laughter at his own expense. Even saints like Matthias needed a share of attention, Jacob supposed.

"You lads show your father more respect," Brother Ernst chided pleasantly. "They want us over there." He pointed to the long, narrow table where the Elders usually deliberated, backed up against the wall and doubling this late Sunday afternoon as a groaning board for a community feast that followed the candlelit service.

The boys scooted after him. Jacob followed, pacing himself so Anna Johanna wouldn't lose her grip on his knotted breeches.

Halfway across the room, Traugott Bagge, recently back from Pennsylvania and still without a mate, stopped him with congratulations, joking that Jacob's bride had been much nearer after all. And pretty. Jacob smiled. He knew that.

As they neared the table, Philip Schopp in jest begged Jacob not to rush to swell the number of boys that he would have to teach. Yet he sounded envious. As well he should, Jacob thought, savoring tender, heated thoughts of his bride in his arms. If he had any say about it, he and Retha would indeed increase the schoolmaster's burden. Jacob aimed for them to start tonight.

The two men merged into a clump of earnest Brothers waiting for the food to be served. Dismissing fragments of conversation he overheard about "No sign of rain" and "Hard on the troops," Jacob anxiously watched the anteroom. For such a simple task as changing Retha's ribbons, Sister Ernst was taking her own sweet time. He wanted his bride back now. In the five long days since Retha had accepted him, urgency had consumed him despite all doubts. The wait had reduced him, an experienced man, a Widower, to youthful eagerness.

A smattering of decorous claps silenced the talk as Sister Ernst pushed his bride into the chamber, a new blue ribbon tied under her chin. His wife now. His beautiful wife. Untrammeled by oaken buckets and willow baskets piled with linens, she moved with newfound grace, shy and regal as a doe in the woods. As she walked toward him, her friends among the younger of the Single Sisters each handed her a wildflower until a bouquet filled her hands. Ducking her head sweetly, she acknowledged each tribute. He thought he saw her blink back tears.

She came to his side, taller than the other women, taller than some men, yet shorter than the bear he knew himself to be. Ah, how she would fit in the circle of his arms. And he was back where he had been all week, consumed, with Retha urgently on his mind, pulsing through his veins, sighing on his breath.

He took in her wild, golden eyes. The tan and amber stripes of her new dress darkened them, enriched them.

"Fetch that man a brandy!" Brother Bagge

laughed heartily, beating on his back to remind him of the occasion, the other men laughing along good-humoredly. Caught lusting after his bride in public, Jacob felt his face heat. He was that far gone.

Samuel Ernst stuck a cut-glass goblet of the town's best peach brandy in his hand as Eva handed one to Retha, and passed the bottle on. In three large swallows, Jacob drained his glass and set it down.

Nicholas, who had hovered impatiently near the food, came over and asked for a glass of his own.

Jacob shook his head, as much to clear it from the brandy as to tell his son no. But Matthias told Nicholas for him. "We're too young, Nicholas. You know that."

Nicholas glowered at his brother. Not here, Jacob thought, putting a warning hand on the older boy's shoulder. He should not have insisted they be allowed to come. "It's our father's wedding," Nicholas hissed at his brother.

"We're still Little Boys," Matthias spit back, maddening in his pious command of community rules.

"No brandy or arguments for any boys," Jacob said firmly.

Together they glared at him.

Bodily he separated them, putting one on one side, one on the other. He should have considered their incessant bickering before insisting that they come. As quickly as his sons arrived at camaraderie, so quickly would it vanish into petty rivalries. But he had wanted them here, as much for their own sakes as to welcome Retha.

"Can I have brandy, too?" A watery voice wafted

up from just above his knees. Jacob dug his fingers into his neck. She didn't even know what brandy was.

"You're just a baby," Nicholas taunted.

"Everyone's too young for brandy," Jacob said, wishing he could dose them all with it and be done with their moods.

Anna Johanna's lower lip trembled. He darted Retha a desperate look. His children would mar her day.

But she broke into a sunny smile and knelt down before Anna Johanna. "You're not too young for . . . for . . ." Retha surveyed the piles of food behind them, a teasing hesitation in her voice. ". . . dumplings! Strudel! Sugarcake!"

Anna Johanna's damp eyes sparkled.

"Which one do you want?"

"Sugarcake," she whispered.

Retha snatched a small square of sticky sugarcake off the table and presented it to his daughter with a flourish. "We need to feed those boys, too," she confided in Jacob.

Samuel Ernst overheard. "I will take care of that, Sister Retha." Using his watchman's voice, he called out that it was time to eat.

"Toasts first!" Brother Schopp cried.

Retha's eyes met Jacob's in a quick glance filled with dread. No toasts, she mouthed.

Jacob felt a surge of pleasure at the understanding that passed between them. He knew what she was thinking as surely as if she spoke the words aloud. Feed the children, and take me home. In her way she was as shy as his daughter, but she had held up better, bravely, in public, for him.

"One toast," he said in a voice of command. Quiet rippled across the noisy, happy crowd as all faces looked toward him. His years of leadership counted for something.

"To my bride. Her courage in marrying us, and her beauty." He thought of Single Sister Krause's hope for her most unusual charge. He turned to Retha quietly and said so she alone could hear, "I pledge to make you happy in our home."

Her amber eyes widened in surprise, reminding him uncomfortably of her wild wolf. And how much she might be like it.

CHAPTER 4

Cries of "best wishes" and "a long and happy life" rang out from the steps of *Gemein Haus.*

"You'll regret it," Eva Ernst teased. Her plump hand clinging to her stocky husband's arm belied her friendly taunt.

"Gratulieren!" Philip Schopp cried out as Retha and Jacob escaped the festivities and crossed the parched square to Jacob's house. Stately Brother and Sister Marshall led their way, Jacob's children romping close behind.

Neither the hour nor the sultry evening heat stifled their high spirits. Anna Johanna, skipping along beside the Ernsts in her trusted old dress, waved a sprig of indigo that she had salvaged from the floor. Nicholas, eating a huge piece of cake, rudely defied all good manners by hiding his free hand in a pocket. Meanwhile, sober Matthias—usually sober Matthias—gawked at two Little Girls of his own age as they wove in and out around the bridal party.

At the heavy green door of Jacob's half-timbered home, Retha paused and faced the happy crowd with her husband. The Little Girls hurried up, shrieking as they sprayed the couple with rose petals and a bit of precious rice. Retha and Jacob fended off the light barrage with upheld hands and laughter. When it ended, Retha eyed first the giggling girls and then the rowdy family that she had acquired so abruptly.

Always before, she had loved being among the Little Girls and younger Single Sisters, full of joy and bent on play. Now, self-consciously fingering the new blue ribbon under her chin, she felt matronly and apart. A Married Sister, with a home of her own.

Red-faced from the heat, a few members from the brass band struck up a spirited folk song from the homeland they had left behind. Familiar with the tune from other weddings, Retha couldn't keep her toes from tapping.

Soon Jacob's arm settled approvingly around her shoulder. For the first time. Her toes stilled. He was touching her for everyone to see, conspicuously, she realized with alarm. She suppressed an urge to lurch away, to retreat from the public view, escape to the meadow and run down to the creek.

Instead, tall and solid, her new husband backed her up a step and squeezed her into the protection of his small doorway. She didn't feel protected. She felt exposed. The band began a softer tune, a romantic little air.

Jacob leaned over and whispered in her ear. "Brace yourself."

A surge of white-capped Little Girls and Single Sisters rushed them.

"This is for you, too, Sister Retha. Open it," the youngest Little Girl trilled importantly, holding up a present. Anna Johanna sidled in to see, eyes bright with interest.

"Must I?" Retha pressed against the bulk of Jacob's hot body. She knew what was coming.

Little Catherine Baumgarten held up a tome-sized package wrapped in a scrap of dyed cloth and tied with a vine string. It was very light. Taking a deep breath, Retha undid the bow.

Loosed, the cloth fell away of its own accord, and a foam of fine white linen unfolded in front of her.

A gown for her wedding night. Linen so fine that her laundry-roughened skin picked its fabric. Deeper ruffles than she had ever seen edged its neck and sleeves. She didn't want to be caught staring, but couldn't stop.

Applause rippled through the crowd. To cover her flustered state, she looked down. Her new stepchildren watched the show with avid interest. The oldest and the youngest, at least. Smiling smugly, Nicholas stuffed both fists in his pockets as if he had a deep dark secret. An enthusiastic Anna Johanna clapped in time with Sister Ernst. Matthias, oblivious to his father's wedding, was grinning foolishly at the little Baumgarten girl.

Someone cried out for another toast.

Nicholas's sneaky grin widened. "Here, here," he chimed in, letting fly a second barrage of rice aimed mainly at his father. Retha took refuge behind Jacob's great body.

"Enough for one day!" Speaking with firm good humor, Jacob scowled at his older son as he swirled Retha through the door. He closed the door behind them and clicked its latch with a flourish. "That rascal!" he said. Still, she heard the pride of love in his voice.

"The word is out, they're all rascals, Brother Blum!" Retha teased, crowding with him into a narrow entry.

"You too, I think," Jacob answered. He swooped in on her, larger than ever in the confining space, and close enough to kiss. She clutched the gown up to her neck.

Gently he pulled it away. "You have no need of hiding from me now."

"I'm not hiding." But she felt her face heat.

He bent his head for an even closer look. "You are blushing, *Liebling*, at the very least."

Of course she was! She peered at him in the shadowed entryway. His sober tone couldn't mask a grin tugging at the corners of his mouth.

Caught teasing, caught blushing. She lifted her chin. Would the rest of her life be embarrassment with this man!

"You would blush, too, if they held your night-shirt up to the whole wide world," she sassed, jerking the gown behind her back.

"*Nein*, with me, 'twould only be from heat." Playfully he tipped her chin before reaching around to snare her gown. "Let me see it."

"Not for a moment," she cried, stepping back-wards and stretching the gown as far away from him as possible.

He caught up to her, gripped her tightly around her waist, and danced her into the middle of a large room, smoothly dodging scattered chairs, a table, a desk. He was still laughing, laughing harder. To him it was a game. She hadn't played with boys since childhood, but games she understood. She wriggled in his arms to keep him from the gown.

"Yield," he gasped, pausing to snatch a kiss.

"Never!" Twisting, she flung the gown into the air, away from his control. Like a giant white heron, the gown sailed to the front of the room and fluttered to roost over a slanted desktop.

Fine brass implements clattered to the floor, and a small globe of glass shattered.

Shocked at her own recklessness, she skidded to a halt.

"A spirited wench. I like that." Jacob's eyes glinted and dropped to the strict lacing of her bodice.

Under it, her breasts heaved. She was acutely aware that he saw that. Then he went after the gown, brought it back, and held it up as if for measurement against her wedding dress.

"I'm going to like this, too." He looked her up and down. Under his new possessing gaze, she wanted to shrivel up and blow away.

Without a thought, she flattened her hands across her bosom.

"No, don't," he said. His voice deepened, softened. With one finger, he gently moved her hands away, leaving her uncovered, fully clothed. Her breasts felt heavy, conspicuous. One hand moved back to cover them. He frowned. "Please don't."

She dropped it down. Somehow she had pushed the game too far. "What must you think of me?"

She bit into her lip. Jacob Blum was a man, a father, a pillar of the town. Why was she always and ever again a silly girl in front of him? "I was frolicking like a fox cub."

"A vixen. A very pretty one," he insisted.

She shook her head. "I have always been too wild."

Sudden tenderness softened his handsome countenance. She couldn't fathom why. Misconduct was her besetting sin. She couldn't hope to hide it from him now.

"Oh, Retha. Not too wild." As if to comfort her in her dismay, he calmly draped the gown across a black-sleeved forearm. "We will use this soon enough. I will just put it on the bed."

He stepped down into a room beyond the parlor and disappeared. Alone for the first time since morning, Retha examined her surroundings. Except for the scattered instruments and broken glass, the room was immaculate. Its paned windows opened to the east, but smaller ones in adjoining rooms admitted the last slant of evening sun. Yellow light warmed brass fittings on desks and glanced off glass cobblers' lamps on shelves.

Off those, that is, that had survived her assault.

Hastily she stooped to pick up his tools, not knowing what they were or what they were for, and replaced them at the lipped edge of the slanted desk. She wrinkled her brow. The shards of glass were another matter. She gathered up her skirt and was cautiously depositing them in it when she heard Jacob's tread behind her.

"Never mind that." He gave her a reassuring hand up, helped her transfer the broken glass onto a pewter plate, and brushed up the rest with a rag. Feeling useless, she stood by, eyes fixed on the wide planks of the polished floor. A slippered toe peeked out from under her new skirt. She withdrew it from her husband's view and sighed, resigned to confessing her sins.

"I have been careless."

For a moment he said nothing. The day's heat radiated up from the floor, off the walls.

"How do you like your new home?" he asked after what seemed to Retha a long and possibly angry silence. But his voice was mild, even.

She breathed with relief. He was giving her a fresh start. " 'Tis beautiful, so clean, Brother—Brother—Jacob."

He snorted with amusement, overlooking her clumsiness. "An illusion, you can be sure of that. Let's see. The Ernsts have had my children for"—he studied the face of a gleaming watch he took from a waistcoat pocket—"all of nine hours and forty minutes. Their house is now a shambles."

Retha looked up. Surely he was joking. "They were at the wedding the whole afternoon."

"My point exactly. They need much less time than that."

She scanned the immaculate room. "This is no shambles."

"Ah. The Single Sisters' other gift to us was cleaning up the house. It hasn't looked this good since Christina—"

Breaking off awkwardly, he took a step away. Retha could see his throat work. Since Christina *what?* she wanted to know. Would he say *died,* or would he say *went home,* as Moravians usually said? She had been at the funeral herself, and it had been a sad, sad day, those three lost children and the large, grief-stricken man. Even she had felt sad to see a kindly woman gone home so young.

Retha studied her bitten-off nails. At least the

weeks of doing laundry had removed the last traces of dyes, she thought, waiting to hear more about Christina Blum.

After tense moments Jacob gripped her elbow, inclining his head toward the kitchen, and guided her toward it.

"Come. They left us a repast as well."

She made a face. "I could not eat another bite."

Yet more than the thought of food, she resisted his touch. It made her feel strange in ways she didn't understand, tingling, tense. Worse, it made her think of the woman who had gone before her, the woman who used to make him laugh. She wished he had finished what he started to say about his wife. It was no secret he had adored her.

Perhaps he adored her still. Retha touched her new blue ribbon and sighed with heavy doubt. What if he found her to be a poor substitute?

The small kitchen was equally neat, its blocky table laid out with pickled eggs, a bannock board of cold pone, a redware bowl of blackberries.

He offered her berries. "Fresh picked, I'd guess."

"And early. 'Tis not yet July."

"The heat must have hurried them along."

She popped two berries in her mouth, their tartness exploding on her tongue. "Ooh, not ripe," she exclaimed, shaking her head and pursing her lips tight when he offered to feed her another berry himself. His gesture made her think of him feeding children. His square fingers looked too large for such a tender task.

And eating suddenly seemed terribly intimate.

"No more." She tried to smile. "I said I couldn't hold another bite."

He ate the berry himself as if it were the most succulent fruit in the world. "Better. But if that doesn't tempt you, perhaps this will." He indicated a stoppered jug and two bottles filled with ruby and amber liquid. "Cider or scuppernong wine. Or more of that peach brandy."

At the thought of more dizzying brandy, she recoiled in mock horror. "Not spirits! I would fall off my chair. My head still spins."

"I might like for your head to spin," he chuckled warmly.

She furrowed her brow. He was recovering his humor, but his meaning eluded her. Save for the unfortunate mention of his wife, he had seemed happy, had been full of caged energy all afternoon. Standing to prowl the confines of the kitchen, he seemed to make a quick decision, and grabbed two mugs from the topmost shelf of a high cupboard. He didn't even have to stretch, but his reach left her admiring his wide, deep shoulders. He filled the room.

She didn't know what to make of his taut haste. The wedding was over, the celebration ended. They could rest now. She had one whole day to learn her way about the house and prepare to meet the children formally. To meet them, she thought worriedly, and the Marshalls tomorrow morning at breakfast.

He plunked the mugs down on the table, filled them from the jug, and took a swallow. "Cider then, as the milder of the three. I do not want a drunken bride."

"Drunken! I've never been drunk in my life. I'm a perfectly sober Sister, Brother Blum—" She clapped a hand over her mouth. "I will find it hard to ever call you by your given name."

He pushed her mug closer to her.

"I do not have the habit," she explained weakly, ignoring the cider.

He smiled. "Then I will teach you."

Setting his own mug down, he drew her to him. His body was damp from the heat, thick, long. Its unanticipated contact shocked her. He had been so upright over the soldiers that day. She could scarce believe that he would show so little restraint here. After all, that physical business was for making babies. Even she, green as she was, knew that. He had three children already, and they were more than he could handle.

Perhaps not. Tenderly, seekingly, his mouth touched hers. And she was distracted. The skin of his lips was as tender as a new spring leaf, she mused. Who would have thought that? They moved across her mouth. A quiver she had never felt before snaked into her stomach. A little alarmed, she pulled away and heard him groan.

"There." His soft, sweet tone was musical, the voice she had always admired, and his face so very close that she saw only shadowed planes and golden angles lit by the setting sun. "Say my name."

"Jacob," she whispered obediently.

"Good," he whispered back, managing to sound like a teacher until his mouth covered hers, humid and urgent. She closed her eyes. He was too, too close. Too pressing. A pressing heat, heat like the brutal summer's day that lay thickly over the room, enveloped her body.

He pulled at her lower lip, released it, then parted her mouth with his wet tongue. Its tip touched her teeth, then probed around them and searched above them and between them. He touched her tongue. She gasped. He tasted of the cider.

She had seen people kiss, a little, but hadn't imagined it would feel like this. Nor had she thought that a kiss would taste—that a man would taste—so good. No matter that he did, his invasion sent an unexpected ripple down the back of her neck. A frightening sensation. A faint memory of some bad dream, some nameless fear flitted across her mind's eye. She wondered—no, worried—what would happen next.

But he broke off.

And she felt his terrible absence in the cool air on her damp lips.

"Jacob?" She whispered his name again, confused by yearning and an unspeakable fear that strummed through her at once.

"Beautiful." Jacob started to touch his new bride's lips with his finger until a look of feral caution flashed in her amber eyes. He withdrew.

Perhaps he had imagined that look. She tasted sweet as a summer peach plucked from a tree and hot from the sun. Yet she pulled away. Twice. He gave a sigh and let her go again. Noticing the heavy confinement of his black coat for the first time all day, he unbuttoned it with fumbling fingers and shrugged out of it. Hot air hit him like a blast from a forge. God help him, he hated summers in his new country. They had never been this bad in Germany.

He turned to hang his coat on a peg. Not a second too soon. Under his damp waistcoat, hard desire for Retha pressed against his breeches. His virgin bride was not yet ready for evidence of his arousal. She could barely handle a drink of cider. Behind him, she choked merely sipping it. He hoped coughing would occupy her while he adjusted himself inside his breeches.

She walked away, striding lightly across the floor into the parlor. He pivoted in time to see her tip a curtain aside. For a long time, he watched and wondered as she gazed into the night. He must have frightened her away.

He blamed himself. He had assumed too much and rushed her. She could not be like his first. Christina had been a distant cousin and his closest childhood friend. With their families, they had sailed to the Colonies together and never been separated after that. Once married, they had come to loving as naturally as water flows a well-planned course.

Retha started out a stranger.

That had to be her problem. Simply welcoming her here must not have been enough. Women took to houses in bits and pieces, room by room, table by chair by bed. Except for the scary night he found her, she had never seen his home. He could only hope she didn't remember that. She had been only ten or twelve, and straight from years of living in bark houses under stars. How alien his home must have appeared to her.

He joined her by the shadowed parlor window, knowing she saw nothing. "'Tis dark out," he reminded her quietly.

"Everyone's gone home." She sounded lost. His heart twisted. He could think of nothing in his life for which he had been as unprepared as she must be for this. For him, for his whole family, overnight. Christina had been playmate, confidante, long before she became his wife. He must not assume that anything tonight would be the same.

"Come," he said. He thought better of trying to lead his bride. Wild she might be, but innocent, too, unused to a man's touch. He was sure no man had ever kissed her.

He lit a golden candle, releasing its honeyed scent into the room and casting a pale light. Already it was dark enough to spook his daughter. But his new bride was a grown woman, as his senses told him relentlessly.

"This way. The children sleep here." Reversing their steps through the entry to the stairs, he led the way to the loft's two rooms and gave her time to look around.

"That's a fine tile stove." Her voice sounded controlled.

"In winter, it heats both rooms."

The candle's light muted the intricate designs on the stove's sleek tiles. She asked if it had been made here or imported. He didn't know, he hadn't built this house. And then she was full of questions about who slept where and whether the boys took care of wood and fire and ashes and how Anna Johanna slept at night in a room alone.

Delaying questions. He started down the stairs before she had a chance to interrogate him about what was stored under the eaves. When he took her hand it rested in his, compliant but passive. He gritted his teeth. He was in this marriage for the rest of his life. He would make it work.

Back in the parlor, she walked straight to his drafting table and held up the compass that had fallen out of its shagreen case when she had flung the gown.

She winced as she inspected the jointed instrument. "I hope I didn't break it. What are these things?"

"My drafting instruments. This is a compass." He traded it with her for the candle. "I use it when I work."

She gave him a blank look. She didn't even know who he was. Large scrolls of paper stood in a deep basket against the wall. He unrolled a stiff sheet detailing his latest project.

"This is one of my designs."

Her eyes politely scanned the curling paper. She couldn't make out the object represented. Girls learned geography, but he couldn't expect her to have a feel for drafting.

" 'Tis the mill's new water wheel."

"It had a water wheel the last time I went by," she said smartly.

"A wooden one. Ours has to be improved if we're to meet the army's demand for grain."

She smiled vaguely, uncomprehending, unimpressed. He felt his loss. Christina had been his friend when he had discovered his knack for invention. Scarcely a one of his plans had escaped her helpful emendations.

With Retha, he realized with an inward groan,

such a point of commonality might be far to seek. For weeks, months, he had steeled himself to the notion that his new wife would be a different woman from the one he still privately grieved. But he hadn't steeled himself for this absence of familiar ground. He had to give Retha time, to learn, to adjust. To him. And himself to her.

His last sense of the afternoon's lively celebration waned like a setting moon. He determined to recover it.

Restless, he escorted her to the kitchen and poured another mug of cider. Gamely she came along, inspecting a rack of dried herbs hung along a wall.

He mounted a workstool and listened, amused, as she proceeded to talk about each and every one. To chatter. Any mature man would recognize a nervous bride. Stretching his legs in front of him, he relaxed as she rambled.

Thyme, she insisted, was the easiest to grow. He couldn't agree or disagree. He was watching her pretty chin.

"That's an annual"—she pointed to the marjoram—"but the Sisters have little success with it."

It overran his garden, but he couldn't say so. His gaze had moved to her slender neck. Which invited his caress.

She touched a sprig of horehound. "Isn't this medicinal? Have the children had sore throats?"

"Not lately," he muttered. Her shapely fingers deftly sorted through the rack.

Jacob was on a rack of his own. Those fingers ought to be on him, deftly sorting through layers of hot, heavy clothing, through to where his body burned. He quaffed the last of his cider and touched her shoulder.

"Retha, 'tis time."

She spun around, wide-eyed. He thought she swayed—a little away, a little toward him, he couldn't tell.

"You've had a long day." In the candle's glow, her breasts lifted as she drew a quick breath. He shut his eyes against a stab of desire, then acknowledged what her quick breath must mean. A bride's nerves, not arousal. Nothing more. Even Christina . . .

Nein! Not again! To himself, he vowed the end of all comparison. Christina had been dear friend, beloved wife, the mother of his children, but he had to let her rest in peace. He squeezed his eyes shut against the lingering hollow of her absence, and loosened the stock that tightened around his neck.

Retha was not merely another woman. She was his sanctioned bride. And simply scared of what would come. An understandable trepidation in a woman, any woman, he told himself, but the more so in a young one taking on a family nearer her age than his. His arm circling her slim waist, he aimed her toward the large room behind the parlor where he had stashed the gown.

Alarmed, Retha felt her body throb. She sensed possession in Jacob's guiding touch.

"Lead the way," he said.

She couldn't. Already exhausted from the effort of forestalling his next intimacy, her mind raced to seek another delay. She didn't know why she had to, only that she did.

Hot candlewax dripped onto her forefinger. She let it burn, grasping for a way to postpone the inevitable. None came to mind. She was going to have to sleep in his bed. The honeyed scent of beeswax filled her nostrils.

Acutely aware of his wife standing woodenly at his side, Jacob lowered the hinged press bed, retrieved its mattress from the floor, and tossed it onto the bedropes with a single sure motion. He snapped out freshly laundered sheets. He had become expert at this maneuver these last months. They puffed with air and settled with a sigh. He smiled. He doubted that the Sisters had meant to add that touch.

Beside him, his bride gripped her candle like a cudgel.

He took it back and secured it in the chamber candlestick. Wax had dribbled onto her forefinger. He peeled off the wax and drew her finger to his mouth, watching her expression as he tenderly kissed the mild burn. She trembled like a trapped fawn. But her amber eyes had the look of a wolf too smart to run, too wise to trust.

He did not understand. He was taking every care.

"Allow me only to free your hair . . ." he said. He released a breath, anticipating a fall of red-gold riches. She neither consented nor turned away. A light tug undid the new blue ribbon under her chin.

When he eased the starched *Haube* off, she lowered her eyes, sunk her chin to her chest. He didn't have to wonder why. His limited experience told him to ease her past this dawdling, this reluctance.

His fingers strayed into her tightly bound hair, scavenged for pins, and extracted them one by one, as if he—as if she—had all the time in the world.

They did not. In his mind, the children galloped back into the house, filling day and night with needs. He summoned his powers to make the most of this rare and private evening.

At last the silken mass tumbled down around her shoulders. In minutes it would cover his face, his arms, his chest.

"I have wanted to see you thus since that night." His fingers combed thick tendrils, arranging them across the snowy collar of her dress, over her shoulders, down her back.

Truth be told, he wanted to feel it against his skin.

He unlaced the ribbon that threaded the length of her bodice, careful not to startle her with an inadvertent touch. Released, the stiff new linen stood out from her bosom. Memory led his fingers to the pins that fastened her neckerchief. He removed them carefully. Only when he tried to slip her bodice off did he realize how stiff she was.

"Helfen mir, Liebling," he coaxed in his native tongue.

She helped, lifting one shoulder forward, then the other, absently, as if she were not actually there. She let her tan, striped bodice drop to the floor, revealing the top of her white shift. His eyes fell to her thinly covered breasts. High and firm, they barely moved. She barely breathed.

Concern deepening, he studied her face. With its arched brows, high cheekbones, fine nose, it was the prettiest face that he had ever seen. Her expression, however, was painfully blank. Not scared or nervous, but blank. Like a sleepwalker's.

"Retha." He waited. He had a sense that she was far, far away.

Her coming back was slow. She focused her gaze on him, and a little light returned to her eyes. He took that to be a response.

"Let me," he coaxed again. "You are my wife. I am your husband. This is what comes next. Look." He shucked his waistcoat and untied the stock that bound his shirt's damp collar to his neck.

Her eyes went glassy again.

Bewilderment and a terrible desire to chastise her besieged him in equal parts. Trying to keep both out of his voice, he ended on a tone of impatience. "This is what married people do. Kiss. And undress. And kiss some more."

She stood as rigid as a stone.

He swallowed a black Teutonic oath that he had forgotten he knew and forced a gentler word. "Your new gown's on that chair. Why don't I leave you alone to change?"

He left the room, safely feeling his way on the blessedly dark, blessedly short walk to the kitchen, only to stub his toe on the table's thick leg. He gave a caustic laugh of pain. He had already used the blackest oath he knew.

What could he do? Something told him he had more than a reluctant bride on his hands—or rather slipping through his fingers. And only these two nights to get her past the difficult part.

A drink would help. His fingers searched the

table, skipping over the cider in its squat jug and going for a more serious kick. He took a burning swig from the uncorked brandy bottle.

Leaning his torso's considerable weight against the table's edge, he covered his face and sucked in air through his teeth. He had been in a state of rut for a month, and his ever-so-promising bride thought him an ogre. Sudden, deep fatigue walloped him. Sorrow and loss and loneliness, three impossible children, war raging around him—he had come through all his trials. Surely he could manage a resisting bride.

Humid night blanketed the room, almost too thick for love. They had seen too many weeks of heat and no rain, and this night afforded no respite. But he would love her. He tore open his shirt, rubbed a hand over his chest.

As she would learn to do. She was so near.

A room away, fabric rustled and landed on the floor with a thump. Her skirt. He imagined her next removing her shift, then gliding to the chair that held her wedding present. He heard her shuffling around. Under candlelight, her skin would glow, her form would be perfection. His manhood hardened against his dark Sunday breeches, and he let out a groan of hot desire.

Damn his unruly body. For months he had been without release. He had ached for Retha since the day he saw her. He would have to ache a little longer. He downed a draught of brandy.

From a distance, the bed creaked as it always did when he crawled into it at night. She had taken the first step. Relief mixed with anticipation.

He wanted her. But he would have to be careful,

he would have to take it step by step. He gulped a last swallow of brandy and headed toward the light, treading a fine line between uncertainty and bounding hope. He even smiled. She would be under the scented sheet, coverlet pulled up to her nose, he'd wager.

And he would teach her why she wanted them pulled down.

But Jacob walked in on a startling sight.

Against the far post of the bed, eyes closed tight, his bride sat on her heels, naked as the day she was born, her body rocking from side to side.

"Retha?" Disbelief careened down his spine.

She rocked.

Trying to make sense of what made no sense at all, he scanned a room in disarray. Only her prim white gown lay untouched where he had left it. She had folded the bodice and skirt of her amber wedding dress and laid them in the cupboard, leaving its door ajar. Her crumpled shift lay abandoned on the floor, midway between cupboard and bed. One threaded stocking dangled across the nearest chair.

He tugged hard at the ribbon that tied his hair and looked around for other garments. After a moment he spied the second stocking flung across the spinning wheel that sat in the room for daytime use. And her *Haube*—she had tossed it into a basket of flax.

Gott im Himmel, he prayed. She had gone mad. Never in his wildest dreams. Darkest nightmares. Desperate, he tried to recall what Sister Krause had said about Retha's aberrations. She went out at night, sleepwalked. This was not sleepwalking. This was worse, weirder.

What had Rosina Krause failed to tell him?

For moments that seemed like hours, Jacob watched his bride. The steady rhythm of her rocking sank into his body like an ax hacking green wood, hacking into hope, hacking down desire.

At a loss for what to do, he collected all her clothes and mechanically stacked them in order on a spare chair. Then he sat with great care on the edge of the bed. She paid him no notice. He wanted to make her stop, but hesitated to touch or speak to her. Sleepwalkers, he had heard, could be startled into harming themselves. Yet what could she do?

She was in no danger here. They were alone, bride and groom, in a safe room in the quiet night. Besides, he was sworn to protect her. And he had to find out. Her slow, steady rocking would fast drive him to an asylum. To Bedlam, he remembered, dredging up the English word for it.

Gently, gingerly, he laid one hand on her nearest, slender shoulder.

She didn't miss a beat.

He brought up the other hand, touched it to her opposite shoulder.

"Retha." He paused, then spoke purposefully. "You have to stop now."

She rocked.

He firmed his grasp, but she didn't react.

"Retha, 'tis Jacob. Open your eyes."

Under delicate veined eyelids, her eyes moved in a restless, troubled way. Her lush lashes fluttered, eyes opening to reveal white edges. And nothing more.

If only he could remember everything Sister Krause had said. Had she known anything of this peculiar madness? Had Retha always had such spells, such fits? Or given such performances? He prayed not, for they were beyond his ken.

Even so, however she acted tonight, he tried to console himself that her conduct was an aberration. She had been sane enough, able enough to establish herself in the community. He knew of nothing that had actually interfered with her work. Under the Sisters' care yet ultimately on her own, she had been schooled, mastered the art of dyeing, taken on laundry, and even made friends, however ill-advised.

He was unconsoled. She could not go on like this. Nor could he let her. But he knew so little of her. Earlier, in the kitchen, she had responded to tenderness, he remembered. A kiss might rouse her where a touch had not.

Leaning forward, he brushed his lips across hers.

The rocking stopped.

Encouraged, he kissed her again, watching her even as he lengthened the kiss, aware of thick fringed eyelids, sweet breath, silken skin beneath his fingertips . . . and a resisting mouth.

Her eyes flew open, filled with that terror he had seen before, and she wrenched herself away.

"No, no. No, no," she chanted in a singsong, childlike voice. "No, no. Don't hurt. No, no."

And she resumed rocking.

He jerked the string that bound his hair and freed it with a savage shake. She was beautiful—

fawn fragile, snake sinister, wolf mad. She could be having a fit, staging a performance, or going insane: He could not tell the difference.

With such a woman, he feared for his children's safety.

He feared for himself.

Her nakedness displayed a healthy, luminous body that would tempt any man. It tempted him. Against all reason, ungovernable desire swept him like a hot wind. He did his best to tamp it down, but it assaulted him in unholy gusts, buffeting his chest, lashing his skin, burning his loins. He had waited so long, and her body was perfection.

And it was his. He clenched his fists against a primal urge to take her. He had the right but would not stoop to do it. He would never, ever force a woman in such a state, real or imagined, acted or felt.

In an agony of frustration, he stripped the coverlet from the bed and wrapped her in it despite the heat. Later, when his mind cleared enough for him to ponder what he had done, he would know that he acted from a sense of decency, all he had to offer.

Concealing her sweet body muted none of his desire. He sat down heavily on the chair where she had flung one threaded stocking. And waited for morning to come, and burned.

CHAPTER 5

Sun warmed Retha's face, the mild heat of early morning. She let it, taking another moment to enjoy the clamor of summer birds—the surprising blast of tiny wrens, the haunting coo of mourning doves, the caw of crows. Perhaps they thought this day would not be hot, she mused lazily, lying on her side and stretching like the cat that guarded the grain from rats at Steiner's Mill. How well she'd slept. How lovely to wake up to the sun.

She never woke in sun.

Cautiously she opened her eyes and studied the unfamiliar room. Jacob Blum's bedroom. Uncurtained windows admitted morning light. It brightened whitewashed walls. Last night there had been but one candle, a valuable beeswax one Jacob had considerately provided for their wedding night. She remembered sipping cider, touring the rooms, being burned by candlewax, undressing hastily to get into the bed—but nothing clearly after that.

Surely, she hadn't fallen asleep on her own wedding night. Worried to think she might have done precisely that, she raised up on an elbow. Coarse sheets abraded her skin. She stiffened, realizing with a small shock that she was naked.

Naked in Jacob Blum's bed. How had that come to be?

And where was he? Nearby. Propped up so she could see him, he sat in a chair at the foot of the bed, wearing his shirt and breeches from the day before, dozing. He could not be comfortable, she thought, though his shirt was open at the neck, its untied stock dangling. Curious beyond measure, she stared with unaccustomed freedom at her first sight of a sleeping, half-dressed man. Under his summer body linen, she could see the strength of his wide shoulders. And under the breeches he must have slept in, the awesome power of his heavy thighs.

She sank under the sheets, not sure that gawking was within her rights. His bed was wider and longer than her dormitory cot. It was big, of course, because he was so large. The mattress was thick with new cornhusks. They were for her, she realized.

He had prepared his bed for her.

And he must have taken off her clothes. So that's the way married couples did it. Whatever it was that they did. That duty must have been a lot simpler and quicker than she had dared to hope. Or perhaps in the end, he had agreed with her. It was much too soon for children. Even so, she had expected some shock, some pain, some embarrassing exposure. There was nothing but this bird-bright morning, and a man she barely knew sitting in a chair beyond the foot of her bed. She looked at him more boldly. His open shirt revealed a thatch of sandy hair at his throat. His deep chest rose and fell evenly, peacefully.

A shiver of appreciation coursed down her neck, followed quickly by a quiver of fear. Drawing the coverlet to her neck, she apprehensively studied this private, intimate side of Jacob Blum, her husband. Her husband.

Suddenly, urgently, she wanted to be dressed when he awoke, and she scooted out of the bed. On another, smaller chair beside the bed, her wedding clothes lay stacked and folded, but neater than the laundry she used to fold for the tavern. It was not her work at all. She thought she remembered what she had done last night, but what had Jacob done?

Surely nothing . . . harmful. Shaking off that doubt, she hastily pulled on her shift and secured her stockings with linen garters. She felt better already. Safer. When she had tied on her skirt and laced her bodice tight, she smoothed the wrinkles out with a sigh. Ready for the Marshalls' breakfast, she turned to straighten the tumbled bedding. And gasped.

No blood this time.

She reeled at the thought.

What blood? There was no blood.

She closed her eyes.

That blood. Blood on the sheets, and splattered on the wall. Stumbling to a stool beside the bed, she curled into a small ball of misery.

Make it go away, she used to say to Singing Stones.

Close your eyes, Singing Stones would answer, until you see only gray, and rock yourself to sleep. Don't let fear rule. It's only memory. No harm will come of it.

No harm had come. Silent this morning, Retha

hugged her knees. This time, it was not so bad that she needed to rock, but she must have done so last night. She had tried so hard to keep her secret. At least there was no blood. The wild beating of her heart slowed as she summoned birdsong to ease her fear. She concentrated, not on the doves' sad music but on the bold blast of little wrens.

After a time there was nothing but song, and she opened her eyes to her husband's stony gaze. Embarrassed to be caught hugging her knees like a little child, she quickly stood and smoothed her skirts.

"*Guten Morgen,*" she said sunnily. He need not know how shaken she was. "I dressed. Should I not wear this to the Marshalls' breakfast?"

In her wedding dress, she turned for him.

Jacob glared at his fully dressed wife. He couldn't help it. So that was how it was going to be with her. But did she not remember? And what was this new performance, or was she truly mad? He rubbed his hands over his aching face. During the night, each and every tiny muscle had contracted into a grimace of disbelief. He could not scrub it out. A grown man would not, should not give in to adversity, yet at the sight of his wife's determined cheer, he felt a moment of despair so profound he wanted to weep.

His wild, sunny wife was mad, or beyond redemption. And he had committed the gravest error of his life.

"You look like a sullen bear who spent all night in a chair, which I hope you did not," she said brightly.

He jerked his head up at the cruel remark, but her cheerful expression showed no intent to wound. Determined not to let her see that she had any power over him, he forced a light laugh. "It won't happen again. You'll not turn me out of my bed again."

"Oh! I never intended that." She flushed deeply, her cheeks like peaches. "I—we must have fallen asleep." Doubt flashed across her face, but that damnable cheer soon subsumed the doubt.

"Determined to make the best of it," he muttered, more to himself than to her. Certain that fatigue lent a sarcastic edge to his words, he pivoted and stalked into the kitchen. Let her follow if she wished.

"Yes, of course," she said after him, on a questioning note.

He had questions, too. Behind him, she trod lightly, as if she were an Indian. But she smiled like a conniving virgin. Or an innocent one. Which was she?

To slake his thirst, he filled a dipper with water, but checked himself when she looked at it longingly. She was his wife, his care. Wordlessly he offered her the dipper, watching closely as she drank deeply, wiped a drop of water from her mouth, and cleared her throat to speak. He couldn't guess what she might have to say.

"This is a fine home, Jacob, and I am proud to be its mistress. And the children . . . I promise I will work hard . . ."

Dry-mouthed, stiff-necked, and disbelieving, he dropped the gourd onto the table with a solid thump.

She jumped.

"Why don't you tell me what was going on last night?" he said evenly, but with a faint hope of startling the truth out of her.

A tremor in her chin betrayed her confusion. "I'm sorry about the glass."

He had thought he couldn't bear her all-denying cheer, but he didn't want tears. He softened his voice. "The glass is not important."

"Oh." To his amazement, she fixed him with a sincere amber gaze and touched his hand. "I forgot to thank you for a beautiful wedding day." She blushed. "And night. I hope I didn't drink too much."

Speechless, he ground his teeth against that oath he hadn't used in years before last night. He was, he had always thought, a man of exact measurements. He knew things of the material world by weight and size and substance. He could bend them to his will, shape them to his imaginings. He could dam rivers, turn the course of streams, supply a town at the frontier's edge with precious running water.

Retha left him at an utter loss. What could a man do? Wait, and watch her actions, and try to gauge her intent, he told himself. Protect his children. Protect himself. And keep his hands off the only part of her he had not yet taken a measure of—that delectable body.

"I . . . um . . . have to dress," he said, and retreated to their bedroom. Knotting his stock at his throat, he thought about what lay ahead, not in the distant future, but today and tomorrow. Shortly he would take her to the Marshalls' breakfast. There he would reveal nothing. Then tomorrow, at the

Ernsts', he would introduce her to his children as their mother as if all were well, regardless of the miserable truth.

"The Ernsts are ready for us. Past ready by now." Retha heard the exasperation in her husband's voice the next day as he urged her to dress to go with him to fetch the children home.

But she didn't answer him. Her mouth was full of pins. As her fingers struggled to fasten the bodice of her best work dress, another pin dropped to the floor.

At least he had left her alone to dress. She would hate for him to see her shaking at the prospect of being formally presented to his children as their new mother.

Perhaps she should wear her wedding dress, as she had done yesterday for breakfast with the Marshalls. No, she had decided to put it away for fall Sundays when she would need something heavy and warm. Besides, wearing such a fine new dress on an ordinary Tuesday morning might be prideful.

She was proud, though, proud to be married, even if Jacob seemed not to share her feeling.

"Children don't wait!"

"Ouch!" she cried out as a straight pin lanced her thumb. She stuck it in her mouth and sucked the coppery blood.

Jacob thundered in. Off and on since their wedding night, he had been a dark cloud. He had tried for fair weather at the Marshalls', but she could tell he was feigning good humor. She had not the slightest idea why. Something had happened on their wedding night.

Or had not. She pushed the thought away.

"You may as well learn this now as later. The children's needs can't wait on our—" He studied her, scowling. "What's the matter with you?"

"I was hurrying," she said through pins, and held up her thumb, hoping it still bled.

A fat drop of bright red blood welled up.

"I think you will survive this." He examined her thumb thoroughly, as if she were a child.

" 'Tis only a pinprick," she said, irritated by his unexpected condescension.

"Do you usually mistake your appendages for pincushions?"

She looked up doubtfully. Was he mocking her, or teasing? His tone was Sunday sober, but a corner of his mouth crooked up.

Squeezing the edges of her bodice together and inserting two final pins without mishap, she tried to sound casual. "Perhaps I'm not prepared to become a mother."

His dark demeanor lightened. "Some days I'm still not used to being a father. 'Twill come to you soon enough."

She sighed and shook out her skirts. "I'm ready."

"Wait . . ." With a quick movement, he tucked a loop of hair under her *Haube.*

She shrank from him when the brush of his fingers tickled her neck. Since Sunday night, he had avoided touching her, sensibly acknowledging, she assumed, that now was not the time to engage in those married matters that led to children.

Part of her feared he did think it was time. Last night he had insisted on sharing the bed, stripping down to his crisp body linen in full candlelight. Sitting on the bed's edge, she had not been able to watch. But she had listened. He told her this was how it would be between them every night with the children home. They would go to bed together, strip to their body linen, and sleep side by side. She need neither fear his touch nor worry that he would hurt her.

But he had lain so close beside her, she could feel his heat. His massive body hemmed her in. She could not steady her breathing to match the slow, even exhalations that came from the depths of his thick chest. Once, in sleep, he rolled toward her, stretching out a heavy arm that pinned her in place. A fear had washed over her like floodwaters engulfing the ark.

This hand at her neck in daylight was only a touch, she reminded herself.

His gaze lingering on the very spot that he had touched, he spoke softly. "Although I liked it as it was." He hadn't used that tone since their wedding night.

"Thank you," she mumbled politely, uncertain what to say.

Self-consciously she checked the nape of her neck where his fingers had rested. No more hair astray. No explanation for the tingling.

"We had better go then," she added, and hastened for the door.

The day was sunny, the heat rising. The dusty street slanted uphill to the Ernsts' small cabin at the edge of town. Retha stretched to match Jacob's long-legged stride. In the morning's relative coolness, more people were out than usual, several acknowledging her who never had before. An elderly Single Brother tipped his hat. Abraham, the newly baptized slave who worked at the Tavern, nodded before lowering his head.

Brother Meyer too, scurrying back to his busy tavern, gave her a smile. "We miss your good work on our linens."

"I will not miss the laundry!"

"You will have laundry aplenty, Sister Blum," he laughed, rushing on. But Jacob stopped him, engaging him in business. She caught snippets—*that Hessian . . . a danger to us*—but dismissed them and savored her new last name.

Sister Blum. Her throat caught, her eyes misted, but she wouldn't let on. Overnight, she marveled, her status had changed—had become his, of that she had no doubt. At last, she had a name. It felt so right, she even allowed herself, for once, to ponder who she had been. The Cherokee she remembered vividly. But from the time before them, she recalled only a faint tableau: There had been a tall, brusque, bearded man, a woman with hair the color of her own, a piercing scream, and blood . . .

Enough of that. She monitored herself as she had always done. She had survived by forgetting. Long ago, Singing Stones had encouraged her to believe that wondering where she came from did no good, that hoping to find out did even less. She persuaded herself that that was so. If those terrifying dreams had anything to do with where she had come from, she was better off not knowing.

". . . have to insist that the Redcoats bury their own," Jacob was saying with finality.

"All the more if the soldier were a Hessian." Brother Meyer sighed heavily. "The man would have to be German."

Jacob shrugged. "They will link us to him nonetheless. Germans caring for a wounded German mercenary cannot but look suspicious—"

"Brother Blum!" plump Eva Ernst cried out, flapping her way down the street. "I found you not a moment too soon. Hurry, hurry!"

Jacob had already broken into a run. "Anna Johanna! What's wrong with her?" Retha heard him shout as he sped past her friend.

" 'Tis not her! 'Tis the boys!" Eva yelled, puffing as she bent over, hands on her knees, to catch her breath. "Fighting—the boys are having a terrible fight."

"Where's Brother Ernst?" Retha cried out.

"At the store—I go to fetch him. You—help Jacob—"

Waiting not a second longer, Retha hiked up her skirts and dashed after Jacob. She would not have thought so large a man could run so fast. Far ahead of her, he leaped the steps and disappeared through the open door of the Ernsts' tiny cabin.

She sped up, dismissing a thought about the unseemliness of running through town, past the Square, the Brothers House, the public cistern, and Dr. Bonn's apothecary. Gasping, she arrived, and hung on the doorjamb while she caught her breath.

A ruckus of grunts and clatter assailed her. She peered inside. Nicholas, red with anger, pounded his flailing brother, pinning him to the floor with superior weight and skill.

"Enough of that!" Jacob lifted his large older son as if he were no more than a sapling, gave the thin boy a hand up, and reprimanded both of them. Retha strained to make out Jacob's harsh whisper but could not.

What was she to do? The boys had made a mess, scattering bright new pewter utensils and wedding-gift redware on the table and onto the floor. At least one platter had been smashed.

She felt useless, extra. Then she heard smothered sobbing. Searching the room, she spied Anna Johanna under the table, clinging to one of its legs, weeping.

Had the boys hurt her? A need to protect this fragile child, fiercer than anything she had felt for her wolf, flooded Retha. Scrunching under the table, she crawled over to sit cross-legged beside Anna Johanna. She reached for the girl but checked her hand. Jacob had given fair warning. Touch could set his daughter off like a torch to a dried-out haystack.

"Anna Johanna," Retha whispered, feeling the awkwardness of offering comfort without touch. " 'Tis all right. You will be all right."

Anna Johanna sobbed away. There were no signs of injury, but her knobby spine heaved beneath the thin fabric of her cherished old dress.

"I'm here, sweet potato. Are you hurt?"

"Not hurt," she cried.

She sounded hurt. Retha pressed her. "Do you want to tell me what's the matter?"

"No-oo," she wailed.

"Very well, then . . ." Retha paused, casting about for the right words. She had reached an impasse with her new stepdaughter at their first crisis, and felt perfectly useless. "I shall just keep you company." She folded her hands in her lap, and waited.

Gradually the tide of sobs ebbed. "Anna Slowhanna . . . is not my . . . name," she sputtered.

"Of course it's not. No one says it is."

"M-Matthias s-says so. 'Cause I'm slow."

"You're not slow. They're just bigger and faster. You're Anna Johanna. Everyone knows that."

"M-Matthias doesn't. He calls me Anna Slow." She ran the offending words together in a rhyming, nasal voice.

Retha recognized her imitation of Matthias's voice and understood the impact his teasing would have. Her seven years with the Single Sisters had taught her how effective youthful tormentors could be. How hard to be youngest and slowest and always last. The memory of taunts that used to come her way still raised her hackles. That boys might be as cruel as girls had never occurred to her.

She glanced at her husband and his sons. He was dressing them down in words so soft they almost frightened her.

"Matthias isn't going to say that anymore, Anna Johanna." Carefully, Retha used the child's full and proper name. It worked.

Still crouched under the table, the girl turned on her hands and knees, and looked at Retha with blue eyes trusting as a pup's. "Not ever?"

"I don't think so."

Anna Johanna gave a little smile. It faded quickly. "How 'bout Nich'las?"

"He said that, too?" Retha tried to hide her sudden annoyance, but it was hard to keep it down. She might be new to the family, but in her opinion both boys should be looking out for their younger sister, not driving her to tears. Especially not the elder, and especially not in company.

"No," Anna Johanna said, but her chin trembled.

"Did he say something?"

Retha couldn't catch her breathy mumble and leaned forward.

"He said what?"

Anna Johanna hung her head. "Told me I'm a baby."

"Sweet potato, you're the youngest. That doesn't make you a baby."

She looked up hopefully, tears spangling pale lashes.

"In fact, I would say you're a big girl now," Retha said. When she got her hands on those boys, she wouldn't let them off with a soft-talking.

Suddenly, of her own free will, Anna Johanna surrendered herself to Retha's arms. Retha, her heart swelling with tenderness, folded her new stepdaughter to her breast and rocked her for comfort.

Wild as they were, Jacob had never had occasion to be ashamed of his boys until now. In less than five minutes, he had wrung confessions from them.

After Sister Ernst had sent her husband down to Traugott Bagge's store, Matthias had teased Anna

Johanna, calling her by her baby name. Only one time, he protested. It made her cry.

Nicholas claimed he took up for his sister. He corrected Matthias by telling him he would be the one to help tend the new babies, just as he, Nicholas, had once helped with smelly Anna Slow.

"You called her that?" Jacob simmered.

Nicholas had fueled the flames in both directions. He was expert at riling his brother and his sister. He always whetted his militant spirit at their expense. Not for the first time, Jacob ruefully acknowledged his older son's fire without perfectly understanding it. Nicholas had been born for soldiering, striking out at any opposition from his cradle days. Of late he followed the ceaseless tide of troops from both armies, paying little regard to which side was in the right and much attention to the fit of uniforms to young men and bayonets to rifles.

Or had his interest in things military coincided with his mother's death? It was yet another puzzle Jacob had not had the time to piece together. Until he did, Nicholas would be Moravian under his father's roof, and Jacob would take the same careful steps to snuff out his son's warlike nature that he had long taken to control his own.

He consigned both boys to a month of mucking out Brother Meyer's stables with no remuneration.

"For free?" Nicholas protested.

Jacob silenced him with a look.

Matthias tugged at his coatsleeve. "What about the new babies, Papa?"

"Babies?" Jacob puzzled.

"Nicholas says there's going to be new babies."

Nicholas, still resentful, cut Retha a hostile look. "New wives mean new babies, stup—"

"One more word, son," Jacob warned. "I can find hotter, smellier work for you."

In silent protest, Nicholas pursed his mouth. His split lip made him wince. Jacob buried a smile. Pious Matthias, although overpowered, had landed one solid hit. A further thought consoled Jacob: This time, he need not lecture his firebrand son on the theoretical consequences of fighting.

He ushered the boys to the table, planning to seat them on opposite sides, opposite ends, as he would do at home. Their brotherly brawls had intensified since they had lost their mother and he had been away from home so often. But this brawl he attributed to the marriage, and to the change it was bringing to their lives. As if they—or Anna Johanna—needed more change.

Although his daughter was taking this rather well.

Where had she gone, anyway? He looked around, unable at first to make out where she was. Then, there, he saw her, on the other side of the table. Underneath it, on the floor, and not alone. For a moment, he could not believe his eyes.

Then he could. His heart thudded in his chest. Retha, sitting on her heels, her cap askew, held his daughter in her arms.

And she was rocking her.

Alarm and anger fighting for command of his senses, Jacob strode across the room. He would not let Retha drag his daughter into her . . . what if it were madness?

"That's intolerable."

To his surprise, Retha gave him a look of pain. Or was it innocence? He didn't know her well enough to read her face. He didn't think her in a trance, as she had seemed to be on their wedding night. Yet whatever strangeness she was perpetrating on his daughter, it comforted Anna Johanna. His daughter was quiet.

Perhaps he had overreacted, and hurt Retha to boot. The thought that he had done so cut through his anger to a feeling of consternation that he didn't want to examine.

He searched Retha's face for a clue. All he could see in her amber eyes was warm concern for his daughter.

Nevertheless, the image of her haunting behavior on their wedding night was burned into his brain. When she had rocked then, she had not been herself. And now she was rocking again. With his daughter. To him it seemed purposeful, even mad. He could not trust her with his child. Not yet.

"Let her go, Retha," he heard himself say tautly.

Clutching her burden, she lurched to her feet.

"Here." She offered him his daughter.

He knew not to accept. "Put her down."

Retha hesitated. "She was crying over what the boys—"

"I know what the boys said. Put her down."

She did, whispering first in Anna Johanna's ear. Anna Johanna nodded solemnly, plopped her feet on the floor, and happily took her usual handhold where his breeches knotted at the knee.

"What in God's name did you say to her?" he

said, too sharply. He meant to be calmer, for everyone's sake.

At his tone, Retha looked as if he had betrayed her.

He had lost all control—of his children, his temper, of Retha and her pain. But he didn't think she had been in a trance. This morning, unlike their wedding night, he believed she knew what she was doing when she rocked his daughter.

He would not allow her to do that. "Tell me."

She lifted her chin a trace and straightened her cap. "I told her she's such a big girl she doesn't need me."

Retha's quiet dignity struck him like a splash of cold water in his face.

Raking his fingers across the back of his neck, Jacob said a quick prayer for wisdom to deal with his unfathomable wife.

He picked up a shard of redware and turned it in his hand. The boys had gone well beyond making a shambles of the Ernsts' small home. He would have to apologize, make reparations. He could only hope that Brother Samuel had been spared this awkward family altercation.

Sister Eva poked her head inside the door, Samuel close behind. Their timing—and the deliberate smile on Eva's plump face—said they had been waiting just outside.

"We are back from the store with utensils enough to cook for an army. I mean, a crowd," Eva chattered self-consciously. "We had only enough for ourselves."

Samuel stepped past his wife and warmly took

Jacob's hands in his. "Our heartiest congratulations, Brother Jacob."

"We wanted you to have a moment alone," Eva added. "For the introductions."

Jacob cleared his throat. His kind friends were prepared to overlook his children's bad behavior. He could not. But so far, negotiating trades and sales with Redcoats and Continentals was proving to be a simpler task than keeping his family in line. He apologized for the fight, paid for the damage, and then gestured to his sons to face their hosts.

"You have words for Brother and Sister Ernst."

Nicholas almost rolled his eyes, but Matthias modestly clasped his hands in front of himself. "I was wrong to fight in your house," he said promptly.

"I'm sorry," Nicholas jerked out, a moment after his brother and with a good bit less sincerity. Jacob let the apology lie. A good soldier, Nicholas had said what he ought whether his heart was in it or not.

And he would be wearing that split lip for a week.

Jacob gathered the children to him. "You have met Sister Retha, but now you can greet her as your mother."

Retha felt all eyes turn on her and almost bolted. Not since the night that Jacob had captured her in the Square had she felt so much the focus of attention, or so much out of place. Without a word to her just now, he had settled the boys' fight. But when he found her comforting Anna Johanna, he turned on her for no reason she could see. Mercifully, he made short work of this formal presentation.

Nicholas, who stretched up toward his father's

height, intimidated her with a slightly challenging formal bow. Matthias, paler and thinner than she had noticed before, shifted his feet and blushed. Her stepsons, her new responsibilities. Her new problems. One could not admit that he needed a mother, and one could not hide it. But little Anna Johanna grinned.

Jacob seated them randomly, Retha thought at first. Then she discerned a pattern. Child, father, child, stepmother, child.

She could not like his arrangement. He had placed the boys as far apart as could be and seated his daughter to separate the two of them, husband and wife. While her friend Eva, piling plates with waffles and hefty slabs of bacon, sat snug up to her own new husband.

As I should be to mine, Retha thought. Instead, Anna Johanna and Matthias flanked her. With pretend cheer to mask her chagrin at being shunted aside, she buttered her stepdaughter's waffles. When she passed Matthias honey, he refused. Apart from his finicky eating, Retha reflected, two men and two hungry children made the midmorning meal an entirely different affair from the Single Sisters' simple breaking fast at *Gemein Haus.* Heaps of food were decimated.

Whatever troubled her husband, his appetite was unaffected by the squabble.

"My family still needs your help, Brother Samuel," Jacob said after a while of talk and clatter. Retha wondered what the family could possibly need—apart from miracles for the three children. Miracles were hardly the night watchman's line of work.

He casually took a long swallow of the steaming sweet coffee that even the children drank. "Help? Whatever for?"

"For watching after them. When I'm away."

"Why, Nicholas is near grown," Samuel said. "And now that Retha's in charge—"

Jacob wouldn't let him finish. "They are not that safe, not with me away and so many troops about."

With him away? Retha gaped at him over Anna Johanna's *Haube*-capped head, then filled her mouth with waffles to hide her embarrassment. What did he mean, he would be away?

And what kind of help did he think *she* needed? He had *married* her to help him with the children. Surely, he wouldn't take away her duties before giving her a chance to show she could fulfill them.

Across the table from her, Nicholas manfully sawed off a hunk of bacon. "I'm big enough—"

"But not old enough," his father answered.

Samuel winked at Nicholas. "The two of us will make it doubly safe."

Retha, on being excluded yet again, felt the first seed of anger planted.

"It needs to be you," Jacob insisted.

"I will do it. I am out every night anyway."

"Day is scarcely safer."

Retha bridled. Day or night, Jacob was planning not to entrust her with his children.

"I will be here, Jacob. If any troops are near, my wife and I will come straightaway," Samuel assured him, then narrowed his eyes. "Nevertheless, I fail to see why you must take all the missions."

Jacob gave his friend a wry smile. "Are you volunteering to master English?"

Samuel deflected the idea with upraised hands. "Not I. The night watchman needs little English beyond *halt*."

"I wouldn't let him anyway," Eva said firmly. "What you do, Brother Jacob, is far too dangerous."

Retha had not considered Jacob's work dangerous. Then she remembered how he had fought the redheaded man and realized that it must be.

Jacob lifted a shoulder, dismissing everyone's concern. "The actual missions have not been, despite everyone's fears."

So he was not in danger, Retha thought. If he was not, neither was she. She chafed. Jacob had ignored her during all the friendly breakfast conversation. She hated being left out. Worse, he flatly denied that she could handle her new responsibilities. Why had he even bothered to marry her?

"The night watch is more than enough risk for my Samuel," Eva continued, placing a plump hand on her husband's arm.

Retha noticed Eva's secure, possessive touch, and felt Jacob's exclusion of her all the more. Samuel smiled at his new wife, and Retha longed for Jacob's smile. She wondered what had gone so suddenly, inexplicably wrong between her husband and herself. If she touched him as Eva touched her husband, Jacob would likely push her hand away.

If he would let her close enough to touch him.

She slumped against her chair. Samuel Ernst doted on his bride as Retha had fondly hoped Jacob would dote on her, want her, cherish her. Premature hope and her own indomitable optimism had filled her with romantic notions. For Eva Ernst, such hope had been well placed. Her optimism had been rewarded with a besotted husband.

For herself, Retha sighed, she had acquired an inexplicably distant mate who had forgotten overnight his sweet promise to make her happy in his home.

At her side, Anna Johanna merrily chased a run of honey across her plate and smeared some last crumbs of waffle onto the table and into her lap. Swabbing off the sticky mess while the little girl giggled, Retha consoled herself that one member of Jacob's family liked her.

Matthias pushed food around on his plate. "When will you go this time, Papa?" he said, dejected.

When indeed! Retha disguised her alarm by taking another forkful of waffle. Up till now, Jacob's departure on any mission had seemed a distant future event. Matthias was asking his father to name the day he would go and leave them in her charge.

Or rather, leave Brother and Sister Ernst in charge of her, Retha silently corrected. The bite of fluffy waffle turned dry and fibrous in her mouth.

Jacob intently carved a piece of pork. "Not this week, son. Perhaps next."

Nicholas's eyes lit with avid interest. "What's this mission about, Father?"

"The army wants the grain we promised. I'm to let them know at their garrison as soon as the millrace is repaired and the new wheel working."

Nicholas set his coffee mug down with a decisive thump. "I'd like to see the garrison."

Eva Ernst gave a horrified gasp. "They would snap you up for a recruit before you passed the gate."

"You're big enough to get away with it, too," Samuel teased, clearly thinking the danger less.

Jacob set down his fork and glared at his friend. "Don't encourage the boy, Brother Samuel. He's hardheaded enough about joining the army."

"Well, I do want to be a soldier," Nicholas said.

Jacob huffed. "Last month 'twas a gunsmith."

"Soldier too," Nicholas insisted.

Eva Ernst stood up to pass around a tin plate of blackberry pie. Offering a wedge to Nicholas, she reminded him sweetly, "Moravians don't go for soldiers, Nicholas."

Taking the pie, he looked up stubbornly. "Some boys from Friedland did."

"Those men were drafted," Jacob said. "Some of them illegally. Their families paid the threefold tax, but the army reneged on them, and we had to arrange for their release."

"What's 'reneged'?" Matthias asked. He had left two-thirds of the food on his plate and turned down the berry pie.

" 'Tis when you strike a bargain and turn your back on it," Retha said quietly, reminded of the promise Jacob made her at the altar and then so fast abandoned.

All heads whipped around to look at her.

She had been purposefully silent, collecting her thoughts. Now she purposefully spoke, seeking her husband's gaze and holding it. "Imagine a man consulted the lot about where to build a house. The lot said to build it here, but he built it there. Then he had reneged on his promise to the Lord to abide by the lot. The same way you can renege on a promise to a person. You give your word you'll do something, then you don't. Do you understand?"

Jacob's gaze didn't waver. Retha thought he ought to be ashamed, familiar as he was with reneging on promises. She saw his jaw clench. Perhaps he was.

"I suppose," Matthias answered.

"Here's another example, Matthias," Eva said in her cheerful way. "Imagine that a man consulted the lot about proposing to a particular woman, and it said he could. Then he would have to ask her, or he would be going against his solemn promise to obey the Savior's will."

Retha watched Jacob's expression harden. Perhaps he wasn't ashamed. More likely, he regretted marrying her.

But the deed was done.

"Is that how you married Sister Retha, Father?" Nicholas asked. "Because the lot said you had to?

"Nicholas!" Jacob said sharply.

"Well, it did, didn't it?"

Suddenly determined not to be left out, Retha caught her new stepson's gaze. "It doesn't work that way, Nicholas." She thought his father misunderstood his intent. At the wedding, Nicholas had asked for particulars, too, not rudely, but because he wanted to know. "A man seeking a wife asks the Elders to cast the lot. They can suggest the woman or he can. If the lot says yes, then they ask her if she's interested. Then she can say yes—or no."

Nicholas turned to the Ernsts. "Is that how you did it?"

Samuel shoveled another forkful of pie to his mouth. " 'Tis the way we all do it."

Thank you, Samuel, Retha thought.

"Because you wanted to?" Nicholas probed.

Eva smiled happily. "Because we wanted to, Nicholas. And then we abide by it."

Thank you, Eva, Retha thought again. Then she studied her plate, unwilling to see Jacob ignoring her again. Purple syrup oozed from the edges of her pie. She liked that shade of purple and could produce it, but not from blackberries. It took pokeberries to make it fast.

But Jacob should be pondering what had been said, she thought angrily. Because he was not abiding by the vow he had made to her. Happy in his home, indeed.

The Ernsts' words, if not hers, ought to remind him where his duty lay.

She toyed with her pie. Matthias's abstemious habits must be catching.

Someone rapped decorously at the front door.

Liebe Gott, Jacob muttered.

They had left Brother and Sister Ernst an hour ago, and Jacob had yet to settle his family in. He felt the way Sister Ernst had always looked to him—like a fussy mother hen whose chicks were scooting out from under her in all directions.

When the knock came, Matthias was up in his room, rummaging loudly for a precious book. In the parlor, Nicholas noisily searched for a chalkboard. From the kitchen, Jacob overheard his daughter complaining that she had left her "redacool," her little purse, at Sister Ernst's.

"Little girls don't carry reticules," Retha said patiently. Against his will, he admired her throaty voice.

" 'Twas my real mama's," Anna Johanna answered.

Cringing at his daughter's unkind words, Jacob jerked open the door, prepared to welcome almost any distraction from his flock.

A disheveled Brother Marshall held a tattered missive in his hand. Dispensing with formalities, he pushed his way in and lowered his voice. " 'Tis your cousin Andreas, Brother Blum."

Matthias shouted down that he couldn't find his book, and Nicholas yelled back where to look.

"If we might speak in private," Marshall added.

Half attending to his boys and half to his fellow Elder, Jacob motioned the latter to take a parlor chair.

Marshall remained standing, peering out from under drooping eyebrows. "You would prefer privacy."

Jacob shrugged. Save for his bedroom, every room was full. "This is all I have. What has my cousin done this time?" he asked, resigned to yet another lengthy recitation of his cousin's thoughtless transgressions.

New to Wachovia, Andreas Blum lived in Friedland, one of the Moravians' outlying settlements. There he had interpreted their trading practices to his own advantage, disregarding one of the Moravians' key tenets, that most property was held in common. Communal property was a source of their strength and an article of their faith. His cousin's transgressions had been brought to Jacob's Supervisory Committee, and thus to his attention.

So far, he had barely managed to keep Andreas in line.

Marshall sat down and handed Jacob the missive. "This time, it might not be his own doing."

With a sinking feeling, Jacob read the note. "Drafted." He slapped it against his thigh. "Who brought this?"

"His neighbor, Jonas Reed."

"Did he say which regiment?"

" 'Twas not the regular army." Marshall grimaced. " 'Twas Liberty Men."

"I hope not Scaife's detachment."

"I fear so. They bound him up tight and hauled him off in the night." Intent on persuasion, Marshall leaned forward. "You must go. As with those others, he paid the tax. We have records. You can redeem him. You must."

Jacob crumpled the note in his hand. "Scaife will be difficult to persuade, whether we have records or not."

"Then go to his superior. Scaife is but a captain. He would answer, I think, to that regular army man, Colonel Armstrong. He has sided with us before."

Upstairs, boys' boots scuffled across the floor. Jacob lifted his gaze to the ceiling. " 'Tis too soon for me to leave them. They cannot be ready."

I'm not ready, he thought.

Marshall must have caught the reluctance in his look. "Ah. You have come from Brother and Sister

Ernst, have you not? How do the children take to their new mother?"

"Very well. We are all doing very well." Jacob covered his emotion hastily, wondering at the magnitude of that white lie on a scale of venial sin.

"If another man could go, Brother Blum, I would send him."

"I know you would."

"However, Brother Bagge has but returned from Pennsylvania, and I—"

"I'll go. Andreas is my cousin, and I know what to do."

"I will gather his proof and write the colonel a letter."

Jacob nodded, already organizing the trip in his mind. "I can leave in an hour. I have to take the boys back to school for the afternoon and then instruct . . ."

Instruct my wife, he thought, in her duties, in a thousand and one things she would need to know about each child, each task, each meal.

Brother Marshall gave him a look of kind sympathy. "Now, at least, your children can stay home. Sister Mary Margaretha will care for them. You can rely on her."

Jacob masked his doubt and led Marshall to the door.

Sister Mary Margaretha, indeed. At the Ernsts', Retha had had the nerve to upbraid him over breakfast. He had scarcely had the time during this chaotic morning to digest her pointed looks, her deliberate explanation of the word *reneged*, her disturbing kindness to his daughter.

He stalked to the kitchen. "I need to talk to your

new mama, pumpkin," he said, starting to tug at Anna Johanna's fine blond hair and remembering not to. "Would you go upstairs and take these tallow lamps for tonight?"

Anna Johanna trotted upstairs, proud to have a mission of her own.

He turned to his bride. Her amber eyes shining in the bright sun of early afternoon, she sat expectantly at the kitchen table. Unwanted, unwelcome warmth pooled in his groin.

How could she look like that—so innocent after her strange actions with him on their wedding night and with his daughter only this morning? Was it madness—or a bride's nerves in the one case and a new mother's awkwardness in the other? How could he know? Where could he turn?

She smiled sweetly, and he clamped down on desire. How could he—knowing what he knew, having seen what he had seen—look at her and be overcome with craving?

"An urgent mission has come up," he said brusquely, glad that thoughts were silent. "I must leave today, and leave you with the children. Of course, I will tell the Ernsts, and they will take charge. But if the children become too much . . ."

"What is the mission?" she asked with utter calm.

"My cousin, Andreas Blum. Do you know him?"

"Only by word of mouth. He must be a Single Brother." Her eyes sparkled at her little joke. Single Brothers and Single Sisters lived strictly apart.

In spite of himself, Jacob smiled back. Of course, she would have been kept quite separate from his rather dashing cousin. "Yes, he is. And just drafted by Captain Scaife, apparently. Andreas and I rarely see eye to eye, except in this. He will resist them—so as not to fight. And his resistance will put him in the gravest danger."

"Then you must go." Retha squeezed his hand as if to offer comfort, but her unexpected touch ran through him like fire. "We will be fine."

Doubt flooded him. " 'Tis too much to ask. I will call on Brother and Sister Ernst. You know naught of the children."

"I know their names and who sleeps where and how to cook and where the Ernsts live if I have questions," she said.

Jacob searched her face for a sign of deception.

"And I know Brother Schopp and Sister Baumgarten and the Marshalls, and will call on them if need be," she continued.

He heard only earnestness, saw no attempt to deceive. He wanted to trust her. She was too guileless, too wild for plotting. Now Brother Marshall had added his confidence in Retha to Sister Krause's strong support. Perhaps he ought to give her this first chance. Trust someone else for a change. After all, her logical litany was mightily reassuring.

"Besides," Retha added, unblinking under his gaze, "Sister Rosina taught me all I know of discipline."

A short laugh escaped him. This was too much sense for madness. "I . . . very well then. I have to take the boys to their lessons."

She put her hand on his forearm to stay him. He looked down, confused.

"I know the way to Brother Schopp's house," she said. "If this is so urgent, should you not go right away?"

In the end, he conceded. She sounded both prepared and eager to take on her new role. He rushed her through the house, reviewing all she needed to know. Then he climbed the stairs to the children's rooms and instructed them to remember their regular habits and to obey their new stepmother.

Predictably, Nicholas looked mutinous, although probably more over not being allowed to go than over staying home with a stranger. Matthias, sitting with hands clapped on his knees, withdrew. Anna Johanna, as so often lately, looked a little lost.

Downstairs, Retha met Jacob at the door, handing him hat and money purse and powder pouch. He had to admire her quick grasp of such loving, wifely chores.

"Be very, very careful, Jacob," she said earnestly.

Ah, how he relished the sound of his name willingly on her tongue.

Suddenly she rose on tiptoe and flung her arms around him. "And come home to your family safe and sound."

She breathed her words into the hollow of his neck, her hot, sweet body pressing along the length of his.

Jacob neither questioned her action nor shrank from answering it. He sought her mouth and gave her one quick, searing kiss, all he thought she might allow.

And almost more than he could bear to leave.

CHAPTER 6

Retha swept the yard with a mind to murder dirt. She knew it was a bad idea to sweep in the rising heat. But a deceptively lowering cloud had come up, and she thought she would burst with nervous energy if she spent another minute in the confines of the house.

It was her first full day as mother to Jacob's children, and she had kept a tight rein on her anger. By eight o'clock she had bustled the boys off to Brother Schopp's for lessons, slapped on some pottage and a kettle of beans, and moved outdoors for space to indulge her temper. But only for a moment. Anna Johanna joined her, a child-sized broom in hand, and mimicked her every move.

The day before, Jacob's hasty departure had at first astonished her. How could he leave so soon after their wedding? And on such short notice? Disbelief had changed to anger as he bulleted about the house, leading her upstairs to point out the children's wardrobe and their separate beds, downstairs to review cookery utensils, then down a narrow set of steps to the cellar stocked with early summer food. Through it all, he instructed her relentlessly. Anna Johanna couldn't drink milk. Nicholas wouldn't touch lima beans. Matthias might have nightmares.

Despite Jacob's evident concern that the children would run wild, they had been on their best behavior. But then, of course, Brother and Sister Ernst had visited them at every meal. A nagging resentment settled in Retha's chest as her husband's plan became clear to her. He had asked the Ernsts to check on her.

Finished with the yard, Retha leaned on her broom and sighed with indignation. Anna Johanna propped against her little broom, too, imitating Retha's sigh down to its length and intensity. Retha could not stay indignant long while the child so aptly mirrored her bad humor.

"Too hot for snakes," Retha grumbled, mopping her brow.

Anna Johanna's blue eyes narrowed with curiosity. "How come?"

"Snakes love to lie in the sun, sweet potato, but this stone is too hot for even them. Feel it." Retha knelt and touched her fingers to one of the sizzling flagstones that paved the small backyard where the children played and laundry hung to bleach and dry. Anna Johanna knelt, too, and touched the stone.

"Yee-ouch! It'll scald their slimy bellies," she shrieked, jerking her hand away and shaking it far harder than her quick touch warranted. Her brothers must have taught her such a relish for gore, Retha thought, briefly amused.

"Let's brush off this dust, and go inside for water."

Anna Johanna shook herself like a spaniel up from a lake. Retha took both brooms and followed the child to the house. Standing on a rough-cut stone step, she stretched to unlatch the door.

Blinking in the shadowed kitchen, Retha plunged the gourd dipper into a bucket of water and offered Anna Johanna a drink. The girl took long grateful gulps, the gourd's bowl clasped in grimy hands. Inside her scuffed shoes, Retha thought, the child's feet must be black. Apologizing, Jacob had explained his and Sister Ernst's failed effort to bathe his daughter before the wedding. Neither of them had been willing to risk one of her fits so near the event.

Anna Johanna handed back the gourd, half-moons of dirt under her fingernails. Retha drank deeply, too, wondering how to solve this problem. Jacob's dirty daughter did not reflect well on him and would be no credit to her. Surely the child's fear of baths was nothing so simple as a fear of water. Jacob hadn't given her his opinion. Perhaps he didn't know himself.

Retha smiled as a new plan formed.

"You know what I think we ought to do next?" she asked with an air of mystery, learned in dealing with Younger Sisters.

"Play dolls," Anna Johanna chirped.

"No-o . . ." Retha waited for another suggestion.

The child's shoulders slumped. "Play soldiers?"

"Oh no, not that!"

"Then what?"

"Play pick-lima-beans-from-the-garden and go-wash-them-in-the-creek."

Furrowing her brow, Anna Johanna considered

this proposition. "We always wash them here . . ."

"I'm sure you do. But doesn't this sound like a good game?"

Anna Johanna coiled a curl around a finger. "Not the picking beans part."

"I suppose that is work," Retha conceded.

"The creek part might be all right."

Retha thought her stepdaughter sounded reluctant. Perhaps this was a bad idea. Perhaps she was scared of water. "Of course, you might not want to. We'd have to wade in. We'd get wet."

"How wet?" Anna Johanna's voice trembled with worry.

"I don't know," Retha said lightly to reassure her. "Water wet. No more than ankle deep."

Anna Johanna shook her head with girlish gravity. "Mama wouldn't let us play in the creek."

"You can play in the creek with me."

"No, I can't. I got all muddy, and Mama got sick, and Papa yelled."

"Papa won't yell this time. I won't let him."

Anna Johanna gave her a doubtful look.

"And we can wash the mud off," Retha reassured her. "Come on."

"You mean now?"

"Soon as we pick enough beans."

Picking beans was another matter. Anna Johanna was too young, Retha realized by the time the child had stripped a whole plant of pods and leaves alike. Quickly reorganizing their task, Retha picked the beans herself and let her stepdaughter put them in the wicker basket. She gathered two handfuls for Nicholas, one for herself and, judging from what she had seen of their appetites so far, one for Matthias and Anna Johanna. Then she stood and stretched.

"That's enough. Let's go to the creek."

Anna Johanna stood, mimicked her stretching, then grabbed a finger and followed her stepmother to the meadow. Retha accepted her tentative touch with silent gratitude.

The low creek gurgled feebly, a boundary between Retha's life now and her years with the Cherokee. It reminded her of simpler times. Laundry tubs would have amused them when there were perfectly good streams to use. Bathing using tubs and basins would have made them howl with laughter. They would have been astounded by the Moravians' elaborate waterworks, a system of underground pipes and pumps and cisterns, planned and built, Retha suddenly recalled, by her husband.

Nevertheless, for memory and for her present purposes with her stepdaughter, the creek was perfect. Enough water for wading, but not deep enough to frighten her.

Anna Johanna knelt at its sandy bank, a miniature, feminine version of her father. Her sturdy body bent to its work, her dirty blond curls stringing from under a simple girl's *Haube.* One by one, as if the pods were treasured crystal, she washed the lima beans. At this rate, Retha calculated, they would be washing pods all day. But Anna Johanna's hands would be clean. Still, they had only a short while before the boys would come home for the midday meal.

"Let's try several at one time," Retha suggested,

kicking off her shoes and wading into the shallow stream.

"How?" Anna Johanna asked, taking her own sweet time to wash another pod.

"Watch." Holding half a dozen beans in the cage of her hands, Retha immersed them in the creek and shook them, splashing the water.

Anna Johanna's eyes brightened with interest. "My turn?"

"Your turn."

The child submerged a chubby hand in the water. Her willingness encouraged Retha. She gave her three pods to wash.

Anna Johanna shook her hands in the water to rinse the pods, then set them aside, and took another handful. "What if one gets away?"

"We'd have to wade into the creek and chase it."

Anna Johanna considered. With a careful glance at Retha, she opened her fingers one by one as if freeing a butterfly. The beans dropped into the stream and bobbed away. Biting her lip nervously, she started after them.

Retha stopped her. "Shoes off," she said cheerfully. "Stockings, too."

Much faster than she had undressed for bed last night, Anna Johanna took off her shoes, stripped her stockings, and flung them onto the bank. With a cautious look at Retha, she lifted the skirt of her beloved dirty dress and splashed into the water.

She wasn't afraid; she loved it! Retha shucked her shoes and joined her. Already well downstream, Anna Johanna captured her first pod with something like a war whoop, dropping the hem of her filthy skirt into the water and splashing noisily.

What could have soured her on bathing? Retha wondered at the sight of such unexpected delight. Not any fear of water she could see, and surely not a fear of punishment from her father. Jacob adored her. From the dirt he had left behind, he plainly could not lift a hand to discipline her. But how strange to think that this quick creek bath might have done the trick.

Anna Johanna squealed again in a sharper, higher tone. Retha looked up to see her sitting in midstream, bean pods in each fist. Her skirt mushroomed around her.

Retha ran down the creek's sandy margin. "Are you all right?"

A small but happy smile stole across Anna Johanna's face. "I'm all wet."

Retha had to laugh. "So you are."

Anna Johanna dropped the beans and slapped her hands against the water, drenching herself with spray. A miniature rainbow shimmered across it.

"What are we going to do with you!"

"Hang me out to dry!"

"Now, how do you propose to do that?" Retha asked.

Anna Johanna didn't know, nor was Retha sure what to do next. She hesitated to try to remove Anna Johanna's wet dress for a serious bath. Jacob's instructions on that score had been explicit: no bathing until he returned. Still, with the matter progressing so favorably, Retha felt she had to put the proposition to her.

"When we get home, you can put on a dry dress."

Anna Johanna shook her head vigorously. "I have to wear this dress."

Retha stopped short. She *had* to wear this dress? *Had* to?

"How about the pretty blue one?" Retha countered. She had seen it upstairs in the children's cupboard. "It matches your eyes."

Anna Johanna sat in the creek's thin flow, stubborn and meticulous as she washed a recovered pod. Retha felt helpless in the face of her new stepdaughter's silent refusal. What did she know of mothering? And what, besides her own dimly remembered girlhood, did she know of a young girl's wants and needs?

For no reason Retha could imagine, the child loved her filthy flaxen dress. She clung to it, old and worn, dirty and wet. Nor would she switch to the blue one in the cupboard. Most likely, she had outgrown it, too.

She needed a new one then, Retha thought, suddenly inspired. And Anna Johanna could help pick out the cloth and help her make it.

"I think you need a new dress, sweet potato. Something special."

Ignoring her, Anna Johanna patted down her puffed skirt, careful to immerse all remaining dry spots in the water. "How special?" she mumbled at last.

"Umm." Retha paused, making a show of deciding. "Some different kind of special."

Anna Johanna gave her a doubting sideways glance.

The child's doubt was warranted, Retha realized, as she cast about for a way to make good on her impulsive offer. She had gotten herself into another fine pickle. To replace whatever hold that flaxen dress had on her, Anna Johanna needed something new enough to fascinate, something uniquely hers.

Retha racked her brain. What had she loved most as a child?

Ah. The comforting softness of her first deerskin dress. She had treasured every one of them, even the one she had made shortly before losing her family. Scavenging the countryside as an orphan, she had bemoaned its rapid ruination and then its loss when the Sisters took it away.

Anna Johanna had, after all, been at pains to copy her all morning.

"I was thinking about a deerskin dress like the ones I used to wear when I lived with the Indians."

Dripping wet, Anna Johanna stood up in the water. "For me?"

After the midday meal, Retha sorted through a pile of dusky deerskins at Brother Bagge's store. Like a bee sampling nectars, Anna Johanna danced around her, always returning to her favorite site, the hides. Retha knew selecting a hide would not be difficult. No matter where the animal's wound was, she could cut the small pieces of a little girl's dress around it. But Retha took her time, cultivating Anna Johanna's eagerness to pick out a special hide and giving herself time to master a new and growing resentment.

While they had been eating, Brother and Sister Ernst stopped by. Again. Certain now that Jacob had directed them to watch her, Retha chafed at their surveillance, his lack of confidence, her own mortification. How was she ever to become mother to Jacob's children if he would not give her the chance? She flipped through the hides without seeing them.

He would get an earful when he got back.

After selecting a hide, she let Anna Johanna bundle it up to carry home. But it was too heavy for a child. Retha draped it over her arm.

Halfway home, she stopped at the Ernsts' cabin, deciding on the spur of the moment to confront her friend. The front door was open to the heat. Retha entered, called, and sniffed. They were boiling tallow. In the summer. That was unheard of. Following its faintly rancid odor, she walked through the cabin and out to the backyard, Anna Johanna tagging along shyly.

Eva Ernst scrambled up from a log bench where she had been sitting next to several white, dripping, greasy lumps. "It's too hot to mess with tallow," she said, her plain, flushed face damp from tears. "It won't form for candles."

Retha patted her hand consolingly, unwilling to remind her absentminded friend that tallow candles were made only when the weather had gone cold.

"I am so much better with children," her friend added, sniffling into her apron.

"You could use tallow lamps," Retha suggested gently.

"I know, I know. But I broke our lamp. I meant to be so smart, making these. We have to have them. Samuel comes in at all hours of the night." Eva made a hopeless gesture that swept her small yard. "The Sisters didn't teach us everything!"

Retha nodded sympathetically. "I'm finding that out."

"Is it what you hoped for?" her friend asked eagerly, her eyes suddenly alight.

Confused, Retha shrugged. She had hoped for love, but only Eva seemed to have found that. "It's too soon . . . I . . . my husband—Eva, I don't know how to say this."

In private they dropped the formal address Moravian adults used and spoke as girlhood friends.

"You can tell me." Eva encouraged her with a smile.

Retha shook her head. She couldn't bring herself to accuse her husband of having her spied on, or her friend of spying for him. She tested the greasy tallow. "They might harden in the cellar."

Eva fingered the fat lumps. "How practical you are."

Watching her friend painstakingly mold the lumps into candles, Retha worked up her resolution. "Jacob doesn't trust me with the children, does he?" she blurted.

"Retha! No. Of course he does."

But Retha thought her friend looked guilty. "I want you and your husband not to visit us while Jacob is away."

"But we want to. We love the children. We know them."

"But I don't. And this way, I never will."

"You will in time. There's no hurry."

"Perhaps not. But I want to be alone with them. Then you would not have to bother with all these visits."

"It's no bother," Eva insisted.

Suddenly her friend's insistence on helping made Retha feel like a coddled child. "Eva, please. How else can I get to know them? I have to show Jacob I can be their mother."

Eva concentrated on arranging an uncooperative lump of tallow on the plate. "We're supposed to visit you every meal," she admitted softly.

Retha's resentment turned to a sharp and painful anger.

He should have told her.

But he had not. She recalled his gloomy demeanor after the wedding night and felt more confused than ever. He had even been angry at her for comforting Anna Johanna. For reasons beyond her understanding or control, he was not willing to give her a chance. Did he fear for his children while they were in her care? Was he trying to protect them from her?

Jacob was, after all, a protective man. Her heart warmed as she remembered his hand on her arm, protecting her from the Redcoats. Still, he had no cause then, as he had none now. The only other time had been the night he had found her as a child, dark with filth and stealing from the Moravians' communal stores. But who had he been protecting then? Her, or his community? She had fought him wildly. After that, for a while, everyone mistook her for a dangerous Indian. A few still did.

Perhaps Jacob did.

Jacob, and Eva and her husband, too. That was it. None of them trusted her with the children because of the years she had lived with the

Cherokee. They trusted her to dye their clothes and do the laundry, but not to be a mother.

Angry clear through, she rose from the log bench and faced her friend, who at this moment seemed like a false friend. "I want you to stay away from supper tonight."

Eva's thick brows frowned with indecision. Her expression only reminded Retha of every doubtful look that had been cast her way since the night Jacob Blum had caught her for a thief. Old outrage over injustice arrowed down her back.

"If I decide to scalp them, I promise I'll ask your permission."

Later that afternoon the boys clattered into the house, dashing from school to escape an ineffectual spatter of rain. The cut-out pieces of Anna Johanna's deerskin dress lay on the kitchen table. Retha watched Nicholas and Matthias spot it and exchange knowing glances.

"We don't need leggings," Nicholas said stiffly, shrugging out of his rain-spotted vest. "Especially not in summer."

"Father already has riding gaiters," Matthias informed her bluntly, placing his vest on a peg beside his brother's.

Retha went on guard. How to respond to her stepsons' challenge? Both curious and critical, they were clearly testing her. This would be her chance to establish herself as their new mother. Not quite sure she was adequate to the task, she remembered Rosina Krause in charge of the Little Girls and

Single Sisters and squared her shoulders.

"She's making me a deer dress!" Anna Johanna, who was playing on the floor, poked her head above the table's edge.

Matthias approached the hide and touched it with keen interest. "An Indian dress?"

Ignoring the hide, Nicholas gave Retha a look of disgust.

Retha checked herself. She had not thought how others might respond to her rather novel measure.

"You can't do that," Nicholas said with authority.

"Of course I can," she answered. But his tone surprised her—and her own upwelling of anger.

Withdrawing his hand from the deerskin, Matthias hung his head. "We're already a laughing-stock."

Retha grabbed a rag, lifted the lid on the pot of beans, and stirred. She needed to sort this out. Just who did Matthias think of as a laughingstock? Surely not himself, he was merely thin. Or his brother. A bona fide troublemaker attracted attention, but no one laughed at him. He had to mean his sister, because of her dirty dress.

She felt a pang of sympathy for the poor child. Anna Johanna was just old enough to catch their meaning. Surely, Jacob wouldn't allow the boys to say such things to her face.

Nor would Retha. The beans had thickened nicely. She hoisted the heavy pot onto the table and told the boys to sit down. They sat, and she stood over them, feeling right and angry and anxious at once.

"You had better explain what that means."

Nicholas glared, but Matthias wouldn't meet her gaze.

"Matthias?" she prodded the one she judged more likely to answer.

He huddled against the table, his lips shut tight.

"Nicholas? What's this about your sister?"

"It's not about her," Nicholas said, still glaring.

His father's indigo glare. Retha met it and was struck with sudden, unwelcome knowledge, like the lightning that hadn't brought rain. "It's about me."

"We didn't ask to have a squaw for a mother," Nicholas ground out.

In her heart, Retha almost felt old scars tear. Old prejudices bounded to life. Squaw baby. Squaw wife. Old hurt throbbed anew. Now the children would feel it, too. She wondered if Jacob had realized the taunting would begin again. She certainly hadn't. She knew children were cruel but had convinced herself that her tormentors had all grown up. Clearly, new ones had taken their place. For her new family's sake, she struggled to recover her forbearance, once acquired at such great cost.

"I was never a squaw, Nicholas," she managed to say calmly, ladling beans into redware serving bowls and carrying them to the parlor table. He was still glaring when she returned. "Tell me what happened."

"Naught happened," he snapped.

Matthias laced his fingers in a pious gesture and set his hands on the table. " 'Twas Thomas Baum—"

" 'Twas naught," Nicholas cut him off and stood in stony silence. Retha recalled doing the same in front of Sister Rosina. Telling tales was worse than taunting.

And Retha was sure he had been the one more injured by the taunts. She reached inside for wisdom, for heart's ease. "Sometimes people don't know any better, Nicholas. It hurts them more than it hurts us."

"It didn't hurt," he said.

But he looked hurt, she thought, the exact same way his father had. She probably had a better chance to help the son. "We can't stop them from saying things, but we don't have to believe them."

Nicholas rolled his eyes. "You grew up with Indians."

"Yes, I did, and I loved them very much."

"You loved Indians?" Matthias sounded incredulous.

"My Indian family was very good to me," Retha said, passing out plates and pewter utensils for the boys to set the parlor table.

Nicholas hung back, but Matthias, amidst a clatter of tableware, wanted to hear more about the Indians. With relief, Retha told of her life with the Cherokee, stories the Little Girls used to relish. Matthias did, too. But Nicholas joined them at the table with evident displeasure, sitting at attention like a soldier but refusing to meet her eyes. Matthias piously offered to say grace, then picked at his food, asking for more Indian stories. Nicholas scorned the stories, but Retha noted that his appetite was unimpaired. He wolfed all of his two handfuls of limas and a pile of bacon and bread.

Perched on a stool by her side, Anna Johanna copied her, as she had done all day. Bite for bite, bean for bean. At least, Retha thought, flattered by the imitation, she had made some headway in winning over one of Jacob's children.

Matthias lined up a row of beans on his plate and looked up. "Did you have an Indian name?"

"I did indeed," she said slowly, noticing that Matthias was eating one bean at a time. No wonder he was skinny. "They called me Wanders Lost."

"I got lost," Anna Johanna perked up. "In the meadow—"

"Why did they call you Wanders Lost?" Matthias overrode his little sister's chatter, much more interested in pursuing exotic Indian names.

"They said, which I don't remember, that they found me alone near a cabin in the woods. Wandering, and lost. That's how they name children, by something that's happening when they're born," Retha explained, changing the subject. She rarely let herself think of her Indian name. It reminded her of being lost that second time and losing all again.

Nicholas, who was sulking, flashed his sister a wicked grin. "You'd be Rats in the Cellar."

Anna Johanna's face crumpled in confusion.

"Nicholas!" Retha said, rushing to her stepdaughter's rescue. All she needed was one child sulking, another pining, and a third in tears.

Nicholas feigned innocence. "But there were rats. Father and I were trapping them the night that she was born."

Retha stifled a smile at the image of her large, dignified husband scuttling in some cellar after rats. "Anna Johanna," she assured her, "they'd probably have named you Starry Night."

Anna Johanna smiled shyly, placated. "I like that."

"I'd be Born in a Wagon," Matthias announced proudly.

Retha blinked. She knew so little of her new family. "In a wagon! Were you?"

"When we moved here from Pennsylvania." He giggled. "But I don't remember."

Nicholas snorted at his brother's silly joke.

"And what would you be named, Nicholas?" At this very moment, Retha thought, they could have named him Smoking Musket.

Defiant, he shook his head. Obviously, he wouldn't admit to wanting to join in this game.

But Matthias kept it going, shoving his nearly full plate away. "Did you have an Indian mother?"

"You might say that. I lived in an Indian family, and they treated me like the other children."

"Did she have a name?" Anna Johanna whispered.

"Singing Stones."

Anna Johanna let out a contented sigh. "Pretty. Can I be Singing Stones?"

Retha tapped the tip of her nose. "You can be anyone you wish, sweet potato." Both boys groaned.

After everyone but Matthias had cleaned their bowls, Retha set out a bowl of blackberries.

Matthias waved them off impatiently, even though he seemed to look at them with longing.

"There will be that much more for the rest of us, Matthias," she teased him, starting to relax a little in spite of Nicholas's refusal to join in.

Her joke fell flat. While the others ate, Matthias

steepled his fingers and studied them. "What should we call you?" he asked abruptly.

" 'Mother?' " Anna Johanna whispered in a tremulous voice.

"No!" the boys spoke as one, and exchanged a glance. They had discussed the matter, Retha was sure of it.

"We called our mother 'Mother,' " Nicholas announced.

"Of course you did," Retha said, taking a deep breath. "I suppose you could call me Mother Retha."

"No," the boys said again.

Then Nicholas stood up and leaned forward, his hands flat on the table, almost as tall as his father.

"Not 'Mother,' " he said, defiance tightening the line of his shoulders. "You're not our mother. Our mother's dead."

Their mother was dead, Retha acknowledged that. But where did that leave her? She now served in Christina Blum's stead, and they would have to call her something. She had to propose that something right away. Thinking again of Sister Rosina in charge, she matched her militant stepson's pose and stood him down.

"I am your father's wife, and I will be a mother to you. You may call me 'Mama' or 'Mama Retha.' Or 'ma'am.' "

Nicholas twitched with indignation.

"I like 'Mama,' " Anna Johanna said.

Retha smiled down at her, grateful for large favors from small people, and then addressed her older stepson. "Sit down, Nicholas, and finish your meal."

Nicholas glowered, and in his expression, Retha glimpsed his father. Nicholas might well grow up to be as handsome and powerful as Jacob, but he was neither yet. He was mounds of food running up to height and awkwardness. None of it yet formed the taut self-command that marked his father as a man to reckon with.

Still, the son's anger swamped the room. Retha was shaking. It seemed that she had won some war of words, but she had never felt less adequate to a task. Perhaps Jacob's insistence on the Ernsts' help had not been a matter of distrust. Perhaps he had been wise, knowing his own children—and not knowing her.

But at this moment, she was on her own with Nicholas, who stood resentfully. She said a silent prayer that he had more respect for his father than he had shown for her.

"Nicholas, you honor your father by setting an example for your brother and sister. Sit, and finish your meal." Retha watched his face as the discipline of young years battled with his own wild will. She had fought such battles herself as she strove to become a good Moravian child.

"Yes, *ma'am,*" he said emphatically. Though one hand fisted, Nicholas took his seat.

Exhausted at the end of a long day, Retha stripped to her summer body linen and dragged herself to bed. Luckily, despite her rudeness to her friend in the afternoon, Brother and Sister Ernst had walked with them to *Singstunde* for the evening song service and kept them company in the *Saal*. Luckily, too, Eva's forgiving disposition diffused Retha's tension, and Brother Ernst teased Nicholas about tripping on his lower lip until Nicholas had to smile. Most luck of all, heavy clouds brought darkness early, so Retha hustled the children off to bed before another incident could occur.

Jacob's bed was still newly crisp and inviting. Its cornhusk mattress crackled as she settled in alone. But not without an overwhelming sense of his presence. It had shadowed her all day, as if he were watching her, evaluating her, quick to prod, correct, protect. He had become her conscience, and her critic.

She slipped into the bed, weariness deepening as she listened to the crickets' heated chirping. She wanted to be a good mother to Jacob's children, to be for them the mother she had lost not once, but twice. She wanted to care for each one of them equally—ragged Anna Johanna, pious Matthias, defiant Nicholas. No matter how difficult mothering half-grown boys was proving to be.

She wanted to do so without anyone's help because she had always made her way. If she could do it on her own, they would seem—would be—her own family all the more. But getting all three of them to accept her as their mother was going to be very, very hard. She pulled up the sheet, then flung it off. The bed was hot, and she was frustrated and confused, for Jacob had sent help in the persons of the Brother and Sister Ernst.

Humiliated as she had been on first realizing his ploy, she was less so tonight. She had to admit, he had not been all that wrong to enlist their aid. They had helped. Their presence had deferred Nicholas's explosion and afterwards doused his fire. If Jacob stayed away long, no doubt she would need them again.

Deep inside, she wanted more. She had to prove herself worthy of being Jacob Blum's wife. Whatever she had done on her wedding night had cost her his respect. She wanted it back. She twisted her body on the half-empty bed, in the heat, in the dark, lonely night. She imagined his body beside her, strong and solid and peaceful in sleep. She wanted him back. To whisper *Liebling* again, his lips warm at her throat.

CHAPTER 7

"Ah, Blum. You have news about our grain?" Inside his field tent, a tall, fastidious Colonel Martin Armstrong relinquished his smoldering pipe to its stand.

Jacob bowed courteously to the Continental officer. Until now, his every contact with the man had shown him to be fair and reasonable. Cousin Andreas's latest stupidity might well put the man's reason to a test. Mentally, Jacob shifted to English.

"No, sir, I have not come about your grain."

Eyes narrowing, the colonel stood up behind a battered but much polished field desk. "What other reason could bring you here? I doubt you come to enlist."

Jacob stiffened. "You know our community does not bear arms in this struggle, Colonel. Wherever our personal sympathies may lie. Indeed, my cousin, Andreas Blum of the Friedland community, has been wrongly drafted."

The colonel fingered his pipe. "Not wrongly, since your Friedlanders did not pay the tax required of men who do not wish to serve."

"Some paid it. My cousin paid. I have the proof."

Jacob slid a hand inside his coat for the duplicate certificate, forgetting caution in his haste to be about his business. In a flash, Armstrong's aide and another soldier pinned his arms, wrenching them back. Too large and strong for them to actually hurt him, Jacob tightened his muscles against an angry compulsion to retaliate.

"Check his coat," the colonel ordered, his voice calm.

Jacob tried not to resent their roughness as they patted him down and probed his coat pockets, ignoring the crackle of paper.

"No arms, sir."

"Release him."

The men stepped back as if reluctant to lose a potential prisoner. Armstrong walked out from behind his field desk and stopped three feet in front of Jacob. "Proof, you say?"

Jacob retrieved the bishop's certificate of waiver for his cousin from his pocket. No one stirred as he handed it over.

Scanning the waiver, the colonel tossed it onto his desk. "Very well. We can check the roster. Corporal!"

The aide handed the colonel a large sheet of parchment. The colonel inspected it. "I see no Private Blum. But for you, I will send a man to look among the new recruits."

Jacob weighed the colonel's response with frustration and hope: Andreas was not here, but the colonel would help look. He ordered an aide to go, motioned Jacob to a worn camp stool, and busied himself with papers on his desk. Finishing, Armstrong set down his pen and picked up his pipe.

"We must not waste your visit," he said.

Jacob waited as the colonel nursed the pipe to smoldering life, not trusting the casual tone of his remark. "If I can be of use . . ." he said cautiously.

Armstrong made an obliging gesture. "You can deliver the grain we ordered or at least account for your delay."

"Our mill-race was destroyed in the spring floods. We can grind no grain until it is repaired."

The colonel popped his lips around his pipe's stem. "In lieu of our grain then, you can tell me what you know of the Tory encampment on the Atkin."

Jacob bit down on quick anger. "I am no spy, sir." He neither supported the British nor sympathized overmuch with the Tories who did. Nonetheless, he could report nothing without compromising his community's strict neutrality, and the colonel knew it.

"They're nearer Salem than Salisbury, are they not?" the colonel probed.

Resolutely Jacob met the man's gaze. " 'Tis widely *rumored*"—he stressed the word—"that several hundred men are camped there."

"That agrees with our reports. And the British approach from the south. I take it you have word of that."

"Yes, sir. Salem is a hotbed of rumor."

"No doubt," the colonel said wryly.

Relieved that Armstrong accepted his answer in good humor, Jacob had to smile. "If your officers found other towns more to their liking, we might know less."

The fastidious colonel shrugged obligingly. "Everyone knows there are no finer accommodations to be found in this bloody wilderness. But what of military traffic through your town?"

"It increases. Unlike spring, troops pass through nearly every day. Some stay, but not for long, and rarely very many."

"British? Or ours?"

Probing again, Jacob thought. But this information he could give without betraying his beliefs. Which army or which faction passed through town was common knowledge. "A few British officers, usually on the run. Lighthorse, occasionally. All the rest are Continentals and militia."

For a moment, Armstrong chewed the stem of his pipe. "What of your actual danger?"

Surprised at his concern, Jacob replied, "We tripled the night watch."

"Comprising how many men?"

"Three."

The colonel shook his head. "Not enough, Blum, to protect your people or our grain. Did you arm them?"

"They carry conch shells to sound a warning. And since Brother Horner was beaten in the street, we keep clubs at home to protect our families."

"Clubs!" The colonel snorted. "They'll not stop a raid. But you are foolhardy, to neither fight nor arm yourselves."

"With respect, sir, our beliefs . . ."

"Your beliefs will be the undoing of the most successful trading community in the backcountry, Mr. Blum."

"Or our salvation. We do not bear arms, colonel. That is why I have come for my cousin, taking time from needed repairs."

Armstrong glared. Jacob waited, his expression impassive, he hoped, over the impatience that drove his pulse.

"Oh, very well," Armstrong snapped. "You may wait outside. I have much work."

Satisfied to have won his point, Jacob sat out the rest of the afternoon in front of Armstrong's tent. But after four days of fruitless travel, it was hard to bear the waiting and the bold taunts of soldiers when his body burned for action and his heart yearned for Retha and his children thirty-nine miles away.

The Lord only knew what havoc his family would wreak in his absence. During Jacob's last trip, Nicholas had teased his sister to tears with wriggling skinks, Anna Johanna had tried to run away, and Matthias's nightmares had terrorized the Ernsts.

Now Jacob could add his bride to his other worries. How would she contend with skinks, runaways, night terrors? It was some comfort to recall that she had once quieted his daughter and later held her own in altercations with his sons.

Leaning his elbows on his knees, he stared past troops gathering for drill near the river. Instead of doubting everything, he should try to trust Brother Marshall's reassurances, depend on the Ernsts' steadiness, take heart in Retha's confidence when she saw him off.

Such confidence, and such unexpected concern.

Abruptly the texture of their departing kiss flooded back to him. He could not fathom it. What had brought on such a change from her terror of his touch? After all but turning him out of bed on their wedding night, she had bid him good-bye with a soul-shattering embrace. It held a lingering sweetness, a trace of trust, and a hint, he hoped, of desire. Beneath that, he sensed a wild promise in her kiss as well. Across the miles, that promise tugged at him.

But her touch, that chameleon change, held her secrets, too.

He mopped sweat from his brow. It did no good to sit and stew. When he returned home, he would have her many mysteries to solve: her cheerful, concealing competence and the wild temptation of her touch, both set against her clawing fear.

Perhaps that fear would dissipate. Unlikely, he told himself. As his search for Andreas had lengthened to days, he had had little to do but recall the events of his wedding night. Her fear appeared to be an old one, fueled by forces he might never know. Even so, what could he do to forestall such another scene? Could he do anything?

He shifted uncomfortably on the cramped camp stool the colonel had consigned him to. His bride would share his bed, if not her body; he insisted on it. He entertained the idea of investigating. Sisters Krause and Ernst, perhaps even old Sister Holder, could shed some light.

But he dare not ask any of the three. Retha's secret was, in honor, now his. He would not shame her to any Single or Married Sister by casting the slightest doubt on her suitability to be his bride. She had done no wrong. She had not hurt his children. She had not hurt herself.

At last the aide returned, bringing neither Andreas nor good news. His cousin was not among the newly drafted men.

His patience raveled, Jacob demanded another interview. Armstrong's head bent over papers as Jacob strode to his desk and placed his palms on Armstrong's desk. "Allow me, Colonel, to question the recruits regarding my cousin's whereabouts."

Raising his head, Armstrong gave Jacob a sharp look. "You presume on our acquaintance and waste our time and your own."

"Sir, we are within the law."

The colonel jammed his pipe into its holder. "Very well. It is your time after all. The sooner you are satisfied, the sooner you will return to your mill, will you not?" To the aide he said, "Take him to the new recruits."

The aide tucked the roster under his arm and marched with Jacob toward the river through lanes of packed red clay and choking red dust. In the harsh sun, tents gleamed, haggard infantrymen lounged, and a few mounts rested. The smell of supper cookfires hung over the encampment—strong coffee and scorched beans, reminding Jacob he was hungry, reminding him he was far from home. Downstream by the riverbank, he caught a glimpse of unbound amber hair so near the color of his wife's that his breath lodged in his throat.

She couldn't be here. Blinking, he peered through the shimmering haze of campfire smoke and summer heat. No, this woman's hair was shorter, straighter than his wife's untamed mane. But suddenly he longed for Retha, his groin telling him in no uncertain terms exactly what he wished for: her presence, her body, here.

Trailing the aide, he neared the gap-toothed,

grinning woman, a bedraggled camp follower doing laundry. He hurried past, vexed to be so vividly reminded of his wife and then to have that vision spoiled.

On the camp's outskirts, three sweating men dug ditches under the broiling sun. The stench hung, concentrated, in the still afternoon. Jacob suppressed his planner's impulse to tell them how to alter the entrenchments to improve conditions. Below his knees, flies swarmed thickly, a few escaping the throng to light on the bare skin of his face. He swatted at them.

"There's naught but three," the aide said, then barked an order to the straining men. Surprised, they turned, dropped their shovels, and tiredly stood at attention, facing the sun's glare.

One of them shielded his eyes and grinned. Relief and exasperation welled in Jacob's chest. Could the man take nothing seriously?

"That one is my cousin," he told the aide. "In the middle."

The aide studied the men and then ran a finger down the roster. "That man's Pope, or Richards, or Andrews," he read.

"Not Andrews," Jacob snapped, seeing the military's error in a flash of irritation. "Andreas. Andreas Blum."

The aide stubbornly clung to the name on the roster. "Private Andrews, fall out."

Andreas looked from the aide to his fellow ditch-diggers, clearly puzzled.

Jacob spoke in German. "He's releasing you from duty, Andreas. Get out of the ditch."

At the sound of his mother tongue, Andreas perked up and squinted into the sun. "*Kusine* Jacob!" Eagerly he slogged through the muck to Jacob's side and gave him a disgusting, smelly bear hug. "I had not expected you for days—no, weeks!"

"The war comes closer to us. I could not well leave you to kill and be killed," he growled.

"*Ach,* but for you to come and leave a beautiful new bride at home . . ." His cousin's dark eyes danced, for Andreas enjoyed a joke at anyone's expense.

Jacob ignored him. "It has taken me four days to find you. And it will be as many hours before we are free of this mistake."

His prediction proved all too true. A setting sun reddened the sky by the time Andreas strolled up, dressed in plain farm clothes and flanked by an armed infantryman and the aide.

Armstrong saluted his men. "Andreas Blum is hereby stripped of all rank, privilege, and duty to the Continental Army and released and relinquished to the custody of Jacob Blum."

"I thank you," Jacob said formally, trying to balance a deep-rooted dislike of military procedure with grudging gratitude for Armstrong's help. "And for our community, Brother Marshall thanks you."

Armstrong nodded. "Neither your gratitude nor theirs impresses me, Mr. Blum. All I want from Salem is our grain."

Jacob reined in anger. "You shall have it," he promised.

"I can afford you no more favors," the colonel warned.

Jacob bowed curtly. "We shall ask no more, only our rights under the law."

Arms hugging her knees, Retha sat on a large rock. Jacob had been gone four long days, and she was fighting worry.

For years she had come here for a respite from the too orderly enclosures of a Single Sister's life. The rock was still warm from the day's heat. The bright half moon was near to setting, and water lapped lazily in the creek. She had only precious minutes to herself. She had left the children in bed asleep.

Her wolf had not yet come for the hunk of fatback she had placed on a nearby log. She waited anxiously, craving a sight of its free spirit. A sight of something purely wild and not so demanding as the children. She had ridden herd on them all week. Or them on her. Anna Johanna wanted her hair brushed, her face washed, her "deer dress" completed now. Matthias would accept no food on earth but demanded more Indian stories.

And Nicholas wanted Retha to leave him alone. His father gone, he sulked. Daily she invoked the sixth commandment, the only measure that seemed to work. *Honor your father, Nicholas. The more so while he is away.* Grimly her stepson set out dishes. Stubbornly he hoed his row as she had struggled, with the children, to restore the garden to order and rid it of weeds. Mechanically he apologized to his sister each time he thoughtlessly reduced her to tears.

But, Retha told herself tonight, taking comfort

where she could, he had gradually begun to do so with less prompting from her. And without the intervention of Brother and Sister Ernst.

She heard a splash and looked up. Its coat streaked silver by the moon, her wolf bounded through the creek, gulped down its trophy and paused, head held high. The night was too dark for Retha to make out the color of its golden eyes. But they peered at her. She hugged herself with relief and awe. It must have watched for her for days!

Then it trotted off, tail wagging in the air. Until the woods' dark recesses swallowed up its shape, she studied its gait. The limp was almost gone.

Wonder of wonders! Strong and well and on its own, it remembered her. Retha let out her breath and gulped in the still, sweet night air. Memories of peaceful woodland nights in Cherokee bark lodges refreshed her as no close room and cornhusk mattress could. Stepping down from the rock, she gathered the damp hem of her gown in her hands and hurried home to her children. Moments later she slipped into the house, lit a tallow lamp, and mounted the stairs to check their rooms, confident they were sound asleep.

Home safe. Jacob paused at the foot of the stairs. He had made it back, nerves on edge from coddling his lame, feckless cousin and exhausted from dodging bullets. Whether fired by Whigs or Tories, Redcoats or Continentals, he had not paused long enough to tell. Beneath hot stockings and heavy boots, Jacob's feet burned, raw from a forced march of forty miles with his cousin on the horse.

Weary, Jacob mounted the stairs to his children's rooms, one step at a time as best he could. Before collapsing in his own bed, he needed the reassurance of their peaceful slumber, sweet breath, and warm innocence.

Halfway up, he stumbled and grabbed the handrail. Its polished surface spoke of domestic comforts. Bracing his weight on the railing, he pulled himself up another step. It took all his attention to ignore the pain and keep on climbing.

He barely registered the sharp inrush of breath before a hissing whirl of white slammed into him.

"Not in this house, you don't!"

Sharp nails clawed his face. Teeth sunk into his coat sleeves, scraping skin. He grabbed for arms, and found them, fine boned, small, flailing.

"Retha, it's—"

"Not on my watch, you miserable, benighted wret—" She whispered a barrage of oaths and curses, half in English, half in Cherokee. He could not make out her garble.

"Retha—" He swallowed his words in a consuming effort to master her frantic strength. But the fear behind her fury rang clear as a bell.

He softened his voice. "Retha, it's Jacob. You're safe. I'm home. You're safe."

She wrenched her arms free, struggling against him as he banded her body with his arms, resisting his words as if some desperate rage propelled her past all reason. Struggling on the step above him, she seemed larger than life, formidable, a fury.

But he was heavier, stronger. Conscious of his advantage, he drew her down against his chest, pinning her arms between them, preferring to absorb her battering there than about his face. A smaller man could not have conquered her. Secured against him, she did not stop.

"Retha! Wife!" He addressed her sharply, suddenly afraid—suddenly certain—he had lost her to another fit. To an outraged panic worse than her withdrawal on their wedding night. " 'Tis Jacob. I'm home."

Silent, she writhed against him, recognizing nothing.

This was his homecoming, she was his wife.

He shook her, hard, speaking all the while, frustration lashing his body at this terrible new face of her resistance to him.

Reaching Retha seemed as futile as trying to commune with Anna Johanna in her fits. Yet worse. His daughter, he hoped, would grow out of them. He had seen Retha this way before, years ago, the night he found her in Salem Square, a frantic, savage fighter. What made her so determined then? What inspired her now? Could this oblivious violence be linked to her mute, sightless rocking in the bed?

Force once calmed the lost child, he reminded himself, but she was no stranger now.

He spoke as he would to Anna Johanna, softly, reasonably. Retha did not recognize him. Gradually her frenzy subsided, then her resistance slackened, and he explained again that he was home. She made a noise low in her throat, the small cry of a surrendering animal, and he eased his hold.

She jerked free and stumbled to the top of the

stairs. There was just enough light from some taper she had left that he could see recognition return to her face, then bewilderment, then anger.

"Jacob, good God! I heard someone enter. It scared the life out of me!"

Her words came out in English, broken and strained. But the thought arrested him with perfect clarity: her response was honest. In her frenzy, she had not known him.

Beyond the fatigue that weighted him, he grappled to comprehend all he had just felt and seen: she-wolf rage, feral strength, blind devotion to his children's safety.

And again, that inexplicable madness.

Chilled, he sat her down at the top of the stairs and pulled her to his chest. She was soggy with emotion, rigid with the aftermath of fighting whatever demons stalked her night. Rigid, but no longer resisting.

"I thought . . . you were . . . them . . ." she whispered, her breath hot at his neck in the folds of his stock.

He pressed his face to the crown of her head, his lips to her hair. The faint sour smell of fear lingered there. It was fear of him. He clenched his jaw against regret that that had come to be. "I am so sorry. 'Twas no one but me."

"I see that now." But she didn't sound as if she quite believed it.

He hastened to reassure her. "You're safe. There's no one, no one in five miles."

That is, he amended, no one had shot at him in the final five miles of his trek. He gave no hint of that to her. The truth would plunge her back into that state.

"They were here today. I saw them leave. They're gone. I know they're gone. But I thought they had come back."

"I saw Samuel. He said it's been clear."

She slumped against Jacob. "I couldn't know when you would be back."

He accepted her weight. "I couldn't find my cousin. I went to all the wrong places. Armstrong had him outside Salisbury."

She became heavy against him, her body firm and strong except in its womanly soft places. Lucky for him the stairs were dark. He couldn't hide a grin of relief. It slid into place. He could help her change. She needed only reassurance. He was more than willing to give that.

He ventured to move a hand against her back. "I never dreamt it would take four days."

"You're home now." Subdued, she folded her hands in her lap.

"All of a quarter hour. I did not expect such a welcome." He gave her hands a quick squeeze, hoping she would hear the lightness he attempted in his voice.

With a shuddering sigh, she relaxed into him. "You were gone so long."

"Too long," he forced himself to say agreeably, as the weight of her trust brought him to throbbing hardness. "Too long." But perhaps not, he thought, if absence brought me this.

"And then I heard some soldiers fumbling with the latch."

"That was me," he said. She didn't need to know that exhaustion had made him clumsier than a drunk. He had broken the latch in sheer frustration.

"And then one of them came in, and I heard him walking across the kitchen, and then I heard his steps on the stairs. He was coming so slow."

"That was me, Retha," he reminded her again.

A frisson of worry skittered down his spine. What would he do if she persisted in confusing him in the flesh with the *them* of her fears? What if this were merely the still before another storm?

Gingerly he patted her shoulder. If he could only keep her talking. Perhaps she simply needed to repeat her story. He prompted her to continue. "So you heard noises, and you came upstairs to protect the children."

Against his chest, she shook her head. "No, I was already here. I was coming down to find the club."

"The club?"

"You forgot to show me where you keep it."

He dragged his hand across the back of his neck, annoyed. He had not forgotten. Samuel Ernst was supposed to defend her. Jacob had not imagined her strong enough to wield it. Now he could. If she would zealously fend off an attacker with nothing but nails, fists, and teeth, she wouldn't hesitate to wield such an awkward weapon.

"It's below, under the bottom stairstep."

"I couldn't believe Brother Ernst had let anyone past him. Not after the way he hounded us while you were away."

"He *promised* to keep an eye on you."

"He did more than that." Edginess seeped into her tone.

"He acted in my stead, Retha. I couldn't leave you all alone." He put an arm around her shoulder, helped her up, and started down the stairs. "Let's take you to bed. And me to bed."

"No, the children." Quickly wary again, she slipped from his grip and tiptoed into the small front room where Anna Johanna slept.

He followed. His daughter lay as she often did, tucked in sleep as she had curled within her mother's womb. She had been Christina's heart's delight. Jacob's throat closed on a lump of sorrow at the memory of her, here, bending over her baby. He thought of the tragedy of Christina's too, too early death, of Anna Johanna's loss, his own long year of—

Retha reached out a mother's hand to smooth a lock of hair from the child's innocent forehead. A wave of tenderness washed through him. Despite Retha's inexplicable frenzy, her simple maternal gesture gave him hope.

He turned to his sons' room, a few steps away. Leaning over, he touched the older boy's cool face. Nicholas whimpered as a much younger child would do. *Ach,* Nicholas, who wanted to go for a soldier. Who wanted to grow up too fast. All day, Jacob had seen the soldiers his son inexplicably revered, some scarcely older than he, and a good number not so large. Jacob rubbed the back of his neck. What could he do for this one?

Matthias lay on the far side of the small shared bed, the light coverlet snarled in his arms and legs, even in sleep his small, wiry body mirroring his perpetual struggle with the angel of God. Quiet as a whisper, Retha leaned forward and freed Matthias from his tangle.

"He does this every night," she whispered, laying a hand on Jacob's arm.

"All his life." Jacob felt his throat tighten with unexpected gratitude. While he had been away, she had noticed his son's habits. She had taken care. She had cared for him, for all of them. He patted her hand on his arm and surveyed his reconstituted family. Safe and at rest.

Angels in the moonlight, every one.

Downstairs, Retha scrambled into their bed like a frightened rabbit into its hole, vanquishing Jacob's moment of hope. Setting the tallow lamp on the windowsill, he hid discouragement in a Herculean struggle to take off his tight-fitting boots. Pulling up his chair, he sat and crossed his left leg on his knee and worked his heel out of his boot. Pain seared him. By the time he had worked his heel into the boot's narrow ankle, he was sweating. He gave the boot another jerk and it came off, thumping onto the floor as he fought for balance.

He eased off a bloody sock, picking it away from the flesh where blood had clotted and dried. He lifted his right ankle across the other leg and applied himself to his task, cupping the boot's heel in his hand and rocking it. Needles of fire shot through his foot. The other boot was even tighter, the other foot worse.

Through gritted teeth, he sucked in his breath and began again. The smallest movement scoured his open wounds.

The boot was stuck. Under the last thin light of the setting moon, he glanced at Retha's shape, huddled on the bed. He could not tell if she were awake or asleep. He could not expect her help.

Muttering a mild oath, he closed his eyes, exhausted. He would just sleep here, in the chair, as he had done on his wedding night. Tired to the bone, he crossed his arms across his stomach, stretched out his legs, and nodded his head.

He could not do everything, be everyone he was expected to be.

And he could not do it alone.

Her face to the bedroom wall and coverlet up to her ears, Retha heard Jacob's grunt of pain. Something thumped onto the floor. A boot, it had to be a boot. He muttered an angry phrase she couldn't understand. And then he was silent. She waited, listening. He had to come to bed. When he did, she would be awake.

She lost track of time. Tree frogs croaked and crickets ticked seconds, minutes. He hadn't moved to join her. In the waning heat, an owl hooted.

What was he waiting for? She unbent cramped limbs, propped up on one elbow, and squinted at his massive body outlined by the light of the lamp. He sat in that same chair where he had sat the morning after their wedding, half-dressed, his chin rested on his chest. Was he asleep? Or had he been badly hurt?

She slipped out of bed to go to his side, tripped over a boot, but righted herself. One boot was on, one off, she noted, looking down with some confusion. Worry overtaking caution, she sank to the floor at his feet.

And smelled blood, the thick tinny smell of blood. Quelling ripples of revulsion, she stood and placed a shaky hand on the back of his chair. Think, think. He needed help. She needed better light. She moved a candle stand nearer to him and set the tallow lamp on it. Then she sucked in her courage on a deep breath and knelt at Jacob's feet, forcing herself to inspect the foot he had bared.

His heel, toes, even the ankle bone were raw.

More blood, she thought, quivering in anticipation of the queasy feeling that had overcome her since the day the Cherokee had found her, wandering and lost. The feeling hit her full force, but it was not the same. For this was Jacob's blood. And he was hurt, and needed her.

"Jacob," she said softly, testing her voice for steadiness. He must not know how much the blood unsettled her. She gently tapped his shoulder. "We have to take off your other boot."

"Hmmm?" He was barely conscious.

"That boot. We have to take it off."

"Cannot," he mumbled. "Tried, before."

"We have to." She tugged at his sleeve to make her point. "Now. And you should be in bed."

She looked at him. Weariness and pain scored new lines in his handsome face. She had to act. Her heart raced as she knelt, boldly draping his arm around her shoulder, and urged him to stand. Bracing on her, he pushed himself up.

"Come," she said. "Lean on me."

Slipping an arm around his waist, she guided

him to the bed, trembling inside. He was so large, so hot. So close. She felt vulnerable, yet oddly powerful to have such a man relying on her.

Retha's arm around his waist jolted Jacob awake. His wife was touching him of her own accord. Though unsteady, her hands had been firm and caring. But as much as he wanted to prolong the moment, he could barely stand on his miserable feet. After easing himself down on the edge of the bed, he mutely stuck out his booted foot.

She looked at it. "You said it wouldn't come off."

"Not for me, it wouldn't. You try."

Facing him, she grasped the boot's heel and pulled. He relished the fierce concentration on her face, half-hidden by her hair falling free. But the boot wouldn't budge, and her tugging hurt like sin. A hiss of pain escaped him.

She stopped, shaking her hands in frustration. "I cannot do this."

"You can."

Her tone brightened. "We could cut it off and spare you."

"No." He was alert enough to know he didn't want her slicing up his only good riding boots, not with footwear at a premium because of the war. But her concern warmed him. "The worst damage is done. Try the other way."

"What other way?" she asked in a small voice.

Ah, he thought. She wouldn't know how to take off a man's boots. A small fissure of tenderness opened in his heart at this reminder of her absolute innocence of men, their habits and their needs.

"This way. Turn around," he said softly, as if to a

newly broken filly. He placed his hands on her hips, finding them round and firm, and turned her about. Stiff but showing no other reluctance, she let him position her straddling his leg as she faced into the room.

He leaned back on his elbows. "Now, I brace my foot against you for balance. You grasp the boot by the heel and pull."

She even allowed his free foot to brace against her behind. Her firm, shapely behind. The sight of it so near, its feel, took the edge off his pain.

Until she started pulling in earnest. A poker of pain branded his heel.

"The slower you pull, the longer it hurts," he said between clenched teeth.

Obediently she leaned her weight into the boot. For a moment he banked his senses against pain by focusing on the slimness of her waist. His ploy almost worked. But as the boot came off with a tearing wrench, the black oath flew, unbidden, out of his mouth.

"Jacob Blum!" she scolded, hanging on to the boot as she spun away and faced him. "Sister Krause would never have let me marry a man who said things like that!"

"Hurt like the Devil," he said meekly, although he managed a slight grin over the biting pain. He did not believe in false heroics where there was such delicious sympathy to be gained.

But she hurried to pick up his other boot and stood the pair at the foot of the bed, escaping contact with his body. He regretted the loss, but decided to take his small gain.

She had touched him; she had let him touch her.

He flopped back on his bed, her bed, and laughed. He wanted to introduce Retha to every pleasure he knew and consign Sister Krause to . . . the sanctity of *Gemein Haus* with the Single Sisters.

Retha rounded the bed and loomed over him. "Don't you laugh," she said with mock severity. He loved it.

"Wouldn't dream of laughing," he said, struggling to hide his grin.

"I'm not through with you." Picking up the lamp, she whisked into the kitchen.

Jacob was so tired and so pleased by her caring touch that he drifted off to sleep, smiling, only to be shocked awake sometime later.

A cold, wet *something* touched his feet.

"Wh-at?" He tried to sit up to see. Faint light filtered through the window.

She had come back.

He was instantly attuned to her presence by his bed.

Coral sunlight profiled her face, turning it into a cameo for his own private viewing. He wanted to trail kisses down her high forehead, to the bridge of her fine, strong nose, down her nose to its tip, all the way down to her shapely lips. Where the kissing would not stop.

"I made you a compress," she whispered, as if she did not wish to rouse him. But he was aroused. She bent to her task at his feet.

He watched. A thick fall of hair, its amber depths tinged gold by the dawn, floated over his feet. The slanted sun outlined his bride's body, slender in pristine white, and meltingly desirable. His desire stirred, quickened. Astounded and yet pleased at the morning urgency that pooled and throbbed in his erection, he shifted himself in his thick traveling breeches.

"Hold still," she whispered again, snugging his leg to her rounded hip as if to steady it.

How? he wanted to shout. At the moment all he felt was the inevitable urge that had plagued him every morning since the afternoon he noticed her in the Square.

But this time was the sweetest, and the worst. She was here, at his side, touching him of her own free will. And with no sign that he could detect of the panicked, unfathomable woman-child of their wedding night. Or of the she-wolf who had defended his children only hours ago.

It was too soon, he warned himself. Too soon to hope her fears had been put to rest. He breathed in through clenched teeth. He would master this desire, subject it to his will and train it to her need.

She grasped the ankle of his near leg in her hand, and he winced. But she lifted it gracefully and tenderly and set his heel onto a soothing compress. Although his mind made quick note of its wet coolness, it wasn't the compress his body affirmed. Her slim hand rested on his leg, her round hip heated his calf.

With the purest frustration he had ever felt, he groaned. His fatigue vanished, transmuted into more energy than he had had in a decade. He wanted to touch, kiss, claim every inch of his bride's body; he wanted her skin rosy from touching, her face pink with exertion, her very being quivering on the edge of where he was now. He wanted her with him. Surrounding him.

Methodically—and quite skillfully, he thought—she wrapped his other foot in some damp, cool vegetation and swathed it in a cloth.

"There," she said, brisk and competent. "Almost done."

Don't be done, he wished but did not say. His senses on edge, he willed himself not to complain, but to lie back and wait, turning every ounce of the desire that thrummed through him into a plan of action.

"Thank you," he said.

"Those fresh comfrey leaves should do the trick," she said proudly.

Fresh comfrey? He didn't even have dried comfrey in the house, universal as the herb was as a compress for scrapes and bruises. Half wild Indian that she still was, she must have gone outside to fetch some fresh. Outside, where Moravian Sisters were forbidden to go alone at night. Outside, where embattled men prowled the woods. His trip had shown him nothing if not that. Common sense overcame the delectation of his arousal.

"Where did you find the comfrey, Retha?" He made himself ask gently, needing to know but unwilling to break the tender spell of solicitude she had woven around him.

"Down by the creek, of course."

He sat up. *"Liebe Gott,* Retha. You're not supposed to go there."

"You needed it."

"Perhaps so, but not enough for you to risk being seen and captured. Or worse."

She dismissed his concern with a smile as naïve as morning light. "I didn't see a soul."

"Retha . . ."

"Except my wolf!"

"That beast be—"

"And no one saw me. You forget, Jacob. I know how to look out for danger. You're the only man who ever caught me."

The only man who ever caught her! She must be thinking of that night years ago when he captured her in Salem Square. Had she escaped others? But when and where and how? And could they have anything to do with her troubled mind? The thought intrigued and then dismayed him.

He pondered the matter as she washed his face, untied his stock, and diligently sponged road dirt from his neck. He would probably never know. But he railed against the sense of honor that bound him not to ask another soul. He had to protect her from the shame of others knowing her affliction, as Sister Krause had done. More, in some strange way he did not yet understand, he had to protect her from herself.

"Retha," he growled, "no one's safe out there . . ."

"Be still." She dipped a cloth in a basin of water and covered his mouth with it. "I'm not finished yet."

For the moment, Jacob closed his eyes and gave in to his wife's gentle ministrations, torn between his duty to correct her and his desire to let her have her way with him.

Any way at all.

Tomorrow he would deal with her rash foray into the night.

Her husband was beautiful, Retha thought, lingering by his side in the brightening dawn. Roughly beautiful under the sheets, like a great slumbering bear. And perhaps as dangerous, for all she knew, although he didn't seem so now. His sleep deepened, and she watched with satisfaction. He had come home to her, let her nurse him, and drifted to sleep as if their life together was a matter of long habit. Clearly for him, life with a woman was. Life with Christina had been . . . She clamped down on that thought. She would not, could not think of his first wife.

Yet for her, being intimate with a man was all new, alarming, and . . . interesting. She had all but sat on his rock-hard thighs, felt his power, and managed not to flinch. She had snugged her hip up to his naked calf, felt its heat through her thin gown, and managed not to jerk away in shock. She had laved the bloody wounds on his bare feet and managed to control her queasiness.

But she could not suppress her fascination with his body. For under the fall of his breeches, she had seen him . . . thicken. Even now, as she remembered what she had seen, warmth spread through her belly, low, where she usually ached each month. This new ache alarmed her, except that it was sweet, not hard and pinching as her monthly pangs would be. Instead, it made her breath shorten, made each intake of air tickle her nostrils.

She looked back at him, searching for a cloaking, denying word for his visible response. For that . . . swelling. She looked away, embarrassed at the idea, at the word, yet scarcely knowing what else to call it.

She loathed being ignorant. Even more intrigued, she looked again. Had it . . . gone down? Perhaps. It wasn't quite so large. Then, and now, she wanted to explore him there. Perhaps even touch him. Her curiosity rose, making her as tremulous and irreverent as any silly, giggling Younger Sister.

Mostly, she knew of mating through barnyard animals and creatures of the wild. She had seen panthers coupling in the woods, bucks with does, mares with stallions. She had covered her ears to the caterwauling of cats. Once she had cringed to see a pair of mating dogs get stuck. A shudder of disgust ran through her.

Still, she wondered what her husband's private parts looked like under his nightshirt, under the concealing sheet.

Just as much or even more, she wondered what it was that men and women really did. And what Jacob had done to her on their wedding night. He could not have done exactly that, but what? He must have done something different, but how?

She wished she knew. Perhaps if she had not been such a troublesome charge, Sister Rosina would have told her outright, instead of turning her over to her husband's capable . . . hands. Perhaps if she had made friends among the older, unmarried women in *Gemein Haus,* they could have explained.

But what did any Single Sister know? Eva must

know now, but Retha's chance to ask her in the nighttime secrecy of their dormitory room was lost. Her friend was married and living in a house of her own.

A mother might have told.

But both of Retha's mothers were dead. That faintly remembered white woman who smelled of pine and lavender; and her Cherokee protector, Singing Stones, who taught her to walk in the wilderness.

Exactly what either might have told her, Retha could never be sure. All she knew of people mating were the sounds, last heard when she was ten or twelve and with the Cherokee. Disturbing, unexplained sounds: mysterious moans, grunts, cries. Sounds heard always in the dark. Always from inside bark huts.

Sometimes she had heard her Indian parents, sometimes others nearby. Their cries had haunted her, the men poundingly angry, the women keening hurt. Yet always the next day, to her great puzzlement, everyone had gone about their work as if nothing were wrong.

Surely something had been.

From upstairs, the first footfalls of a child awake jerked her back to the present. Wishing for more time to steady her thoughts, she listened anxiously. Whichever child was wandering about stopped. Almost tripping on the low step up from the bedroom, Retha hurried to the kitchen, hoping practical matters would crowd out her concerns. She lit a low fire and set on a kettle of mush for the children's breakfast along with a pot of coffee for Jacob if he should wake. Later she would go to the children. She had not finished with her sleeping husband.

She scurried to his side to check on him. The compresses had slipped, and she painstakingly adjusted them. But his injuries were not what had drawn her back. She wanted another look at his massive body against the flaxen sheets. Another secret, lingering look at his power and awesome male beauty. And she wanted to touch him again, purely to feel his hair-roughened, heated skin in the utter safety of his slumber.

Stretching out her hand, she brought it barely close enough to feel the fire of his flesh. And slowly, insidiously, again, the warmth spread downward into the private center of her self, but sharper, wider, lower than before. Wrapping her arms around herself, she hunched over, alarmed.

She had never felt this way, ever. Unnerved, she slipped to the open window and leaned out, gulping in cool morning air. A heavy dew damped the dirt yard, and she breathed in the rich humus of earth, the rich freedom of the world outside, the strength and consolation left her from her wilderness life.

Gradually a sense of well-being seeped into her soul. She rested her head against the window jamb. At last she noticed the first birdsong of morning, the bobwhite chanting his monotonous dawn lament. Poor bobwhite, it shrilled. Poor bobwhite. It must have been singing since first light, and she had been too occupied to notice. She, who noticed, who longed to be a part of everything that happened in the world outside.

Oh, how her world was changing—from twig

pallets in bark lodges to a cot in the Single Sisters' dormitory to her husband's bed. But she would listen now while breakfast warmed, the sky brightened, and the children slept.

Inside her, the pleasurable, alarming ache ebbed. In its place, worry flowed.

What was happening to her? Again she thought of confiding in Sister Eva. But her friend would not do. She was in such a ridiculous flutter over Samuel, she would probably blush or giggle or tease. Retha didn't think she could bear that.

Then who? Sister Rosina's words from Retha's wedding day came back. We leave you in your husband's capable hands, she had said. He was capable, yes. But capable of what? Leaving her to him had not worked. What was it that she did not remember of her wedding night? Not only had something gone wrong then, but something was wrong with her now. Something dark as sickness, sharp as fever. Something powerful as sin.

Wringing her hands with frustration, she knew it was up to her to find out what, and soon, before too many days had passed.

Sleepy footsteps scuffed down the stairs. She hurried from Jacob's side to meet the boys, relieved to be distracted by practical matters. A drowsy Nicholas had tousled hair. A worried Matthias had slicked his back and tied it.

She held a finger to her mouth. "Your father's home—but sleeping!" she hastened to add as both boys neared the narrow landing by the front door. Like a cattle drover, she held out her arms to stop them.

Nicholas cut her a dark look, and Matthias's sleep-creased face produced a pout.

She stood her ground. She didn't have to understand her sleeping husband, she thought with wifely satisfaction, to defend him.

CHAPTER 8

Faint harmonies drifted through the window, softly humming Jacob's body awake. He opened one eye. Dust motes danced in the slant of late afternoon sun. The blend of voices and brass horns in the afternoon meant vespers underway in the Brothers House a few doors down the street. Groggy and drenched in sweat, he propped up on one elbow. He had been in bed all day, alone.

But not alone for long, he thought. After his wife's soothing attentions last night, he couldn't help hoping she would soon willingly share his bed.

He flung back the sheet and swung his legs over the edge of the bed, scattering bandages and vegetation.

Vegetation? He raised a battered-looking foot to his knee, picked a crumpled leaf off it, and sniffed. The melony smell of crushed comfrey. Forbidden comfrey, which Retha had collected in the night. He tried to rouse up the indignation he had felt earlier, but the memory of her expert ministrations prevailed instead, swamping his sleep-clogged senses.

She had been tender, determined, tantalizingly close.

Smiling, he hobbled to the washstand. He had liked coming home to her touch, her earnest concern, her brisk bossiness. More than liked it. He wet a rag and mopped sweat off his face, neck, and body, coming fully awake as the aroma of ham and cabbage cooking triggered the onslaught of ravenous hunger.

The music trailed off, marking the end of early service. As predictably as a clock's chime, children's whoops punctuated the quiet conversation of adults passing beneath his window. Whoops contributed by his boys, no doubt. He had about two minutes to dress before they hit the house, Jacob realized, hastily pulling on his breeches and tying his stock. He had to be up and dressed. The children must not see him injured, however mundane and humbling his wounds. It was enough that they had lost their mother. He rummaged through the clothes cupboard for his outer coat and a pair of clean stockings.

The front door slammed, and his chattering children were home. Home. His heart twinged with sadness and relief. Since Christina's death, they had had to stay elsewhere whenever he was called away. Now, with Retha, they stayed here. It pleased him.

"Hush, hush." Retha's whisper squeezed through the cracks of their bedroom door. "He's sleeping."

"I waited all day," Matthias complained.

"Everyone waited all day," she answered mildly.

"You said he would be up at noon."

"It's almost time for supper!" Anna Johanna added.

Jacob scowled at no one. His daughter's remark

was beside the point, as she so often was, and Nicholas was testing Retha. Jacob almost rushed to her defense, coat and stockings in hand.

"I let you look in on him, Nicholas," Retha said, perfectly calm. "But he was sleeping."

Retha held sway. With relief, Jacob shrugged on his waistcoat, then looked down at his battered feet. He had no plasters to protect the wounds. Very carefully, he eased one stocking on and winced at the sharp pain. At least his everyday shoes were better broken in than his riding boots. On the other side of the door, the children clamored.

"He must really be hurt." Identifying worry in his younger son's words, Jacob felt a twinge of remorse. He was not hurt, not compared to how he was hurting his son by this allegiance to duty that took him from home and placed him in constant danger.

"No, Matthias, he wasn't so much injured as exhausted," Retha assured him. "He said he hardly slept."

"Bah!" said Nicholas. "I'll bet he had a terrible fight."

Jacob bit down on the pain as he stuffed his feet into his shoes. What would it take to sway Nicholas from his determined, contrary fascination with war? He had been embattled since his cradle days, taking on his mother, his father, even his brother from the day he was born. Yet somehow after Christina's death, the boy's interest had intensified. But why? Jacob understood this son's passion no better than his other son's affliction.

No matter what Jacob said, Nicholas's enthusiasm for gore never flagged. Indeed, the sight of lads little older than himself trooping through town in British red regalia or Continental blue whetted his appetite for battle. Jacob knew he wouldn't be admitted to the ranks of his son's heroes without bashing in the brains of some unfortunate Redcoat.

"There wasn't any fighting." Retha laughed, denying his older son's fondest hopes. "He blistered his feet from walking all night long to get back home."

"Blisters?" Nicholas sounded crushed. Jacob's worry lifted. With dispatch, his clever wife squelched his son's fantasies of heroism.

"Yes, blisters. Now you boys wash up for supper."

"What about Hanna—" Nicholas started to complain.

"Anna Johanna is clean," Retha interrupted briskly.

Clean? Anna Johanna was never clean. The words propelled Jacob through the door to face his family. Matthias eyed him keenly while Nicholas glared at Retha, but Anna Johanna's face pinked with pleasure at the sight of her father.

"Papa!" she squealed, charging him. "You woked up!"

Suppressing a fierce urge to crush her to his chest, he knelt to greet her. "I surely did, pumpkin, just for you."

He winked at his sons to remind them he had come home for them, too. Nicholas snorted, and Matthias shrugged rudely.

He started to correct them, but Retha cleared her throat. Both boys lowered their heads as if she had scolded them. Jacob observed, confounded, amazed.

"You were gone way too long, Papa."

He turned to his insistent daughter. Her round face scrunched up severely.

Her *clean* round face. He let the surprise seep in. In the past, he had managed to make a swipe or two at that face himself. But for Retha to succeed where he had so often failed?

"I know, pumpkin," he said, trying for normalcy.

"You were gone for days and days."

"Only four."

Her eyebrows contracted into a practiced scowl. "Even Nich'las thought it was too long, and he wanted you to have a 'venture."

Jacob's heart swelled with pride. His daughter had never made such a complicated speech, and he didn't care a fig if she made it while scolding him.

"'Twas no adventure," he said solemnly. "And I am very glad to be home with you."

Anna Johanna's scowl widened into a grin. "Me too," she said, and grabbed one of his fingers.

Jacob's throat caught, and his gaze fell. A plump white hand circled one of his large, sun-bronzed fingers. A clean hand. He felt as dislocated as if he had been gone a year.

"Come *on*." She tugged him toward the dining table in the parlor.

Rising carefully so as not to dislodge her grip, Jacob shot Retha a questioning look. She stood in the doorway to the kitchen, smiling benignly.

What happened? he mouthed at her from his high post above his daughter.

Retha shrugged, avoiding his question. "Supper's ready," she sang out, and crossed the floor to the table carrying a platter piled with bacon and a host of other food.

He didn't have time to identify any of it before

the boys crowded him with questions. He put them off, promising to tell all after grace. Anna Johanna clung to his finger until the boys were noisily seated and silenced and they had finished grace. At last she released him, giving in to the temptations of a full meal at suppertime.

Retha dished food onto his plate, then spoke to him directly. "I thought you would be hungry."

Surveying ham, dumplings, lima beans, and the usual evening mush piled on his plate, he smiled. "Ravenous," he said, unable to overlook a mild lift in his other center of hunger as he gazed into her amber eyes.

She must have caught his meaning, for she blushed. The sight of her rosy cheeks filled him with unexpected pleasure. And expected anticipation. This too was what he had come home to. But his fantasy was brief.

"What did it look like, Father?" Nicholas asked eagerly. "Was it a big encampment?"

For a moment, Jacob shut his eyes. He saw tents stretched out before him, white flags of tranquillity that belied the wretchedness of battle. He saw youthful faces reviling him, one reckless with bravado, another haunted, another drawn with fear.

Jacob studied Nicholas, a premonition of disaster banding his chest with dread. His son's summer blue eyes burned with envy for a chance at the heroic deeds that fueled his imagination. Choosing words to squelch his fervor, Jacob said flatly, "An encampment is a miserable place, rain or shine."

"Oh, Father. You always say something like that. What was it like?"

"Choked with dust. Vile with stench. The lanes between the tents were so rutted you could hardly walk."

"Tents? How many tents?" Undaunted by the thought of military hardships, Nicholas wolfed a forkful of beans. He didn't eat beans, Jacob recalled.

"Didn't take the time to count, son."

"What about the men? Were there Lighthorse? Was it just infantry? How many?"

"Mostly infantry. Hot, stinking, hungry infantry, nervous as jackrabbits about the British coming up from Camden."

Nicholas smashed a fist into the tabletop. "We'll lick them this time, not like Camden."

Matthias rolled his eyes. *Danke Gott,* Jacob thought, he was not on his brother's path. One warrior offspring was tribulation enough. Jacob cast about for words that might douse Nicholas's fire. For wisdom. Wisdom, if he could yet lay claim to any, had come slowly.

"There's no 'we' to it, son," Jacob said quietly. "They're the army. We're Moravians. Our allegiance is to this land, yes, and to the Continental government, but more to our community. Colonel Armstrong understands this. He respects our decision not to fight."

Even if Sim Scaife did not, Jacob amended to himself. But he refrained from further explanation. He remembered only too well that his response to parental logic at Nicholas's age had been rank rebellion. And he was loath to mar his homecoming with a pitched battle.

"But did you see any Lighthorse?"

Jacob repressed an oath of dissatisfaction. Wisdom was lost on Nicholas. "One division passed me on the way home," he said, answering again as if the matter were of no importance.

"British?"

Retha intervened. " 'Twas probably those Continentals that rode through yesterday. Nothing to be excited about. Nothing to worry about either."

"Who's worried?" Nicholas said with adolescent bravado.

Retha raised an eyebrow, and Nicholas subsided.

Jacob looked at his wife in mild surprise, wondering what he had missed while he was away. Had Retha spoken to Nicholas about his attitude toward war? Jacob had had no success in dampening his son's interest. He had explained the community's neutrality. To that, he had regularly added discouraging tales of the misery and injustice of war. Nothing had worked. But Nicholas seemed to respond to Retha.

For the present, Jacob accepted his son's silence and addressed the food piled high on his plate. Good food. Hearty food. Retha could also cook.

"But Papa—" Matthias pushed back his nearly full trencher and steepled his fingers. "We thought you were wounded."

"Not wounded, son." Jacob speared a fat dumpling. Nicholas's rebellion quelled, he really was hungry.

"Then why did you sleep the whole day?" he asked in a small worried voice.

"Because I was bone tired."

"Not wounded?"

"Wounded? No!" Jacob bit into the salty, tender fruit of Retha's labors, half attending to his son's innocuous question.

Eyes glimmering, Matthias stammered. "But you—you always say we're not supposed to lie."

Jacob set his utensils on his plate. From his younger, milder son, such a statement was tantamount to revolt. "That's right, son."

"But I saw your bloody socks," Matthias accused.

"My socks . . ." Jacob repeated.

"When she—" He sounded out the word awkwardly, as if unsure what to call his stepmother to his father's face. "When she let us look in on you."

"Blisters," Jacob answered, taking care to be very serious. "You saw blisters."

Matthias jutted his chin out. "They bled."

"That's not the same thing as being wounded, son. I wasn't attacked and I didn't fight."

"You were hurt."

"But safe, son. I'm home safe, and you're safe, too," he said, reaching out to reassure his most serious child with a hand around his shoulder.

He could hardly bear to keep it there. His once vibrant, healthy son had wasted away to skin and bone. Rail thin.

A pox on Dr. Bonn's easy assurances. Jacob promised to plant himself on the good doctor's doorstep in the morning.

Jacob glanced up at Retha. Concern was printed across her features like a map. She knew Matthias was starving, and cared. Squeezing his son's shoulder, he gave her a look of gratitude.

"And so," he said, aiming for lighter conversation

than wounds and war, "what did everyone do while I was gone?"

A smile broke through her concern. "We picked lima beans. And then we hoed the garden. And the boys went to school every day, and we went to vespers once, and to *Singstunde* every night."

She stopped and smiled mysteriously.

What else? he wanted to ask, but the children chimed in about games and blackberries and school. Retha brought out a fruit pie, served up thick runny wedges, and everyone feasted, save Matthias.

In the parlor for the short wait until *Singstunde*, Jacob watched the boys play at spillikins while Anna Johanna dressed and redressed her little doll with its porcelain face, wishing he could spare each child the pains and trials of growing up. He sighed contentedly, cherishing this quiet moment. By the dwindling light, Retha worked a small, shapeless piece of material. He was too tired to notice what.

But not too tired to notice her. Serene as a swan, she arched her slender neck over her work. Ah, she was a treat to come home to. She was making this her home. She looked domesticated, calm, transformed from the wild creature who had attacked him on the stairs last night.

The children were transformed, too. To his astonishment, Anna Johanna had touched him. His strictly proper Matthias had voiced a worry. Even Nicholas had said, "Yes, ma'am."

A small hand tugged at his shirtsleeve.

"*Hilf mir*, Papa." But his daughter didn't need help. Before he could figure out what she wanted, she had clambered onto his lap and snuggled against his chest.

He scarcely dared to breathe.

For the first time since her mother's death, Anna Johanna wanted him to cuddle her.

So he wrapped his arms around her, throat clotted with feeling. He held her little body as if it might break. She giggled, wiggled, and settled in with a sweet sigh. Tentatively he lowered his head to plant a fatherly kiss on the *Haube* that hid a froth of blond curls. Beyond the smell of starch, he detected the scent of rosewater.

Even her hair was clean!

With gentle hands, he steadied her shoulders and held her away a little to inspect her face. Scrubbed clean! Before dinner he had been too occupied with her touch to look this close. It was just as well. He would probably have said the wrong thing.

He looked to Retha for an explanation, but she stayed maddeningly engrossed in her work.

Then he examined Anna Johanna's ragged dress. Up close, it was brighter than usual. Up close, it didn't smell.

She didn't smell.

"Pumpkin," he croaked. "I think you had a bath."

Vigorous nods rocked her whole frame and dug her little seat bones into his thighs. His heart expanded. His emotionally fragile daughter was sturdy as a cart horse.

"When and where did this wonder come to pass?" he teased.

Suddenly shy, she ducked her head and mumbled. "In the creek."

Taken by surprise, he laughed. "You fell in!"

"Oh, no." She shook her head earnestly. "I waded in."

He raised a paternal brow. The creek had been off-limits since well before her mother died. Could that be why she'd shunned all water? To keep a promise to her mother?

"I got 'mission," Anna Johanna said hastily.

"Permission," he said absently, resting his face against her starched cap.

"Right. 'Mission. To wash beans. From Mama Retha."

Mama Retha? Washing beans? In the creek? He hadn't felt so emotional since he last wept for his wife at the end of a long Christmas day. He was close to crying now. But these would be tears of joy, of relief. He couldn't shed them here. He had to make sense of what had happened.

In the creek! What if . . . He remembered now. Not long before the epidemic that carried Christina away, she had scolded Anna Johanna royally for wading unattended. During her mother's illness, he too had found her in the creek again and scolded her himself. What if, in her child's mind, she somehow twisted her wading in the water into guilt over her mother's death?

"You smell like roses," he whispered to Anna Johanna, sure now he understood and hopeful that his daughter's ban on bathing was ended.

"Rose *water*," she pronounced proudly, dragging out the word as if it felt good on her tongue. "Mama Retha said you'd like that."

"I like it, pumpkin." He took the liberty of tweaking her cheek, but she slid off his lap like a boneless kitten and started rummaging in Retha's sewing basket.

Again he looked to Retha for some clue. Diligent, she bent her head to her work. But he thought a corner of her mouth crooked up. Was she pleased? Amused? Proud of herself? And what had really happened? he wanted to ask for the second time that evening. The creek! The creek?

Anna Johanna came back with a nondescript scrap of material and scuttled onto his lap, this time more confident.

"Look, Papa. Mama Retha's making me a deer dress."

Nicholas sniggered. "That's *deerskin*, you numb—"

"That's enough, Nicholas." Retha's firm order cut him off as effectively as Jacob could have done himself.

"Yes, ma'am," he grumbled.

Jacob's mind whirled. Nicholas obedient and Anna Johanna clean! If Retha had another week, Matthias might start gaining weight.

Perhaps he should return to the battlefield.

"You have to explain these miracles to me, Retha," Jacob said quietly a quarter-hour later as Retha shyly took her husband's arm.

He was escorting her down the street to attend the final song service of the day—limping slightly, although only she could tell. The boys ran on ahead. Anna Johanna skipped up to her and Jacob, and inserted herself between them.

"Later," Retha promised, tongue-tied with pride

that each child's behavior had so greatly exceeded her expectations on this, her husband's first evening home. But she could not explain Anna Johanna's transformation. She would not if she could. In truth, she feared speaking. She was afraid to break the spell. It was their first outing as a family, and she relished it.

From Sister Marshall to Brother Bagge, people greeted them as Brother Blum and Sister Blum. Even Rosina Krause, who always called her Sister Retha, dignified her new status by calling her Sister Blum. Retha smiled with secret pleasure, too, that she had acquired a surname after years of having none.

Eva Ernst fluttered up, giddy with inconsequentials, until she knelt to Anna Johanna and saw her holding her parents' hands. "Retha! Anna Johanna's hold—"

"Anna Johanna's glad her father's home," Retha blurted, meaning to keep Eva from saying something silly.

Eva seemed to fluff up her feathers, but instead of being affronted, said, in her dithering way, the perfect thing. "Why, Anna Johanna, aren't you grown up tonight?"

Anna Johanna danced in place. "Mama Retha's making me a deer dress," she boasted.

"Isn't that nice?" Eva gushed, although she looked confused.

Retha felt a moment of panic over Eva's response to the dress, but Anna Johanna beamed and Jacob was smiling, too. Retha squared her shoulders and tried to savor both her accomplishments and her new status. She would just have to get used to being seen in public as a mother and a wife.

Especially wife. Unfortunately, she felt more natural being with Jacob's children than with him. With Jacob, she still felt like gawking. His manly bearing was beautiful to her, and paternal pride sat well on his broad shoulders. She wondered whether he would have the same pride if they had children, given that they had now done what married people do.

She felt a flush heat her face. Such thoughts, she chastised herself as she entered the *Saal* for *Singstunde.* Such thoughts, when it was time to resume her duty as mother. With her free hand, she straightened her apron.

"I will keep the children while you sing." She hoped she struck a note of maternal competence.

"Ah, but I planned not to sing tonight." Jacob nodded tellingly down at Anna Johanna whose death grip on their fingers had not slackened.

Retha looked up questioningly.

"She's the reason. I don't think she'll allow it."

He called the boys, who joined them as they took their places on the bench. Nicholas, Matthias, Jacob, Anna Johanna, and herself. The boys to Jacob's left and his daughter to his right, separating Retha from him. But surely, when he sat with the family for services, her place was beside him. She squashed a blossoming disappointment. Or was it resentment? For four solid days she had done nothing but tend his children's needs—and a great many needs they had. Except for a few stolen minutes at dawn, her husband had given her no more attention.

Suddenly she recognized her churning emotion for what it was. Childish jealousy. She sank her chin to her chest and laughed at herself. The children would always come first with him. Had to come first. She married him knowing that. She had to accept that. And she couldn't allow childish emotions to turn her into a child.

Without his powerful voice, the choir sounded thin, but she still tried to lose herself in its song. The congregation sat, then stood, and Anna Johanna released Retha's hand. When everyone sat down again, a new chorale began and Anna Johanna claimed her father's lap.

Jacob gave Retha a glance of blinding gratitude. Thank you, his lips said. Then he patted the empty space between them on the bench.

Her heart skipped a beat. Manly and beautiful and mine.

Self-conscious now that she was getting what she wanted, she edged nearer to him. As at dawn, she could feel his heat. She did not mistake this radiating warmth for summer weather. It was his man's heat, a physical power, a pull he had over her that she did not understand.

When the choir paused before its next chorale, he whispered in her ear. "You're the other reason."

His breath spiraled a warm shiver down the side of her neck, and she completely missed his meaning. "Pardon me?"

The choir's song swelling to fill the room, he whispered again. "I wanted you beside me."

Her face flushed, and then her stomach twisted with those scary, pleasurable feelings from the night, from the morning when she had lingered beside his half-naked body. Not here! She bit into her pressed lips, but the feeling spread below, to the depths of her stomach, and deeper, to the parting of her thighs. Mortified, she wanted to wrap her arms around herself and crawl under the bench.

How could she have such unworthy feelings while hymns were being sung? There must be some renegade Cherokee part of her heart that the Moravians had never touched.

She dared a glance at Jacob. He looked steadily ahead, his strong profile undisturbed, except for a slight strained downturning at the corner of his mouth. She had an uncanny sense he was reining in runaway mirth. At her? Had he seen her flush? Could he know about her predicament?

What if he could feel her heat? As she felt his.

Heaven help her.

Her husband, it seemed, would not.

Jacob shifted his wriggling daughter on his lap. Now that he had shocked his innocent wife to her bones, it was all he could do to honor the solemnity of evening service. He couldn't say when such a wicked playfulness had overcome him.

On second thought, he could. He had probably been about seventeen, and Christina, already his best friend, had been his willing partner in irreverence. Unlike her, poor Retha had had the most irregular upbringing, her white parents of unknown background lost, savage Indians schooling her for untold years, and the Moravian way of life. As a Single Sister, she had conformed to proprieties her parents might not have approved of and the Cherokee would not understand. Proprieties no longer appropriate to a Married Sister. Surely more than her upbringing lay behind the fear she'd shown him. Jacob muted a clarion of worry and determined to take heart. Whatever her fears were, she had made great strides with his children.

He resettled himself on the plain bench seat and felt her shift of attention.

In the coming days, if need be in the coming weeks, he thought, it would be his pleasure to teach her all the ways, all the delights between a man and a woman. If this interminable service ever ended. No wonder he had spent every night for years singing in the choir. Without that sanctified discipline, his attention strayed.

By dark the children were in bed, and Jacob waited in the parlor to talk with his wife. She whisked about in the kitchen, plunking washed supper dishes into the cupboard and then readying breakfast. Something pinged into the iron kettle. Hominy, he guessed, for morning. She splashed some water in. Yes, she was soaking hominy.

Wondering what excuses she would drum up for tonight, he closed his eyes and hummed a complicated bass line from his favorite hymn. It helped him bear the wait. It helped him bear her clattering pokiness.

But he could not rush her, he reminded himself. He had had days to think about her bizarre behavior on their wedding night and after. Last night, except when nursing him, she had again been nervous, strange.

He had arrived at no conclusion, a place where he, as a man of reason, did not like to be. Her deft handling of his children had scotched his theory that she suffered from an excess of fancy.

Beside him, Retha's skirts rustled. He looked up, ready with compliments, ready to cajole her, if need be, into his arms.

Tight-lipped and pale, she stood before him. "I'm going to bed."

CHAPTER 9

In the morning light, Retha lay across Jacob's bed, abandoned to sleep. She had flung off her sheets to the cool of the night and lay on her side facing him. One arm cradled her head, and the other reached across the bed toward where he should have been. Like an Indian runner at the top of his stride, Jacob thought, she had drawn up one leg.

She looked wild. And free. Without her *Haube*, she reminded him of the untamed child he had caught and saved, of the woman seen dancing in the moonlight, unfettered by fear.

He couldn't ignore the weight of desire that pulled at his groin. Last night, on seeing her distress, he had let her go, compliments unspoken, questions unasked. He was too tired. She was too—too repelled by him. Frustrated, he had thought of storming that bed, her citadel of resistance, her fortress of rejection. But her pallor argued stronger than his need. He willed himself to sleep, into a shallow, restless sleep. By morning, when he woke with his desire in his hands, he retreated to the chair, watching her as if he were her sentinel.

If only he could free her from whatever haunted

her, free both of them from the torment he had seen on their wedding night. But he would not free her from himself. He stepped up to the bed. A slight breeze stirred through the open window as first light flickered over her sensuous curves, playing along the long line to her waist, her generous hips, her shapely legs. But the gown and her position concealed her intimate charms.

He longed to see more but thought better of making so much as a gesture. Last night, she dove under the cover's protection.

Retha made a high, anxious sound in her throat and twisted uneasily onto her back. Her high breasts pressed into the thin cambric of her gown. He took a slow admiring breath. Her nipples were taut, tempting. He let his gaze travel down. Beneath the fabric, at the juncture of her thighs, he could make out a sweet shadow of pleasure. Her legs were slightly ajar, as if some lover had entered her and left her so.

He should be that lover.

For long moments, he let longing fuel desire, a wrenching but delicious torment that overrode the weariness of his body, the lingering pain in his feet.

Battling need, he left the bedroom, bare feet slapping the planked floor, and set his mind to other matters. He had to finish repairs on the mill. Armstrong was breathing down his neck. Using an ember from the kitchen hearth, he lit a tallow lamp, set it on a shelf above his drafting table, and took out a set of plans.

For more than a week, the important work he undertook as planner for the town had gone untended. But then, if he had been less obsessed with improvements, repairs on the mill-race could have been finished days ago. The heavy drafting paper crackled as he unrolled it. Rubbing morning stiffness from the back of his neck, Jacob reviewed the dam's design. While searching for Andreas, he had reworked it in his mind.

His new plan would withstand any deluge short of the one that had sent Noah to the ark. Not only that, the mill could grind grain all the faster for Armstrong's needy troops. In half the time it usually took him, Jacob marked his changes, rolled up the scroll, and tapped it impatiently against the slanted desk. So much for conquering desire with work.

He thought of his reluctant bride in his bed. Her rejection struck at his pride. Her resistance forced him to smother his growing attraction. Her fear went against everything he knew the union of a man and a woman could be. He wanted her trust, her love, her passion.

He wanted her to come to him.

He snuffed the lamp and left the house. Down the street, Dr. Bonn, an early riser, might have a new remedy for Matthias.

The children woke Retha, the two younger ones tumbling onto her bed like a litter of pups.

"Where's Papa?" Anna Johanna burrowed worriedly under the sheets.

At work, Retha guessed, groping for consciousness. She didn't know for certain where he was, so she did not say.

A fuzz of early light haloed Matthias hugging a stray pillow beside her. "He didn't have to go away again, did he?"

"He'd better not." Nicholas hung back at the foot of the bed.

"He didn't." The resonance of their father's voice made the children whirl to greet him.

Retha scrambled up to see Jacob duck his head under the door. Caught sleeping late. Caught half-dressed. She thought of joining her stepdaughter under the sheets. "I'll have breakfast for us in a minute," she stammered.

Jacob's amused look acknowledged her confusion. Then he clamped a hand on each boy's shoulder. "Time to dress for school," he said indulgently, pushing them out of the room.

"Wait for me." Anna Johanna leapt from under her covers and grabbed for his breeches at his knee.

"You too, pumpkin. You can't say morning prayers in your shift." His hands reached to lift her, then closed to fists as if unwilling to trust the change in her he had witnessed last night. "We'll be back," he said over his shoulder.

Retha felt left out but had no time to dwell on that. Dazed by her new family's energy and demands, she hastily pinned her bodice and buttoned on her skirt before the thunk of children's feet had reached the top of the stairs. There was always so much to do and so little time to do it.

Last night she had had time aplenty. For hours she had lain in bed, anxiously awaiting Jacob, fearing he would join her and fearing he would not. Any minute he could have touched her. Or left her alone.

But throughout her vigil, her body kept on betraying her, sheer shaking nerves alternating with warm, unexplained pulsings that brought on the nerves again.

She felt doomed to this incessant cycle of sensation, without knowing what caused it or when it might end. She wanted to end it today, if only she knew how, if only someone would tell her what was wrong. If only she had someone to turn to.

Preoccupied, she went to the kitchen and set the table with tinware plates, cups, and utensils.

Alice! She could go to Alice. Her married Chero-kee friend would know what was happening to her, would tell the truth and not scorn her or giggle. In one morning, Retha could trek to the Voglers' cabin and back. Soldiers would be on the roads, but they didn't frequent the woods, and no one knew Indian trails or deer paths as well as she. Still, she didn't have the pass that the Continental Army required of travelers of late, and she would be going behind her husband's back. All in all, she would be taking a terrible chance.

But, she told herself, gathering her resolve, she was going for his sake, for the sake of their marriage.

She put out milk, bread, and cold green-apple pie. One quick trip was well worth the risk. Eva could keep Anna Johanna for a few short hours. Retha needed dyestuffs anyway and would be sure to find some. She would be back by noon when the boys came home for hominy.

Four hungry, dressed Blums noisily descended the stairs. Their racket made a comforting domestic clatter, Retha realized, relaxing for a moment. She was starting like having a family. She almost liked being a mother.

But Jacob caught her eye and cocked his head toward the table, amused and questioning. She followed his gaze, staring blankly for a moment at everything she had set out, feeling stupid. Wasn't it enough? After all, there were only five people. . . .

And four plates! In mock distress, she hit her forehead with the heel of her hand.

He laughed. "Is someone not welcome here?"

"Someone is not awake." With a hot blush, she retrieved a fifth plate from the cupboard and set it out with a flourish. "Everyone's welcome."

After prayers and breakfast, they shuttled the boys off to school. Jacob picked up a large scroll of parchment from his desk in the parlor, headed for the door, but turned to Retha, speaking so low that Anna Johanna could not hear. "Ah. I talked with Dr. Bonn. He suspects consumption."

"But Matthias has no cough."

"So I reminded him. He offers to examine the boy, but he has made up his mind. Consumption." Jacob's eyes glinted. "I will not have my son frightened into thinking he has a deadly disease."

She agreed. "Because he doesn't. There's no cough. He's thin, but he is not sickly."

"He merely will not eat. 'Tis not the same at all."

"Perhaps some concoction to stimulate the appetite."

"I asked the good doctor for one. Matthias, the man said in all his pomposity, is too young to lose his appetite. 'We must seek the underlying disorder.' " Jacob imitated Dr. Bonn's droning voice, but Retha heard a note of disgust in his tone. "That means *we* must find the cure ourselves."

Jacob's *we* heartened Retha. "We will. We'll find it."

"I know. Somehow. But naught I've tried has worked so far . . ." He paused at the door, looking defeated.

Unsure of what wives did when dejected husbands left for work, Retha stepped nearer, reaching out to soothe him.

Apparently not this.

He wielded his scroll like a weapon. "I have to go," he said briskly.

Alice sat under a giant oak that arched over her small cabin, a waist-length fall of jet-black hair obscuring her face and the work in her lap.

Having walked for an hour through morning dews, Retha untied the skirts she had knotted up to keep dry. Her shoes, *Haube*, and neckerchief dangled in her hands. She decided not to put them back on. Even in the deep forest, it had been sweltering. Her Cherokee friend would understand her effort to be free of white women's hot, confining clothes.

"Alice," she called softly.

Alice didn't respond. Retha walked closer. Her friend's attention was given over to beading a very large moccasin, at odds with her simple gingham shift.

Retha called again.

Alice jumped up, spilling beads onto the hide spread over the weedy ground.

"I am come," Retha said in German, the traditional Cherokee greeting of a guest sure of being accepted.

"You are. It is well," Alice said, welcome in her words and in the smile that flashed across her still pretty, pockmarked face. But her hands moved nervously to recover the scattered beads.

Retha dropped to her knees to help. "I didn't mean to alarm you."

Alice's gaze skimmed the large clearing. Retha could see nothing but crops, planted on land that Indians had burned for hunting years before. In the distance, Gottlieb rhythmically swung a great scythe, single-handedly harvesting wheat in a parched field.

"We have so many . . . intruders," Alice finally explained, searching her hard-earned German for the right word.

"I didn't see a soul all the way here."

Alice scooped the last of the beads into a small pouch and surveyed Retha's state of undress. "Militia," Alice explained. "You should not come here. Redcoats march from the south, Gottlieb says. And many others."

"They aren't here yet."

Smiling cautiously, Alice gestured to her to sit on the hide blanket. "Why do you come?"

"To see you, of course." Retha sat down, folding her neckerchief and beribboned *Haube* on her lap.

"You travel with pass?"

Retha shook her head, her loose hair sticking to her bared shoulders. "No pass. I didn't come by the roads."

"Woods are not safe."

"I avoided clearings, too, until yours."

Alice scowled ever so slightly, the reproof a severe reprimand from her. "The Sisters would not like. They take good care of you."

"They try."

Retha saw the moment Alice's eyes widened at the sight of the new blue ribbon on her *Haube.* A blush of self-consciousness warmed her face.

"Your ribbon. It is blue." Alice touched it and grinned. "Married?"

Retha nodded.

Alice's limited German seemed to fail her, and she burst into her loud native tongue. "But when? And who? When I saw you at the market, you said naught of marriage!"

Retha eked out her story in rusty Cherokee, hoping the earthy tongue would make her intimate questions less embarrassing. "I knew naught. But even then, I believe Brother Blum had conspired with the Elders to cast the lot for me. Imagine that. Imagine a man like Brother Blum asking for me."

"But he's the one—isn't he Gottlieb's friend, the one with all the children?"

"Only three." Retha giggled, then bit her lip. She had to be serious. She needed to know about men and women, and even more—if she could bring herself to ask—about these strange new feelings. Suddenly feeling terribly naïve, Retha retreated to safer ground. "In truth, I've scarcely thought of children."

"Tell me about them," Alice entreated. She and Gottlieb still had none. "Is it difficult to be a mother?"

"Yes. And no." Sometimes switching to German to explain a nuance, Retha unburdened herself of all she had come to feel in her first week with Jacob's family—confusion, commitment, and pride. Alice *ahhed* over Anna's dirty dress, commiserated over tales of Nicholas's intransigence, wondered aloud why Matthias was so thin.

"You should feed him good Indian food," she said.

"Perhaps I will."

"But you never spoke to me of marriage."

Retha ran the blue ribbons through her fingers, thinking what to say. "I wondered why no one ever asked," she confessed. "To them, I was an orphan and an outsider. So I never spoke of it. I thought perhaps my past repelled them."

"It could not have. They never would have kept you. Besides, you are not born Cherokee." Alice patted her hand, then took up her work. "Well, well. A bride of a week. And so, my friend, is he a gentle man?"

A gentle man. Retha sat back on her heels. What a peculiar notion. Jacob was a large man. A strong man. A busy man. And a good father. What was Alice asking? "I think he is a good man. He loves his children. He works so hard for everyone."

Alice smiled slyly. "That's not what I meant." She lowered her voice to a whisper. "Has he satisfied you? Is he a gentle man?"

Retha withdrew her hand. "Oh, you mean his temper. I think he has quite a temper. But he keeps it under control."

The smile slipped off Alice's face. "He's hurt you."

"Oh, no," Retha said, truly puzzled. "I don't believe Jacob would do that."

"Of course, it hurts the first time, and the blood—"

"It didn't hurt, and there was no blood," Retha assured her, hastening to one of the worrying points she had come to address. "But with three young children already, I hope and pray we'll not soon have another—"

"No pain?" Alice set aside her work and studied Retha with piercing black eyes. "You would have felt some pain."

"No. None."

"You would have seen blood on the sheets."

Blood on the sheets? Retha shivered. She could only shake her head. There had been no blood.

"Something is amiss, my friend." Alice's voice softened. "Are you sleeping with your husband?"

"Of course I am. Except when he was away. When his cousin was drafted and he had to go and bring him back. The four days he was gone, I slept alone. Which is what I'm used to, but not a whole room to myself . . ."

She was rambling.

Alice stopped her. "I mean, lying with him. You know. As husband and wife. As woman and man."

Retha's hand shook. "I don't know."

"Did no one explain to you beforehand?"

No, she thought to herself, that's why I came to you. But Retha sat mute, shaking her head stupidly.

Gently Alice wrapped her arm around Retha's shoulder. "Wanders Lost, has your husband loved you?"

Tears sprang to Retha's eyes. This was awful.

When she tried to speak, the words scratched her throat. "I don't think he loves me."

Alice looked uncomfortable. "I am serious. Has he mated with you?"

"I told you. On our wedding night."

"Ah." Alice paused. "Tell me what happened."

Retha steadied herself with a deep breath. She had come for this. "He kissed me and held me and took me to the bedroom and left me alone to undress."

"And then . . ."

Fierce heat flooded Retha. Instinctively she began to rock. "I don't remember."

Her friend's brow furrowed with doubt.

"I mean, 'twas over so quick . . ."

Alice made a clicking sound of disapproval.

"It must have happened fast."

"My friend, it doesn't happen fast."

"Oh."

"I think your husband has not yet loved you."

Retha didn't think she could feel hotter. Embarrassment, consternation, bewilderment washed through her. She was so sure something had happened.

Why else would Jacob have been angry?

Alice stood, extended her hand, and helped Retha up. "I have some sassafras tea. Let's go inside and talk." She rolled her needlework up in the hide and led Retha into the cabin.

Inside, the night air lingered, the day's heat held at bay by thick log walls. Retha wiggled her toes against the cabin floor's hard clay and let its coolness seep into her body through the soles of her feet. She needed to ground herself on the simple earth, and chill the hot confusion that raced through her veins.

"This tea is not quite what you need but it is all I have," Alice said, seating Retha away from the small room's huge hearth where a stew simmered in a covered kettle over embers. Then Alice took out the moccasin she was beading, and sat, too. "If you had come of age with us, your mother . . ."

"Singing Stones of the Wolf Clan . . ."

"Would have told you. But I will speak for her."

Alice proceeded with a simple yet earthy description of the marriage act that left no doubt in Retha's mind: Her husband had not yet joined with her. He hadn't entered her, it hadn't hurt, she hadn't bled, and nothing, nothing had made her body feel like water rushing over rapids and then plunging over falls. Except perhaps . . .

Self-consciousness skittered along her veins. She had already had those feelings—*for* Jacob but not *with* him.

She was a wife and not a wife.

Alice had detected her failing to fulfill a woman's duty to her husband like a hawk sights prey. Not that Alice would use that knowledge to harm or hurt her in any way. But Retha dared not look at her friend. She tried to conceal the turmoil of her thoughts by sipping her tea. What did it all mean?

And why was Jacob angry? Because he did not love her or did not want her? Or because she somehow truly repelled him? And if it were the last reason, did she repel him because of her past or in some other way? If so, how could she ever change what had already gone so wrong? She had ruined her chance for happiness with her husband without even knowing she had done wrong.

She set down her cup to steady it. But what had she done? Nothing. She had gone to bed and gone to sleep.

And he had shared their bed.

Perhaps there was hope to be had in that.

Listening to the sigh of thread as Alice stitched the moccasin, Retha cast about for a positive sign that Jacob still wanted her as he had on their wedding day. Happy then, he had kissed her in front of the world. Again, before he left to find his cousin, he had kissed her with feeling. And when he had returned, he had accepted her nursing with gratitude, with . . .

The image of his large, powerful body, lying on the bed, came to her.

He had wanted her.

If not waking, then at least in his sleep. She had seen him, under the sheet, swollen with what Alice had just described as the most powerful of all human desires.

But Alice hadn't said one thing about the size of a man.

"It won't fit!" Retha protested, covering her face with her hands, mortified by her own outburst, but also appalled by this startling new notion. Jacob would have to fit that part of him inside her, into a space inside herself she barely believed existed. Surely Alice had it wrong. No wonder cats cried out and dogs got stuck.

"Man was made to fit woman," Alice assured her.

Unable to look up, Retha heard beads clink as Alice stirred in her leather pouch for another one.

"You're certain?" Retha said weakly after a while.

"I would not lie about that." Retha looked up to see Alice smiling warmly, a little bit amused. "Men and women do it all the time."

"And all those moans and groans I used to hear . . ."

"Were sounds of pleasure."

Pleasure. Retha grabbed her cup and gulped her tea to hide the thought that swept her. She had felt pleasure. Those alarming new sensations felt good. She had only to think of him for them to wash through her again. Like water over rapids, rivers over falls. Exactly as Alice said.

But it was so very hard to ask Alice about the rest.

"I wonder . . ." Retha twisted the cup in her hand. "This pleasure . . . is it . . ."

Alice patiently plied her needle to the soft deerskin.

"Do you feel . . . this pleasure . . . with Gottlieb?"

Abruptly Alice stood up.

Retha watched closely as her friend lay her work on the mantel, her copper skin reddening. "You're blushing."

Alice covered her face with outspread fingers. "I never blush."

But she did. And her blush was partial confirmation, and it gave Retha the nerve to ask about the deepest secret she had. "Do you ever feel it when you think about him?"

Bending her head over her work, Alice nodded, but Retha detected a shy grin.

"When I am with him and when I am not," Alice finally admitted in a breathless voice. "He is a very gentle man."

For a moment Retha could say nothing. Envy swirled through her. Although diffident, Alice sounded happy, sure of herself. Satisfied.

Suddenly she felt Alice's strong arms around her. "Wanders Lost, I have met your man. You are a lucky one. I think he too will be very gentle."

Retha buried sharp doubt in her friend's embrace, inhaling the strong yet comforting smell of bear grease that protected Alice's skin. The last questions were the hardest. "But how do I start? What do I do?"

"Trust him. Touch him. Reach for him. Let him know you will not shrink—"

Alice broke off and moved toward the window, listening.

"What is it?"

"Visitors."

Retha heard nothing, but the tension in her friend's stance sent an old, raw terror slithering down Retha's spine. "Redcoats!" she whispered.

"No. Worse." Alice strained on tiptoe to look out the cabin's one small window. " 'Tis the militia. They hound us. They believe me to be a spy."

Heavy steps pounded the small front porch. Gottlieb, a massive porcupine of cut wheat stalks and clinging chafe, burst through the door. His chest heaved as he strode to his wife, gathered her protectively in his arms, and swept her from the window. Then he saw Retha.

"Sister Retha! *Gott im Himmel!* How do you come to us?"

"I came . . . I came . . ." Retha wrung her hands and looked from friend to friend. Alice's face tightened with resistance. Gottlieb braced his body with a warrior's determination.

" 'Tis too dangerous for you here," he scolded in German. "The Sisters should not have let you come."

"They did not, Gottlieb. She is married. To your friend Jacob Blum."

"He should not have let you," Gottlieb said sternly. "But you are married! This is good, Retha?"

She swallowed quickly, hard. Did her own doubt and confusion show? "Yes, good."

Again footsteps thundered on the porch. Her heart flapped in her throat like a trapped bird's wings.

One man's peremptory steps, three men's, four. A lot of men, a band, a troop. She couldn't count. She couldn't breathe.

Gottlieb extended her a ham-sized hand. *"Stehen zie hier,* Retha, *bitte. Mit uns."*

Retha went to stand with them, a thin, uncontrollable shaking suffusing her limbs and her belly. In town the sight of soldiers never bothered her, but she barely had time to register that thought.

"And let me speak with him," he went on. "Moravian Sisters don't know English. He will think you a spy for sure."

Retha bridled. Jacob said that, too. She hadn't wanted to believe it was true. She couldn't hazard that it was not.

A tall, skinny man pushed his way inside. Road dirt streaked his rough militia linens. He circled the three of them as if they were prey, his thin lips curling over stained teeth.

At Retha, he halted. Her furtive glance caught him ogling her, and she purposely stared past his gaze, only to see his bony fingers slide through his unwashed, carroty hair.

CHAPTER 10

The man called Sim Scaife paced the clay floor. Four sweaty Liberty Men lounged behind him, their heat and their easy, edgy menace swamping the cool room. Retha fingered the blue ribbon on her *Haube* for reassurance but felt none. Gottlieb's hand came to rest protectively on her shoulder. His stolid presence comforted her only slightly as an eerie sense stole over her.

She struggled briefly to remember another hot day, another tight room. She had been in this exact predicament once before. A man behind her, a woman beside her, the thin stench of danger. Unwashed men, spent powder.

"Reckon we caught your wife at it this time, squaw lover," Scaife drawled.

Retha's images vanished, and she saw only the redheaded man.

"Cherokee Alice consorting with a white woman. Two skirts." He spat. "Nothin's worse'n a female spy."

Gottlieb's hand tensed on Retha's shoulder, but still he didn't speak. His silence riffled her nerves. How much of Scaife's crude, backcountry English could he understand? He should have let her talk. It wouldn't prove she was a spy. Besides, she could clear this up with a quick explanation. She had simply taken a walk, looking for dyes. As everyone knew she had always done.

With the muzzle of his musket, Scaife flipped one of Alice's black braids over her shoulder. "Naught's prettier. And naught's sneakier, neither."

"*Nicht* spy, Captain Scaife," Gottlieb said at last, his profound bass straining against his meager English. "*Sie ist nicht* spy. Not when you come here last month, last week. And not today."

"Ah, but this one—" Scaife made an insolent quarter-turn to Retha and snaked out a hand, untying the ribbon on her *Haube* and dragging the cap off her head.

Freed, Retha's hair slumped around her shoulders. A small, wiry militia man laughed restlessly. Hot blood rose to her face.

"Blue ribbon, too . . ." Scaife examined the cap and its ribbons before tossing it to his men like plundered spoils. "One of them Moravians got him a wandering *Frau.*"

"Maybe Vogler here just likes his quim in different colors," a fuzzy-cheeked militia man taunted, taking his cue from Scaife.

"Naw, it's all pink inside, Calloway. Mebbe you ain't had none yet," the wiry man said.

The young man reddened and went for his comrade's linens, but Scaife separated them with a growl. "It's my arrest, Calloway."

The men slouched back. Retha looked down to hide confused embarrassment. She didn't understand the words but caught the implication. Gottlieb didn't seem to.

"*Das ist* Mary Margaretha Blum," he said carefully. "*Ist Frau* of *Bruder* Jacob Blum."

"*Brooder Bloom's* woman?" Scaife raised an insinuating eyebrow as he mocked Gottlieb's heavy accent. "We know *Brooder Bloom*. You and Blum taking turns now?"

Gottlieb did not take the bait but drew Alice and Retha nearer. Tension crackled across the room.

Scaife turned to Retha, touching her loosened hair with bony fingers. "You spying or running away, little house *Frau*? I'll find you out." Suddenly he snatched back his hand. "Yellow eyes! Where'd you get them yellow eyes?"

Chin high, Retha refused to answer a question meaningless to her anyway.

"What's he saying, Retha?" Gottlieb muttered in German.

"I'm not sure." She was worse than not sure. She was mystified. Her eyes were strange, so Eva always teased her, as pale a brown as if they had faded.

"Didn't he say something about yellow—"

"No plotting, squaw lover," Scaife rasped, even as he stepped away and spoke in an undertone to one of his men.

Retha strained to hear. The words *garrison* and *crowded* floated up to her. Did he mean to arrest them all and haul them off to prison? The thought of being locked up chilled her. Then she detected a phrase about taking her to Salem.

"What else, Retha?"

"He means to escort me back to Salem, I think."

"I can't let him take you—"

Scaife returned, glowering. "None of that

babble, Vogler. You just tell Cherokee Alice to dish us up some of that stew over there."

Gottlieb lifted his hands in question.

"Food, you ham-handed German dunderhead." Scaife pointed at the steaming kettle. "Feed my men."

Omitting the insults, Gottlieb told Alice what to do. She began setting out bowls.

"You too, *Frau* Blum. Serve up." Scaife pointed her toward the table.

Retha hefted the kettle to the table so Alice could ladle out the stew. Any task was preferable to standing still. War-thin and hungry, Scaife's men crowded around, tearing off pieces of corn bread, soaking them in broth, spooning up stew with chunks of meat.

Scaife spit out his first bite. "What the hell's this slop, Vogler?"

Gottlieb raised his shoulders. "What's wrong with the stew?" he asked Retha in German.

"He doesn't like it," she translated promptly, almost amused by Scaife's sputtering indignation. "Maybe he never had turtle stew."

"Don't talk." Alice concealed her warning to Retha by looking straight at her husband. "You give yourself away. You show you know English, and they will think you are spy." Silently she walked over to the hearth, picked up a turtle shell, and held it out to Scaife.

"Turtle soup? Pig swill!" he barked, swatting the shell aside. It cracked onto the floor, rocking like a spun top. "You men finish up and meet me outside."

Grabbing Retha's elbow, Scaife jerked her toward the door. She almost stumbled.

Gottlieb prevented her fall, catching her with large, gentle hands and wresting her away from Scaife. "She stays here. She is our friend."

"We're taking her to her husband," Scaife purred derisively. He removed Gottlieb's hands from Retha's waist like a dandy plucking lint off his waistcoat.

Gottlieb swelled with indignation. "I myself take her to Jacob Blum."

Scaife's free hand whipped his pistol from his belt. At the table, one soldier plunked down his bowl, reclaimed his musket from the wall, and snapped its bayonet in place.

"You can make this easy, Vogler," Scaife said. "Or you can make it hard."

Gottlieb's hands lifted, fisted.

Scaife eyed the fists and raised a brow. "Another threat from you and we'll take her, too." His head twisted toward Alice. "To the garrison where she belongs."

Retha watched defeat and anger play across Gottlieb's face. "I'll be all right," she assured him with a confidence she did not feel. But she was mortified that she had so endangered her friends and would do anything to set that right. "Let me go. He'll take me to Jacob." Slowly Gottlieb lowered his fists.

"Don't you men tarry," Scaife barked, and pushed Retha through the doorway. Outside, he flopped her onto his ribby nag like a bundle of deerskins, squashing her breasts under his bony arms as he lifted her. She swallowed hard against the bruising insult.

As she struggled to right herself against the saddle's crude wooden framing, her skirt flew up.

"Nice gams," Scaife mocked, eyeing her bare legs.

She understood the tone if not the word. With an angry flourish, she shook her skirt down to her laced shoes and straightened in the saddle. Bared legs, bare throat, bare head. Her *Haube* would be left behind, her neckerchief was inside. She refused to ask for them. No brave-hearted Cherokee woman would stoop to supplication, and her heart had learned courage from them. Defiant, she lifted her chin above her naked throat and unprotected chest.

"That's right, *Frau* Bloom." Scaife's leer lingered on all the female parts of her that Alice had just spoken of so earthily. Lips, breasts, and the juncture of her thighs. Her offerings to her husband. "Get yourself set. You ride with me."

She shot him a flaming look.

He barked a laugh. "Thought so, little liar. You understood pert' near every word."

Just outside Salem at Steiner's Mill, Jacob slammed a sledgehammer into one of the new pilings for the frame dam. Usually he took comfort in doing his full share of communal labor, and the spillway's renovations were, after all, of his design. But today he had spent the two hours since noon trying to ignore the way the sun crawled across the sky, poking in and out of dark, gathering clouds.

His wife had not returned for the midday meal. Sister Ernst had puffed the furlong down the road to deliver the message to him here. Retha was gathering dyestuffs in the forbidden woods and had convinced her friend that she took no risks. Unconvinced, he listened to the Sister's arguments, thanked her, and sent her back to care for Anna Johanna. The boys would spend the afternoon in school. So he wasn't worried about his children. But he was starting to worry about his maddeningly independent wife.

What if something had gone wrong? For weeks, as the war moved up from South Carolina, soldiers had swarmed the roads and woods. Of late, he would admit, there had been a lull. Still, he could have, should have, gone after his wife. If she were harmed, he had no one to blame but himself. For now, he was treading a fine line between encouraging his young bride to stand by his side, newly married and all grown up, and gently guiding her in her new role, so as to help yet not interfere. If he fell on the wrong side of that line, in either direction, he would further jeopardize their fragile relationship.

She had made a decision, and he wanted to stand behind her. As the town dyer, she had scoured the countryside for plants. She knew the woods.

But it was late and getting later, and distant thunder threatened a storm. Any minute now he would give in to his growing conviction of her danger, fling his sledgehammer into the muck, and tear out after her.

He struck another resounding, satisfying blow, and another.

And heard hoofbeats. The mopey slap of water against his pilings did not mute the rhythmic threat of horses tearing up the main road that ran to the mill.

Jacob looked up, in no humor for soldiers, red or blue, fleeing or charging, needing grain or change of—

Clothing. From this distance, he could make out a person in a dress astride a horse. A woman, leading a band of men.

Amber hair furled out behind her, and skirts buffeted her horse's sides. Flanking her, a small band of Liberty Men galloped in tight formation. Above her head, a tricorn swayed and bobbled. Jacob squinted. A man rode behind her, his arms around her body.

Retha was a prisoner. They had found her, captured her, and done to her—God only knew what.

Jacob's hands tightened on the shaft of the sledgehammer as he fought a mad desire to maul the man who clasped her to him.

They galloped up, five ragged, bearded Liberty Men and his windblown wife. Their heaving horses skidded to a halt in front of the drained millpond, at the wet bare feet of Jacob and his men.

In the part of his brain that had gone on full alert, Jacob noted the hired deserters had vanished behind him while Brothers Hine and Rausch held back. Beside him, Brother Steiner was already sloshing through the muck to tend to other business.

These soldiers were not Steiner's business.

With a sudden wave of anger, Jacob charged past him to claim his wife. A wiry soldier spurred his horse up against Jacob, cutting him off from her, but the small horse's arched neck didn't block his view. Anxious, he scanned her face and her alarmingly bared throat for signs of injury. And gave a quick sigh of relief. No harm done, on the surface at least.

But she sat in the saddle like a wild thing cornered, too smart to bolt before her way was clear. Sunlight streamed through storm clouds, lighting her untamed amber hair. *A sight for her husband and no one else.* A memory of his first glimpse of her glorious hair flashed upon him. Here it was unbound for all the world to see: both those reckless, grinning soldiers and his Moravian compatriots, the upright Brothers Hine and Rausch and Steiner. Men who would leer and men who would look away.

A possessive rage, the likes of which he had never known, spiked his gut. He sidestepped the soldier's mount to claim his wife, her eyes flashing and her chin held high above her bare chest. Where her neckerchief should have been.

Who had removed it? Jacob swore the black oath under his breath.

From behind her, Retha's captor vaulted off the horse, revealing his face for the first time. Sim Scaife turned to Jacob and tipped his rumpled tricorn, showing a carrot-red tangle of hair. "Brought your wife home, *Brooder Bloom.*"

Jacob almost choked on his anger. It would have to be that man, mocking his good German name, giving him a thorough once-over, spoiling for another fight.

Scaife sneered at Jacob's sledgehammer. "That weapon ain't no match for muskets."

But my fists are more than a match for yours, Jacob thought, priming himself to sink his knuckles into that grinning jaw. Slowly he became aware of his warlike posture, legs apart, arms braced with the shaft of his hammer held straight across his hips. Answering Scaife's derision with hostilities could not help his wife. He let the hammer down at the road's edge.

Behind him, Brothers Hine and Rausch came dripping up. To help defend his wife? No. A restraining hand landed on his shoulder. "We must have no fighting, Brother Jacob," one said.

No fighting? To the devil with that. He was ready for a fight. He was wet and hot and nearly naked, stripped to nothing but body linen and breeches, barefoot from slogging in the mud.

And that troublemaking Liberty Man had dared to touch his wife. Scaife had no right. Not to be dragging innocent Moravian women about the countryside with a rowdy detail of militia.

Jacob's empty hands curled into fists. "I'm not aware of any military orders to take our women into custody, Captain Scaife."

"Seems like your bride is Cherokee Alice's best friend, *Brooder* Blum," Scaife said silkily.

Jacob clamped down on the anger that caped his shoulders and stood up for his wife. "Yes, we know Alice Vogler. Gottlieb Vogler belonged to our community."

Scaife grinned thinly. "Just like I thought. I found me a Tory spy ring. Your wife and the squaw."

"We have no spies among us, Captain. No matter how hard you try to make it so." Jacob repeated his usual message to the hard-headed Liberty Man.

Colonel Armstrong might rely on Scaife to flush out recalcitrant recruits and even think the captain beyond reproach in fulfilling his duties. But Jacob had always sensed meanness in the zeal with which Scaife caromed about the countryside, seeking spies under every cornhusk mattress.

Scaife ignored Jacob's answer. "And Mr. Vogler

says that Mrs. Blum, 'she speak nik English.' I think he's lying, but I brought her home for a little translation."

Translation? Jacob ground his teeth. Small likelihood that he had come for that. He knew in his gut why Scaife had brought her home. To humiliate him. Ever since their fistfight in the Square, Scaife had been his undeclared enemy. Now he had declared his enmity.

Well, Scaife could try to embarrass him, but he couldn't shame his wife. "I can translate—" Jacob gritted.

"Then, let's get her down—" Scaife stretched long arms up toward her.

Through a purple blur of fury, Jacob lunged.

Laughing, Scaife sidled out of range, and Jacob hit the ground, tackled by his own men from behind. Flattened under the Brothers Hine and Rausch, he rolled and rocked and bucked, struggling to his knees and winning until a third man joined the fray. Jacob's face scraped the graveled roadbed before their grunts and protests registered. They were spewing platitudes about bending swords into plowshares and the meek inheriting the earth.

" 'Tis not our way, Brother Jacob."

"You are an Elder, Brother Blum."

Jacob couldn't sort out one man's voice from the other. Someone pinned his left arm, someone twisted his right wrist up to his shoulder blade. He spit dirt out of his mouth. "Let me up," he growled.

"Very well." Heaving for breath, Brother Steiner eased the grip he had on Jacob's arm. "But you cannot fight the militia."

Jacob knew he couldn't. He only wanted Scaife. But he was outnumbered. By Liberty Men—and a militia of righteous Brethren.

"I quit," he grunted, resting his cheek against the road. "Let me up."

Someone gave him a brisk, understanding pat on the back, and someone else tried to help him stand. He shook off aid and sympathy, and rose.

Scaife shoved his face close to Jacob's. "I'm just helping her down, Blum. For our little translation exercise."

Jacob ignored the derision in his words and looked up into his wife's golden eyes. Are you all right?

Her gaze met his. "I can get down myself, Jacob," she said in impeccable, reassuring German.

He honored her ruse and translated. "If you're letting her go, she wants to dismount by herself."

Scaife nodded permission. Lightly, gracefully, Retha slipped off the horse, bundling her skirts with such skill that no man got a glimpse of ankle.

But on the ground, she wobbled toward Jacob. He caught her and pressed her to him, her breasts so soft, her hair so like a cloud that he fought an absurd fear that she might vanish. He buried his face in her runaway mane. "*Liebling,* are you hurt?" he whispered in German, but quietly so not even the Brothers, hovering protectively near, could hear. "Did they hurt you?"

"Nein," she muttered. "My pride only." But she shuddered against his body, her heartbeat aflutter against the dirty wet shirt that clung to his ribs. "I am terribly, terribly sorry."

"Never mind that," he rasped into the shell of her ear, holding her tighter, longer, despite the men surrounding them. Profound relief thudded through him: She was safe, she was home, she was in his arms. He would do what was needed to set her free.

"Now, about her friend Cherokee Alice . . ." Scaife began.

Jacob moved one arm to surround her shoulders, composing his expression as he turned with her to face her accuser. The zealous Liberty Man would pick at a weakness like a crow at a carcass.

"I can translate," Jacob said evenly. "What do you need to know?" His three townsmen bracketed them, crowded him. He needed no more help from them.

Scaife cleared his throat officiously, playing to a captive audience. "What she was doing with that spy. That's all."

Jacob weighed his answer, ripped by an angry conviction that Scaife cared not a jot if his wife and her friend were spies. No, his real purpose was to discredit Jacob in front of the community. "I take it you think Alice Vogler is a spy."

"Know so, Blum."

"Do you have proof?"

"Your wife may be my proof. Ask her what she was doing there. She won't tell me."

He didn't need to ask. Thank God for Sister Ernst's busybody ways. "She was seeking stock for dyes."

Scaife growled a blasphemous oath, unknown to Jacob but graphic and immediately clear. Good. A ready explanation for Retha's trip from home had to weaken Scaife's trumped-up charge that she was a spy.

"Why not use her garden? Like any other woman?"

"She dyes cloth for the town. She is the town's dyer."

"Then where's her plants? I never saw naught. And I searched her."

Jacob bristled. Scaife meant to taunt him with the fact that he had touched his wife. Jacob forced calm words for her in German. "Retha, I told him you do the town's dyeing—"

She lifted her face to his. It was pale. Scaife must have had at her with his insulting touch for hours. In Jacob's chest, rising anger threatened to explode.

"I understood you, everything," she said.

A quiver in her voice pierced his heart. For her sake, he softened his tone. He would not add hurt to hurt. "I know you went out for dye stock. Eva told me," he said tenderly. "Where is it?"

"I'd not collected any yet."

Retha's excuse sounded lame, even in her own ears. When she had left this morning, she hadn't given dyes a thought, nor danger, nor capture. Inside, she withered like a picked plant at the thought of how much trouble she had brought onto herself. To say nothing of the trouble she had made for Jacob. She had almost collapsed in relief when she had stumbled into his strong arms, safe from Scaife's meandering fingers.

"She had not yet gathered them," her husband said stoutly.

Scaife's eyes narrowed. "Ask her why not."

Jacob asked.

"I hadn't gotten there yet. I was going to the waterfall for indigo." She did not want to lie, but how could she tell him the embarrassing purpose of her visit? She couldn't, not even in private. Surely not in front of these men.

Luckily, Jacob didn't doubt her. He explained to Scaife.

Scaife made a honking noise of disbelief. "All I know's I found her with that Cherokee woman, tight as clams."

"But you found naught on either one of them."

"Your female spy knows the secret of hiding things. In her house. In her person."

Retha felt Jacob stiffen at Scaife's crude insinuation, but to her surprise, he spoke as before, with calm authority. "My wife and Alice Vogler are not spies, Captain Scaife. The Voglers' cabin was on the way to her destination."

Scaife pounced on that idea. "You tell me then, how come a carefully brought up Moravian girl knows where a pair of outcasts like them lives?"

"Vogler is no outcast. He was a Moravian, and he comes to market still. We trade with him. The army trades with him. You know that, Captain Scaife."

"His squaw's the outcast, then. She's Cherokee," the Liberty Man scoffed. "They hate whites."

Retha bit off an indignant protest. With reason, the Cherokee hated backcountry oafs like him, who had raided and ravaged them. Scaife distorted everything.

"She married a white man," Jacob reminded him.

Scaife scowled. "I'll get her yet."

"You say yourself you found naught on her. You never will. You have never seen her with a Redcoat, either. You should leave her alone, Captain Scaife. There's enough for you to worry about with the Redcoats marching from the south."

Scaife snorted, but had no rejoinder.

"As to my wife, I suggest you let me handle her."

Outtalked but far from daunted, Scaife smiled thinly and ogled Retha, secure by dint of superior force from even Jacob's wrath. "That one needs handling, Blum."

It was too much for Jacob. From his place at Retha's side, he lunged forward with a roar, filling his fists with the militia linen of Scaife's collar. A heartbeat behind Jacob's angry impulse, Brothers Steiner, Rausch, and Hine tore him off.

Doubt furrowing their faces, the three Brothers released Jacob while Scaife spun off, hand to his bruised throat.

"Him too, good *Brooders*," he jeered over his shoulder. "You handle him, too. I done had her."

He hadn't, she thought, revulsion rising in her throat. But his words mocked her, and the Brothers' looks accused her. She had been handled. Scaife's hands had been all over her dress, her body. In a vulgar mockery of the sacred intimacies Alice had just explained to her. It made it worse to know exactly what insults he intended. Or perhaps it made it better. For, at the very least, she understood the taboos Scaife had broken.

Inside, she quaked with outrage at the thought of his invasions. She wanted to wash her hands, arms, breasts, belly, everywhere he had touched. She wanted to bathe herself in a racing, cleansing stream. Her body belonged to Jacob, but that snake had defiled it. She closed her eyes, wishing, wishing she could rip out his viperous heart. She tried to steady her breath. In her own heart, she knew for sure he had done nothing to her past remedy. She could forget hands touching her, body pressing into her. He had not stripped her clothes. He had not raped her.

Still, his rude hands had pawed her breasts and poked her belly. On top of that had come the talk. Coarse, intimidating talk. His men had laughed, likening what they proposed to do to her to sows and boars in breeding season.

But Jacob had rescued her. Rising out of the mud and muck like a massive, maddened bear from a rain-soaked winter den, he had mastered rage and talked Sim Scaife to a standstill. Jacob held her now. She burrowed under his sheltering arm, against his powerful torso, taking comfort in his body's solid differences from the bony, punishing angles of Scaife's sour invasions. Taking relief, claiming redemption.

On Jacob, the clean smell of a recent bath mingled with the sharper scent of honest labor, and the damp of his worn body linen soaked through her sleeve to her skin. They were all but flesh to flesh. His massive arm, his humid heat, enveloped her like a thundercloud.

Across the road, under darkening skies, Scaife mounted, then sidled his jigging horse over to her. Tilting back her head, she saw his filmy yellow teeth and matted, carroty hair.

"Just remember"—he smiled thinly at her—"I know about you."

She clenched a fistful of soiled skirt in apprehension. He knew about her? Knew what? What was there to know? He couldn't know she was a spy because she was not. He couldn't know that she spoke English because he had not heard her say one word. His parting salvo puzzled her, weighted her. Frightened her. He was not through with her.

Then Scaife rode off, he and his small gang spewing up a billowing dust that rose to meet the lowering black sky. We need rain, Retha thought, absurdly, randomly, grasping at anything ordinary and obvious and certain. She was losing control. All afternoon she had fought panic, a distant yet familiar nightmare she somehow knew would make her mind spiral into a bleak gray numbness. She wanted that, not thoughts of Scaife, his repellent touch, his leering words.

Just remember, he had said. Remember what? His accusations? Or his touch?

Just remember. She spoke English. He had figured it out on the ride. She hadn't been able to hide it from him. She hadn't been able to hide . . .

Jacob felt her slim shoulder pitch into his ribs, and he hefted her into his arms before she could slide down his body to the ground. "I am taking my wife home," he called out.

"You need help," Steiner offered, but not kindly. All through the confrontation, Steiner, Rausch, and Hine had stood there, useless. Or perhaps not. He would never know if their presence had saved him from doing worse.

"Finish the pilings," Jacob snapped.

Steiner's mouth dropped.

Jacob was never harsh, but this time he didn't care. He would countenance no more public scrutiny of his and Retha's private troubles. "Before the storm hits," he punched out over his shoulder. Clouds had thickened, darkened, and the air had gone very still.

He strode up the road toward the tannery, toward town, one arm circling his wife's back, the other cradling her knees. He felt careless, enraged, all the control he had mustered to deal with Scaife spilling out of him with each lengthening step.

What had his wife been thinking, to go out on her own?

And what had those men done to her in one short day?

His burden was not heavy. An angry man has all the strength in the world. He crossed the log bridge over Tanner's Run and came out behind the barking sheds, away from the men who worked in them, on the far side of town.

"I can walk, Jacob."

"You only just now fainted." He wasn't about to let her go again.

"I swayed. They gave me no time to eat. Let me walk," she insisted, writhing to be free.

But he was much the stronger. "I want you home safe."

"I am not hurt. Set me down."

Every taut, sweet curve of her demanded that he set her down. He bent his knees, lowered her legs, and her feet patted lightly on the ground.

"Not hurt?" He reined in rage, rage born of fear of what he did not know. "You could have been lost or shot or ravaged. You could have been killed."

"They didn't really hurt me," she asserted, her face set.

In the lee of the tanning yard, without a soul in sight, he pulled her to him. She felt so slim. So stubborn.

"Never, never, never go where I cannot protect you." He ground out the words from the depth of his heart into the froth of her hair.

She pulled away as if to read his face. "You're angry with me." Her golden eyes brimmed with tears.

"I was terrified for you. I didn't even know which direction to go looking for your body."

"I see that now."

She ducked her head, her chin dimpling. He lifted it, brushed her lips with his. Hers were unresisting, yet they trembled.

"Ah, *Leibling,* what did they put you through? You were so, so brave." She had looked like some flame-haired Indian woman warrior. He didn't think he should tell her that.

She cleared her throat and straightened against him. "They talked. They said rude things. In English." She gave a small, brave laugh. "Much of which I didn't understand."

He stifled a snarl. "What else? What did Scaife do to you?"

She dropped her head again.

He lifted it, saw her distress, and lowered his voice. "You can tell me. I will not hurt you over this. He's the one I want to throttle."

"No, Jacob! No!" She clutched at his shoulders with sudden alarm. Precious alarm. His heart lurched with gratification at the gift of her concern. "You are already hurt because of me."

"I will do naught," he promised. But his promise went against the grain. He had a new, knife-sharp understanding of homicidal purpose. "This time. Some day, some way, one of us must stop that man from plaguing innocents. I pray God 'tis me."

"Jacob," she said earnestly. "Don't do it for me."

"Then tell me what he did."

She shook her head and lowered her hands, withdrawing. He thought she would not speak.

"You can tell me," he urged. A few fat drops of rain splattered in the dust.

"Touched me," she whispered finally.

"God, Retha," he whispered back. "Touched you? Not only while he was riding behind you?"

Her head bobbled a faint negative. He could not bear her pain, her determined, embarrassed isolation. He wanted to share it. With care, he drew her back into his arms.

"Where then? Where did he touch you?"

"Mouth." Her voice went small, childlike. "Fingers in my mouth."

"Liebling," Jacob consoled her, rubbing circles of comfort into her rigid spine. Anger streaked down his. "I would have done aught to spare—"

"I bit them," she confided.

That startled a laugh out of him. "Brave wife," he said, then sobered. Scaife would not have stopped with that action. And Retha needed, Jacob felt, without quite knowing why, to carry no more secrets than those she already bore. They needed none between them. "Was there more?"

"My—breasts. With his hands. All over." She buried her face in his chest, and he took the trusting gesture to heart, plotting revenge, planning mayhem, even knowing he would likely never have the chance. He rested against her, swaying slightly to release his turmoil.

"Is there more, Retha? You must not endure this alone." He cupped the crown of her head in his palm and steadied her against him, feeling his own head would burst if she had worse to reveal.

"My stomach. He . . . We stopped to water horses. The other men were in the creek."

Jacob could not suppress a growl, and she lifted her head against his palm, her eyes shining with determination. "He did not touch me . . . there . . . where no man has the right but you."

No man had the right to touch her anywhere. But she had not been raped. *"Danke Gott,"* he murmured, for her sake, not merely for his own. Despite her ordeal, she was safe at home with him. And suspected of being a spy. "Dear God, if only he hadn't found you at the Voglers."

Retha lifted her chin. "Alice is my friend."

"Your Cherokee friend, suspected of spying," he pointed out gently.

"She had not heard that we are married."

"What has that do with—"

"I wanted her to know that you married me."

"*Gott im Himmel,* Retha! That was no reason to risk your life."

She touched his face, placing cool, experimental fingers along his jaw. "She is very happy for me."

He relished her touch but not her reasons for

taking her excursion. "War is no time for social niceties," he said in the patient, paternal voice he used with the children.

"She says you are a good man." Retha's fingers edged his jaw, his chin, and touched his lips.

Every fiber of his being flashed like lightning in the distant sky, and he dragged her fingers from his lips and crushed her mouth with his.

CHAPTER 11

Jacob's kiss was firm, demanding, hot, but the day's events collided in Retha's mind, distracting her. Alice's earthy counsel clashed against Scaife's invasions. Yet Jacob had stood up for her against the militia men. Her husband had defended her. Her spirit soared.

And now beneath her cold, wet dress, her skin warmed to his caress. But the captain's hands, too, had roamed her back, her neck, her breasts, the very places Jacob claimed. Valiantly she struggled to shake off those vile images. Her husband's confident embrace, she told herself, was not her captor's insulting clasp.

Jacob prolonged the kiss, his appetite seeming voracious, unending. A corner of her mind struggled to understand his hunger and her own sense of floating. To understand this kiss. It went on and on, lasting far longer than any they had yet shared. Alice had not warned her that a kiss could last so long. Retha wanted to answer his intensity, his enveloping embrace. She wanted to yield to the claim he made. She wanted . . . air. Under his mouth, she gasped for breath.

With a low baritone growl, he released her, granting her one breath and then beginning again, softer. His hot, moist tongue edged her lips. When he had kissed her so before, she had been startled. This time sensation skittered over her lips, the tingling as acute as if he had touched an open wound. Yet for all the race of feeling, she felt no pain, nothing but his effort at restraint and his reassuring warmth. A whimper of surprise sounded in her throat, a small, strange animal sound she had never before made.

Chagrined, she parted her lips to apologize. His teeth clinked against hers. She cringed at her clumsiness, but he held her tighter, reassuringly.

What did he want? Alice had said nothing of this. *Trust him,* she had said. Trust him to do what? Retha wondered. She didn't know.

His breath caressed her face. Her skin shivered. His damp, broad chest lifted and fell, flattening her breasts under the stiff bodice of her dress. They tightened strangely. His tongue probed against her teeth. Her very teeth, she marveled, could feel his touch.

He broke away, his mouth a thread's breadth from hers. "Open for me," he rasped softly. "*Liebling,* open your mouth."

With a small, speechless shock, she did, slackening the jaw she had clamped shut unawares. The tip of his tongue pushed against her teeth. He must really mean for her to open her mouth, and so she tried, uncertain of his intent and awkward in this unaccustomed position. Then his tongue touched hers.

He tasted rich, she mused, rich and manly, of hearty bread, ripe cheese, strong ale, not the stale tobacco fumes Sim Scaife had blown into her face. Retha shuddered at the awful thought. She would not let that man intrude, not with her husband comforting her. Sustaining her, like daily bread, as necessary as the air she breathed. She would not.

Jacob's tongue swirled in her mouth, inviting her to let him kiss away the thoughts, the fear. She opened her eyes, fighting the insidious image of Scaife with the pure sight of her husband's face. So close, so intimate. His still-lowered eyelids were lightly veined, and his lashes thick and golden. Sun had flecked the hint of skin that she could see. Nothing Alice said of kissing measured up to this glory.

The mounting urgency of his hot tongue burned away the images of her captivity, the endless gallop home. The iron certainty of his massive arms banded her, blotting out her skin's memory of Scaife's cruel fingers. Soon, for Retha, sensation overpowered thought. But still she did not know what he expected her to *do.* Tentatively she moved her tongue to meet his. He groaned, and tightened his arms. She yielded, relaxing her body into his strength and finding wondrous freedom in his close embrace.

A blade of lightning cut the distant sky. Moments later its thunder rumbled toward them.

Lifting his mouth from hers, Jacob glanced at the looming clouds as if he had forgotten they were there. Then he gazed into her eyes with a slight, self-conscious smile. "Ah, Retha. Forgive me. I am a selfish man."

Hardly selfish, she thought. His embrace seemed a generous gift. He was offering her his world, protected and secure. She shook her head against the landscape of his chest.

"You must be tired and hungry," he went on. "And I am caked with mud."

She couldn't speak. Her fatigue didn't matter, or his disarray. Only this mattered: the unexpected refuge of his arms.

"Are you truly unharmed?"

She looked up into his caring blue scrutiny. "Yes, unharmed. Truly."

Fat raindrops splattered on her exposed skin. Icy raindrops. She shivered.

Tenderly, futilely, he brushed her wet cheek. "We'll get drenched."

She smiled and found her voice. "You needed a bath."

Jacob chuckled with relief. The kiss had done her no harm, had done him much good. His wife was in his arms, accepting the best comfort he could give her. Perhaps she even asked for more. He bent to her and whispered, "I never meant to come to you like this, all dirt and sweat."

"The rain will rinse you off." He thought he heard a plucky note of teasing in her remark.

"Not if we outrun it," he tossed back, doubting that they could make it home before the heavens broke, not caring. A curtain of heavy rain marched up the meadow, drenched the peach orchard, and overtook Sister Baumgarten's plump *milch* cow.

Retha pushed her glistening long hair over her shoulder. "I couldn't run a step."

Taking that as a challenge, he scooped her up. "I can," he said, and strode off briskly. His anger was only a coal of memory at the back of his mind, for his wife was in his arms.

Halfway home, the sky let loose. Cooling raindrops pelted his old work shirt and splashed on her upturned face, her still-uncovered throat and chest.

"I'd rather run, Jacob!" She laughed, wriggling to be free.

Scarcely missing a stride, he set her down, keeping one hand in his and pulling her to the house. Once she stumbled, but he helped her to her feet, bracing her with his arm. Once she almost jerked him off the road.

"Stop here!" she urged, veering toward the wide, protected porch of Brother Meyer's Tavern.

"No need. We're almost home."

He ran on, exhilarated by the unrelenting rain and his young wife's mettle. By the time they reached the house, she had caught his spirit. She laughed at him—with him—when he fumbled with the latch. They huddled under the tiny roof that failed altogether to shelter the front stoop. He shepherded her into the narrow entryway.

Hands on knees, she bent over, panting. He supported her, confidently clasping her slim waist in his large hands for the first time since their wedding night. And he watched, fascinated, as her thick flame of hair, darkened by the downpour, fell forward, trickling rainwater onto the floor.

" 'Twas but a shower, wife, and 'twill soon be ended." He chuckled as she shook a spray of water into the air.

Straightening, she removed his hands and glared. "'Twas a thunderstorm."

With her apron, she blotted her wet face and then dabbed self-consciously at the tops of her breasts, ungauzed, unguarded. He could not resist the sight.

He did not have to. She was his wife.

"Small wonder they invented neckerchiefs," he said wickedly, running a finger along the square neckline just above her cleavage. "The sun has burned you."

Already flushed from their run, she blushed still deeper and touched the angry pink skin of her chest. "I took it off . . . in the heat . . . to walk . . . they gave me no time . . ."

Then he remembered. "We haven't time. The boys will be home shortly," he interrupted, ushering her into the bedroom and latching the door behind them. He plucked his clinging shirt away from his body. Muddy water puddled around his bare feet. "It won't do for Nicholas to see me looking as though I've been in a fight."

"What about Anna Johanna?"

"Sister Ernst will keep her safe until we fetch her," he said, peeling his shirt over his head.

Retha did not move. She gaped, dazzled by the sight of her husband stripping to bare skin, talking all the while. What was she to do? *Trust him,* Alice said. That had been easier outside with him fully clothed.

"Don't I have a clean shirt in the clothes cupboard?" he said in a normal voice.

Somewhere, Retha thought, so distracted she could only nod. The sight of him mesmerized her.

Shirtless, the body that had held her and consoled her was all mountains of strength. Tawny hair whorled around the bundled muscles of his chest, drawing her gaze to his dusky nipples. She had never seen them on a white man, she realized with a start. She had never thought about seeing them on a white man. Their small peaks mimicked hers as if he were chilled.

Or aroused, as Alice had explained that *she* would be.

Oh, her friend had not told her everything.

He wadded the shirt and dropped it on the floor. "I'll have to rinse this for tomorrow. I have not finished at the millpond. For *Singstunde* tonight, my Sunday clothes will have to do."

Turning to his basin, he quickly poured water into it, wrung out a cloth, and began washing his body, speaking of inconsequentials. Retha did not hear. At least his back was to her so that she could gawk unseen. She wished, she craved for him to slow down. When he raised his hands to sponge his face and neck, his muscles rippled over his shoulder blades. Like water over rocks, she thought. As Jacob disrobed, minute sensations streamed throughout Retha's body, overwhelming her.

Clumsy as a schoolgirl, she stepped backwards, stumbling over the willow sewing basket, thumping against the door.

With a warm, quizzical smile, Jacob set down the cloth, closed the distance between them, and took her hands. "Are you all right?" His knowing gaze searched hers.

She felt her neck heat, then her face. He had

caught her again looking at him. This time shamelessly.

"I am your husband, Retha, you can look at me," he said softly, earnestly. "I want you to look at me."

But she couldn't. Alice's advice was far too simple. Trusting him was difficult. Looking at him—and knowing that he knew she looked—was . . . was . . . Retha dropped her gaze.

It stopped at the fall of his breeches.

At that swelling.

"There too, wife," he said, his voice smoky. "I want you to look at all of me."

She swallowed hard and curled her hands into fists.

"No, *Liebling*, don't. Don't be afraid. I don't want you to be afraid of me ever. Not of any part of me. Here." With strong fingers, he uncurled her fists and flattened her palms against his naked chest. "Touch me."

Touch him, her friend had said. And now he was asking her to do just that. Embarrassed, emboldened, she did. She spread her fingers—they were not quite still—and let them sink into his flesh.

She heard his sudden inrush of breath.

Her fingers sizzled. The tawny hair crinkled as she shyly glided her hands across his immense breadth. His chest was damp, hard, manly. Private. But what did he want her to do to it? She stopped.

"More," he said. "I won't break. You cannot hurt me."

He was twice her size and strength. Larger, more powerful unclothed than dressed. Gingerly she pressed her palms against his solid chest, testing for texture, for knowledge. He radiated heat, warming her cold hands.

Touching him was not so difficult after all, she mused. Surprised at the silky skin of his nipples, at their hard pebbles of arousal, she paused. She could have sworn his heart leapt to meet her trembling, cautious hand.

"Lower," he grated softly.

She hesitated.

"Please."

Reach for him. She let her hand slide down.

Lower, he was just as solid, just as hot. At his rib cage, his skin was clammy to her touch, and lower still, his hard abdomen was ridged. Sanctuary, she thought with wonder at the sheer strength he held in check for her. She lifted her gaze to his.

With a shivering breath, Jacob sucked in his stomach and pulled her hands away. It was a mistake, he realized, seeing the first light of desire in her eyes. Her simple, trusting touch had almost spun him out of control.

He knew she wasn't ready to see him, let alone love him.

He knew there wasn't time.

A sudden frown spelled her confusion.

"Thank you. I love this, Retha," he said, kissing the frown away. "I love it so much I want more. We had best stop while I still can."

He had to wash and change. With grim determination, he poured water from the pitcher to the basin and began to scrub.

He had never made love in the afternoon. He had never wanted to this badly. Outside, the rain had stopped. School would be out any moment now, and the boys would soon be home. They had to go to services, united as a family. Rapidly he unbuttoned the fall of his breeches and loosed their ties.

Before Retha could think to avert her eyes, her husband had stepped out of the rest of his clothes. Fascinated, she studied him, his exposed body vulnerable—yet to her invincible. From a thicket of fawn-brown hair where his powerful thighs met, his manhood jutted out, proud with wanting her.

She averted her gaze. A surge of blood pooled in her belly. Now that she had an inkling of what his desire and her response meant, she didn't know, at this moment, what to do.

He ran the cloth over his most private parts and down his legs, bending to swab caked mud off his thick calves and sinewy feet. As he turned and bent and flexed, he neither hid his arousal from her nor tried to protect her from the sight. She could not watch, even though he showed none of the reserve or modesty she felt herself. But did he really mean for her to watch? Or should she honor his privacy? At her sides, her closed hands felt large and ignorant.

But her friend had told her not to shrink, to let him know that she was willing. Retha summoned all her nerve and edged up to her naked husband.

"Do you still want me to look?"

He gave a strangled laugh and wheeled to face her, glorious in the flesh and feral as a bear. "*Gott*, yes. I mean no. Not just now." He clamped down on her arms. "I want to look at you."

"At me?" Her voice wavered.

His voice lowered, deepened. "At you, wife. At all of you. I want to love you in the middle of the afternoon. With the children almost home from school. And Eva doubtless on her way with Anna Johanna. And the bell about to ring for vespers."

"We cannot," she croaked with new and inexplicable frustration. They had come so far. So near. But Jacob's children would soon be home. Already shouts of boys at play echoed in the nearby Square. She was a terrible new mother, she chastised herself. Jacob's compelling presence swamped her senses, and the children had slipped her mind.

"No, not now," he agreed. But he did not move.

"Can I help?" She reached for his cloth, but he wouldn't let go of her arms.

"No." He grinned. "You can only make it worse."

"Oh." Heat suffused her face. "I didn't mean to."

"'Tis in nature for you to make it worse. 'Tis your role. Your duty."

His ruddy manhood was still swollen. One glimpse told her it was much too large, she thought, for human comfort, his or hers. "It must hurt."

His eyes darkened with desire. "'Tis a pain men die for willingly. For after this comes pleasure. Pleasure beyond your imagining until . . . well, just until."

He spoke as Alice had, Retha thought, vexed that there was some part of the experience neither one would put in words. She didn't like not knowing. Releasing her, Jacob stepped into fresh breeches and shrugged into a long, clean shirt. Its pale summer flax cloaked his magnificent body. She felt a stab of disappointment, a twinge of relief.

Swiftly he finished dressing, adjusted his stock

with a flourish, and grinned. "All done. My turn to help you." He looked around the room. "Where are your clothes?"

She retrieved them from the cupboard and nervously shook the wrinkles out of the skirt. He slipped her soiled skirt over her petticoats, letting it fall into a circle on the floor, and knelt down, placing her hand on his shoulder so that she could balance herself.

But she didn't feel balanced. She felt dizzy, restless, too high above him as he knelt at her feet. His head was at the level of her belly, yet he did not seem aware of the strangeness of his position. Of her strangeness teetering above him, nothing but empty space in front of her face, her arms, her body. He lifted her plain petticoat, its hem limp with mud, and slid it down from her waist.

"Step out," his voice rumbled up.

She did, catching a toe in the folds of cloth and gripping his shoulder all the harder. When she was clear of the fabric, he stood and bent his head over her breasts, concentrating on them or on the bodice that covered them. She couldn't tell.

"And this." He slipped his hand beneath the bodice, knowingly sought the pins that fastened it, and took them out.

She stifled a shower of impulses: to help him, to stop him, to face him. She didn't want her body to change, the way Alice said it would. Yet she wanted that change fiercely. She wanted to know the ultimate pleasure that even now tugged at her womb.

With a will not hers, her freed breasts sprang

toward his waiting hands. He covered them, released them, and his knuckles gently rubbed her nipples taut. A pull of yearning took her breath away.

He gave her a broad, pleased smile. "I heard that. Tell me, wife. Tell me you feel it, too."

She nodded, unable to say the words: I want you too.

Retha's silent, bashful nod satisfied Jacob. For now. He was a planner, a builder, and would construct her desire by degrees. It was enough that she did not retreat, that she acknowledged feeling.

With detached dispatch, he stripped her down to her simple shift and then dressed her again in her clothes, a fresh petticoat, pockets, dry skirt, clean bodice. She almost raced to pin her dress before he could touch her there.

He loved her virgin awkwardness. He hadn't expected her to charm him when all he wanted to do was ravish her.

"I can do that," he said. "Let me. I want to finish dressing you."

She raised a doubtful brow.

"Then I will undress you. Later on. Tonight—" he began, hoping to woo her with words. But the front door banged open.

Retha's eyes widened. "They're home."

They were. Jacob sighed, reluctant to return to his children's demands. This time he had come so close. They had come so close.

Footsteps trudged into the kitchen. Slates clacked onto the table. Matthias's voice rose in complaint.

"Brother Ernst said Papa would be home."

"He is home, stupid," Nicholas said.

"Where? I don't see him."

"In there," Nicholas hissed, loud enough for them to hear him.

Behind the closed door, Jacob watched his wife press the edges of her bodice together.

"The door's locked," he reassured her, and commenced to pin her dress, one pin at her trim waist, another at the hollow between her delectable breasts. He clenched his jaw. This was why a man should never woo his wife in the middle of the afternoon.

Through the door, he heard Nicholas continue.

"With *her*."

"What for? He's not hurt again! Brother Ernst did not tell us that he's hurt."

"What do you think for, then?"

"It's too early to go to bed," Matthias reasoned.

"Not for married people, you dunce," Nicholas taunted.

"Only babies sleep in the afternoon," Matthias snapped back, innocent but petulant.

Nicholas went for the kill. "What would you know? You're still a baby yourself."

The closed door muffled a blow, a grunt, a boy's high cry of pain. Jacob rolled his eyes, parental duty warring with a state of arousal only slightly impaired by his sons' spat.

"I have to stop them," he said reluctantly, setting the pins on the windowsill and hastily kissing her hand. "We are not finished."

Breathless with haste, embarrassment, and desire, Retha turned her back to the door while Jacob plunged through it. Stern baritone murmurs engaged the boys' soprano excuses, but she didn't try to follow Jacob's soft admonitions. She wasn't fully dressed. And the boys' brief squabble told her that young Nicholas had a fairly clear idea of what she and his father had been doing. Being a mother to boys that age—there was so much she hadn't thought of. What exactly did Nicholas think parents did in the afternoon? And how did he know? And what did Matthias have yet to learn?

Her dress pinned, she braved the domestic scene and entered the small kitchen. Jacob sat with the boys at the work table, his back to her. Two miniatures of him looked up at her, although without his tender acceptance.

She smiled. Tried to smile.

Matthias frowned back. "Where's her *Haube?*"

"Matthias . . ." Jacob's tone sounded a warning.

Retha touched her hand to her throat. No ribbon, no cap. She had forgotten. She wasn't sure she had another here.

"She's not wearing her *Haube*, Papa," Matthias stated in a grown-up, censorious way.

Retha sat beside Jacob, facing her accuser across the table. Since the Younger Sisters slyly used to mock her going barefoot and braiding her hair, she hated being talked about. Or scolded. "We were caught in the rain, Matthias."

Jacob nodded, apparently approving of her simple version of the day's events.

But Matthias slid his eyes away from her quiet rebuke. "Don't women have to wear *Haubes?*" he asked his father stubbornly.

"As men have to wear hats," Jacob confirmed.

"But not all the time. And not when their hair is dripping with rain."

Nicholas butted in. "It wasn't rain that kept her away from lunch."

"No, your stepmother had to be out. Sister Ernst brought you your lunch," Jacob said evenly.

Retha blinked in gratitude at Jacob's defense of her. She admired his way with the boys. He didn't punish; he reasoned, answering their questions yet telling them no more than they needed to know. Nor did he blame her or allow them to. Even though he could have. A heavy burden of remorse lifted from her heart. He had protected her from the militia in front of the Brothers, and now he was upholding her in front of the children.

But she had lost the precious ground gained with them while he was away. There was no help for it but to get to the end of the day. She started up from her seat. "Perhaps I should fetch Anna Johanna. Sister Ernst should have brought her home by now."

"Ah . . ." Meaningfully, Jacob scratched his head, reminding her that hers was bare. "Let's send the boys for her."

They crowded out the door, bumping each other in an excess of youthful energy. In a moment, they were back.

"She's here," Nicholas said, dejected.

A woeful Sister Ernst followed them inside. Anna Johanna trailed behind her ample skirts. "She refuses my touch," Eva confided.

Dismayed, Retha closed her eyes. She could not shut out recrimination. The old Anna Johanna was back, and Retha blamed herself for disappearing, just as the child's mother had.

Jacob approached his daughter, speaking softly. She glared and wrung the hem of her worn dress. Hoping to appease her, Retha retrieved the porcelain-faced doll from the parlor and offered it. Anna Johanna snatched it away and marched off, shutting everyone out as she curled up in a chair.

Not quite the same old Anna Johanna, Retha amended her thought.

This one was angry.

For supper, Retha cobbled together a modest meal of stale bread and breakfast hominy. Jacob ate heartily, but it was a poor supper by anyone's standards. The children poked at the warmed-over mush, Nicholas and Anna Johanna as finicky as Matthias at his worst.

After Retha's thick hair had dried, she riffled through her few clothes for a spare *Haube* to wear to the evening service. She had only one, worn but clean. She folded her still-damp hair up under it, tied its frayed ribbons in a modest bow, and returned to the parlor.

"Pink ribbons! Married Sisters wear blue ones," Matthias, the keeper of rules and regulations, pointed out.

Retha firmly squashed a teary flood of exasperation. She didn't want to wear her old *Haube*, but she had neither new ribbons for it nor the time to sew them on. And she didn't want Jacob defending her again.

"Sometimes Married Sisters haven't put new

blue ribbons on all their old *Haubes* yet. They have to wear the ones with pink ribbons until they do," she told Matthias firmly.

Bested, Matthias picked up a small puzzle and jammed its wooden pieces into place.

Retha took refuge in the supper dishes, swabbing them furiously. Jacob sneaked up behind her, feathering a kiss at the nape of her neck.

"I have dreamed of taking liberties with a Single Sister," he whispered.

She couldn't suppress a giggle at his playfulness—or stop the tiny thrill that ran up her neck to her ear. She grabbed for a cup to dry. "That's a wicked thought, Brother Blum."

"I have others . . ." he said, planting another kiss, evoking another giggle, teasing another thrill up her neck.

But any other wicked thoughts her husband had would have to wait until after evening services. The bell sounded for *Singstunde.* Retha flinched, and the mug she was drying clattered to the floor.

Soberly Jacob picked it up and carefully returned it to her hands. "Perhaps you would rather not go. 'Twas a hard day for you. Perhaps you're not ready."

"Not ready for services? Of course I am. I'm not that tired."

"No, I mean that you may not be ready for this. Everyone will know what happened. You don't have to go."

She studied the dull pewter of the mug. Surely he understood that she had to. But perhaps he wished she wouldn't.

"I have to go, Jacob."

"Some will talk," he warned gently.

"They can't talk about your wife if she's there. I won't let them," she said, suddenly savage, thinking of every insult and outright lie she had ever endured. But she had endured them. She would again.

"You cannot stop their talking." Cupping his hand at her ear, he mimicked a gossiping Sister in a high whisper. "Did you hear about Sister Blum? She ran away today."

"I most certainly did not run away," Retha said, laughing aloud at Jacob's apt banter. "Of course, if I am present, they will point at us as well."

"Let them." He raked his fingers through his hair as if the thought, once spoken, irked him. "Let them. Retha, this is not about you. You made a small error in judgment in leaving town today. Sim Scaife turned it into a large mistake. He's after me. Through you, through them. I won't let it bother me."

"But it will, it must. I never should have gone. It seemed so simple, 'twas but a walk. I had been cooped up so long. But he seemed almost to have been looking for me."

"I know, *Liebling.* Perhaps he was, but we cannot control that now."

"We can't even control Anna Johanna." Retha returned to her dishes, stacking them in exceedingly neat piles. "I blame myself, Jacob. She's so upset, just as she was before."

"Not quite as before. At least this time, she is merely angry. That marks an improvement over her fits."

"But she was so much better. We had done so well."

"You had done so well. You could not have known how she would react. You came home as soon as you could."

"Perhaps I should stay home with her."

Jacob rubbed the back of his neck. "No," he said thoughtfully. "No, she should go. She already let me touch her, even if she's still upset with you." He took Retha's hand, holding it fast. "And you should go. Although I can't stop tongues wagging, however much I want to."

No one but her husband had ever tried to stem the flow of gossip that pursued her. "Tongues always wag about me. Since the night you caught me."

He grinned as if remembering that night, and then his blue eyes darkened. "They cannot hurt my wife."

Retha felt old scars begin to soften, and she squeezed her husband's hand in heartfelt thanks.

"I won't let it hurt, Jacob. I want to be at your side."

"Good. That's where I want you to be." Securing her hand in the crook of his arm, he led the family out the door.

Outside, the thunderstorm had cooled the day and wet the dust. In the Square, Nicholas marched off to reconnoiter his troops for a few moments before services, with Matthias thoughtfully behind him. Anna Johanna resumed her former handhold at her father's knee, ignoring Retha with a swish of her skirts. Retha was so focused on her stepdaughter's anger that everyone was seated before she noticed any untoward looks in her direction or suspected that any of the usual hushed whispers were about her.

"Pink ribbons," she heard from the bench behind her.

"That Scaife," from a bench in front.

"All day?" a woman walking up the aisle was saying. "Not all day!"

It was worse than Retha had anticipated from the safety of her home. For years as the orphan whom Indians had raised, she had borne curiosity and even censure alone. But tonight they were talking about Jacob Blum's wife. Mortification heated her cheeks. The buzz of disapproval absolutely proved that she had let her husband down. That she had let his children down. She couldn't sing a note. Not even Jacob's resonant baritone recalled her mind to worship.

At last the service ended. Nearby, the band members put their instruments away. Beyond them, the three Brothers from the mill clustered, the ones who had witnessed her humiliation.

She stood up, the better to face them if they turned her way. She was sure they would.

The men summoned the head Elder, Frederick Marshall, and all four bent their heads in conference. Looking up, Brother Steiner pointed to her. Looking down, Brother Marshall's brow furrowed. She was indeed their subject. Squaring her shoulders, she left the *Saal* with Jacob and the children. Retha did not want to look at her husband just yet. She did not want him to look at her. Not until she composed her thoughts.

Outside *Gemein Haus*, the boys scooted off, but Anna Johanna clung to her father when Samuel Ernst cornered him. Retha hid her eagerness to go home, her anger mounting as she surveyed the crowd. She met people's looks even as they tried to look away. It was not fair. She had done no real wrong. If she had, Sim Scaife would not have let her go. Retha stood alone as men chatted with men and women with women, but she was in no mood to join her friends among the Single Sisters. They sought her out instead. Rosina Krause and Sarah Holder took her aside.

"Are you quite all right, my dear?" Sister Sarah asked with sweet concern, taking Retha's hand in knobby, trembly fingers. "Those militia men can be so fearsome."

Retha winced. Now that she was married, she had assumed she would put misadventures behind her. Her actions had worried poor Sister Sarah, too. And not for the first time.

"They were not so bad," she tried to assure her. "They brought me home."

With a *harrumph*, Rosina Krause rejected Retha's version of the event. "Word is out, Sister Retha, that they were bad," she said firmly, wagging her head. "You could have been ravished. Such an incident has long been my fear for you."

Retha gritted her teeth but humbled herself as befitted Jacob's wife. "I know. You always warned me."

"But my dear, what happened to your new blue ribbons?" the older woman asked.

Retha's pink ribbons suddenly seemed to strangle her. At home, the missing *Haube* had been an inconvenience. Here, faced with the Sisters' concern and the Brothers' impromptu meeting on her account, Retha forcefully felt how far she had compromised her spotless status as Jacob Blum's bride. How far she had compromised him. The pink ribbons proclaimed her indiscretion.

"I lost my cap, Sister Sarah."

"Lost it?" Sarah inquired gently.

"Lost it!" Rosina demanded.

Retha squelched her pride. "It was my best one. I do not yet have blue ribbons for this old one."

"Oh, dear," Sister Sarah said. "Ribbons, with the war, are in such short supply." A sympathetic frown crinkled Sarah's face.

Impatience lined Rosina's as she turned to the old woman. "No doubt the soldiers had a hand in that. Come now, Sister Sarah, 'tis time to go home. As for you, Sister Blum, this small reminder of your folly"—she touched the offending pink strands—"is better than the injury they no doubt contemplated."

And she led her aging Sister away.

Unable to allay the sting of Rosina Krause's censure, Retha waited by herself. Across the Square, she could see that Jacob, shackled by a cranky daughter, had rounded up his sons. Retha wanted to join her family, to help with Anna Johanna, but thought any aid from her might well provoke a tantrum. She smothered an outburst of self-recrimination. Leaving home this morning had been her decision, and her stepdaughter's relapse was her fault. With each of her new stepchildren, she would simply have to start all over.

They hiked across the green, Matthias leading, Anna Johanna dragging, and Nicholas under his father's affectionate arm. When they neared, Retha realized that all was not well. Jacob, tight-lipped, had his hand on his son's neck, and a defiant Nicholas, one eye swelling shut, was being firmly marched toward home. Quelling curiosity, she fell in, aware that the dwindling crowd made way for them to pass.

Then Frederick Marshall, stern in black, stepped into their path.

"Brother Blum," he said, without a glance at Retha or the children, "the Elders meet tomorrow to discuss your offense. These are serious charges." And he marched off.

Nicholas whistled in admiration but winced as Jacob pulled him closer.

"What offense, Papa?" Matthias asked.

Jacob did not answer his earnest, legalistic younger son. Retha's mouth went dry. She turned to him, taken aback by his stony demeanor as much as by the Elder's severity.

"Charges?" she said. "Against you?"

CHAPTER 12

At home in the kitchen, Jacob smeared lard onto his militant son's cheek, already turning purple. "Hold still," he said impatiently to the very large and still very angry boy on the stool in front of him. For once Jacob wished himself anywhere but here in the sanctuary of his home. It was too much—Marshall's injunction, his wife's worried question, and his older son's fight all at once.

"But it wasn't my fault!" Nicholas protested. "Thomas Baumgarten started it. He called her a spy!"

Jacob glanced over his son's battered head to see how his wife was taking this. Badly. The tallow lamp she held illumined her set features. Beside her, his daughter lingered to catch her brother's scolding, but Retha nudged her forward. Anna Johanna snatched up her doll and swished her ragged skirts upstairs to bed.

"I would hit him again," Nicholas insisted.

"Hit him again, son, and you will be in more trouble than you are in now."

"She's the one who's bringing trouble to our family."

"You're the one bringing trouble to it now, son.

It's not your place to judge what your elders do, especially not your stepmother and especially not in front of her."

"I was fighting for our name."

Jacob gritted his teeth. For a moment he wished he believed in corporal punishment. But the one time he had lost his temper and spanked the boy, it hadn't helped either of them. Physical chastisement was the worst possible recourse to take with a born pugilist. Reason, he reassured himself, would turn a hotheaded boy into a reasonable man. Only reason.

"You were fighting with one of our Brethren. That's the worst thing you can do."

"Spying's the worst," Nicholas muttered doggedly.

Jacob laughed and turned his son's face to the light for a final view of the damage. "Recalcitrant sons are the worst." He dabbed more lard onto a smaller bruise above the boy's left eyebrow.

"Ouch!" Nicholas wrenched away. "What's recalcitrant?"

"Stubborn and disobedient."

Jacob returned the crock of lard to the cupboard. He had brought Nicholas around before. "Now, about your fight, son."

His older son thrust out a mutinous chin. "You fought."

"Not since I was a lad like you. And I paid for it."

"Today. You fought."

If Brothers grinding his face in the dirt constituted fighting, Jacob had to concede he had fought. And more, he had wanted to land a volley of punches in that Liberty Man's gut.

"Who told you that?"

"William Steiner, the miller's son. He said you fought the Liberty Men. He said they captured *her*—"

"They brought her home, son."

"—and when they brought her home, you had to fight for her. What I want to know is, did you win?"

Jacob sunk his aching body into his railback chair and told both boys to pull up stools.

"No one wins, Nicholas, when a disagreement comes to blows. I was working on the dam when Captain Scaife brought your mother home. I never struck a soul, and she was safe." Technically, Jacob amended to himself, if not fighting meant never landing a blow, and safe meant the nervous silence she had displayed since they had come home.

"Why did William lie?" Matthias asked.

Jacob regarded his pious middle child with amused exasperation. Matthias the theologian would know how many angels fit on the head of a pin.

"There are many ways to tell a story, son, especially when so many saw the event. Captain Scaife made me very angry. I wanted to fight him, I admit. But I was wrong."

"I can see that," Nicholas said. "The captain's a Whig. He's on our side."

"We don't have a side, Nicholas, hard as that is for you to accept right now. Moravians have always supported whatever government is in power, and Captain Scaife supports it too. But unlike him, we don't bear arms for it."

"I don't understand why they had to bring her home," Matthias said.

Jacob sighed heavily. Retha's brief absence had

disturbed his sons as much as his daughter.

"They *brought* her home because she *left us*," Nicholas spelled out.

"Our real mother would not have left," Matthias said.

"That is not true, Matthias. They brought her home because she belongs here."

"Our real mother was always home to feed us," Matthias said reprovingly.

Jacob saw Retha before he heard her, entering the kitchen behind the boys, her face set.

Before he could intervene, she stepped forward to touch his son's shoulder. "And I will always be home now, Matthias."

Startled, Matthias jerked away, then craned his head to see her. Tight-lipped silence told Jacob that the boy had doubts.

"I'm sorry I was not here when you came home," she said softly.

Matthias's chin jutted out another notch. "We had to go to Brother and Sister Ernsts' house for our dinner."

"I know you did," she said with sympathy. "Sister Eva is a good cook. What did she feed you?"

Matthias shrugged uncomfortably. "Just food."

Retha smiled gently. "What did you eat?"

"Not much," he mumbled. Then he brightened, as if struck by a means of diverting Retha from her questioning. "What I wanted to know was, did you see any Indians?"

Retha looked at Jacob.

He nodded. If Indian stories would placate one son, or both of them, Jacob could think of no harm in telling of her visit.

"I saw my friend Mistress Vogler."

Matthias snorted. "Mistress Vogler is not an Indian name."

"That's Cherokee Alice. The spy," Nicholas said with authority.

Jacob bit off a caustic reprimand. There would be no placating the boys tonight. "Nicholas, you must not pass on wild schoolboy rumors. Alice Vogler is no spy, and neither is your stepmother. It's been a long day, and it's time for bed."

"I want to hear more about the Liberty Men," Nicholas persisted, his larded cheek shining in the candlelight.

"To bed, son. By the time this war is over, we will have soldier stories enough for a lifetime."

Nicholas shuffled up the stairs, defiance muted by defeat, Matthias behind him. Jacob went up to tuck them in. When he came back downstairs, his wife had moved to the parlor and taken up her sewing, but it lay rumpled in her lap. It hardly seemed the time for conversation. Jacob needed to settle down himself. The day's wild swings of worry, anger, lust, and tenderness had him on edge. Her too, obviously.

He turned to the basket of plans at his drafting table and spent some time in silence reorganizing them by weight and length and timeliness, reminding himself what work was urgent and what he could postpone. Very little. His rolls of parchment crackled, and Retha's thread squeaked through the seams of Anna Johanna's dress.

"I didn't mean to cause us so much trouble. I didn't know I could." She dumped a deerskin sleeve into a shallow willow basket, stood, and slung the basket to her hip. "I—we—should go to bed, too."

He searched her face for a clue: Her shift from *I* to *we* was unexpected but welcome. "Yes," he agreed, snuffing out every light but a tallow lamp and trailing her to the bedroom. Her back was straight and stiff, her shoulder blades pinched. In spite of the pleasure they had shared, they both had had a wretched day, hers even worse than his. On which part of the miserable day were her thoughts trained now?

She set the basket down beside the idle spinning wheel that dominated the center of the room. Then she made her stand beside the hinged press bed, which he had not let down yet for the night.

"I have not been a wife to you, Jacob Blum," she said, her throaty voice lower than usual, her words clipped.

A bolt of pure lust, latent since afternoon, streaked from his heart to his manhood. Her thoughts were on him, not misery. He offered her an encouraging smile although it felt as toothy as the smile of a retriever unleashed on a covey of quail. Then a dozen questions assailed him. Why now? Why this sudden change of heart? How much change truly was it? What wonder had wrought it? And how far was she prepared to go?

Mentally he leashed himself. It would not do to speculate. It did not serve to inspect gift horses. "You made a fair start this afternoon."

"I did?" She turned a becoming, alluring shade of red. "But we didn't finish. I know that. I want to." She reached down to her waist to untie the tapes of her skirt—her clean skirt, the one he had promised to remove. The tape knotted. She tugged at it, carefully at first, then roughly, knotting it worse. She held it up and gave a nervous laugh. He took it as a sign of her excitement. He reined in his. He would take it slow.

"It's tangled. I can't . . ."

"You can," he murmured, bringing her hands to his mouth and trailing kisses across cold knuckles. "But your hands are cold. Warm them here." He slipped them inside his shirt against the skin that covered his ribs.

She let him guide them there.

"Besides, I promised I would do your clothes."

Once he had untangled the tedious knot, he meant for her disrobing to be a torturous seduction, but pieces of fabric fell as fast as autumn leaves. Hands warmed, arms circled, mouths met, and she clung to him as she had done in the afternoon—evidence, he was sure, that she was ready. He held her at arms' length to survey his handiwork, his wife revealed.

"Schöne Frau," he marveled. "Beautiful."

Loosed from her *Haube,* a nimbus of wild hair framed her face, half hiding bare, proud shoulders. In the flickering light of the tallow lamp he had set upon the windowsill, her round breasts gleamed. Her arms and legs were long, long enough to pair with his own great body, their womanly muscling sleek with health and vigor. His rapt gaze rested on a fiery triangle of fleece at the base of her belly and then rose to meet her golden eyes. They looked slightly wild, a little hunted. He would soothe that look away.

"I promised I would make you happy. I have not forgotten. 'Twas my solemn oath."

He urged her hands to help him shed the burden of his clothes. She did so almost efficiently this second time. Or was it the third? Had she not helped him before when he was half-asleep? Tonight her task of divesting him of his garments absorbed her. With a slowness that pained him, she seemed to strive to meet some exacting standard of housewifely care.

"Don't fold them," he muttered.

She hesitated one shy moment before flinging his breeches over a chair. They landed, falling as if some broken soldier had sprawled over a stump. And then, slightly ahead of his own intent, she gave him her virgin's version of a kiss. She pressed her lips against his, too hard and too still. He waited, knowing she was learning, hoping she would remember, growing aware of her quickening breath. Her hands found the sides of his face and angled his head a little to the left and then a little more. She seemed to have a plan, and he would indulge her. She moved her mouth against his, slightly, slowly, as if seeking some perfect alignment.

Then he felt her lips part. He stifled an urge to direct her kiss, for he wanted her to come to him. On any terms. At any speed. From any angle. Whatever he had to endure. She couldn't know her nipples brushing his chest burned him like hot coals. She couldn't feel the rush of heat in his groin.

"Would you open for me?" she whispered, the words almost too soft for him to hear.

He obliged, relaxing his jaw, and her tongue

entered his mouth. She seemed curious and reticent at once. She explored the biting edge of his teeth, the tip of his tongue, before she ventured deeper. Never deep enough. He felt that he would shatter right in front of her, that he would spill his seed into the narrow, empty space where she held her body away from his, that he would die and be forever happy.

She pulled back, a secretive smile playing across her rosy lips. "Was that right?"

He could barely speak. "I want you over here."

Putting his arm around her waist, he led her to their marriage bed. She waited as he lowered the hinged press bed and pulled back the coverlet. Suddenly stiff as starch, she sat beside him.

Ah, he thought tenderly, she was more frightened of this than she wanted him to know. Kissing was the easy, the familiar part. In the most chaste terms he knew, he spoke to her of every move that he would make. She nodded faintly, her head against his chest as if she needed reassurance.

As if her sweet desire for exploration had simply withered in her limbs.

"We don't have to finish this time, *Liebling,* if you're scared of being hurt," he assured her, contrary to the impulse behind his pounding pulse. "Not tonight, not all at once."

"I want to be your wife, Jacob. Wholly your wife." To him, her pale body glowed an invitation. But her jaw clenched with resolve—or resistance—or fear—or even, perhaps, repugnance. He did not know which. He simply could not tell.

Frustrated, he stood and walked a small circle in

front of her, his hand rubbing the back of his neck, his eyes trained on the narrow black cracks that defined the wide planks of the bedroom floor. "It won't hurt that bad or that long, Retha, and it will only hurt this first time." He instructed her in a bland, patient voice utterly at odds with the tumult of desire inside him. But he could not, would not, have another evening like their wedding night. "Truly, we can wait," he said, although the thought was bitter gall. "I can merely hold you."

He turned to look at her.

She scuttled to the center of the bed and sat, tucking her heels under her buttocks.

"*Mein Gott*, Retha. Don't start that."

She blinked her eyes. In innocence, defiance, fear. He could not guess which.

"Don't start what?"

"That. What you did—" Casting his gaze to the low, beamed ceiling, he floated up another desperate prayer.

When he looked back, she was rocking, her slow pace rhythmic, mesmerizing. As before. He grabbed her shoulders, digging in fingers with the force of his desperation.

"Don't. Rock."

Her golden eyes widened. Her head tilted. "Don't what?"

"Don't rock. As you did on our wedding night."

Her face crumpled with unmistakable dismay. "Our wedding night," she whispered. "Oh, Jacob, something awful happened. I knew it. What did I do wrong?"

You went utterly mad, he wanted to say. He hadn't known what to do then, and he didn't know

now. But he would not let her start this again if there were anything—anything—he could do to stop her. He wanted to hold her, to help her. Moving to her side, he reached for her hand. "Can I—"

With a slight nod, she gave it to him, palm up. In the silence that stretched between them, he rubbed small, relentless circles into the damp, cold hollow of her palm. Her breathing was short and shallow—from fear, he believed.

She swallowed hard. "I have to know."

"Yes." But he did not stop the circles. They were a lifeline. He had a premonition that if he stopped, she would rock again.

After a time, he told her. How he had left her to undress, honoring her maiden reticence. How he had returned to find her rocking. How angry he had been when she pretended not to hear him.

"I heard naught." Her fingers tightened on his. "I remember naught."

"I realize that now. But the next day, you were as ever, even cheerful, and I was sorely confused. How could you be one way and then the other?"

"I don't know. I do not understand myself." With her free fist, she struck the cornhusk mattress. "This bed. 'Tis but a bed. This room. I am no different here from when you kissed me by the tannery. But I *am* different here. And you . . ." Tears tracked down her face. "You are my husband. My strong, handsome husband. I believe myself fortunate. I want to be with you. I believe our union is the will of God. And I am ruining it."

To assuage her, he disagreed. "We are not ruined yet."

She drew a shuddering breath and lifted her chin. "I am not afraid, Jacob. It isn't that I am afraid. I want to be your wife. *Bitte*, Jacob. Please."

Given her fragility, Jacob thought making love to her just now seemed neither wise nor right. But he could not deny the sincerity of her plea. Soberly, filled with doubt and hope, he kissed her lips and lowered his mouth to the beaded nipples of her full breasts. First one and then the other, when he kissed them, quivered with her eagerness.

He was too aware of the strangeness that lay between them to recapture his sharp arousal right away, but this was sweet. It mattered not that harsh lye soap perfumed her breasts. When his hands wandered over the infant-soft skin of her naked buttocks, she shuddered. He deepened his touch, and her firm muscles, resilient with animal health, trembled.

She trembled all over.

She was trembling whether he touched her or not.

He ceased even the tenderest of touches, and his hands dropped empty to his sides.

"Don't stop," she begged.

But her cry was not that of a woman driven by desire. Her eyes were glassy. With apprehension? He hoped only that.

"If we can only do it this once, then perhaps . . ." Her voice cracked, and he heard her fear.

"*Meine schöne Leibling*, you are terrified. I will not take you in this terror. I cannot."

"I want to love you, Jacob."

"Not this way," he said softly, laying her against the sheets and surrounding her stiff body with his.

Flesh of my flesh, he thought. A dew of anxious perspiration covered her soft skin. If he could not stay her fears, he would absorb them. Racked with unfulfilled desire, he tried to take comfort in how far she had come. She had not retreated into that eerie, rocking silence. She was accepting his arm around her shoulder, his belly to her back, his fiery arousal against her buttocks.

"Sleep, *Liebling.* We will find another way. When both of us are willing."

But he could not imagine how that would come to pass.

Inside *Gemein Haus*, the meeting room already smoldered in the August morning. With scholarly precision, Philip Schopp squared his ever-present papers for the specially called meeting of Elders, and gave Jacob a pinched smile.

"Tell us, Brother Blum. Is your bride a spy or is she not?"

Jacob pressed his steepled fingers to the bridge of his nose. "She is not." He would not explode over the distortions and innuendoes of the tirade that Brother Steiner had just leveled against him over the unpleasantness at his mill. Nor would he submit to Brother Schopp's terrier-like attempt to sniff out a scandal.

"Evidently Captain Scaife thought her one, or he would not have taken her into custody."

"He never formally took her into custody. He escorted her home," Jacob said. Scaife had set out to embarrass Retha and flaunt his power in front of

Jacob. How well he had succeeded. By now everyone in town knew what had happened. After months of grim reports about the encroaching war, such fresh, delicious local gossip would entertain those good Moravians who frowned on backbiting.

"*Escorted* her home . . ." Schopp repeated silkily.

With simmering impatience, Jacob retold the story. His version was not the one that Brother Steiner had just reported to the Elders. Jacob's wife had not run away to confer with the Cherokee informer. She had not arrived, circled by a soldier's arms, immodestly astride a horse, wanton without her neckerchief and *Haube.* She had spit in no one's eye, not even in the dirt. And he, Jacob, had not attempted to tear an admittedly rough but entirely reputable captain limb from limb. Not quite.

"Perhaps," Elisabeth Marshall said, frowning, "you could explain the sling around poor Brother Steiner's arm."

"And Brother Hine's black eye," her husband Frederick Marshall added, not bothering to conceal a note of reproach.

"Captain Scaife was going to put his hands on the body of my wife."

Schopp bared his teeth. "A gentleman is always in the right to assist a lady from her horse."

"Captain Scaife meant no help. He intended further insult."

"But you charged into him," Schopp said. "*Attacked* him."

"I rushed at him. I admit it." Jacob looked to Frederick Marshall for understanding. "You, sir, would have protected Sister Marshall. 'Tis allowed to protect your wife. You too keep a club at home. We can defend our wives, our children, and ourselves if need be from direct assault."

Marshall lifted his drooping brow. "No one has confirmed that she needed actual protection. Was not Captain Scaife returning her to you?"

"Her honor, then," Jacob growled.

Marshall gave Jacob a reproving look. "Brother Blum, you endangered everyone. You wrestled our own men. You fought Brethren."

Jacob met the Elder's gaze. He was not sorry. But he would offer no defense and no excuses.

Marshall straightened on a deep breath. "We have no choice but to admonish you for your rash and hasty action."

"Although we are thankful Sister Blum is safe," Rosina Krause added. Sister Marshall nodded in agreement.

But a punctilious Schopp spoke up. "Should we not take a vote?"

"There is no need," Jacob said, roiling. They could not understand, but he was outnumbered. "I accept the judgment of this body."

He also accepted that he would take the exact same course again to ensure his wife's safety. Whether to protect her from mere rude insult or from more grievous harm, to him it mattered not one whit.

"Brother Blum," Marshall continued gravely, "you realize that another incident will force us to consider your disassociation. The more so as you are an Elder. You of all men lost your temper. You to whom we entrust our dealings with both armies. Not only do you set the worst example for our hot-blooded young men, you jeopardize your credibility as a negotiator and thus your most essential contribution to our community."

"I recognize that."

"Perhaps now you can make an effort to ensure that your older son understands this as well," Schopp added, with ill-concealed triumph.

Jacob bridled.

"Not to the point, Brother Schopp," Marshall said crisply, and turned to Jacob. "The upshot of it, I fear, will be further repercussions, Brother Blum. Nevertheless, this committee has other pressing matters." Marshall smoothed out a small, hand-carried note, piecing together a tear at its official military seal. "I received this missive this morning. Colonel Armstrong is in town and requests an interview before he returns to camp."

"Demands one is more likely," Schopp said.

Rosina Krause shushed him as if he were a smart-mouthed schoolboy. He had the grace to blush—while Jacob had the grace not to gloat that someone had thwarted the man. Some time ago Jacob had decided that God had put Philip Schopp in his path in order to measure his progress in forbearance of his fellow man.

Marshall slid the note across the long, narrow table to Jacob. He trailed his finger down its center, silently translating the demand from English into German and then addressing his fellow Elders.

"The colonel asks if the mill is ready for the grain, and has a new order for us. This is more a matter for my Supervisory Committee than for the Elders. It needs little notice to meet."

Marshall took the note back. "As we are gathered here, I see no reason to assemble your group. Any serious request the colonel makes will come to us next. He awaits word at the Tavern."

It was a short walk. Jacob volunteered to go. The room weighted on him, and he could use a private moment with a man to whom he still owed thanks. He crossed the Square, passed Bagge's store, two neat houses, and Samuel Ernst's leather shop, and mounted the steps to the Tavern. Martin Armstrong's elegant form, bedecked in full dress regalia and bewigged and powdered for official travel, stood at attention on the porch. He had been less imposing in his field tent.

Jacob made a formal bow, and the colonel bowed and smiled.

"The Elders await you, Colonel."

"And it is good to see you," he jested as the two of them made their way down the dusty street and across the quiet Square, matching stride for stride.

"I owe you a great deal of thanks for releasing my cousin. He has run us a merry race before although this one was his most harrowing to date."

"You made it home in good time, I trust."

Jacob smiled wryly. "Indeed. If two men sharing a horse for thirty-odd miles can be said to make good time after one man goes lame—"

The colonel's mouth crooked up. "You walked."

Jacob laughed aloud. His miserable trek amused him now. "I limped. Crawled. Succumbed to blisters long before we arrived in Salem. Then I dragged myself upstairs, kissed the children, and stumbled into bed."

"You have . . . how many children?"

"Three."

"And a new wife, I understand."

"Yes. One," Jacob said as soberly as he could muster.

A hearty laugh erupted from the dignified colonel's throat. "I thank you, Mr. Blum," he said, becoming serious with an effort. "War affords us few amusements. I do not fully understand how your cousin came to be pressed into service. Captain Scaife is . . ." The colonel seemed to search for a word.

Jacob supplied it. "Zealous."

"Um. Thorough."

"Yet not always careful."

The colonel ran a knuckle through his powdered mustache, considering. "Perhaps not. None of the militia officers, however, has a better record of tracking down reluctant recruits. Legitimate ones, I might add. He has a keen eye for Tory spies as well."

Jacob went on alert. But they were at the steps to *Gemein Haus*, and they went in.

Inside, the colonel dwarfed the staid Elders, a fact Jacob found curious. He thought of them as his equals, but they were not, not in size. He and the colonel were of a height, although the colonel's war-lean physique made Jacob feel the lumbering bear. Shoving the brief mention of spies to the back of his mind, Jacob addressed Armstrong's stated business, the opening of the mill.

"Barring rain or invasion, Colonel, you can bring grain no later than the beginning of next week."

Armstrong nodded, apparently satisfied. "Very

well. We have commandeered but half the wagons we need. Many can be, I regret to say, pressed in a week."

Although Marshall and Schopp were less fluent than Jacob, they understood the colonel's spoken English. Jacob swiftly translated his reply for the women who, like all Moravian women save Retha, had yet to learn their new homeland's tongue.

"Your orders bring severe hardship to poor back-country folk," Marshall said, not a man to mince even unfamiliar words.

"Less so, it is to be hoped, than British rule," the colonel observed, unperturbed.

Schopp colored, but said nothing. Dared nothing, the milksop, Jacob thought uncharitably. At heart, Schopp had all the inclinations of a Tory.

In the silence, the tall colonel raised a brow. "You would not turn rebellious on this matter?"

Half smirking, Philip Schopp regained his facility with words. "Rebellion, my dear Colonel, has been taken care of."

The officer's brows snapped together. "Explain yourself, sir."

"There was a scare of Tory spies amongst us."

Anger flooded Jacob's chest, cloaked his back, raced the length of his legs. The man was not a Tory, merely a fool.

Evidently, Marshall thought so too. " 'Twas naught, Colonel. 'Twas but a rumor, less than a scare."

"Captain Scaife did not think so," Schopp insisted.

Indiscreet, incontinent scoundrel! Jacob's hands

fisted, knuckles blanching under the tan that bronzed his skin. He launched himself out of his chair, then thrust his fists into his pockets. He should master such emotion.

He had to. Anger, in part, had brought him to this pass.

Stupidity had brought Schopp to it.

Jacob felt the colonel's keen gaze assessing him. Did the man assess Schopp as well? Then Armstrong stood, taking his plumed regimental tricorn from the table and bowing with courtesy to the company—and to Jacob.

"We have needed the grain for weeks. Perhaps, Mr. Blum, you could demonstrate your progress at the mill as I take my leave of your town?"

Jacob acceded readily to the command couched as a question.

But what, in truth, did the man want of him?

CHAPTER 13

"Papa's not never coming home," Anna Johanna fretted.

"Not *ever* coming home," Matthias corrected her.

She burst into tears. Retha held hers back. Jacob was late for lunch, and her hands were full of fussy daughter and rambunctious sons. Sometimes Jacob missed the midday meal altogether, though always with good reason. But half an hour ago, she had glimpsed the Marshalls walking home. The Elders' meeting was over. So where was her husband?

Nicholas snared a hunk of cheese off the half-set table. "No need to carry on, Anna Jo. Matty didn't mean that. Papa's coming home as soon as he finishes talking to the officer."

"What officer?" Retha asked, masking a stab of alarm.

"The officer I saw him with when we were walking home. General, I think," Nicholas said, as if proud to link his father with the military.

Anna's cries swelled to fill the small kitchen.

"Talk of soldiers frightens her, Nicholas," Retha chided. "You'd best not take that tack."

"You were with the soldiers yesterday," he said

unabashed. "Did they scare you?"

"No," she said repressively, not about to indulge him in his favorite subject at his sister's expense.

By the time Retha had set out the meal, Anna Johanna's lament had subsided into hiccups. Brooding, Retha watched her little diners eat. Or rather, she watched Nicholas eat. A dead-on copycat of her starving younger brother, Anna Johanna pushed beans and cabbage into symmetrical piles on her redware plate. For now, the task absorbed her, so Retha tolerated it.

But she saw no easy remedy for the little girl's distress. As soon as the boys left, her stepdaughter would no doubt revert to her weepy worst. Retha's ill-timed foray had provoked a relapse, disarming her surest weapons against childish misery, hugs and kisses. Once again, Anna Johanna would not accept a touch.

Retha decided then and there that she would escort the boys to school herself and take Anna Johanna to see her father in the flesh.

"We shall find your papa," she told her. "You boys clear the table."

"Aww," they grumbled in unison.

She deftly flung Nicholas a damp cloth, her accuracy surprising him enough to set him straight to work.

"Papa's probably just gone to the mill," Matthias guessed, scraping his and his sister's mangled vegetables into the slop bucket and setting its cover back on.

Anna Johanna's mouth thinned. "No, he hasn't. He's gone where Mama went."

The despair of certainty rang in the child's pronouncement. Retha's heart compressed in her chest as she knelt beside her, feeling every inch of her own maternal failures. "He has not gone with your mother, sweet potato. He positively, absolutely has not gone with her. In fact, he's probably waiting for us to bring him his dinner."

A surprisingly adult skepticism filled Anna Johanna's indigo eyes. No hug would reassure her now, Retha thought. "Let's fix him some food, and then go find him at the mill."

Woodenly, Anna Johanna slapped fresh bread and slabs of cheese onto the square napkin Retha set before her. Retha knotted it into a bundle, called the boys, and directed her stepdaughter out the door.

In the wake of yesterday's debacle, Retha held her head high as her family walked through town, enduring veiled curiosity and uneasy snubs. Halfway across the Square, Sister Baumgarten prodded her troublesome cow toward home, averting her eyes as Retha and her band approached.

Retha wished the woman good day and stood smiling till she coughed up an answer.

At the door to Brother Schopp's house, Retha spoke cordially to a curt schoolmaster. He rushed his charges inside as if to protect them from her influence. Let him, she thought in disgust. She answered to her husband, not to him.

Crossing the log bridge over Tanner's Run, they ran into Samuel Ernst. Anna Johanna hid behind her. Even from him, Retha felt a distance. Politely he offered to escort them and tried to tease a greeting out of the child. She whimpered and clung to Retha's skirts. Retha clung to dignity, learned as an orphan with the Cherokee, until Brother Ernst remembered urgent business elsewhere.

There was no sign of Jacob at the millpond. Brother Steiner slogged toward them through stinking mud, one arm in a sling. Scowling with suspicion, he eyed the cloth bundle. "Brother Blum has no need of that, Sister. Colonel Armstrong ordered him to dine with him at the Tavern."

"The colonel?" she asked softly, evenly, hoping not to spread her sudden alarm to Anna Johanna. But what if Nicholas were right? What if her actions had redounded against Jacob? She had to ask before rushing to him with his daughter at her side. "Is my husband in trouble?"

"I don't know. While they were here, they spoke of naught but how fast we must complete all this." His arm swept over the disordered millpond scene. The wooden dam was still a skeletal frame awaiting planking, little advanced beyond what she had vaguely noticed yesterday. "We would accomplish more if he weren't taking care of other kinds of business."

Retha clenched the bundle's knot. No doubt Brother Steiner resented her role in his injury, but she would not apologize for herself or make excuses for her husband.

"They're at the Tavern? Then we shall go there, too," she said resolutely, reaching for Anna Johanna before recalling the child's state of mind and retracting her hand. Words would have to do. "Let's go, sweet potato. Your papa's waiting for us."

Anna Johanna whimpered but clutched the skirt again and trudged solemnly along, untouched and uncomforted. All at once, Retha thought her heart would break over the little girl's obvious pain. For she understood it. Even though Anna's fear for her father's life was groundless, Retha could only sympathize, unwillingly recalling her own misery on a long-ago day like this. She had trekked alongside Singing Stones, a stranger, and stranger still, an Indian, hoping that around the next bend of some narrow woodland trail, beneath the spreading branches of the next mammoth oak, her parents would be there, smiling and holding out their arms to her—instead of sightless, breathless, bathed in blood, the way the men in militia linen had left them in the cabin.

The way she had last seen them.

Gasping at the crisp, stark horror of her long-forgotten memory, Retha took a misstep in the road.

Anna Johanna gave a cry of alarm. Oh, what would the poor child think if she gave in to this old terror that raked her body! Retha determined not to let on to it. She had to protect Anna from her old, secret, fruitless fears. Catching her balance, she sank to her knees as gracefully, as naturally as she could, scanning Anna's startled face for signs of an imminent explosion.

"Tell you what, sweet potato," Retha said with what felt like transparently false cheer. "When we find your papa, you can give him his meal." She offered Anna Johanna the bundle.

The girl refused it, wringing her hands.

Retha offered it again. "He'll like that. He'll be proud of you."

A small hand closed around the knot at the top of the bundle. "He will?"

"Absolutely, positively," Retha said, smiling

encouragement, trying to hide her own shaking. The memories. She had always hidden from the memories. "Are you ready?" Retha stood.

Anna Johanna nodded cautiously, and they climbed the Tavern's steps.

Jacob spooned up another bite of tavern stew, savoring the gamy aroma of fresh-cooked venison before tasting it. Good enough, he thought, but not as good as the simple fare Retha now provided in their home. Mealtime might be calmer here, too, but he should be there, especially after yesterday. Colonel Armstrong had inspected the mill as if he had a stake in its profits and then insisted Jacob join him in the gentlemen's dining room at the Tavern.

In the spacious room, the colonel's dark blue uniform stood out against immaculate white linens on small, round tables set with the best pewter and good stoneware plates. Bright midday light streamed in through tall windows and glinted off the polished brass buttons of Armstrong's uniform. There was no more civilized spot in all the Carolina backcountry. Jacob had to appreciate the officer's condescension in inviting him.

He had to wonder why Armstrong had insisted that he come.

The colonel commandeered the nearest table and a seat facing the door. "You must indulge me. I cannot sit with my back to the door. A military man's superstition."

Jacob indulged him. Despite his own sometimes

martial inclinations, whole areas of military life were a mystery to him. "I don't mind, but we like to think you safe among us."

They ate and tried to talk. Given the colonel's professional caution, Jacob could find little common ground with him, beyond the grain and a new and unexpected order for a thousand pairs of shoes. The war interested Jacob mainly as it affected Salem, and one issue interested him more than others at the moment though he did not want to raise it. To his surprise, the colonel brought it up.

"The town's abuzz over your rescue of your wife, the spy."

The colonel had revealed his true purpose for this shared meal. Jacob smiled guardedly. "Fresh fodder for the gossips."

"Enlighten me. I would prefer the story from a man I trust."

Jacob told him in terms as neutral as he could, omitting anger, insult, personal bias. He gave the colonel Retha's explanation: Scaife had long harassed the Voglers and had taken her for a spy simply because he had found her there.

"The captain is, as you may know, our most effective man with spies."

"I suppose a man who pointed at every bush he passed would flush out an authentic turncoat from time to time," Jacob said caustically.

"Ah, yes. His enthusiasm for his task. 'Tis well known. He did no harm, I trust, to your wife."

"She was not injured."

The colonel's raised brow acknowledged Jacob's careful choice of words. "Why do I not believe you?

No one tracks down more runaway recruits. He broke up the spy ring in Wilkes County. And yet . . ." The colonel ran a knuckle over his mustache and lowered his voice. "He is dangerous, difficult."

"Is he?" Jacob replied, surprised by Armstrong's confiding tone, by his admission, and by the promise of more.

"He's been with me since I was a captain in the War of Regulation, and before. More than fifteen years, during the lawlessness that led to it. I keep thinking I have him under control, and then he pulls a caper like this. There was a day back then . . . a young couple murdered . . ." Armstrong shook his head with regret. "I could have court-martialed him that day. His lawlessness went beyond the rest. I thought I had reformed him—"

The colonel broke off, his eyes widening. That was Jacob's only warning. With a sob of "Papa!" a froth of blond hair and a raggedy dress catapulted onto Jacob's lap, ending the officer's dark reminiscence.

"Anna Johanna!" Jacob pulled his daughter to him for a welcoming, fatherly kiss, too flabbergasted by her unexpected appearance to worry if her ban on being touched, held, and hugged had been lifted for this public place. "Sweet potato! What in the world are you doing here? Why aren't you at home? And where's Mama Retha?"

Retha appeared at the door frame. "*Hier*, Jacob," she said in tense German. "We worried when you did not come home." She nodded toward his daughter, whose cheeks were stained with tears. Retha didn't need to point out her own concern. It was stamped on her taut face. Jacob's heart warmed: His wife had worried about him.

"We brought your meal," she said. "Anna Johanna, show him."

Opening her bundle, she wrinkled her nose at the pungent scent of warm cheese. *"Der Käse, Papa, und das Brot."*

Armstrong gave Jacob's daughter an amused, avuncular smile. "Bread?" he guessed. "And cheese? That's a good girl." Turning to Jacob, he added, "One of your three, no doubt?"

Pride warmed Jacob. "The youngest. The only girl."

Then he saw the colonel train his penetrating gaze on Retha, saw the danger a fraction of a second after he smoothly spoke.

"And are you well, Mrs. Blum, after yesterday's ordeal?"

"Quite well, sir, I thank you," she said in perfect, if accented, English.

And then she blanched.

Armstrong looked from Retha to Jacob and back. "Ahem. May I congratulate you on your recent and prodigious mastery of English, madam?"

Jacob admired the colonel's clever trap as much as he resented it. It wasn't last night's Tavern gossip or loose talk around the town that had alerted Armstrong to the charge of Retha's spying. He must have seen Scaife. Perhaps they had passed yesterday on the road. And then the colonel came straight here to investigate Scaife's charge.

"Mr. Blum, I must question your wife."

"In public, sir? In front of the child?" Jacob asked, over his daughter's head. He couldn't gauge the depth or nature of Armstrong's suspicions. But he didn't like them. "Is this a formal inquiry?"

"No, not formal, no. The child is no obstacle. I have questions only."

Retha squared her shoulders, feeling not unlike a Single Sister called to account for sneaking out to her beloved wilderness. But facing the elegant, somber colonel demanded a deeper resolution.

"Your command of English is excellent, madam," he said.

"I never denied it, sir."

"You misled Captain Scaife."

"I was merely silent."

"Would you care to explain why?" he asked with cold, implacable courtesy.

Retha looked at her husband. Yesterday he had honored her ruse. What did he want her to do today?

"Tell him, wife, as you told me," Jacob said in English, quietly, a confident, loving look in his indigo eyes.

That apparent confidence, that unexpected love, lent her the extra bit of courage that she needed. She let out a breath.

"Captain Scaife believes the Voglers are spies, but he cannot catch them at it. Indeed, he has no proof. He merely supposes that Mrs. Vogler, who is Cherokee, is motivated to spy against the Continental Army because Colonials killed her family. But how could she be a spy? She speaks no English, and Mr. Vogler does not speak it well."

"Whereas you do," Armstrong said expressionlessly.

"I do. For that reason, Mr. Vogler asked me to

conceal my knowledge of English from Captain Scaife. If the captain heard me, he would no doubt think the worst and conclude that I was the missing piece of his puzzle—her liaison."

Lounging in his chair, Armstrong paused ominously. "And are you that liaison, madam?"

"I am no spy, sir," she said stoutly.

Jacob caught her eye and nodded his support, huddling a restless Anna Johanna to him.

From inside his coat, Armstrong retrieved his pipe, methodically tamped tobacco into it, took out his flint box, and tediously produced a flame. Only after he had puffed the pipe to life did he pin Retha with a martial glare. If he meant to make her nervous, he was succeeding.

"What proof can you offer that you are not?"

Retha touched the ribbon of her *Haube* with a steady hand. The pink ribbon of a Single Sister, the visible mark of Scaife's invasion. "None, sir. Except that I have no motive, no knowledge of military affairs, and"—she looked down at Anna Johanna, fidgeting on her father's lap—"no time."

"Captain Scaife thinks you have the knowledge."

"How, sir? I know naught of military matters."

"Ah, but you do. Anyone in Salem, even you, can report our movements to the British troops that come through town, can receive messages from them and deliver messages for them. We have always known that."

"Surely not a woman, sir," she offered in her own defense.

Armstrong drew on his pipe, letting out a cloud of smoke around its stem. "Were you not recently a laundress for the Tavern?"

Retha felt betraying blood heat her face. He had investigated her. He suspected her.

He smiled coldly. "This morning I spoke to your replacement. You were a laundress. You came here to fetch their linens, wash their clothes . . ."

"Briefly."

"And before that, a dyer for the town. You are said to know more of the woods and paths beyond Salem than any woman in it."

Jacob sat forward, his manner gentle as his strained words were sharp. "You go too far, Colonel. If you have formal accusations, make them."

"Nothing formal yet, Mr. Blum, I assure you," Armstrong said mildly, nursing his pipe.

Anna coughed from the smoke, and Jacob patted her back, glaring.

Retha could not read the colonel's courteous tone. Her throat tightened like a rabbit's caught in a snare.

"In other words," he said, turning back to her, "you have special knowledge and opportunity."

"I know of plants and roots and bark and seeds, but naught of war. Except that it has largely robbed me of the opportunity to do my work."

Armstrong shrugged off her explanation. "The captain thinks you also have the motive . . ."

"I wish for the war to end, sir, but have neither the power nor knowledge to affect its course," she bit off, frustrated by the calm, implacable way he wove his web of implication around her.

"The same motive, Mrs. Blum, as Alice Vogler's. The Cherokee raised you, did they not? And we Colonials, not the British, mounted a campaign against them."

"My wife came to us as a lost child—a white child, rescued and raised by the Cherokee, but as much a Colonial as you or I," Jacob said, controlled anger in his voice.

"Let me, Jacob," Retha said hastily, heartened by his quick, unquestioning defense of her. "I will answer him." She faced her interrogator.

"I lived with the Cherokee, yes, Colonel. And I loved them. They would give you the shirts off their backs, but they are quick to avenge murder. Local troops, not British, murdered my Cherokee family cruelly before my eyes. Men who went on to fight for you. Were I not Moravian, I would have motive enough to spy against your army."

Tears sprang to her eyes, but she lifted her hand to forestall her husband's intervention—and include him. "But these good people found me and took me in, raised me Moravian, and allowed me to join their community. Which I did when I was but . . ." She paused, ever aware of the awkwardness of not knowing her own age. "When I was but a girl. I am Moravian now. Revenge is not our way."

"You claim Moravian neutrality, then?"

"Yes."

"In your particular case, that plea may not wash." Armstrong gave her a small, inscrutable smile and turned to her husband, dismissing her avowal. She bridled, but listened. "Mr. Blum, what assurance can you give me of your wife's innocence?"

"I stand by her words."

Armstrong gave a short bark of doubt and fiddled with his pipe. "What assurance then that she will not spy again?"

Jacob stood up slowly, not disturbing his daughter in his arms. But Retha felt the anger pouring off him.

"My wife is not a spy. Sim Scaife wants to harass me through her. But with respect to you, she will not leave town without me."

"Very well." Armstrong smiled tightly. "You sound convinced of her innocence."

"You, sir, have not convinced me of her guilt."

Retha marched with Jacob up the street from the Tavern to home, past houses, shops, the Single Brothers House, and a few wagons already arrived for tomorrow's market day. Jacob carried Anna piggyback, and she alone seemed to enjoy the short trek. Mortification streaked through Retha's body. First Scaife, then Jacob's fight for her and censure, and now the colonel's accusation. The entire muddle was her own doing. She should have stayed at home.

"Jacob—"

"Wait until we're alone." She couldn't tell whether his anger was for her or the colonel.

Inside the house, they put Anna down for a nap. Jacob practically dragged Retha back downstairs and shocked her with a hot, possessive embrace.

"They can't have you, it's not your fault," he ground out. "Scaife is after me."

"I shouldn't have left home," she muttered into his shoulder. She would not cry, but her body shook against Jacob's stalwart strength. "When you weren't here for our midday meal, Anna took a notion you were never coming home, as her mother left and never came back."

"I couldn't refuse the colonel's invitation, and you couldn't prevent her distress," he said into Retha's ear.

The heat of his body radiated into hers, sustaining her.

"Brother and Sister Marshall had long since passed the house, so I knew the meeting was over . . . And you—so much went wrong yesterday . . . We went to the mill, and Brother Steiner told me you were with the colonel. I couldn't imagine why. I was worried—so worried."

Jacob pulled back, and a slow grin spread across his face. "You worried about me. You tracked me down. I like that," he said on a note of wonder, and kissed her deeply.

Confused by his ardor after her many blunders, Retha simply accepted his kiss, let herself ride the wave of his intensity away from her misery.

At last he stopped, tucking her head under his jaw. "I have to go. They do need me at the mill."

But Retha couldn't simply let him go, the issue unresolved. "The colonel thinks I'm guilty, doesn't he?"

"I'm not so sure. Given Scaife's slander, he had to question you. Given Armstrong's position, he must wonder. But I have not lost all my credit with him. However . . ." He pulled her to a kitchen chair and sat across the table from her. "I have lost credit elsewhere."

Retha's stomach plummeted. "Where?"

Jacob extended his beautiful strong hands to her, and she gave him hers. He seemed to study them, palms first, then knuckles. After a long pause that she found precious and yet alarming, he spoke resolutely.

"We will face this together. Do not think it your fault."

"What is not my fault?"

"The Elders have admonished me for my actions at the mill."

Admonishment, she knew, was the first step to being disassociated from the whole community, as Gottlieb Vogler once had been. But Jacob had done what he had done at Steiner's Mill because of her. She wanted to withdraw her hands in shame.

"No, Jacob, not you. The fault is mine."

He brushed off her protest with a quick shake of his head. "I accept their judgment, wife. 'Twas I who lost my temper, injured Brethren, and jeopardized our uneasy relationship with the militia."

"Because of me."

"Because of Scaife," he corrected. "And I would do it again. I will always protect you, as I see fit, whatever the other Elders say. Your life, your honor, are my responsibility. If we must break with the community, we would not be the first. I will not have you threatened or afraid."

He seemed indomitable to her. She looked at his beautiful hands, strong and broad and yet graceful. She took them to her mouth and kissed them, out of gratitude, out of newborn respect for his courage. "I won't be afraid."

"We will go to services tonight. We will go every night. We will tell the children—the boys, at least.

They must not hear of my misdeeds by rumor."

She agreed. "As Nicholas heard about me. But will the Elders do aught to mark this censure?"

"Very little."

His hands on hers were firm and sure. She did not believe his all-too-casual dismissal of the gravity of censure. "Are you still an Elder?"

He grinned wryly as if it didn't matter. "Quite probably not."

"Will you still serve on the other . . . ?" She did not yet know its name or Jacob's function on it. There had been much of the tightly organized society's communal workings that she as a Single Sister had never needed to know.

He shrugged. "The Supervisory Committee will consult me, almost certainly, for advice and plans as they need them."

"What about your travels?"

"As an envoy, I remain indispensable. No one among us knows English better. 'Tis certain I will still deal with the army."

Rivulets of guilt washed over Retha's body. For her he had suffered a humbling loss of the status he had earned while shaping and protecting the community. Yet he accepted his disgrace with stalwart calm.

She hung her head. "This is all my fault. You cannot say otherwise."

"But I can, and I do. 'Tis not your fault. You are not to worry." With a light and reassuring touch, he tipped her chin up. "You are not to hang your head."

"Oh, but Jacob, when I think I could have prevented you this embarrassment—this loss—"

"Do not think of it. Not like that. You went in search of plants and found a demon."

Her little lie needled her, and his trust made her uncomfortable. It was too late to confess the real reason she had left town.

"Someday soon," he went on, "I will go with you to search for plants and roots and bark to your heart's content."

Retha braided her hair. Jacob had gone to the mill for the remainder of the afternoon, Anna Johanna was sleeping upstairs, and Retha had stripped off the *Haube* with the old pink ribbons. They only reminded her of her troubles. In the bedroom, she tossed the cap to the back of the clothes cupboard, knowing she would wear it at *Singstunde* tonight and whenever else she went out. She didn't want to embarrass Jacob further.

But she need not wear it here. She sat down by the open bedroom window, parted her thick tresses down the middle, and methodically braided first one side and then the other, Indian style, her fingers speeding up as they remembered the simple, rhythmic task. She wished she had moccasins to wear and a deerskin dress of her own again, and she longed to see her wolf.

Jacob's forbearance of her many blunders astonished her. Humbled her. Heartened her. Somehow his feeling for her had survived her rashness as well as her rejection of him and her fear. For his sake, as well as her own, she longed for a moment's reprieve from the community's strict ways. No, she argued with herself, even she honored and respected the ways of the community. If an individual here or there were difficult, most were not. Most were kind and trustworthy, hardworking and fair. Most had risen to the challenge of raising her when she had come to them, wild and abandoned. They had schooled her in the Christian virtues that they themselves practiced. They had taught her to read and had instructed her in womanly chores. They had given her a new life.

Then why did she yearn so for wilderness?

A wagon rumbled by, another settler early for market. Standing in front of the window, she leaned out to see if it could be the Voglers. It was not. Through the open frame, the afternoon sun seared the pink, burned skin on her chest. It would be another day or two before she could comfortably wear a neckerchief. In the forest she would not need one. She longed to be in the thickest groves where sunlight filtered in so thinly that she would not burn but could be cool. She wanted to smell the rich humus, feel a faint breeze on her face, rest her back against the mossy bark of a venerable oak.

She tied off her braids with rawhide thongs.

She wanted to be free of the memories that dogged her.

"You can't go out like that!" Matthias said as he walked in the back door from Brother Schopp's lessons later that afternoon.

"Like what?" Retha asked.

"With your hair . . . like that," he said.

"Like an Indian," Nicholas scoffed, grabbing an apple from a bowl on the kitchen table and heading upstairs.

Retha touched a braid. She had forgotten. Her braids felt so natural, so cool and right, that she hadn't noticed them.

"I don't intend to go out like this. For services, I'll coil them up under my *Haube*. But I like them. On a day like this, they're cool. Almost as cool as hair like yours." She ruffled Matthias's short hair.

That she had made such an unthinking gesture surprised her. She wouldn't have thought that braiding her hair would lift her spirits so. Or that Matthias would accept a motherly hand. His attention riveted on her fascinating braids.

"Did you wear your hair like that before—with them?" he asked with hushed curiosity.

"Well, yes, I did. I mean, I must have. Probably from the day they took me in. But you know, I wasn't much older than Anna Johanna then. I don't remember everything."

"I thought you were as old as Nicholas when you were with them."

"By the time I came here, yes, I was about his age. But I was very young when my parents died."

"What do you remember?"

"About my parents?"

"No, not them." He shrugged, his show of indifference not convincing. "About aught with . . . the others."

Briefly she closed her eyes. How could she convey to him the sharp memories that assaulted her senses? The thwack of the ball in the ball-play game. The coppery smell of a butchered deer. The softness of her deerskin clothing. Ah, was she nostalgic today. But what to tell him? She was no storyteller. But then, perhaps she could be. Each night, Singing Stones had lulled her to sleep with endless legends of the tribe.

"Well," Retha began, "do you know how the possum lost its beautiful tail and ended up with that sad little stick?"

"Is that an Indian story?"

"Yes."

Matthias brightened. "I never heard of that."

As Retha made supper, Matthias listened raptly to that tale and the next. He even helped to set the table without being asked. By the time Jacob came home and everyone sat down for supper, Matthias forgot to insist on saying grace. As they ate, she told the story of how the poky terrapin defeated the speedy rabbit in a race.

The entire family listened, Jacob included. Nicholas, however, took pains to look as if he didn't care. Retha was racking her brain for her next tale when she realized that Matthias's plate was empty—he had wiped it clean! Anna Johanna, the copycat, had cleaned hers, too. Retha caught Jacob's eye, directed his gaze to the miraculous platter, and then pretended to ignore it.

Her Cherokee tales had lulled Matthias into eating, not into sleep. Her mind raced over more stories she could tell him, the animal tales, the story of creation. She supposed Jacob would have to approve the latter story, as it did not follow Genesis. But it was a good story, one she still half believed alongside the Bible teachings.

Services had ended and the children had gone to bed before she could bring it up. Jacob hovered behind her as she sifted through tomorrow morning's hominy and put it on to soak.

He considered his answer. "I don't think the story will harm them. It didn't harm you."

Then he feathered a kiss just where a braid skimmed her shoulder. She shivered.

"But I never dreamed that I would have the chance to kiss an Indian maiden," he whispered huskily. And she heard passion in his voice. Heard it, and responded to it, standing there.

Retha dreamed of spiders in close spaces. One crawled along her jaw and began a delicate trek along the edge of her ear. It tickled. She had fought a fear of spiders since the night that Jacob found her, a lost child in his woodshed, cowering amongst some sticky webs and spiny legs.

"Not afraid of you," she murmured, sleepily brushing it away.

But the spider became a hand. Her eyes flew open.

"I never meant for you to be." Jacob's words were melodic on the morning air. He lay next to her on his side, his head propped up on one arm.

"Good morning." The resonance of his voice vibrated into her flesh.

"Am I supposed to say good morning, too?" she croaked.

He grinned. " 'Twill do for a start."

"Good morning."

The warm tip of his finger outlined her mouth, sparking needles of sensation no spider leg could ever rouse. "You're not afraid. I'm glad. I'm going to kiss you good morning."

She was not afraid of spiders. She was afraid of this. Of being touched in her marriage bed.

She closed her eyes, resolved to accept his kiss. Warm, dry lips touched hers briefly, chastely, and went away. She looked to see where he had gone.

Nowhere. His face was so close that she could see his morning stubble glinting in a first ray of sun. She smiled at the surprise.

"I'm always going to kiss you in the mornings, Retha."

"Oh." The very thought of being kissed, here, in the bed, each morning set alarms ringing in her head. What would it mean? How would she bear it? How could she be prepared?

"Starting now." He bent his head to feather kisses across her cheek, around her ear, and down her neck. Her skin tingled as it had the night before. Deliciously.

A small sigh of tension escaped her, and he stopped, arose and dressed, and left the room, leaving her alone in bed.

Nor had Alice mentioned this! Kisses! In the morning! When they were both still warm with sleep. When he was so large, so near, half-clad. In places the hair-roughened skin of his arms and legs touched hers. Her stomach fluttered and then curled with the sensation that she now had a name for. Desire. It almost hurt. She pressed her hands into the ache. What would she have done if he had not stopped?

CHAPTER 14

"The wagons, Papa, they're here!" Matthias banged the door open, and the boys, who had left for morning classes only moments before, clattered back into the house.

"Three of them," Nicholas added, breathless from dashing home. Or, Retha thought, from excitement. She looked up from her work on Anna's dress. Nicholas lunged into the parlor ahead of his brother, skidded to a halt at Jacob's drafting table, and grabbed his father's hand. "Come *on!* They're almost to the creek, heading for the mill. Soldiers driving them, and everything!"

Leaving his morning's work spread out before him, Jacob stood. "Whoa, son. Where do you think you're going?"

Revolutionary fervor sparked in Nicholas's blue eyes. "To the mill. It's the Continentals. Come for grain. The troops must be close behind them."

Jacob smiled, a little too indulgently, Retha thought. He knew Nicholas worshiped all this. She knew Jacob didn't approve.

Down the hill, the first wagon clattered noisily onto the log bridge that crossed Tanner's Run.

"The troops are no doubt miles away, waiting for food," Jacob said. "But troops or no troops, I cannot let you stand up Brother Schopp."

Instant mutiny darkened Nicholas's face. "What's school when the war is coming to town?"

"The war is not coming to town, son," Jacob said quietly, and Retha's concern grew. She had been raised by Sister Rosina, who doled out swift retribution to budding mutineers.

"Only a few wagons are coming," he continued mildly. "And we were expecting them today, if not tomorrow. Come on. I will walk you back to school. Then I will see what I can do to help out at the mill."

"But Papa—"

Finally Jacob raised a monitory brow. "No *buts*, son. The crowds make it dangerous." He put a guiding hand on Nicholas's shoulder.

"All the men will be there."

"All the boys will be in school. School is where boys learn to become men. And you will be one soon enough. Then you can spend your days slinging heavy sacks of dusty grain from the hopper to the wagon until you think your arms are dropping off."

"Aww, Papa," Nicholas groaned, surly but relenting.

Jacob gave Retha a quick, firm kiss, promised to be home at noon with the boys, and marched Nicholas toward the door. "What's your first class, Matthias?" Jacob asked his more tractable son, who followed them out of the room.

"Latin," was all that Retha heard as they closed the door behind them.

From her parlor window, she watched them

walk up the street, the towering man, his large son still in hand, his smaller son strolling along compliantly. A week had passed since the Elders admonished Jacob, and he had not said another word about it. Released from most of his duties, he spent more time at home. Family time, healing time. Matthias kept on cleaning his plate although he almost wore Retha out with questions about the Cherokee. She ran through her stock of animal fables, and recreated the universe. Soon she would have to start on the stories of the plants and herbs. Anna Johanna, still aloof from Retha, at last deigned to notice progress on her deer dress. Nicholas sulked, plotting, Retha thought, the overthrow of paternal power.

But most disconcerting to Retha were Jacob's attentions to her. They had became both lighter and more demanding. When the children were not looking, he feathered kisses on any bare spot on her body that was within his reach: hand, palm, throat, the nape of her neck, the curve of her ear. At any time of the day or night. Once he took the tip of one of her braids and used it like a finger to outline her lips, her chin, her throat. She shuddered.

He must have made it a rule that his attentions please her, for if she so much as flinched, he stopped cold. She couldn't tell what he was thinking or feeling, but he kept her in a thin shiver of anticipation. And it was heaven.

The invasion was hell. That first morning, as she watched the street from the parlor window, two hunched soldiers in ragged uniforms drove a large farm wagon toward her house. Over the broad blond rumps of their draft horses, one man looked up, caught her eye, swept off his hat, and grinned an unmistakable invitation. Heart pounding, she snapped the fine batiste curtain closed, wishing it were the thickest flaxen cloth dyed the darkest indigo—or heavy sacking, anything to hide the sight.

The man was another redhead. Not Scaife, but to her the reminder was just as bad. Jacob's attentions, welcome as they were, heightened her awareness of the ways of men. And of the risk that soldiers might present.

Slipping back into the room's shadows, Retha braided her hair and kept to home. She took small comfort in her family's prompt return for the midday meal, in Anna's occasional mild interest in her nearly finished dress. For she couldn't close out the creaking of the wagon wheels, neither this one nor the next. Throughout the day whips cracked, men shouted, oxen bellowed, ill-matched teams of conscripted horses neighed, and mules brayed in stubborn disapproval of it all.

By day's end the stench from a multitude of passing animals seeped into the house. Salem's main street became impassable for people on foot. *Singstunde*, rarely canceled but for weather, was not held that evening or the next. The inconvenience was too great. To say nothing of the danger. The teamsters, rowdy soldiers, camped their mismatched rigs behind the Tavern, in the meadow, in amongst the peach trees in the orchard. The evening hours they spent drinking in the Tavern.

Their carousing spilled into the streets, and their caterwauling poured through the open, curtained windows of Retha's home.

She could shut out nothing. Her only comfort was that they had not actually entered her home. She bent her head to her work. What if they did come here? A wave of nausea swept her.

By the second day, everything tightened around her. Her world of safety—the world Jacob had created for her—shrank and crumbled. She did not want to hear more soldiers. The incessant creaks and whip cracks and bellowing of men and animals made her edgy, cross. The stench, made worse by summer heat, permeated every corner of her house.

That night she slept fitfully, waking in the moonless night from horrid dreams of blood.

During the two days of wagons clattering and three nights of soldiers reveling, Jacob watched his wife. Last week his few quiet days at home had seemed to restore her calm. And, he thought with a rush of virile pride, his attentions had piqued her maidenly curiosity. More than piqued it.

Now, subtly, her calm deteriorated. Her interest ebbed. He couldn't put his finger on how he knew. Once, as she put the finishing touches on Anna's dress, she jerked the thread through the deerskin, breaking it. Once, when Matthias asked for another story, she was short with him. Once, at bedtime, a knock came at the door, and Retha muffled a gasp behind tense white knuckles pressed to her mouth.

Jacob opened the door to Samuel Ernst. Whom

had she expected? What did she fear?

For she was frightened. He was sure of it.

Brother Samuel delivered his message—they would have half a dozen men out on this third night of occupation—and left.

But she did not recover. In bed, she drew herself up into a tight, defensive ball, and slightly, ever so slightly, rocked herself to sleep.

In the morning, the last wagons left, the onslaught ending as suddenly as it had begun. Save for the lingering odor and the disordered streets, the town enjoyed a day of tranquillity. By nightfall, the streets were shoveled and swept. That evening Jacob and his family joined the rest of the community for *Singstunde* and sang songs of thanks that they had safely weathered this storm.

But Jacob went to bed anxious. Retha, he noticed, had not sung the songs of thanks. She had not safely weathered this storm.

He drifted off, seeking the soothing void of sleep. Beside him, the mattress dipped. He roused but did not move. Retha sat up and stealthily crawled to the end of the bed, cornhusks crackling. Jacob feigned sleep. Whisper quiet, she padded out of the room into the kitchen. Through the black dark, he heard a muffled grunt as chair legs scraped the wooden floor. The door latch snicked, a hinge creaked.

She was running away again.

He leapt out of bed, striding into his breeches, stuffing in his nightshirt, grabbing a lantern as he tore through the house. Armstrong's accusations flooded back to him. As did his own promise to watch his wife.

Outside, the thin arc of a newly waxing moon shed little light. He would not believe she was a spy. He prayed that she was sleepwalking, though that was bad enough, and not mad. This was his chance to prove her innocent, his chance to prove to himself that she was sane.

Standing in the middle of his dirt yard, he held the lantern up. He had to guess what direction she had taken. The meadow, no doubt. In some fashion he could not understand, that place comforted her. It did not comfort him. He lurched and stumbled across its long downward slope, railing at the near-darkness, which she must have navigated like an owl.

A ragged weeping drew him to her, seated on a large rock, arms wrapped around her legs, chin on her knees. Crying like a broken-hearted child.

He whispered her name, softly and then louder, before he touched her. "Retha . . . Retha . . ."

She wasn't even startled. She accepted his presence beside her, his arm around her, but the crying did not stop.

"She's gone," she sobbed.

His heart tripped. "She?" Retha couldn't mean Anna Johanna. Could Retha, in some mad way he did not understand, mean herself?

"Damnable soldiers. They frightened off my wolf."

Her wolf? She had turned irrational on him. She hadn't been out long enough to attract it, but the creature would have forgotten her weeks ago. He could scarcely believe its failure to appear would actually make her cry. But in one respect at least, her tears reassured him. No spy would cry like a child because a stupid beast had failed to show its muzzle.

Gingerly he sat on the rock beside her, ready to catch her if she bolted. "I'm sorry. You could give it a little more time."

"Not with you here. She won't come."

"I had to follow you. You're not safe out."

She turned to him, but he could barely see the contours of her face.

She sunk her limp body into his. "Make me safe, Jacob. Make me safe."

He had never felt so helpless in his life. Safe from what? This sorrow? The pain of loss? He wasn't safe from that himself. Or was it the soldiers? After her humiliations at Scaife's hands, perhaps she was afraid of capture. But if that were so, why would she have come this far from home alone?

Perhaps she was afraid of him. He thought not, given the way she had accepted him just now. With the greatest care, he tightened his arm around her. No, she didn't feel afraid of him. She felt full of a hot, desperate need. An emotional need, he thought regretfully, not a physical one. Still, he would support her.

"Safe from what, *schöne Frau?*" he said, more lightly than he felt.

She gave a small, surprised laugh and swiped her swollen eyes with the back of her hand. "I am not a beautiful wife just now, Jacob Blum."

"Come home with me. Truly, we're safer there."

"I'm safer in the woods," she argued, but she complied. He stood and lifted her off the rock, feeling her as light and vulnerable, feeling that she needed him without knowing how to ask. He scarcely knew how to offer but wanted to allay her fears.

"You miss the woods, then."

"All the time. I miss my walks. I miss my work."

It struck him how close she had stayed to home since taking on his family, how locked up in town since that night in the meadow when he had seen her dance.

"I could go with you. In a day or so. With the boys in school. Leave Anna Johanna with Sister Ernst. When things are back in order at the—"

She flung her arms around his neck and gave him a smacking, enthusiastic kiss. "Oh, take me, Jacob. Will you?"

Take her, he thought wryly, his manhood lifting, willing. Too bad she wasn't ready to receive what he was instantly prepared to offer. He returned her kiss simply, modestly.

"Tomorrow," he promised. Together they walked home.

With a confidence Jacob had not seen since their wedding, Retha led him into deep woods. The forest transformed her, he thought, into a being at one with nature and slightly wild. Surefooted as an Indian guide, she trekked down paths he could scarcely detect. Paths he had never had the time or inclination to explore. She moved fast, leaning right or left to avoid the spiky holly leaves, ducking under scuppernong vines laden with fruit not yet ripe, breaking through spider webs with her upheld arm and fist. Above them, everywhere, massive oaks and stately poplars barred the midmorning sun from cool forest floors.

Feeling like the great bear he knew he was, Jacob crashed through the underbrush. She moved silently ahead. It wasn't hard to keep up. It was hard to keep his mind on their destination, the secret waterfall she enticed him with. Goldenseal grew there, she said, and wild indigo. But in the week since the wagons left, days and nights of patient seduction had so filled his senses with Retha that he cared little for her dyestuffs. All he saw before him was the embodiment of his desire: her grace, her vigor, her fragility.

She stopped at a ridge. He could not see down far. Below them was all summer verdure, dense and damp. "Listen."

He cocked his head. From far away, a high *shree* broke the hum of forest insects. It was a hawk, that he knew. Nearer, he made out scraps of birdsong—a trill, a warble—he could not identify.

"That pair of hawks has nested here for years," she said.

"They have?" He felt his ignorance. If she knew of the lives of hawks, she would know the birds by song. He did not ask her for their names.

"But listen. The waterfall is near. Can you hear?"

He strained to hear past hums and chirps, and was rewarded. It sounded like breathing, or the wind. "That rustling?"

She nodded. "That roar. Or it will be after we cross the next ridge. But you won't hear it again for a while."

The path disappeared. She took his hand. In places, low bushes overgrew the slope. "The huckleberry's spent." She stepped carefully through them, sparing wiry branches, balancing herself on the fulcrum of his arm. He was careful, too.

The ridge gave way to a steep-sided hollow. Retha went down it sideways, holding his hand in an awkward dance of slip-and-slide. She would have done better on her own, Jacob realized, but she wouldn't relinquish him. He noticed the pounding of his heart. It was from the pace she set, he told himself, unwilling to admit to rising hope, mounting anticipation. For her manner toward him was new. New trust, new confidence, new voluntary touch.

Together they descended to the slight flat of the hollow. Ankle-high, umbrella-like, four-lobed plants covered the ground. Giant clover, he thought.

"Don't step on the mayapple either. I can pick some on the way back."

"What color do they make?" Jacob tried to relate to her purpose on this journey.

"They're not for dyes. They're for Sister Sarah. Her arthritis. Watch out." She pointed just ahead. " 'Tis wet here. There's a spring. That's why there are so many ferns."

Well, he knew that. Ferns loved springs, as builders did not. Jacob's gaze was fixed on the curve of her hip. He looked down the lush hollow. Waist-high ferns arced into the air.

"Anna Johanna would love this," Retha said. "She'd find fairies under toadstools, make them moss beds to recline on, and pluck fronds to fan them in the heat."

Jacob was not thinking of his daughter. His gaze traced the spreading wetness that Retha called a spring. Springs were the bane and boon of his labors.

He built bridges over them, routed roads around them, changed plans for building sites where he had unearthed a dry one. He turned them into wells for needed water.

But this spring belonged to Retha. It bespoke her. Its generous moisture fed a wild garden of fanciful ferns, healing mayapple, and—the Lord only knew what else grew here that he had never taken time to learn the names or uses of. The spring's dampness spread down the hollow. He thought of women's life-giving, mysterious fluids. He thought of his young wife at her untouched woman's center. Of the moisture he would find there, arouse there. He thought of touching her. He had not done so yet, not in any of the husband's ways he knew.

He tried to wrest his attention back to wherever she was leading, but his mind could not convince his body that he had embarked on this walk for her sake, to gather dyes she needed. He wanted his wife with a fierce new appreciation of her, here in the wilderness where she seemed more at home than in his house—where the plants were her utensils, the trees her walls, their overspreading canopy her ceiling, which was no ceiling at all.

"Jacob! We'll never get there at this pace," she said, laughing as she turned her bright gaze on him. Her eyes flashed, wild and golden in the forest's green shade.

He wanted her like this, uninhibited, untrammeled by whatever losses plagued her or fears pursued her.

Avoiding plants, he walked through the wet to her, the soggy earth cooling his feet through the soles of his shoes. She all but dragged him up the next ridge, stopping only at the top, and gasping.

"There!" She spread her arms to include the scene. "Isn't it splendid!"

The waterfall was sublime. Tall and wide as a house, it roared over slate rocks stacked like plates, into a deep and roiling pool. Above it, a rock-strewn lazy stream widened. She led him in exploration, walking across the rocks and stretching back her hand, inviting him to follow her to the opposite bank. She slipped under a low overhang.

"My cave," she said, beaming when he joined her.

The waterfall he knew by rumor, but he had not heard of this. He would have to stoop to enter. He lifted an eyebrow. "Yours?"

"In a way. I think I was here before I ever found it."

He frowned.

"When I found it, I remembered it. I had hidden here once before. When I was lost, before I found my way to Salem."

Taking his hand, she invited him in. They moved through the narrow aperture into a small opening, more a recess in the rock than a cave, its contours just visible in the midday light that filtered through. She had hidden here, a child no older than Nicholas, much smaller and more vulnerable. His heart squeezed with a powerful urge to protect the brave and frightened child she must have been, even knowing he was years too late.

His head butted against a ceiling beaded with dampness. A drop of moisture fell onto his forehead. He took another step and could not stand upright.

He reached out to touch the wall and encountered a stubble of damp moss.

Gradually a feeling of wonder stole over him. Albeit little more than a depression under a ledge, it was an honest-to-goodness hideaway, the likes of which boys dreamed of.

"Retha, we must bring the children."

She nodded. "I thought you might like it."

"Me? I mean the boys." He knew he meant himself as well. A boyhood dream of pirate hideouts had manifested in front of his eyes. A little embarrassed, he shifted the topic. "Do you suppose anyone ever lived here?"

"I did, for one. For a few days that summer. Until I tired of living on rotten acorns and despaired of eating frogs and lizards. Then I came looking for Salem. So I could steal your potatoes." She looked at him sideways, teasing.

"You knew naught of Salem! You stumbled on us!" He laughed at her patently false story. Her bravado.

"Of course I stumbled across you. I don't remember how I got to Salem. Or even how I found this cave. 'Twas years before I came upon it again." She paused, touching the damp walls, reflective. "Oh, Jacob, I was very lucky that you were the one who caught me in the Square. You didn't tell a soul about the potatoes."

"Christina knew," he said gently. "We agreed the town might not understand, and naught required us to report it."

"So you protected me. So did she." Retha was silent for a while, exploring—perhaps remembering—the space that once sheltered her, breaking small clods of dirt off the walls and crumbling them with her fingers before turning to him. "You never say a word about her. Everyone knows you loved her."

Ah, he thought. All this was about that. His first wife. Whom his new wife never mentioned. To deny that he loved Christina would be the worst kind of lie.

"Yes, I loved her," he said simply.

"Sometimes it feels so strange that she is gone and I am here. You must miss her."

"For me, she lives on in the children."

Doubt creased Retha's brow. He could see it even in the low light of the cave.

"But you miss her still—you mourn her."

He couldn't back down. She deserved the truth. He hoped she had some store of wisdom on her own. "I remember her. Just as the children do. Better than they do. That doesn't mean I can't love you."

Turning away, Retha pressed her hands against a patch of moss on the wall and then pressed her head against it. He was a clumsy oaf. He did not have the right words. It wasn't as if he had a map for charting new territory like this, he thought, frustration rising.

"You know the way of mourning, Retha. You have endured many losses. 'Tis not over in a week, a month, a year."

He waited. Still no response. Still she was talking to that wall. Cupping her face in his hands, he insisted on her gaze. "You know that you don't forget them."

"I remember my Cherokee family." Tears seeped out of the corners of her eyes.

He wanted to kiss them away. "Of course you do."

"But I don't remember my real family."

"Naught?"

"I think not. Perhaps. Flickers, shadows. Sometimes a dream. He was a tall man. She was a . . ." She shook her head and fell silent. "A woman. Hair like mine. The dreams, they never last."

"But you were very young when the Cherokee found you."

"I was very hungry. And lost. Singing Stones guessed that I had four summers, perhaps five. Five years old," she explained. "Perhaps I knew then. But she didn't speak English, nor did anyone in her clan. By the time I learned enough Cherokee to make myself understood, no one thought to ask. If I indeed remembered."

Tears leaked down her cheeks, freely, sadly. Without a doubt, she understood loss. Jacob didn't know what else to say. Or to do. Though cool on this hot day, the cave had not turned out to be a happy place. After all the difficulties of their first weeks together, he wanted her to be happy, today of all days. He put his arm around her and turned her toward the light. "Let's go back out. We should eat."

After stepping on the stones for a while to cross and recross the sunlit stream, Retha recovered her bright demeanor. Relieved, he clambered with her down the steep side of the waterfall and sat at the edge of the deep pool carved out by plunging water.

She took bread and cheese out of her pocket, and he divided it between them. Beyond them, sunlight danced on the pool, its surface disturbed by the water's ceaseless flow.

"I can't see the bottom," he said.

She chewed her food as if it were long-awaited manna. "Yes, you can. There it is. Look." She pointed to a shaded area of calm where he could, in fact, see bottom if he squinted. "I swam in it."

He looked at her, astonished. "In your clothes?"

"Of course not. Who'd want to walk home in wet clothes?"

She had startled him. Swimming naked was a bold act for a woman, although not, perhaps, for one raised by Indians. What did he know of them? What did he know of her? Only that this wild, unknown side of her character and experience attracted him, drew him, called to him like the hawk to its mate.

Or like a wolf. Wolves, he had read, mated for life.

In his mind's eye he saw her here, naked in the sunlight, hair freed from its braids, water streaming over the dips and valleys of her body he had more guessed at than seen. He felt the sharp, unmistakable lift in his loins of pure, hot desire. He kissed her. Her mouth, not her image. And broke off, curbing frustration in his voice as best he could.

" 'Tis no place—"

"No place for . . . ?"

"What I want to do with you."

She gave him a quizzical look. "I don't see why not."

He scanned the scene. Thorns, brambles, rocks. Panthers, bears. Her element, perhaps. Not his. " 'Tis not safe."

She watched him, laughing. "There's no one

here, Jacob. 'Tis the safest place in the world. I swam here many times."

"I suppose," he conceded. But he did not take up the kiss again. "You even came that day, before Captain Scaife . . ." He trailed off, railing at himself. Stupid, callous of him to remind her of that day, of Scaife's accusations, when she had turned into this tempting, free-spirited, illusive wood sprite, glowing with her forest freedom.

Glowing, perhaps from his touch.

She lowered her head. But not before he could see a blush steal over her countenance. A sweet, innocent blush. Relief flooded him. Spies didn't blush. Virgin brides blushed. At the thought, he hoped, of swimming naked in front of their husbands. The very idea brought his excitement to a fine edge.

"No. I didn't come here that day." She spoke deliberately, softly. "I never meant to. I went to see Alice. Only to see Alice."

The unexpected words dropped into his heart like stones. She was a spy. He waited. She was going to confess it. Everything he had denied, all his defense of her came to this.

"To ask her about the feelings," Retha muttered, sounding embarrassed, almost ashamed. She did not look up.

"The feelings?" he repeated dully.

"To ask her about being a wife," she whispered, the words droplets against the water's roar.

Jacob's heart started to beat again.

No one had told her.

No one had ever told her.

He hadn't helped either, he realized, chagrined to have failed her, too. His virgin bride had come to him in ignorance. And she had sought out a friend to find out how to be his wife.

"You could have asked me, *Liebling*," he said, his voice grating against a tension of desire that rose in his manhood like a burst of song. "I would have told you everything."

"Yes. Sister Rosina said you would, about that."

"She did, did she?" He bit his lip against untoward amusement at the thought of the staid Single Sister broaching the subject.

"Yes, she said you knew what to *do*," Retha said solemnly. "But I thought you would know naught about my feelings."

"Ah," Jacob said, intrigued. What had she been feeling?

"So I went to Alice. And asked."

"You went to Alice and asked." He waited with growing impatience.

"And she explained . . . how a woman feels . . . about a man . . . as a woman."

For Retha, he had exerted iron control for weeks. But control had never been his forte. No, with a woman he was thunder, lightning, great gusts of rain.

"And how does a woman feel?" he croaked.

"Like that." She made a sweeping gesture that included the raging waterfall. And then she put her hands where her skirt folded over her womb. "Here."

The fall of water roared in his ears, the way his blood drummed through his limbs, his chest, the trunk of his body, into the root of his desire. Alice, and his wife, had the image right. His desire felt as inevitable as that ceaseless stream, as urgent as that heavy downward rush.

And Retha must have felt it, too. Whatever happened in their bed, or had not happened, she felt what he felt. She wanted him.

He covered her with his hands: her face, her throat, her shoulders, down across the fading tan above her breasts, to the breasts themselves. His trembling hands.

Any moment she would rock away, rejecting him.

She sighed, leaning into him, and gave him her golden gaze. "Is this right?"

CHAPTER 15

"'Tis right, Retha. And I will make it even better."

Jacob's baritone rumbled through Retha's being, more powerful than the surging falls. Her head spun from all she had told him, all he had accepted, even forgiven—and her heart sang from his response. He could love her. He had as much as said so when he had confessed that his love of his first wife did not mean he couldn't love his second.

His touch rippled through her like a stone skipped across water. She shook her skirts to dispel the heat and looked down at the small ledge where they sat.

He waved a hand over their makeshift bower. "We won't do much in this jumble, however," he grumbled amiably. Briars and branches hemmed them in while deadfall and cracked stones littered the ground.

Hardly a bed for him, she thought. She laughed, standing and giving him a hand up. "We don't have to." She felt airy, light, a buzz of anticipation humming in her brain, through her veins. She had brought him here for this. Here in the open air where she felt safe and free.

His breath warmed her neck, and he reached for the tapes that tied her skirt.

His touch at her waist surprised her, yet she did not want him to stop. She was ready, now, to delve into the mysteries her friend had told her of. He freed the top pin from her bodice, and she leaned toward him, shivering with an eager hope when his hand brushed her breast. He flung her rose dress and white petticoats over the tangled bushes that grew to the water's edge. Sunlight poured down on her exposed skin.

Instinctively her arms folded over her breasts.

Gently he lowered them to her sides.

"Bitte," he said. "Please. We talked of this. Do you remember?"

Everything, she thought. All too well. She nodded, feeling brave, but not brave enough for words.

"Let me give you this pleasure. Don't be afraid."

She did not want to be afraid. She wanted to be free. She wanted to explore this craving rising within her, this tension pulling her to him. This delight in her body, his touch.

He untied the rawhide thong around her braids, unraveled the plaits with his fingers, and draped her hair over her shoulders and down her back. A reluctant tendril encircled the sensitive tip of her breast. He swept it away and took a short step back, frankly admiring her. "I have longed to see you so."

Shyly proud, she stood for his inspection, her nipples puckering into hard points. His gaze traveled down her body. The triangle of fleece at the base of her belly seemed a glaring red, the weight of his attention there almost too much to bear. Moonlight had been far less revealing. And the day he had bathed and dressed before her, she had been too shy to truly take in the sight of him. Today she would try.

She slid her hands under his waistcoat and eased it over his shoulders. He rewarded her with a smile of incredible sweetness. Before, she remembered, he had not wanted her to fold his clothes. Following his example, she tossed his coat and shirt over a nearby limb, and he shucked off his boots, his breeches.

Her husband stood before her, naked as Adam in the garden, and more beautiful. He seemed even larger than when his clothes contained him. Her civilized town Elder was the golden bear she had first thought him to be. The midday sun dappled the work-bronzed skin of his massive torso.

She hardly knew where to rest her eyes. As before, her gaze skittered down his body—just so far—and retreated up to the familiar safety of his face.

"Look at all of me, Retha. I want you to."

She made herself look down. The thicket of hair around his manhood was a darker gold than the hair on his head. And his arousal—

She saw that he was aroused, felt him watching her. She turned away from this intimate knowledge.

He turned her back. "Look again, wife," he said, his voice softer, entreating. "Think of me as you. We are one. All of me is yours. This too."

Her eagerness—her courage—deserted her. The concept was too grand, the sight too personal. Despite her intention to seduce her husband, she had to stifle an urge to bolt into the woods. Briars seemed safer than this leap into the unknown. She cast about for words that might distract him.

"Alice never said to do it standing," she ventured.

His grin was indulgent. "No, not here. I wouldn't try to love you standing here."

Relaxing his grip on her hands, he bent, scooped her up, and waded into the pool that the waterfall had carved into rock. The creek bank dropped off sharply. Suddenly her toes, her trailing arms, her buttocks skimmed cool water. She squealed and struggled playfully against him, even knowing that it was hot and summer and that she was safe.

"I've got you," Jacob said, wading in deeper, immersing her to the tips of her breasts. His head bent toward them. She closed her eyes.

His mouth seized one taut nipple in a tender, suckling bite. Pinpoints of feeling like a driving rain rushed through her breasts to the center of her being. She cried out in surprise, opening her eyes to his brilliant indigo gaze.

His own fierce pleasure glowed as he murmured encouragement.

Under the mist that the falls churned up, he released her legs. They drifted down. Her feet came to rest on his large, corded ones, securely planted on the rock bottom of the pool. He flattened her body to his. In his arms, she felt like a leaf floating down the stream. Above her, the falls roared, drowning out his breathing and her own. There was only his body holding hers, his chest rising and falling against her, his massive thighs rigid against her thighs, and at her belly, his swollen shaft. An urgent pulsing flooded her deep inside, bringing back the feelings that had frightened her before, the ones for which she had no name. She named them now: Longing. Craving. Desire.

Jacob's eyes could not disguise his want; she saw a hunger to match her own. "Wrap your legs around me, *Liebling*," he said, his voice grating.

She hesitated, not quite understanding what he asked. He slipped her body inches higher. She reached out for balance, grasping air. He claimed her hand and brought it to his mouth.

"I want you holding on to naught but me."

And there was nothing, no one but him. With a shiver of anticipation, she parted her thighs around his slick hips and hooked her legs around his. Her arms draped over the reassuring shelf of his broad shoulders. He held her effortlessly, his awesome strength her refuge as the water lapped around them.

But he was so still.

Was she supposed to still herself likewise?

Perhaps. She hadn't been instructed in the art of loving her husband while they were standing. She struggled not to move. But her body, opened to him, demanded contact, pressure, movement. Despite herself, her hips curled into him.

With a groan of surrender, he pressed against her belly, and a sense of wonder surged through her. And of her own power. She had driven him to that. Then, rigid with tension, he stilled himself again.

"You stopped," she gasped into the mist from the falls.

"Not my turn," he said hoarsely. "This is for you. Move as you wish to move."

As she had to move, he might as well have said.

He helped her glide her mysterious, private center up and down along his ready shaft. Her body felt weightless in his grasp, but a heavy heat pooled between her legs. He mumbled encouragement, his hot words exhorting her to crush herself to him, faster, harder.

This was far from gentle, she thought, exulting at his power. At her own. Yet, no matter what he said, this had to hurt, and so she slowed.

With a low growl, he shifted her tighter to him. "Don't stop, Retha. Your body knows what to do."

His strong hands on her buttocks guided her to a shorter, tenser movement. Thrills showered into her core, leaving her breathless, pressing her center into him, seeking something unknown, unnamable, something just out of reach.

"I can't let go," she cried.

"Danke Gott," he said, and spun her under the falls, drenching them in its spray. "Where is your fear now, *Liebling?*"

"Gone, all gone," she laughed, still seeking his heat.

He returned them to the sun. With a newfound joy, she shook streams of water from her hair, its wet tendrils lashing both of them. His voice thickened.

"You're so close, so close to where you're going. Let me send you over the falls."

Slipping one hand between them, he touched her hungry flesh with deep, gentle pinches. She almost screamed as an upsurge of sensation poured through her, as her very center contracted around him. Of its own accord, her body arced out of control, wrenching a cry from her that she recognized even as it scraped out of her throat. It was the cry of women in the night, the cry that she had taken for pain. But this was not pain, this was torrents of pleasure, slaking desire, fulfilling need.

And she was whole, and she was his, and she was free.

She sank her head into the safe haven of his shoulder, clinging, shaking, shaken. She marveled at her power, the forces flooding her senses.

"Ah, Retha," he groaned. "I wanted this for you."

She could feel the hot pulsing of his body, but he remained as still as stone.

Consciousness, memory trickled back. They were not done. She had been too eager. Too selfish. He had not entered her.

"You didn't . . ." She trailed off. Their awesome act of loving had been easy, compared to putting anything in words.

"Finish?" he said for her. He grinned down at her, looking not in the least put out but like a very hungry man. "Not yet. We have all day. We have a lifetime."

"Shouldn't you? Now, I mean?"

"We could do it now," he drawled, as if considering.

"You don't want to?" Perhaps she had done it wrong. But how could she have, when it had felt so wonderful?

"I want to. And we will." He gave her a hard, convincing kiss, then simply held her in the stream as if she were a treasure, a cherished woman. The water eddied around them, cooling her. She heard a scolding jay, a noisy wren. The sun dried her face. Finally he began again. Nipping, where he had kissed before. Kissing, where a tender bite had flamed into her body. In minutes she was trembling, and he was no longer still. Or quite so steady as he had been.

"But can we really do this here?" Standing? In the water? She still felt ignorant, but she was game.

A wicked grin strained across his face. "We can try."

She braced her arms on his shoulders, opened her legs around him, and he guided himself in. She quivered at the newness of this inmost touch, its rightness, her stunning satisfaction.

"Ah, *Liebling*, you're so tight." From the rapt tension in his voice, she gathered that this was good. He pushed inside her, feeling hot and hard and slick all at once. The pressure was delicious and then suddenly, sharply painful. She gave a small cry of surprise, and he withdrew. Cold water filled the empty space where he had been, and she felt the loss, the deprivation.

She wanted him in her. She wanted his pleasure. She wanted to be his.

"Alice told me, Jacob. I can bear the hurt. Make me your wife."

Remembering all she knew of Cherokee courage, she fortified herself. But before she could think another thought, he entered her, arching up and tearing her maiden barrier. The stabbing pang brought tears to her eyes, but she did not pull away. He waited, his manhood throbbing inside her. The hurt stung, lingered, ebbed. She felt herself contract around him. Only then did he begin to move, slowly at first, and deeper, until she enfolded all of him.

Surrounded by the pounding fall of water, she rode his driving rhythm until deep shudders cascaded through her. He met her ecstasy with a fierce growl, a final plunge into her depths. This time, at last, she relished all the satisfaction and the triumph of his cry.

Sweet lassitude, Jacob thought, reclining on the ledge beside the stream, waiting for Retha to finish collecting plants. He had pulled on his breeches, helped his wife dress, and sent her off for dyestuffs. That was what the children would expect to see. Someone's expectations should be met today. His had not, thank God. He had expected a long day's trek through the woods and had hoped for a kiss or two. Instead, he had gained a lover. He had lost his heart.

Arm raised, he measured that the sun had moved a hand's breadth across the heavens. Suddenly Retha's image filled the sky. She leaned over and offered him a wildflower.

"Indigo." She smiled. "The blue matches your eyes."

"You found that here?"

"Just wild. Here and there, above the falls. I'm not supposed to use it."

He had forgotten that. Even before the war had exhausted the supplies of this most common dye, only men had worked with indigo because of the urine used to fix the color.

"But you do?"

She gave a sly shrug that neither confirmed nor

denied it. "'Tis the last bloom." She gave it to him.

Its delicate flower was a hearty, vibrant blue. His daughter's eyes, Nicholas's, and, he supposed, his own. He threaded the sprig over Retha's right ear. In the golden light of early afternoon her beauty shone, her pale brown eyes sparkling like honey in the sun, her amber hair aflame where it had begun to dry. He reached for his shirt and stock dangling from branches overhead. She sat on the ledge, braiding her damp hair and watching as he put on his clothes.

Her intense attention charmed him.

"Do you like what you see?"

She sighed sweetly. "I liked everything."

His heart turned over in his chest. When she had shattered in his arms, it had felt as though her blood pulsed in his veins. When she had ridden him, driving him to his own explosion, he had felt a passion as pure and wild as uncharted wilderness.

Their union this day seemed the miracle he had prayed for. It seemed that she accepted him at last, whole and unafraid.

But was she whole? And had she truly overcome her fears?

The day Scaife brought her home, Jacob thought she invited his love, only to freeze again when he approached her in their bed. Perhaps his morning kisses helped dispel her fears. And his daily barrage of kisses and caresses. Perhaps.

He smiled a covert, satiated smile. He would take her home and hope that this was so, but he could always bring her back. He would be content to seduce her this way for the rest of their lives.

"Jacob, look." Her whisper broke his reverie. She pointed to the opposite bank.

"Where? I see naught," he said quietly.

"In the ferns, beneath the elm."

He squinted. A gray shape stood statue still, head high, alert. "'Tis a wolf." He put out a restraining, protective arm.

"My wolf. She found us," Retha whispered, digging into her skirts and retrieving a knotted bundle of food from her pocket. Their lunch.

"Not our meal, not for that beast." He grabbed for the bundle, but his concern was not their food. Retha never heeded warnings; she invited danger. He wanted her to be careful.

"Just the bacon," Retha said. "I have to see if she is truly well."

He was not quick enough to stop his wife. She climbed the steep incline to the top of the falls, crossed the stream, and descended the other bank, using vines and branches for handholds. With far less caution than he could approve of, she approached the wolf, stopping a few paces from it and kneeling, hand extended. He could see Retha's lips move, but the water's roar drowned out her words.

Half-crouched, the wolf took one step and then another toward her. She let it come to her.

Tail wagging like an ordinary dog's, it gobbled up the bacon and snuffled her palm, looking for more. Satisfied there was none, it sat on its haunches as if it meant to stay awhile.

The beast was not afraid of her, Jacob thought, amazed. Nor she of it. She was more at home, more wondrous in the wild than he could possibly have imagined. He had been criminal to keep her home, to lock her away from this simple, savage happiness. For part of her belonged here.

Some part of him did, too. He reclined on his side, content to watch, more content than he had been in years of civilized confinement in his beloved village. His golden-eyed bride had brought him to the wilderness, the dream of which had called him to this country when he was seventeen. The dream that duty had deprived him of. He loved her for bringing him here. He loved her in the wilderness.

He loved her. His brave, wild bride who befriended proud, young wolves, troublesome daughters, ailing sons. Who met her lusty husband's deepest needs. Sister Krause's words from days before the wedding floated back to him. *The well-spring of your happiness.* He breathed in dampness, greenery, and let his chest fill with a new contentment. Then he closed his eyes.

Duty, and the war, seemed very far away.

Even from a distance, Jacob thought Salem unusually bustling as he and Retha neared home. A farm wagon rattled past them, heading toward the Square. A couple of militia men galloped out of town, kicking up a plume of choking dust. Uneasy, he shrugged off his impression of danger. Some days were busier than others. Dust enveloped them, and Retha slowed down. Their lovemaking must have exhausted her. Or hurt her.

"Suppose they can tell," she whispered.

"Tell what?"

"That we have been . . . together."

Anyone with eyes to see would guess as much, Jacob thought. That notion would not set well with her. Her swollen lips, flushed cheeks, sloe eyes all said she had been ravished. Well ravished, he thought with bone-deep, hot-blooded male satisfaction.

"They cannot," he said, assuring himself that God forgives small lies told in kindness. "They assume this part over and done with weeks ago."

"Oh!" she gasped, blushing furiously. "All this time! They thought that."

On the well-trodden road in the settling dust, he stopped her at Steiner's Mill.

"They wished that for us, Retha. This union. 'Tis the way of a man and his bride. Even among the Indians you lived with, surely—"

"That was different."

"Different? How?"

"Just different!" She stomped ahead of him, her sack of goldenseal bumping against her tempting behind with each agitated step she took. He caught up to her at the log bridge.

"If you must know," she snapped, "what they did frightened me."

"Frightened you?"

"The cries at night sounded like fighting. Then after I came here, no one ever talked with me about what people do when they're married."

"Not even your friend Sister Ernst?" he teased.

"No, not exactly. Some of the younger Single Sisters talked about it, but not to me."

"Now you know," he said softly, reaching for the

back of his neck in frustration. Rosina Krause should never have left his wife's instruction wholly up to him.

Beyond the tannery, newly erected tents crowded the meadow, and men in blue milled about idly.

"More troops," she protested anxiously, speeding ahead.

"Within their rights," he reminded her. Reluctant to return to town and public obligations, he reverted to personal matters. "Someday you will wish such a happy union for Nicholas and Matthias and Anna Johanna. And someday, for our children yet to come."

"Our children?" she faltered. "I had not thought you wanted more."

Halfway up the hill to Brother and Sister Ernsts' small cabin, he stopped her in her tracks. "I hope for more children, of course. God willing, we have started one today."

Astonishment lit her face.

"You didn't think of that," he realized.

"I dreamed of it," she whispered. "But the boys don't want us to have a baby. Nicholas practically said so."

"They didn't want a sister either, but look at them with Anna Johanna."

"They tease and torment her!"

"Exactly. They adore her. You should have seen their care of her after they lost their mother."

Jacob tucked Retha's hand under his arm, the hand of his possibly pregnant wife, and smiled to himself. Anna Johanna waited for them. He wondered how fussy she had been today.

On the outskirts of town, Jacob rapped on the Ernsts' door. Eva Ernst poked her head just far enough outside to glance nervously up and down the street, and hurried them inside. Anna Johanna sat by the hearth, arranging saucers of something into rows. Retha rushed to her, leaving Jacob to deal with Eva's fluttering distress.

"What's the matter, Sister Ernst?" Jacob asked with concern.

"This morning they found Brother Bonner," she whispered breathlessly. "Beaten half to death."

"Slow down and tell me," Jacob said through gritted teeth, enraged at such a senseless, random attack. Brother Bonner was seventy-seven years old, living quietly outside Salem on his small farm, no threat to anyone. "Who found him? Samuel?"

"One of the other men on night watch, making his last round."

"Who beat him?"

"Soldiers. English soldiers. Over some cows. They marched off before the new regiment of Continentals arrived from Virginia. Dr. Bonn is caring for him. Then this new regiment billeted some officers with Sister Baumgarten, and she took her family to *Gemein Haus* and the safety of the Sisters. She has no protection now that her husband has gone on. If any officers claimed our cabin, we would have to go there, too. We have no second story to live in."

Sister Ernst was babbling.

"We passed the encampment in the meadow. They look quite settled to me," Jacob said, risking the reassuring touch that only a friend could give. "If need be, you can stay with us."

"Oh, thank you, Brother Blum, I have been so scared since Brother Bonner's terrible . . . misfortune."

"I understand," he soothed her. "But surely that was an isolated occurrence. If those troops presented a real danger, we would all already be clapped in the garrison brig."

She whitened. Jacob's hand went to the back of his tense neck. The day, the week, the summer needed only these extra burdens. When the town had needed him, he had been gone. Or perhaps not, he thought, remembering that he had been admonished, and wondering exactly what was expected of him now. His present, pressing task was to protect his own.

"I had best take Anna Johanna home, then."

"She had a quiet day—until lunch, that is," Sister Ernst stammered. "No, actually, before that, she became a little cranky. Then we ate. Afterwards she started to fuss and I never could get her to nap, and I thought of pies."

Jacob walked over to the hearth where Retha sat, helping his preoccupied daughter put the finishing touches on her culinary creations. Green leafy crusts on—

"Mud pies?" he asked bleakly. Red mud caked her hands and arms, and orange-brown splatters decorated her grimy dress. His touch-me-not daughter had doubtless tested Sister Ernst's nerves. He could hardly scold his friend's well-meaning wife, but how ever would they bathe Anna Johanna?

He bent down. "Time to go home, pumpkin."

She grinned up proudly. "Want some pie?"

He didn't, but when Anna Johanna's chubby, muddy fists slid around his neck, he would almost have taken a bite to please her.

It felt good to be home, Retha thought, unlatching the door for her husband whose arms were full of dirty daughter. Home felt safe. Outside, too many soldiers from Virginia lounged and strolled about the town, and a sense of foreboding nicked at her.

"This is going to take a lot of w-a-t-e-r," Jacob said with surprising cheer as he carried Anna Johanna through the narrow entry to the kitchen.

"And p-a-t-i-e-n-c-e."

"To say naught of brute strength. I will be back shortly." Chuckling, Jacob took up a wooden bucket, leaving Retha with her stepdaughter. The nearest cistern was one he had built a good way down the street. Town planners like himself, he said when she had remarked upon the distance, had to avoid the appearance of favoring themselves.

After settling Anna Johanna down to play with her doll, Retha checked the nearly spent hearth fire and thought about a simple supper. Beans and bread and cheese for all with fresh coffee for her husband. Husband now in the fullest sense. And she herself a real wife at last. A welcome tremor of remembrance gripped her, a mystery no longer but all the more a miracle. Jacob wanted children. Her hand stole to where the gathers of her skirt covered her stomach. To where he might already have planted a child.

Shaking her head at her own dreamy state of mind, she picked up a poker to stoke the fire.

A chair scraped in the parlor. Lifting her head, she listened. She was alone, she and Anna Johanna. Except for the footsteps. Boots, she heard boots. Jacob was always noisy. But he always banged the door open.

A new, raw fear clamped her shoulders and ran down her back. Then a familiar voice shattered her newfound peace.

"We'll be needing supper soon, *Frau* Blum."

CHAPTER 16

The menace in the voice was familiar, too. Her pulse beating in her throat, Retha lifted the latch on the parlor door. The little girl in her—the child who had fled other soldiers, other homes—wanted desperately to run. But the woman, newly a wife and newly a mother, braced to face intruders. For the sake of her stepdaughter, muddy and oblivious, who played with her doll by the fire. For the sake of the boys, who would soon be home. For the sake of her husband, who had entrusted her with his offspring and his home.

Holding the poker high, Retha opened the door.

Captain Sim Scaife, Liberty Man and her tormentor, leered as he pulled up Jacob's good chair, univited. "We got all the pokers around here you're going to need, *Frau* Blum."

"I was stoking the fire for my family's supper," she snapped, ignoring his innuendo as she scanned her disordered parlor.

With a cackle, he reared back in the chair. "You can stoke mine, if you want to."

Then he plunked his scuffed boots on the dining table, one at a time. Against the far wall, his men leaned their chairtops against the whitewashed plaster, marking it and the wainscoting. They had racked muskets against the parlor's tiled stove and tossed powder horns and ammunition pouches on top of it. Three muskets. Three powder horns. Three pouches. Three bedrolls. In hers and Jacob's home.

Anger snuffed out any lingering alarm. Of all the soldiers in North Carolina, Sim Scaife and his disgusting minions would have to be the ones to land on her doorstep. Their presence violated the sanctity of her home. Knowing what they were capable of, Retha steeled herself.

"You remember Calloway, *Frau* Blum," Scaife said in a silky approximation of courtesy.

The fuzzy-cheeked militia youth smirked self-consciously.

"I remember."

"And Pickens."

The wiry man dribbled a brown stream of tobacco into Jacob's best pewter mug, but she did not look away. She would not give him the satisfaction.

"We'll be needing more of this." Scaife shoved a cider jug toward her, scratching the table.

With a glare of anger at his insolence, she set the poker down and took the jug. It was empty. They must have already made a trip to the cellar, she realized, and they were getting drunk. She retrieved a fresh jug from the cellar stores and guardedly set it on the table.

Soldiers had never billeted with her, but after her experience at Alice's, she knew enough to give in to their demands. Serving them here alone was even worse. They were closer, more insulting. And a threat to Anna Johanna, who played quietly in the kitchen. She prayed the child would stay quiet. Her safety could depend on her compliance.

In moments, the back door banged, signaling Jacob's return. Retha shivered, fearing a confrontation. He had no use for the captain. The captain despised him. She reclaimed the poker and hid it in the folds of her skirt.

"Captain Scaife. What a surprise," Jacob drawled over her head.

Scaife took his feet off the table, setting the front legs of Jacob's chair down with a crack. Spite shone in the captain's yellow eyes.

"We're billeting soldiers all over town, Blum, and you got me."

"Luck of the draw, no doubt," Jacob said ironically.

"Could be. Could be your lucky day."

Splashing cider from the fresh jug onto the polished table, Scaife poured his mug to the brim and winked at Retha. "This your best cider?"

With a move too swift, too graceful for a man so large, Jacob closed the space and towered over the captain.

Retha clenched the poker. Don't push him, Jacob, she wanted to cry out.

Didn't he know the hazard of soldiers in the house?

She knew, she realized suddenly, with a certainty that spread through her body like the grippe.

She knew all about them! And knew they could not be stopped. Whatever had once given her this knowledge, had happened like this. To her father, her mother, to her as a child. Coming home on a quiet, hot summer afternoon to soldiers in the house.

" 'Tis our best," Jacob said, leaning one inch closer to the captain. "As is the table. As is the mug."

Scaife scraped a spur into the smooth oiled floor, a deliberate, provocative act.

"The floor too," Jacob growled.

The captain's Adam's apple bobbed in his throat, but he flashed his long stained teeth. "You can't stop me, Blum. I got the right. The army pays to billet me wherever I need to stay. They pay for food and damages."

"Harm aught of mine, and it won't be the army that pays."

"Papa?"

Jacob turned. Alarmed, unthinking, Retha fiercely wrapped her wide-eyed stepdaughter in her skirts, the poker in front of them both, although it offered them scant protection.

Anna Johanna, clutching her doll, allowed Retha's touch. "Who's that man?"

"Just a soldier, sweet potato—" Retha began.

"Never knew you had such a pretty little girl, Blum."

"Get her out of here," Jacob ordered quietly, grimly.

Retha moved toward the door, but not fast enough. Leaning forward in his chair, Scaife lowered himself to Anna Johanna's level, a kindly gesture in a decent man. Coming from him, as far as Retha was concerned, kindness sickened.

"What's your name, honey?" he purred.

Jacob grabbed him by the throat and hoisted him to his feet. "Out. Get out."

Belatedly Scaife's men lurched up in defense. In confusion. Having bullied Retha, they expected to bully her husband. She swept Anna Johanna into the kitchen just as Jacob shoved Scaife into his men.

"Take him," Jacob barked to the stunned soldiers. "Unless you want cold hominy, we have no food for you tonight. Take your supper at the Tavern."

In the kitchen, Retha mechanically set her stepdaughter by the fire to play supper with her best set of miniature tin dishes. Then Retha slumped against the wall, resting her forehead on the hearth's mantel while she collected her frazzled thoughts. Anna Johanna hadn't pitched a fit or panicked; she had accepted Retha's touch, her grasp, unconditionally. Somehow their urgency must have penetrated beyond the child's usual obsession. Retha understood the impact of such urgency on a little one.

And suddenly, memory assaulted her like lightning strikes. She was a little girl again. Their cabin had been small, sheltered by deep woods. Dirt-streaked, smelly soldiers filled it. Her father defended her. Her mother shielded her.

But nothing protected her.

Retha swayed against the mantel. The room around her shimmered, blurred, shrank. She bit the inside of her cheek. She would not faint. Would not retreat. Hot blood spurted onto her tongue. It tasted thick, metallic.

Familiar. Bile rose in her throat.

Not again. Not now. Not here.

Through her veil of memories, she heard boots scuff the floor. The men were leaving.

"Mama Retha?" Anna Johanna asked, apparently confused that Retha kept standing by the hearth.

"It's all right, sweet potato. Your papa will be right back."

But she heard Scaife snarl. "I'm sleeping here. You can't stop us, Blum."

"You can make your bed on the parlor floor. Tonight. After services, after my children are sound asleep," Jacob answered firmly.

Then they were gone, and Jacob was at her side, his hand trailing over her shoulder, his voice still gruff with anger, yet thick with concern. "Are you all right?"

She started at his touch, then covered her moment of weakness with a flare of anger and a controlled barrage of English so that upset Anna Johanna could not understand.

It didn't work. By the hearth, the child stirred. "Papa?" she asked worriedly.

" 'Twill be all right, pumpkin." He took a crock from the mantel and handed over precious coffee beans. "Here. Do you want to play with these?"

Anna Johanna smiled slightly. Counting out beans was a special treat. After she settled down to play with them, Jacob pointed Retha into the parlor.

There she wheeled on him in anger. "What were you trying to prove, Jacob Blum? He's dangerous anytime. But worse humiliated."

"Anna Johanna is safe, is she not?" Jacob strode

around the disordered room, taking a gratuitous kick at the bedrolls the militia men had not bothered to stack.

Retha blazed. "At what price? I was leaving the room. He comes here with two experienced fighting men—"

"Do you think I would not defend my daughter?" He shoved the bedrolls into a corner, out of the way. Out of sight.

"I know you would. You would stand up to the three of them—and die. He would welcome naught more than killing you. Then the rest of us. And we would all die—bloody, senseless . . ."

Blood on the walls. Blood on the sheet.

Nausea rose in her throat. She covered her mouth and clutched her stomach.

Jacob's anger softened to worry. "*Liebe Gott,* Retha. What did that man do before I came? Are you sick? Did he hurt you?"

For Jacob's sake, she had to deny everything. However righteous, however right, his temper could mean their ruin. "He did naught. I am fine."

Doubt filled his eyes. His fingers searched her face as if for fever or for injury. She pushed them away. He had to know that she was strong.

"You don't sound fine. What about my daughter?"

"She's . . ."

Frightened for you. Terrified. Dying inside.

And how did she know that? Retha hid her face behind her hands, wondering.

Blood everywhere. She could not tell Jacob that.

"She needs us to be strong," Retha managed to say.

Jacob removed her hands from her face and held them to his chest. "*Liebling*, are you unharmed? Truly. Tell me."

"I am not hurt," she said hoarsely. She had to be well, strong. For all of them.

"We should take them to the Brothers House, for safety. And Anna Johanna, to the Single Sisters—" she added, trying for facts, control.

"We cannot. Both houses are full. The widows, the elderly, those who cannot retreat to a second floor, as we can. We have to stay upstairs. Us in her room and her in with the boys."

It made sense, Retha realized. Nearer to the stairs, Anna Johanna's room opened into the boys' bedroom. For tonight, the inner room could shelter the three children, and she and Jacob would guard the outer one. Surely they would be safe that way. Scaife might be poison, but he wouldn't dare harm them. Not over nothing. Not with an entire Virginia regiment of regular Continental troops in town and on their best behavior.

Jacob watched the window restlessly, then jacked open the back door. "Their lessons are surely over now. I will bring the boys straight home."

Despite the security his strength had lent her, Retha was relieved when he left. Perhaps he would cool down. She assembled their meager supper and decided to chance giving Anna Johanna a bath during their brief lull alone together. She made the brisk sponging a game, drawing on an old memory of an English lullaby, hoping its novelty would distract Anna Johanna. It worked well enough. It even soothed Retha a bit. By the time the boys were home, the Carolina clay that had caked her stepdaughter's hands and arms had stained the fresh water in the bucket brick red.

"Been making mud pies, Anna Slow—" Nicholas greeted her, but Jacob cut him off with a quick tweak of his upper arm. "—Anna Jo?"

But his father's discipline did not deter Nicholas. Eyes shining, he vilified the evil English for beating Brother Bonner, glorified the heroic regiment sweeping down from Virginia to ensure Cornwallis's defeat, and celebrated it that real militia men had occupied his home and would be back to spend the night.

Finally, tensely, Jacob lost patience. "There will be no more talk of soldiers in this house."

Nicholas flared. "I'd go for a soldier if I could!"

"You could not. You are but a lad," Jacob said brutally.

Retha looked up, shocked. Her husband had just thrown over months of careful progress in counseling his son.

Nicholas opened his mouth to reply, but no words came out. Hurt, angry tears rimmed the eyes of the boy who wanted to be a man. He pressed his lips together and savagely, silently, wiped the tears away. Jacob might be right, she thought, but he had lost this battle.

Matthias slunk into the parlor. When Retha went to call him to supper, she found him perched dejectedly on a parlor chair, thumbing through the family Bible, lips moving as he pored over it. Nor did the slapdash supper whet his appetite. The old Matthias returned with a vengeance, pushing food around on his plate.

At *Singstunde*, the Virginia regiment crowded the *Saal*. Even the fuzzy-cheeked Calloway showed his face, only to leave before the singing started. Retha took small comfort in the orderly, even prayerful, presence of the visitors. No one needed prayer more than soldiers, she told herself. But their peaceful demeanor could not make up for Scaife's behavior in her house.

He did not come to services. He wasn't the praying sort. Mounting anxiety followed Retha home, anticipating Scaife's return. Jacob herded the children up the stairs to bed. She hurried into the downstairs bedroom to roll up the cornhusk mattress. She and Jacob needed a pallet to sleep on.

The hinged press bed, which folded up during the day to save space, was a heavy, inconvenient contraption for a woman. Hands on hips, she studied it for a moment. If the mattress could be pulled out from behind the bed, she wouldn't have to lower it and put it up again. She tugged, but it would not yield. Forcing the heavy linen cover might tear it, she thought. Annoyed, she lowered the bed and tugged again.

Still stuck. Tied to the ropes, she reasoned irritably. From above, she could not reach the tapes. Nor could she heave the bed back up.

She crawled into the shallow space beneath it. Poor skinny Matthias was the child for this task, she thought, drawing up her shoulders and squeezing in. Her fingers explored the bed's rough, roped bottom, feeling blindly along its knots for the ties that bound the mattress to it. One, she unraveled. Two, then three.

She did not like the dark close space.

But there had to be another tie. Under here, her tallow lamp shed little light. Her fingers scrabbled into utter darkness.

Into a net of spider webs.

Smothering the scream that rose in her throat, she scrambled crablike out to the dull light, abrading a knee and taking a splinter in the heel of one hand. Spider webs. They made her shudder. In the middle of the room, she clutched her legs to her body, staring beyond the little flame into a final, clear confrontation with her past, and rocked.

Webs under the bed. Sticky, clinging webs with spiny spiders in their depths. She backed out of her hiding place, creeping, afraid to disobey her mother but disobeying nonetheless. The webby film stuck to her fingers and eyelashes. Uncontrollable shudders swept her. Only her mother could make them stop.

She looked about the cabin. A thin man looked back.

The walls and sheets were splashed with blood.

Her mother and her father sat against a wall, sleeping, their clothes all stained with blood.

"Well, well, well. Been waiting for you," the thin man rasped, his hair the color of the red clay soil her father plowed up in the fields. "You must be Elisabeth."

"Yes," she answered obediently, blinking in the light. She had stayed under the bed till her feet went numb, hands over her ears, unable to shut out brutal grunts, harsh thuds, terrifying cries. And her mother's last broken words, "Hide, Lillibet. Don't let them touch you."

"Elisabeth," he purred, pulling her to him with bony fingers. Screaming, terrified, she kicked and clawed

until he let her go. And dove back into the spiders' lair where that man's hands could never touch her.

After Jacob tucked the children in, he found her in their bedroom on her knees, rocking in front of her little tallow lamp as if it were an altar. His heart failed him. All his prayers, all his patience, all his careful, joyful seduction of her had been to no avail.

"Gott im Himmel, Leibling." He knelt beside her, pulled her to him. "Retha, they'll be back any moment."

She turned wide, empty eyes to his face, eyes that only hours ago had brimmed with desire.

" 'Tis tied down, Jacob," she said weakly.

Her observation made no sense. His pulse thudded alarm in his throat.

"What's tied down?"

He watched her swallow, moisten her lips, and consciously arrange her face into something that looked less distracted. He pinned a small hope on that conscious effort.

"The mattress is tied to the rope springs, and I couldn't reach all the ties."

"Ah," he said, feeling a momentary relief that she could be specific. But then doubt racked him. Something was terribly wrong with her. This relapse swallowed up every trace of her sweet wildness at the waterfall.

He grounded himself in action. "I can. Here." He led her to the bed and lifted it. "You prop it up for me."

She leaned into it heavily while he reached through cobwebs to the last two ties, stood, and wiped his hands. "There, 'tis free." Gently he touched her cheek. "The mattress is a good idea. I didn't think of it. We will sleep well, at least."

But neither of them did.

After Jacob more or less single-handedly dragged the mattress to Anna Johanna's room, undressed, and lay down with his wife, he tried to doze but could not. Not when he expected Scaife and his men at any moment. Not when he was distracted with concern that Retha's mysterious affliction had returned. What could have triggered it? All afternoon since they had come home to Scaife's disrupting presence, her assurances that she was well—even strong—had convinced him that she was.

Clearly, she was not. She had been so joyous in the woods, so abandoned to their lovemaking at the waterfall that her present state was harder for him to bear and more difficult to comprehend.

Twice, but only twice before, she had been this way: on their wedding night and again on the evening after Scaife had brought her back from the Voglers. Both times they had been at home, together, in their bedroom. He had blamed himself for provoking her fear. This third time, however, he hadn't touched her. Hadn't even been there.

From below, he heard Scaife's men stagger in. His home was theirs by military right, he reminded himself, hand on the club he had brought up from downstairs. A chair clattered to the floor, a curse rose up, a drunken, boyish laugh careened up the stairs, and all the rest was muffled. Finally a medley of snores drifted up the stairs.

Jacob rolled onto his back, hanging an arm off

the edge of the mattress they had dragged upstairs. The soft, even breathing of his wife did not allay his concerns. How could she sleep through this? But going to sleep had never been her problem.

For him, sleep would not come. Too many concerns today. But none so devastating as Retha's unexpected, inexplicable lapse into . . . he refused to call it madness. But what was the matter with her? Or rather, perhaps the question should be, what provoked her—what should he call them—spells? Terrors? Each time, she had clearly been frightened. But of what?

He reminded himself that he was a rational, educated man, well versed in orderly thought. But tonight he wasn't even sure of the premise he was starting from. What did her episodes of terror have in common?

Not him, he assured himself. Twice, he knew his presence had triggered them. But not tonight. Tonight was different.

Tonight. Each time it had been night. Night terrors were a common-enough human affliction. One of his own children suffered nightmares. But Retha's aberrant behavior was of a different order. Nevertheless, each time it had been night.

And in the bedroom, he realized. Not merely at home, but in the bed.

No, to be precise, on or about the bed. He twisted and punched his pillow. The solution to this mystery seemed tantalizingly close. And yet so far away. He drifted into a restless, unsatisfying sleep.

* * *

When Retha woke in a strange room, it was still dark and she was already sitting. And rocking. She stopped herself. She did not need to do that anymore. She remembered everything from the day her parents died. The day Sim Scaife had murdered them.

No wonder Singing Stones had taught her to rock herself into a trance to dispel the haunting, horrid memories. No wonder they tormented her. No wonder Jacob's bed, the very kind and size that her parents' bed had been, had catapulted her back in time.

Back to the bloodstained sheet.

Back to the blood-splattered walls.

Back to the sight of her parents' bodies, dead against the wall. What had the soldiers finally done with them? She would never know, she told herself. Never, never know.

Beside her, Jacob's hot, huge frame was restless. How her strange behavior must confound him, when she wanted only to please. Waking him would be a risk, but she no longer cared. Daylight tomorrow would be too late, she feared. Her nerve might fail. Her courage would slip. She had to tell him now.

She shook him lightly. "Jacob," she whispered. It touched her that he awoke so quickly. The great bear, roused, in defense of hearth and home and family.

"What's the matter? Is everyone all right?" he muttered, propping on an elbow, rubbing a large hand over his face.

"I remember," she said solemnly. "More than I told you at the waterfall."

"Tell me," he said, sitting up and taking her into his arms as if to shield her from all harm.

He couldn't shield her from her past. Telling him was hard, the more so whispering in the dark in order not to wake the children. Soldiers had come to her parents' cabin. As tempers flared, her mother thrust her under the bed. Then came the pounding and the terrible screams. The men must have killed them.

Minutes, hours later, fear and the cramping in her legs had driven her from her hiding place. One soldier remained behind. She dared not tell that he had been Sim Scaife. Younger, thinner, and with redder hair, but every bit as mean. Jacob must never know.

"*Gott im Himmel*, did he hurt you?" Jacob's voice was thick with protective anger.

She shook her head because she couldn't speak. Now that the moment was upon her, she couldn't tell him who the man had been. Yet Jacob's low growl reminded her that he was the one weapon she had never had. His righteous rage; his steadfast defense.

The palest moonlight trickled in through the small window under the eaves. Jacob slept shirtless in the unremitting August heat. Her lowered eyes fixed on the strength of his chest.

"You can tell me." With a gentle hand, he tipped her face toward his gaze. "Don't be afraid."

Hot, humiliating tears seeped out of the corners of her eyes and tracked down her cheeks, splashing onto his hand.

"Did he hurt you?" he repeated, his voice soft with pain. She was deeply moved. "Tell me."

No. Yes. I cannot tell. I must not tell you who he was, she thought. She moved her head, a nod, a negative, and found a few words. "He meant to—meant to . . ."

Jacob pulled her closer, murmuring into her ear. "Ah, *Liebling*, I wish I could spare you this memory, this pain."

"I was not hurt." Her voice rang brittle, childlike, in her head. His large warm hand stroked the center of her back, consoling her, urging her to go on. She couldn't.

Anger and confusion tightened Jacob's gut. She was holding something back. Everything he knew of secrets held to the heart urged him to help her find her voice. Everything. His daughter's fear of water. His younger son's inexplicable aversion to his food. Retha's own furtive night walks. Always some terrible secret lurked behind.

Once more, he tried to summon wisdom for his young, vulnerable bride, whom he had so often failed. The very rafters pressed down on him. And no doubt on her. "Let's go outside lest we wake the children," he said, pulling on his clothes. But their slumbers were not his true reason. Outside, where Retha seemed to feel so free, she might talk.

"Leave? With the men downstairs?" she asked anxiously, torn between her reluctance to leave her daughter in the house with Scaife there and her certainty that Jacob must never know.

"They came in late, drunk. They have passed out till morning. But I will bar the parlor doors."

His arm around her waist, they crept downstairs, locking the parlor doors to secure the snoring soldiers, then walking out across the small dirt yard onto the strip of lawn that skirted the garden. The heavy dews of an August morning drenched the grass. In the east, the sky had begun to lighten.

Keeping his arm around her, he settled her on the bench where he once watched her shelling beans. "*Danke Gott*, he didn't hurt you. But you must have been scared. Can you tell me what happened?"

When she finally spoke, she whispered in the strained, shamed voice of a child. "I couldn't help my parents. I couldn't stop him."

Thinking of the horror Retha had endured and the irrational guilt she bore, he struggled to reassure her that she had done no wrong. "You were but a child, *Leibling*. And you were under the bed, where your mother rightly wanted you to be."

"But she screamed."

"And then what?" he prodded gently, dreading to know, determined to find out.

" 'Twas quiet so long and my legs began to hurt, so I came out. Even though she told me to stay. He was still there."

Jacob's insides churned as he imagined the worst. "Tell me, Retha, trust me," he assured her, bracing himself to hear what he did not want to know, hoping mere assurance would conjure speech from the child of her shrouded past. How old could she have been? Young, he thought, her tone reminding him of his once-troubled daughter.

"The sheets were red. The walls. With blood. And then I saw my parents propped up against the wall. I thought they were sleeping." Shuddering, she closed her eyes. "I didn't know. I was just a little girl."

Sympathetic fury flashed through Jacob like a summer storm. "*Jesu*, what did he do with you?"

Her head moved against his shoulder, and she murmured something in words so soft he could not hear. He asked her to say it again. "He said, 'Let me help you.' But blood was on his hands. Like killing pigs. And then I understood."

"That he meant to kill you, too . . ." Jacob prodded, knowing in his heart the man intended more.

To his surprise, Retha raised her head and eked out a small, brave smile. "He did. He grabbed me, but I fought him like—harder than Anna Johanna ever fought a bath. Although perhaps not so hard as I fought you that night in the Square." She burrowed her face under his chin. "You see, I thought you meant to kill me like that, too."

"Ach, Liebling. Mein Gott." He lay his cheek on the crown of her head, reproaching himself that he had ever for a minute added to her pain. "I never suspected that. I never would have hurt you. In fact, although I was the victor in our scramble, my shins were black and blue for weeks. I think I fared somewhat the worse."

"So did he," she said with relish. "I bit him."

He tightened his hold on her, celebrating this trace of humor, hoping it foretold her breaking free of the shroud of memory. Whoever that depraved soldier had been, she had escaped his basest intentions. Of that, Jacob was sure. For she had come to their marriage whole in body. What would ever make her whole in mind and heart?

Her hurt was severe, if after so many years it was buried so deep that she only now remembered. He thought of how profoundly Christina's natural death had affected him and his children, and could scarcely imagine Retha's suffering after all that was loved and familiar had been ripped away.

"What can I say, *Liebling*? You were so very brave that day."

"Hold me, Jacob," she answered. And in a moment every bit as sweet as her surrender to his passion, he held her to his heart.

"Where are all the soldiers going, Papa?" Anna Johanna asked worriedly the next afternoon from her post at the parlor window.

"South, pumpkin . . ." Jacob said absently, his mind on designing a cobbler's bench as he sat at his desk.

With an insulted snort that he had dismissed her, she crossed the room to tug at his sleeve. "What's south?"

"South is that way." He pointed his quill pen toward the back of the house. South was where the Continental troops had massed under Nathaniel Green, fleeing ahead of the British. South was where Cornwallis hoped to catch up to them and end the war.

"Nicholas says there's going to be an awful fight."

Gritting his teeth against annoyance, Jacob looked up from his work. The would-be soldier had his little sister worrying that there would be a battle. At least the rascal was locked away at lessons today.

With the troops packing to march, Jacob had walked the boys to Brother Schopp's in the morning, brought them home for lunch, and escorted them back. And stayed home the rest of the day to ensure Anna Johanna and Retha's safety. Sim Scaife had not cleared out until early afternoon.

Jacob pulled Anna Johanna onto his lap. "Well, we're not worried about any fight coming here, are we?"

She studied his eyes with a penetrating, questioning scrutiny. "No-o . . ." she said doubtfully. Then she brightened. " 'Cause Matthias said he'd be praying and . . ." She clamped her pudgy hand over her mouth guiltily.

"Praying and what, pumpkin?" Jacob prodded, paternal suspicions aroused.

"Praying and . . . praying really hard."

She pasted on a sudden smile. Its falseness pricked at Jacob. Praying—and what? Matthias had always been the pious one, but what was he praying *for*? And what else was he up to?

Jacob abandoned the plans on his drafting table and set Anna Johanna down with her ever-present doll. "Why don't we ask Gertrude for some help with planning supper?"

Anna Johanna refused. "Mama Retha did all that."

So she had. Retha had been conscientiously domestic all day long. Burying herself, no doubt, in sheltering routines since the morning when he had caught her in the bedroom, clean sheets folded across her lap, staring off into space. Fearing another lapse into her state, he had helped her put the sheets away and given her a small, inquiring kiss. She had responded slightly, dreamily, as if he—or she—were not quite there. Work, he determined, was the better part of valor. He left her to it.

"Then I suppose we'll have to do the ark," he said, digging into the children's large wooden box of toys for their replica of Noah's ark. Its few dozen pairs of tiny animals were the scourge of parents with a mind for order.

They agreed to line them up by large to small and then by small to large. Then Anna Johanna thought of separating those that fly from those that swim from those that live off grass.

He grinned. "That ought to be interesting."

Soon geese and ducks and chickens flocked together, fish formed schools in an imaginary pond, and cows and deer and donkeys grazed on a rug, awaiting their turn at the gangplank.

"Whoops! That's not right." Anna Johanna giggled, striking her forehead with the heel of her hand. The gesture, so like one of Retha's, warmed Jacob's heart. Imitation had to be the sincerest sign that a child had accepted her new mother.

"What's not right, pumpkin?"

"Fish swim, but ducks do too. So . . . do ducks belong with the chickens or the fish?"

Soberly Jacob wagged his head. "A duck is not a fish."

Anna Johanna's eyes grew round. "How do you know that?"

For a moment he wasn't sure, and then he wasn't sure how to tell her. "Well, did you ever see a fish with feathers?"

"That's silly."

He laughed, and they applied themselves to their task. Animals with feathers, hooves, and paws soon cued up in rows before the gangplank while those with fins swam in the imagined pond.

Well pleased with at least one of his children, Jacob was stretching stiff muscles when a light rap came at the door.

Checking where he had left the club, he opened it, expecting Samuel Ernst had come to say the coast was clear.

Philip Schopp stood at street level with Matthias, looking up, one hand on the boy's shoulder. "Brother Blum," he began, but had to clear his throat. "Brother . . . Jacob. Your son—your other son, Nicholas—" Sweat beaded his upper lip. "Nicholas has disappeared."

"Disappeared! What do you mean, my son has disappeared?" Jacob's roar reverberated under the low beams of the kitchen ceiling. In front of Retha, dried herbs shuddered on the wall. Heart pounding, she dumped an apron full of half-shelled beans into a bowl and hurried to him.

"How could you let a single one of those boys out of your sight?" Jacob belted out. "Let alone this one. We have a hundred and eighty soldiers milling about our town."

Philip Schopp turned his flat-brimmed hat miserably in his hands. "May I—may we—come in?" An abject Matthias waited behind him.

Jacob inclined his head and stepped aside, controlling his rage with obvious effort.

The schoolmaster slumped through the narrow entry and into the parlor. Eyes brimming, Matthias ran to Retha. Touched by his trust, she held him to her side. Anna Johanna, evidently alarmed by her father's show of anger, took shelter with her, too.

"What makes you say he's missing, Brother Schopp?" Jacob demanded.

The Single Brother gave Retha an awkward sideways look. "Nicholas, um . . . asked to be excused, and I—I suppose he didn't come back."

"You suppose?" Jacob repeated sharply. "Up to now, you have kept an exceptionally keen eye on your troublemakers, Brother Schopp."

The man's long fingers worried the brim of his hat. "I was lecturing. History."

Jacob gave him a withering look, slammed into his coat, and headed for the door.

Schopp extended a bony hand to Jacob's sleeve. "May I ask where are you going, Brother Jacob?"

"To find my son." Jacob angrily punched out the words.

"We looked. I, the boys and I—we checked all through my house, the Brothers House, the barn. I asked at the Tavern."

Jacob exploded. "Then I will search the mill. The tannery. The cemetery."

Retha couldn't bear it. She had a terrible premonition where Nicholas had gone. She moved the children to stand together and stopped her husband at the door.

"Jacob, is it possible . . ." She could hardly bring herself to say the thought that troubled her, to hurt her husband as she knew she would. "Last night, he said he wanted to join the soldiers."

The Virginia regiment had left today. The unspoken thought flashed between them.

She saw the rage wash out of Jacob. "He went south," he said flatly.

"Perhaps," she answered softly. "Perhaps he has not gone far."

"I think not south, if I may be so bold," Schopp interrupted with a hitherto unplumbed humility. " 'Twas the militia men billeted with you, I believe, who captured his admiration."

Jacob's hand worked the back of his neck. "Sim Scaife. Another possibility, I admit. He even left late. But who will know which way my son has gone?"

"I regret to say that I cannot be sure," Schopp said. "If we bring the matter up at *Singstunde* tonight, someone there may know."

"No one can expect me to wait that long!"

Retha risked laying a sympathetic hand on Jacob's shoulder. "You cannot plunge off after him, not knowing—aught."

Gingerly, as if expecting a bear to swat him down, Schopp added, "She has the right of it. We must take the time to gather information."

"We?" Jacob's brow arched. "He's my son."

Schopp moaned with contrition. "But he is my student, and he disappeared on my watch. I will comb the town for aught that anyone might have seen. Aught that someone might know."

In an afternoon of few choices, Schopp's idea seemed to Retha to be the next reasonable step. The schoolmaster left, but his earnest assurance of aid failed to comfort her. Nicholas was in the gravest danger, and Jacob would turn the world upside down to find his son, putting his very life at risk. How odd, she thought. She and Nicholas had yet to exchange a civil word, and here she was, shaking at the thought of losing him as if she loved him like a mother. Not odd, however, that the idea of Jacob chasing through the hazard-ridden countryside made her heart pound with fear.

When they gathered in the parlor, Jacob singled out his younger son.

"What do you know about this?"

Matthias raised a thin shoulder in a defiant shrug.

Jacob almost punched the wall. "I need an answer, son. Not a shrug. Tell me where your brother is."

Matthias gave a small, determined huff. "I don't know where, sir."

"Do you know who he left with?"

"No, sir," Matthias said stoutly. But suspiciously, Jacob thought. Yet the boy's innate honesty won out. "Not exactly."

"You must do better than that."

"I think he went with soldiers."

Jacob clamped down on his rage. He was mad enough to lift the boy off the floor and shake the truth out of him. Desperate enough. Not that such a tactic would work. He couldn't even make this son eat.

"Matthias, I don't need for you to tell me that he went off with soldiers. We have guessed that. I need to know which ones."

Matthias squared his thin shoulders. "He said he couldn't tell me, sir."

"You knew. Since when?"

"Only since Latin. Today, Latin class was after lunch."

"He told you he was going—he had a plan—but would not tell you who he was going with?"

"He didn't want me impre—imprecated—"

"Implicated." Jacob bit off the word, then took a

short, angry walk around the room, coming back under a full head of steam. "You are implicated, son. Listen, I am very angry with him and more than a little angry with you. You knew what he was up to, you knew he was wrong, and you stood by while he ran off. I'm surprised he didn't try to talk you into going along."

"He wouldn't let me go. He needed me to stay behind to . . ." Matthias blurted out loyally but then trailed off.

"To stay behind to what? Spell it out."

Matthias backed up against Retha, and she shielded him behind her arms. Jacob clenched his jaw. Couldn't she see the boy didn't need a mother to protect him now?

"To pray, sir."

"To pray?" To pray for what? For forgiveness after he had run away? Not likely.

Rash, bold-hearted Nicholas never gave a fig for consequences. Then it struck Jacob. Nicholas had asked for his brother's prayers because he planned to fight. Responsible of him, Jacob thought, giving Nicholas grudging credit for making sure his prayerful little brother had a reason to stay home. Outrageous of him, Jacob simmered, to enlist his brother's aid in any way at all in this hot-headed, irresponsible scheme.

Jacob gave the skin on Matthias's thin arm a disciplinary tweak. "He wanted you to pray for him in battle."

"Not for *him*, Papa," Matthias said proudly. "For victory."

"Gut Gott im Himmel," Jacob half prayed, half

cursed. "My son is headed for destruction."

Standing behind Matthias, Retha pried Jacob's hand off him. "They can't take Nicholas. He's too young."

Her well-meant reassurance missed its mark. In a pinch, Nicholas could pass for seventeen, and fourteen-year-olds enlisted. As standard bearers. In the front lines.

"Oh, but they can take him," Jacob said grimly. "They will do so gladly."

"I have no news," Brother Schopp said when he met Retha and Jacob outside the *Saal* before *Singstunde.* Some boys cheered Nicholas's escapade, but only Matthias had been his confidante.

Leaving her husband to canvass members of the community, Retha led the children inside and found a bench.

A few minutes later Jacob sat down heavily. "No luck," he said, still angry but with a new note of anguish in his voice.

She put her hand on his, feeling the inadequacy of the only comfort she could offer.

The choir was singing its final chorale when she became aware of someone large hulking behind her, whispering to Jacob.

After the music ended, he introduced Cousin Andreas. Much darker than Jacob, he too was tall and powerful, and for the moment he was somber. "The new recruit was Nicholas, without a doubt, but I only caught a glimpse."

"They wouldn't let you speak to him?" Retha

heard the slight waver of desperation in Jacob's voice. It was no match for the quake that struck her heart. Nicholas at risk left no doubt that her husband would gallop into the breech.

"That was the curious part," Andreas continued. "They would not confirm his name. Only that he enlisted."

After dark, Retha watched her husband head south with Andreas, he on the little tavern hack and Andreas on a great draft horse. Andreas joked that no one would have to walk this time, his humor irrepressible even in a crisis.

Several Single and Married Brothers had argued that they should come along, threatening to rescue Nicholas with clubs and rusty muskets. But Jacob put the idea of a Moravian uprising instantly to rest. Among them, he was the one accustomed to dealing with armies. The town needed all the Brethren at home. Their numbers ensured its safety. All Jacob wanted was a certificate stating that he himself had paid the threefold tax and another dating his son's birth. Frederick Marshall speedily prepared both.

"You keep the children safe," Jacob implored Retha, tucking the certificates into his coat. Then he kissed her with a resolution that shook her to her core. "I will be home soon. We will, my son and I. Be safe, *Liebling.* I love you," he said hoarsely, then mounted his horse and galloped out of town.

For the children's sake, she curbed her joy. In this crisis, in the presence of her worried children, it wouldn't do for her to spin about the room, breaking into an Indian maiden's dance of celebration.

But her husband loved her. *Loved her.* He had said so.

She also hid her fears. It wouldn't do to rail to the children about the dangers to which Nicholas had exposed himself and his father. With the recent upheavals in their young lives, they needed evenhandedness, a sense of nothing terribly wrong.

Matthias gamely tried to teach her to spin a wooden top his father had made him, but her ineptness defeated him. After a while, upstairs, she helped Anna Johanna dress her doll for bed and say a simple child's prayer, and tucked her in. Then she turned to Matthias's room.

He knelt as he did every evening, Bible open on his narrow cot, his head bent and hands tightly clasped in prayer. Flawlessly he repeated a longer version of the child's prayer and added a request for his father's and brother's safety. Retha smiled, resting a moment against the doorjamb while he finished. He was such a good, serious little boy.

Then he ended fervently, "I promise not to stop fasting ever again. Amen."

Retha blinked, disbelieving, peering into the dark.

Fasting! Sudden understanding flooded her. All along, her rain-thin stepson had been fasting. His puzzling, wasting illness made perfect sense. Who would have guessed? And wherever had he gotten that idea? Moravians were more apt to feast than fast. No one would have set him such an example or encouraged him in this. She sank to the floor beside him, praying the right words would come.

"Matthias, we didn't know that you were fasting."

He jerked around, scowling. "That was my secret!"

"Your secret?"

"Between me and God."

Spinning the top was easier than this, Retha thought, at a loss for Matthias's meaning and for her next words. "But why, son? You could have told us. You should have told your father."

"I couldn't either." He paused, his fingers knotting the bed covers.

"Your father's been awfully worried about you."

"I was doing it for him," he said angrily.

"You were fasting for your father?" she asked carefully.

Matthias stubbornly tucked his head down.

She guessed that meant yes. "You didn't have to fast for him."

"I did, too," he said, disclosing nothing.

Biding time, Retha moved his Bible to the little bedside table where a slender taper burned. Extracting confessions from children was not her forte. After a long while, she said, "Umm. I don't understand, Matthias. Help me."

With a great sigh of defeat, Matthias flung himself into the bed. "Doesn't matter anyway. I don't think it's working."

"Ah. Just how is a fast supposed to work?"

He muttered toward the wall. " 'Twas meant to purify me. That's what Brother Schopp said."

The hair on the back of Retha's neck prickled with anger. Already Philip Schopp was not in her good graces. "He told you to fast?"

"Not quite."

"Then perhaps you could explain it to me." She reached to tuck him in but smoothed the thin summer coverlet instead. "So that I could understand."

He shook his head.

"Seriously, Matthias. We have to tell your father. I would like to know why, myself—before he gets home."

"He's never coming home."

"Of course he will. He always does," she said with a confidence she didn't fully feel. Jacob's wartime missions were always dangerous.

He cast her a withering look. "My mother didn't."

His mother? Retha's mind raced to follow the boy's leap in logic.

"True enough," she conceded. "Your mother died in *Gemein Haus*, where we nursed all the sick Sisters in the epidemic. But your father doesn't have smallpox, and I still don't understand why you've been fasting."

He snatched his Bible from the table, opened to the Book of Matthew—his book, she thought—and pointed her to chapter and verse.

Which he cited from memory, flawlessly, while she read along. Jesus fasted in the wilderness forty days and forty nights and told Satan that man did not live by bread alone.

"That doesn't explain why you're fasting," she said.

He scowled at her grown-up stupidity. "Brother Schopp says that Jesus fasted to purify his soul of all his childish sins before he started on his ministry."

"What sins of yours concern you, Matthias?" she

asked gently, keeping her disapproval of the schoolmaster to herself. She was no theologian, but Brother Schopp had surely skewed the text.

Matthias took a minute to reply. "Sometimes I hate my brother. And even Anna Johanna when she pitches fits. If I weren't so bad, God wouldn't have taken my mother away."

"God didn't take your mother away because you were bad, Matthias. It doesn't work that way."

"But I promised God I would purify myself and never sin again if he would let me keep my father."

Retha felt the sting of hot tears. Once she would have done the exact same thing to bring back Singing Stones, to save her dimly remembered parents. Anything. What a lonely, impossible task Matthias had set for himself.

"God won't hold you to that promise, Matthias. He really doesn't want you to starve yourself to death."

"Even if I sin?"

"He understands we can't help sinning sometimes."

Matthias closed his Bible reluctantly. "Are you sure?"

"Sure as the sun's going to rise tomorrow."

"There's bound to be something I'm supposed to do."

She tilted her head and gave it a moment's thought. "Do what you always try to do. Be as good a boy as you can be."

"That's all?"

"Well, you can keep on praying. You can ask Him to bless your brother and your father and grant them a safe return."

His earnest face relaxed, showing his natural purity. "And I really don't have to fast anymore?"

"Never."

A new shy deviltry lit his gaunt features. "Then, can I have a piece of sugarcake before I go to sleep?"

On the second day after Retha's husband left, Sim Scaife returned and posted young Calloway outside her door.

"You!" she said, taken aback on seeing him as she and Anna Johanna escorted Matthias to school. "What are you doing here?"

The fuzzy-cheeked private shrugged, not impolitely. "Cap'n posted me here, ma'am."

"For how long?" And why? She wondered grimly. Jacob's absence, and the reason for it, were the talk of the town. Scaife must have heard. Why else had he come back? Why else post a guard? The fervent militia man would approve of Nicholas's throwing in his lot with the Continentals as much as he would disapprove of Jacob's intended rescue. Cousin Andreas tagging along would only remind him of yet another able-bodied Moravian whom Jacob had plucked from honorable service.

Again Calloway shrugged. "Long's he says so, ma'am."

His deference made her feel older, established, but his presence jarred her confidence. Now that Scaife must know Jacob had left her alone with her husband's younger children, could she care for them?

Her children now, she thought fiercely, clasping

Anna Johanna's hand while nudging Matthias along. Given Nicholas's disappearance, she would not let these two have a moment unattended.

Except for a midday trek to bring Matthias home for lunch—which he wolfed down—and return him to his lessons, Retha spent the day with her stepdaughter, putting the finishing touches on the deerskin dress.

She should have mended the boys' ever-raveling clothes, Retha thought. Or tended the dwindling garden. Instead, she sought old Indian comforts of satiny leather and soft suede, and hid her growing uneasiness.

In spite of Calloway's presence, Retha refused to take Anna Johanna and go to *Gemein Haus* with the Single Sisters. She and her stepdaughter could stay there together, but Matthias would have been alone with the Single Brothers, safe but not secure. Retha could not abide leaving him alone. She planned to oversee every bite of food he took for the next month.

A rumble of rude voices cut into her thoughts. Armed with only the heavy needle she was using, she hurried to the door.

Sim Scaife eyed it with mock wariness. "Not a very friendly greeting, *Frau* Blum."

"My husband is not here," she explained, then bit her tongue for admitting to her vulnerability.

"The more room for us, then," he grinned, indicating the four men around him.

"The Virginians left yesterday. Surely there is space at the Tavern."

He shook his head in affected sympathy. "New

detachment of higher-ups. Bumped us right out on our—behinds." He tipped his sweat-stained hat as if his choice of a less crude word made him a gentleman.

Unimpressed, Retha stood by, heart thudding with dread. The men invaded her parlor, piling up bedrolls but not yet shedding their weapons. She could not stay here. Her children could not be put in such jeopardy.

The men left, but Scaife lingered. She pretended to ignore his presence as she finished the last seam of the deerskin dress. Anna Johanna played amidst the scattered clothing she had taken off her porcelain doll.

Scaife nodded at her. "Pretty little girl."

Retha clenched her teeth. A needle was no defense.

Without warning, he reached down and swung the child off the floor into his spidery grasp. Too stunned to pitch a fit, Anna Johanna whimpered.

"I still don't know your name, honey," he said, his mouth too close to the child's sweet face.

Flaming to action, Retha stripped her stepdaughter from the man's arms and clasped her to her bosom.

"You never will," she hissed at their tormentor, praying her stepdaughter would not erupt. "You will never, ever know her name."

Remorseless, Sim Scaife showed his teeth. "I always knew yours." Then he sauntered out the door.

He knew her name, she thought with numbing dread. And he still preyed on little girls.

Escape, she resolved, was her only choice.

Shaking all over, she packed a bundle. Food, flint, candles, cloth, and one good hunting knife. She rolled up a quilt off the boys' bed. Retreating to the Single Sisters House would not assure Anna Johanna's safety from a determined Sim Scaife. They had to disappear, not as Nicholas had done. They had to vanish.

She would take the children to the cave. In her memory, the shelter by the waterfall had hidden her, had kept her safe.

Anna Johanna's face crumpled when Retha pulled off her shift, but Retha ignored her protest and jammed the deerskin dress on over her head. Teamed with her sturdy buckled shoes, the Indian dress looked odd, but the combination should protect her over rocks and through the briars and brambles they would face.

"Look at your dress, sweet potato. 'Tis all finished," Retha whispered, fluffing the dress around her, pleased. It fit the girl but gave her room to grow.

Anna Johanna wriggled under the sueded inside of the dress and tested its satiny outer finish. "Feels . . . soft."

"You can wear it to the woods."

A reluctant smile teased the corner of Anna Johanna's mouth. "Can I wear it in the creek?"

"Only for wading, sweet potato, and then you have to take your shoes off."

Calloway was still posted at the front door. With her stepdaughter, Retha gathered the bedroll and the bundle of supplies and started out the back door.

But how would Jacob find them? she thought suddenly. She couldn't leave a note. Scaife's crew would doubtless spot it and attempt to track her.

There had to be some way to leave a message. She paced a troubled circle around the kitchen table, a worrying habit she had learned from him.

A clue. She needed to leave a clue, one so obvious that Jacob couldn't mistake it, but no one else could comprehend it. Her hand went to her hair where she had worn the indigo sprig.

"It matches your eyes," she had said that day, offering it to him beside the waterfall.

Playfully he had hooked it over her ear. "Wear it for me," he had whispered. "I'll be watching over you."

She had worn the sprig until it wilted. But its blue petals had not faded. Today she laid it on Anna Johanna's bed, certain Jacob would search the house when he came back and found them gone.

A nearby alley gave them a shortcut to Brother Schopp's house where Matthias had just been let out. A thundering herd of boys chased a ball across the Square. Retha stood by the rail fence, waiting for Matthias to notice her, afraid to draw the other boys' attention.

Finally he glanced her way. She lifted her bundle shoulder high, and he frowned. Then his gaze took in Anna's dress, and he trotted over.

"We have to leave the town for a while," Retha told him.

Awed, he whistled. "Are we going after Nicholas, too?"

"Better than that. We are going to stay in a cave until Nicholas and your father are safely home."

He gave her a doubtful look. "An Indian cave?"

"Could be," she said mysteriously.

CHAPTER 18

"I'll carry it," Matthias insisted. With a poignant manliness, he took over Retha's bundle. "It ought to be my burden if you've got to carry her."

Gratefully Retha relinquished their supplies. They were halfway to the waterfall and the cave above it. She had miscalculated the hardships of a trek with a skittery five-year-old girl and a sober ten-year-old boy. With them and without Jacob, the woods were fraught with dangers she hadn't noticed as a girl, difficulties she hadn't experienced as a woman: hills too steep, branches too low, briars and vines too abundant. Distances too far. Too far from the joy and pleasures she had shared with Jacob such a short time ago.

But up against those pleasures were the terrible memories she had also shared with him. She had had no time to absorb the awful truth: Sim Scaife, the man she fled with her children, had murdered her parents and tried to murder her.

Deliberately, she blocked that memory. She had no time to linger on old hurts. She had escaped him then. She would escape him now. But they had to hurry. The cave was not so very far, she reassured herself. And it would be safe. It had hidden her before. She hitched Anna Johanna a little higher on her back.

"Mama Retha, did you see that?" Her voice trembled.

"See what?" Matthias called from behind them.

"It looked like a deer to me, sweet potato," Retha lied, loudly.

She, too, had seen something as the children crashed through the underbrush. For the third time, it had flashed alongside them. Her wolf, she hoped, but it had been too quick to say for sure. It could be something else, but her entourage of children would scare off almost anything. Besides, deer were noisier than that flashing shadow, chuffing to alert their herd and crashing through the brambles. Raccoons slept in the daytime, and rabbits were too shy. A turkey would fly up. A bear, unless they disturbed it, would not pursue. A panther would not stalk. Would it?

Just in case, she stopped and shredded her neckerchief and apron, remembering Singing Stone's training. A few pieces left behind would give predators something to attack, and no harm done to her.

An hour of daylight remained when they reached the waterfall. The children oohed and aahed with wonder, their itches, scratches, and fatigue allayed all at once. Retha kept a watchful eye on them while settling their belongings in the cave. Even in its cooler space, the night would be too warm to need a fire. In the lazy, shallow stream above the waterfall, Matthias hopped from stone to stone. Obediently shucking her shoes, Anna Johanna waded in the water, squealing with faked fear when she got close enough to see the pool below.

For supper, Retha summoned them to sit under the mouth of the cave and handed out dried pumpkin, cheese, a hunk of bread.

"There it is!" Anna Johanna whispered, panicked.

Retha scanned the forest at the stream's edge, opposite.

"What? Is it a bear?" Matthias asked eagerly.

"Panther," Anna Johanna choked out.

In the dusk through the brambles, a dark shape flashed.

"Shhh. Be very still," Retha said, now certain she had seen her wolf. "'Tis neither. She won't come if we are noisy."

"She?" Anna Johanna asked.

Retha dug into the bundle for a scrap of meat and held it in her hand. "My wolf."

"Your wolf?" Matthias asked.

"She was hurt, and let me nurse her. Now she's better," Retha assured them. "She likes bacon."

"I like bacon." Anna Johanna giggled.

"Shhh . . ." Matthias hissed, attention riveted on the tangles. "I want to see her. Will she really come for bacon?"

"Perhaps," Retha said. "Just wait." She steered them back with her hand. "Now, you stand well behind me."

A wood thrush's evening song fluted over the low, incessant roar of the falls. Finally Anna

Johanna stood up and dusted off her hands.

"Well, I don't think she's coming."

But the wolf did come. Retha sensed its presence. She looked upstream, then down. It skirted the falls, crossed the stream, and climbed the bank to stand at the edge of the cave.

"There," she pointed, holding her palm out flat for both the children and the wolf to see. "Don't move. She doesn't know you yet." She glanced back over her shoulder.

The children stood stock-still. Slowly the wolf came forward, one cautious, curious step at a time. It snatched the bacon from Retha's palm and retreated to the lip of the cave.

"Is she going to hurt us?" Anna Johanna asked, worried.

"Is she going to stay?" Matthias asked, hopeful.

"She might not stay, but she won't hurt us."

The wolf stayed through the night. In the morning, it lurked behind them as they explored the cave. They could not go far. It was but a few child-sized paces to the back wall, and the slanted morning light penetrated just that far. Later, after they gathered at the cave's mouth to eat, the wolf again edged nearer, waiting for another handout.

It wasn't as if it needed any, Retha thought, amused by the wolf's tenacity. She checked her bundle to see what she could spare.

Another bit of bacon. She offered it. The wolf gave a low, menacing growl. Alarmed, she tossed the bacon over, aiming at the wolf's large paws. It gulped down the handout.

And growled again. Unasked, the children

huddled behind Retha. With a sinking feeling, she brought out her knife from its sheath in her bottomless pocket. The wolf had never threatened her, but she hardened herself for an attack.

Hackles bristling, it snarled across the creek.

Over the roar of the falls, Retha soon made out men's voices. Jacob! She thought with relief. And Nicholas.

Men crashed through the underbrush. Too many to be Jacob and his son. Curses floated across the stream.

"Hide, children!" she whispered, pushing them into the cave. "Hide everything! Hurry! Go back as far as you can."

Quilt and all, they sunk into shadows, silent as little Indians. Grim and determined, Retha clenched her knife behind her back. Scaife splashed across the stream, Calloway and Pickens following him.

Scaife called out to her. "You left us a clear trail."

Her free hand went to her throat. Her neckerchief and apron were gone, left behind to assuage some predatory beast. Instead, her offerings to guard against wild predators had been an open invitation to this human brute.

"You won't escape me this time, Lillibet." He was but an arm's length away from her.

"My name is not Lillibet," Retha gritted out, perplexed and certain all at once.

He took a step closer. "Oh, pardon. We're all grown up and formal now, are we? You were a pretty little thing, Elisabeth Harmon."

Her throat tightened. The name tickled her

mind with an odd familiarity. "You know my name."

He fingered one of her braids. She smacked his hand away.

His eyes widened mockingly. "That hair was a clue. But them yellow eyes was a dead giveaway. Just like your mother's."

Anger raked her. He *knew* her parents. "Who were they, Captain Scaife? Tell me what you knew of them. Before you murdered them."

"We never call it murder when it's Tories, do we, men?"

His men guffawed in agreement. Pickens seemed almost as crude and dangerous as Scaife. Calloway looked on with a panting fascination. Retha would not acknowledge them.

She glowered, however, at Scaife. "Unarmed Tories. That's murder."

"Thieving, lying Tories," he said with dark condemnation.

"You're the thief. You stole their lives."

"They stole my property. Mine by rights. Our father gave it to her for marrying that Tory."

Our father? Confusion crashed in Retha's head, louder than the roaring of the falls below. Did he mean his father? Could he mean her mother's father? Merciful God, could they be the same?

Like a skinny orange cat teasing its victim, Sim Scaife watched her. She would not flinch.

"What are you talking about?" she rasped.

His pale, watery brown eyes glinted with triumph. "I'm talking about my father. Your mother's father. Your grandfather, Lillibet."

Retha's stomach knotted. Brother and sister. Her mother's faintly remembered, flame-colored tresses almost matched Sim Scaife's neglected, brassier hair. And his eyes . . . her eyes, her own unusual pale brown eyes. She almost retched.

"I am no kin to you."

"Yes, you are. My own sweet little niece. Your mother, Eleanor Scaife, married that Tory father of yours and finagled our father, Simon Scaife, out of half my inheritance."

"My parents had property?"

He waved his hand upstream, downstream. "They thought they did. They thought they owned this nice little tract of land, all five thousand acres of it, including this waterfall. And I still want it back."

"This is Moravian land." She was sure of it.

"That, dear niece, is in dispute. It should have come to me. And I will have it. After you and me take care of some other unfinished business."

Absorbing his lurid gaze, she had no doubt what that other business was. She steadied her breathing, buying time. She wasn't raped yet. She wasn't dead. And she would not betray the children. She had fought him once before. This time she would fight him to the death.

Her hand tightened on her knife. He was close enough, but too alert.

"You'll like to do it in the water, Lillibet." He chuckled grotesquely. "I like to do it there. Better than I would have in your parents' bloody bed."

She remembered cowering under it, and suddenly the rest of that horrible day flooded Retha's mind.

"What the hell's going on here?" came a shout from outside the cabin.

Under the bed, the cruel bony hand scrabbled after her. She curled herself into a ball, the bed's slats digging into the bones of her back. "Not a peep, missy." Eyes widening with fear, she watched the hand slap on the floor in defeat and retreat.

"Tories, sir." The purring voice was loud now. "Murdering Tories. Tried to kill me."

Shivering at the touch of spider webs, she looked out. Polished black boots strode up to ragged leggings. There was an oath, words she didn't comprehend.

"Not the woman too, private."

"She come at me with a poker."

"Not bloody likely."

The boots and leggings scrambled. She heard blows struck, grunts, curses. Then they left. And she was all alone.

"Who stopped you, Uncle? That day you murdered my parents?"

He spit into the flowing stream. "Martin Armstrong, the dog. And he's dogged me ever since. But he'll not show up to rescue you this time. Or the little one. I saw the trail. I know she's here."

Snarling with outrage, she lunged with her knife. Grabbing her wrist to save himself, he jumped back, chuckling as if her spirit pleased him. As if he wanted her resistance.

"You will touch her with your last breath," Retha warned.

" 'Course, a grown woman like this one'll fight you, Calloway," he called over his shoulder.

Both men waded to his aid. He waved them off. With one hand on her wrist and an arm snaked around her waist, he dipped her toward the stream. "When I'm done with you," he breathed into Retha's face, "I'll find the little girl."

Fifteen years of anger wrested her knife hand free of his control. She slashed at his face. Connected. Watched as the blade etched a clean, straight line across his forehead, the bridge of his nose, and down his cheek. His blood spurted in her face, blinding her, disgusting her.

He howled, thrusting her away but still gripping her wrists. She tumbled backwards into the stream, onto its rocks, and he stumbled with her. Her wrist struck a boulder, dislodging the knife from her hand. A sharp pain pierced her side, and she gasped for breath. She managed to free a hand and swipe the blood from her eyes.

Roughly he bundled her skirts up to her waist and maneuvered his thin body over the split between her legs. He hovered over her, fresh blood dripping onto her.

This blood did not scare her. This man did not.

He would never breathe another easy breath.

She had lost her knife. She would fight him with her last ounce of strength. With her teeth, if she had to.

Like a wild woman. Like her wolf.

Thrusting up with her knees, she hit his thighs and threw him off balance. A hot poker of pain stabbed her side where she had fallen, rocks scraped her back, and the sand gave way beneath her feet. But she would have her revenge.

Revenge for her lost childhood.

Revenge for her long-lost parents.

Her Cherokee heart demanded it.

"Ha! Little witch," he grunted, struggling to mount her as she twisted beneath him. Her nostrils wrinkled at the reek of sweat, of old, unwashed clothes. "You only get away from me once, hussy."

He lowered his body again and covered her in a nauseating parody of the love that Jacob had introduced her to. Scaife's rail-thin shoulder butted into her face. She sank her teeth into it, tossing her head like a wolf with fresh kill, aiming to tear flesh.

Yowling a scurrilous curse, he wrenched away and landed a fist upside her head. Her ears rang. But she could hear his threat. "All right, we'll do it the hard way. Pickens, get over here. Calloway, you're new at this. You hold that leg."

Men swarmed around her in a blur of bloody buckskin and militia linen. She kicked out, clawed a face, bit an arm, elbowed flesh and bone. They struck back at her head, her jaw, and her torso. Pain ripped through her. Until she had the satisfaction of making a man cry out.

And felt the wild desire for pure revenge.

They would not have her living body.

She would not leave them whole enough to touch her little daughter.

And at least one of them, she vowed, would not live to see tomorrow.

"Hold her, damn it! I can't see," Scaife shouted. Blood streamed down his face.

"God willing, you never will," a deep voice growled.

It was Jacob's voice, rich and strong and furious. Her heart leaped with gratitude and recognition. He had come for her.

In an instant, she was free, Scaife's repulsive weight lifted off her body. There was an awful churning in the water, and despair swamped her sweet relief. What could one man and a boy do against armed soldiers? She tormented herself as the green, watery world around her went black.

Jacob's heart compressed in horror in his chest the instant he comprehended Retha's state. Drenched in blood, the very thing she feared the most, she lay broken on the rocks, unconscious in the shallow stream. Water lapped around her sodden skirts, and her braids floated like twin water snakes around her head.

Her bruised and battered head.

He had come too late to save her.

With a roar, he spun Scaife around and rammed his belly with a fist powered by the full force of his massive arm and shoulder and his outraged heart.

The man doubled over, blood from his head dripping into the stream. Jacob heard grunts and splashing behind him.

"The rest are mine!" Andreas shouted.

"Nicholas!" Jacob ordered. "Into the cave."

Scaife staggered up, clutching his stomach. "No rules this time, Blum. Just you and me. And her. She ain't dead yet."

Hope drove Jacob to check, to see. Retha's arm

floated in the water. Her hand twitched. Her eyes fluttered open. Relief flooded his heart.

"Jacob! Look out!" Andreas yelped.

Too late. Something cracked across the back of Jacob's neck, and bodies tumbled into him, forcing him down on one knee.

"I got one, Papa!"

Jacob glanced up. A very large, frenzied Nicholas rode Calloway like a young bear on an ill-fated buck.

Feet sliding off wet rocks and finding little purchase in the sand, Jacob managed to right himself and join the fray.

"Into the cave," he bellowed, tearing his fiery son off the private's back. Nicholas resisted Jacob as hard as he had fought the private, but Jacob caught him in a chokehold and pointed him toward the cave. Without warning, someone plowed into Jacob, tackling his legs. Scaife. Jacob had no choice. He released his son and engaged the captain. Locked in combat, they fought close, each landing a volley of short jabs into the other's body, thrusting and parrying to the edge of the falls.

Jacob saw the danger first and reached to pull Scaife back.

His old enemy dodged him, slipped on a mossy stone, and grabbed Jacob's arms. For a precarious moment, Jacob balanced them both on the slab of shale that defined the fall's rim.

Under the soles of his boots, the shale shifted.

Jacob gestured with his head. "One move will do us in, man. Leap back," he urged. "Together."

Eyes aglitter with insane purpose, Scaife tightened his hold. "Water'll even my odds."

The shale crumbled. Then there was only air and arms and knees and a punishing wall of water, and then no air at all. End over end, they tumbled into the pool, plunging down to its hard rock bottom.

Unexpectedly, unaccountably, Jacob found himself free, upside down, and struggling against torrents of raging water. At last his feet found rock again, and he pushed off and up, lungs heaving.

"Papa! Papa!" Nicholas's screams descended on him as he broke the surface.

"Get back!" Jacob choked out. What was Nicholas doing at the fall's edge? He could not give way to despair. He sucked in precious air.

Scaife was not in sight. Jacob dove back into the churning, clouded pool. Searching blind. Searching for the enemy. To save his wretched carcass. Something heavy butted Jacob's hip. A tree limb? An arm? A leg? He reached for it. It rolled away. Bursting through the surface of the water, he gasped a lungful of air and dove in again.

The pool was ceaseless turbulence and opacity. He crawled along the bottom, along rock worn smooth. The falling water pummeled his back until his lungs shrieked for air. A third time he broke the surface. Scaife's body floated in the eddies, his yellow eyes dull but open wide. Jacob stroked his way to calmer water and eyed Scaife with profound loathing.

"You're a dead man if you raped my wife," Jacob said through clenched teeth.

Scaife spit up water. "Just wanted . . . one more chance at . . . little Lillibet, Blum."

In the heat of the day, the warmth of shallow water, Jacob froze. "Little Lillibet? One more chance? What do you mean?"

"Came this close before. When she was . . . little girl." Half-strangled, half-dead, Scaife taunted him still.

Jacob cursed the black oath. He hadn't guessed. All along, Retha had protected him from knowing it was Scaife. From his own wrath. "You never had her, you perverted monster," he growled.

Scaife grinned feebly, unrepentant. "Sure as hell tried."

Jacob erupted from the pool, water streaming down his body, lunging for the man with a mind to murder him.

Scaife did not resist. Could not resist. The captain's body was as uncooperative as a sack of sand. Jacob hauled him up to the creek's bank, reminding himself he was a Christian man, reciting chapter and verse. The wrong verse. *An eye for an eye, a tooth for a tooth* ricocheted in his mind. He looked down on his loathsome burden's narrow, corrupt face. His wife's tormentor. Her family's murderer.

Against Jacob's abdomen, Scaife's body flopped strangely, the head lolling back. The man was losing consciousness. Jacob arranged his uncooperative body on the rocky shore.

Jacob fought a raging urge to smother the man in the humus of the forest floor.

"Can't move, Blum," Scaife mumbled. "Can't feel a . . . blamed thing."

Jacob bent over him and checked his arms and legs for movement, for feeling. Nothing. He sat back on his heels.

"Your neck's broken, Captain Scaife," he said, against his will granting the man some final dignity.

Scaife gazed at him unsteadily. "Well, then, the joke's on me," he grunted. "See that my . . . niece don't cheat . . . you out of the damned land."

He was incoherent, Jacob thought. Scaife's eyes rolled back, one last breath rattled out, and he was gone. Solemnly Jacob closed Scaife's eyelids and stood, feeling both avenged and thwarted, both relieved and unsatisfied.

Retha. He wanted, needed Retha, the consolation, the assurance of her touch. He climbed the rugged incline to the cave, pulling himself up the thickly growing vines hand over hand.

Cautiously. He had no weapons, and he hadn't heard a sound since Nicholas last screamed. Hidden by bushes at the top, Jacob paused, heart thudding with new alarm. The stream was quiet, the stones flat, the water low, the sun glancing off ripples. But there was not a soul in sight.

No soldiers. No cousin. No children. No wife.

"Retha!" Jacob howled in anguish.

"Get us out of here!" Andreas's angry voice yelled back from inside the cave.

God help us all, Jacob prayed, charging in without a second thought. Whatever had gone wrong, they needed him. His children needed him. His wife needed him.

Or, if they had been somehow carried off and Andreas left behind, he had to know. He ducked under the overhang and stood, his head bumping into the low ledge. Slowly his eyes adjusted to the light, but nothing was immediately clear.

"Where is everyone?" he called out.

"Shhh!" The warning hissed under the cave's dome.

"What? Who is in here?"

"Jacob, shhh! 'Tis us, your family. All of us."

And there was Retha, standing to one side, a child sheltered under either arm. He looked around the shallow cave, remembering its shape from the day Retha brought him here. Along the opposite wall, Andreas and Nicholas stood pressed stiffly against damp moss. At their feet, bound together back to back, Pickens and Calloway hunched miserably.

Only a couple of paces away stood Retha's wolf—for, with a sudden lift of his heart, Jacob knew it could be no other. Its hackles raised, it guarded its four prisoners, at attention, in complete control.

"What is this?" Jacob whispered to Retha.

"I have to get her out of here," she whispered back. "She thinks all men the enemy. I thought you were dead."

Anna Johanna giggled. "Mama Retha was afraid the waterfall would hurt you, Papa. But I told her that it couldn't."

"We tried to drag her out of the water, but she got mad," Matthias added.

"I did not. 'Twas not the thing for you to see me that way."

"Right," Matthias said with approving relish.

"She was wet, and she got blood all over and had to wash it off. But she's all cleaned up now."

"*Kusine,* get us out of here!" Andreas barked.

Retha scrambled to the floor, ransacking what looked to be remnants of a bundle of supplies. "If I could just find something!"

"We're out of bacon," Matthias said unhelpfully. "That's the only thing she eats."

"Well, I know that," Retha shot back. "She will like something, but I don't see a thing but sugarcake."

"That's my sugarcake! Besides, wolves don't eat sugarcake."

"We better hope she does, Matthias, because 'tis all that we have left."

Jacob's heart swelled with pride as he heard the ease of their exchange. Something had happened between Retha and his children in all the times he had been away. And this time. Something wonderful. In the year since his children had lost their mother, they hadn't laughed or joked or even complained with such lightness of heart. And here his starved son Matthias was, arguing over his right to keep his sugarcake from a wolf.

"We just want out!" Andreas reminded them impatiently.

"Andreas." Retha heard her own voice echo in the small chamber. "If you would but sit down and be less *threatening,* my friend the wolf would back down. I promise she won't hurt you."

"With all due respect, *Kusine,* I prefer to take my chances standing up."

Speaking softly, Retha edged up to her wolf, a

step at a time as always, and placed a small square of sugarcake on the ground.

The wolf lowered its head, sniffed, and gulped the food.

Retha stepped back, set down another bit, and waited, trusting in the bond she had forged with the animal—and its weakness for pantry scraps.

With a hasty look back at the men it had guarded, the wolf abandoned them and followed until Retha's trail of food led it well beyond the cave. The sun struck Retha's eyes, blinding her for a moment, and the wolf slipped away with scarcely a sound. Retha blinked into the underbrush, seeing nothing, until the wolf lunged through the bushes up to the top of the cave. Then she heard panting and a whimper from above the cave's dark mouth.

Another wolf, taller, more robust, with silvered fur. Her wolf's mate, come for her? Their wagging, snuffling reunion gave Retha a tingle of pleasure. She had saved her wolf so it could have this match. They disappeared together into the forest foliage, the wolf she had befriended, whose freedom in the wild had made her long for freedom, too, with its chosen mate.

She herself had found new freedoms, Retha thought, turning eagerly to her family. Inside the cave, Jacob had a son under each arm and a daughter on his back.

"I can help with these appendages, *Kusine*," Andreas said gravely, taking Anna Johanna's hand and bowing formally to her. "If madame would like a ride."

She giggled and flung out her arms. "Gallop?"

"I'd best stick to an old nag's trot. This poor horse has been galloping since the break of dawn."

But Andreas hoisted her up onto his broad shoulders as if her weight and his fatigue were of no consequence.

Retha turned to her husband. "My wolf is gone," she said, feeling a little sad. "My wolf found her mate. I suppose I have seen the last of her."

"I think you know where to find her now," he answered, and gave her a hungry, searching look. He meant that she could come back and find the wolf here. Come back with him. Here, where they had met the wolf. Here, where they had found their passion.

"I hope we do find her again," Matthias said, oblivious to the emotion that flowed between his parents. "That is, if she doesn't want any more of my sugarcake."

"What I want is to go home," Nicholas said wearily.

Retha could see Jacob hug his prodigal son closer. "I want you home, too, son," he said in a choked voice. "You fought like a tiger for our family today, but now we need you safe at home."

Nicholas's arms tightened around his father. "I'm so sorry I ran off with the soldiers, Papa. I thought if you wouldn't fight, somebody in the family had to. But I missed you." Over his father's broad shoulder, his eyes sought Retha's. "I missed you all." Her heart swelled at the tentative invitation in his look. This proud, belligerent boy was now hers, too.

He blushed to be caught out. "Besides, the

food was awful," he added. "Not like yours."

She grinned back at him, seeking words to assure him of her love without embarrassing his boy's pride. "I need you around to keep my portions right. Without you, we've had twice the bacon and twice the beans left after every meal."

Andreas trotted back with his blond-headed rider, a conspiratorial smile playing at the corners of his mouth. "Nick and Matty," he boomed, in a voice not unlike Jacob's, "you come help with the real horses."

What in the world? Retha wondered.

"We left two horses in the hollow to bring you children home. Let's go fetch them while your parents pack up."

With a telling nod to Jacob, Andreas winked at her. She understood the sweetness of his conspiracy. He was giving them some precious time alone.

Andreas and the children crossed the stream, Anna Johanna piggyback, and the boys jostling shoulders as they danced from stone to stone, the blood now washed away. All the blood now washed away.

They had come so far, each and every one of them. Anna Johanna, in her deerskin dress, trusted a cousin she scarcely knew to carry her home. Matthias sneaked a piece of sugarcake to eat along the way. Nicholas, subdued after his fight, accepted his father's protecting arm.

Retha's eyes met Jacob's. They had survived, and he had saved her yet again. "I thought you were dead. I thought you were dead," she muttered, turning to the true shelter of her husband's embrace. The sob that rose in her throat was a cry of joy, of wonder. That turned into a cry of pain as he pulled her close.

He released her instantly. "You're badly hurt."

"I'll be all right."

Jacob turned her face to the sun and examined her scraped cheeks, a swollen eye, a purpling jaw. "You don't look all right."

"Neither does Sim Scaife. I slashed his face."

"Ah, that accounts for all the blood." He drew her back to his chest. Now that he knew what Scaife had tried to do to Retha, he did not know what to say. "Sim Scaife is dead."

A medley of feelings played across her face: shock, shame, regret. "Jacob, I must tell you what I didn't know before. He was my uncle. He knew me. He knew my parents. All along, he knew."

"He told me, too," he said, stroking her, absorbing this unexpected twist.

"I should hate him, I suppose. I suppose I do. But how will I ever forgive him?"

"Not all at once, *Liebling*."

They would neither one of them forgive him all at once.

Retha nestled against Jacob's chest. "I can hardly believe you had to rescue me again. You rescued me so many times."

"I cannot think of a single thing that I have done."

She raised her head in disbelief. "You took me into our community. You rescued me from my life as a Single Sister. You saved my wolf. You defended me from my uncle at the mill the day he brought me home from Alice Vogler's. You stood up for me before the town."

" 'Twas . . . 'Twas naught." He sounded puzzled.

" 'Twas everything to me."

"You are my wife, a mother to my children. Of course I defend you." He lifted her chin and kissed her lips with great tenderness, surprising in a man so large. "No, 'tis much more than that. You are my heart."

And at last, she could say the words that had been growing in her heart and she had not known how to say. "I love you, Jacob Blum."

The steadfast love in his indigo gaze told her no other words were needed.

EPILOGUE

July 4, 1783

"You look like a woman in need of rescue." Jacob's breath feathered the curve of Retha's neck, and she felt a familiar thrill of pleasure spiral down it.

"Harmon is a little tired," she answered, gladly handing over their two-year-old son. The chunky towhead insisted that she hold him while his father finished singing, not understanding the burden that his weight added to the unborn child she carried.

It was the twilight of a perfect, windless summer day. Retha leaned into her husband as they blended into the crowd that filled Salem Square in celebration. Governor Alexander Martin proclaimed the fourth day of July a Day of Thanksgiving for Peace. All the townspeople turned out, and Moravians from the nearby settlements walked and rode and drove farm wagons in. Salemites took great pains to ensure that neighboring settlers also heard the news, and they traveled for miles to join in the feasting and listen to the music.

Jacob was flushed, having just finished performing Brother John Frederick Peter's new cantata, and his deep voice was rich and full from a day of singing. On opposite corners of the Square, brass bands played antiphonally: different songs, started at different times, filled the evening air with a joyous cacophony of sound, more rousing, more abundant than birdsong at dawn.

But night was coming on. Soon Salem Square sparkled with the light of dozens of tapers held aloft as almost two hundred celebrants gathered for a final procession through the streets.

"Where's my candle?" Anna Johanna asked, dragging her escort Matthias behind her.

"Check Mama's pockets, Anna Jo. You know what a treasure trove they are," Matthias said in his grown-up, literate way, his voice breaking. Next week he would move to the Brothers House to begin the seven-year apprenticeship to a trade that all boys submitted to. Flush with anticipation, he had told Retha of his hopes to apprentice to the new dyer. If afterwards he turned to the ministry, she couldn't be more proud that the trade he had selected had once been hers.

"Have you seen Mrs. Vogler?" he asked Retha now in quite competent Cherokee. "She said I could practice anytime."

"Over there." Retha pointed across the Square where she had seen the Voglers last, and he bulleted off.

"At first I didn't think he was serious about learning the language," Retha said to Jacob. "Nor did I think he would stick with it. But Alice adores him. He is the first Moravian to come to her for aught."

"Except for you," Jacob reminded her, laughing softly in the dusk and privately squeezing her thickened waist.

Retha felt a sweet heat rise in her cheeks at the thought of that day with Alice, the memory of what her friend had told her about love, and the certain knowledge of how very much more Jacob had taught her. "She is my friend."

Andreas Blum lumbered toward Jacob and Retha through the crowd, a great brown bear next to her husband's gold. He beamed at them as if he had been the matchmaker. "You two look pleased with yourselves. Your caterwauling must be in celebration of the imminent event, cousin."

Jacob grinned at his cousin's teasing while Anna Johanna danced at Andreas's feet.

Andreas bent down on his knee. "You've grown awfully big for this old nag, madame." He lifted her to his shoulders and trotted her off to see the crowd.

Retha watched him fondly. Cousin Andreas, all strength and might, could probably carry her, great though she was with child.

The baby kicked, and Retha could not suppress a little cry. Jacob's arm immediately encircled her aching back. She smiled, grateful, at his loving concern. "It has been a day of ceaseless motion. He must be tired."

Jacob secretly moved a hand to her stomach, feeling for the baby. "She." He grinned, ruffling Harmon's blond Blum hair. "We have enough of boys with straw-colored mops. This one will be a girl, and she will have your golden eyes and amber hair."

Retha flushed at the compliment. "I would just have her healthy. And I would have you here this time."

"I will be here, *Liebling.* No more wartime heroics, now that the soldiers are gone."

Not all the soldiers. Colonel Martin Armstrong, sharp in military dress, strolled up with Nicholas and greeted Jacob and Retha with a hearty warmth that bespoke sincere respect.

"This one tells me that he has become a gunsmith."

Jacob shrugged, not without pride, Retha knew. Nicholas's road had been the hardest of any of the children's. As the war had dragged to its close, he had with difficulty given up his dream of defending his family. But he had never again run away to fight, and had finally found some direction and, oddly, peace in learning the gunsmith's trade.

"We have always made guns, Colonel. For hunting," Jacob added wryly.

"For protection, too," Andreas goaded genially, returning with his rider from a quick trot through the crowd.

"Not lately," Jacob said. "Lately, everything is calm."

Everything, Retha thought. Even the dreams had stopped. Even her parents' old disputed property was settled. Jacob had pursued the intricacies of its title all the way to the governor's office. It belonged to the Moravians now. But the waterfall would always be a special place for family outings—and a secret escape for her and Jacob when the Ernsts could watch the children.

Then she felt the first clear pang. "Jacob, go find Sister Sarah," she gasped. "I think your Elisabeth is ready."

"Oh, no, I will not leave you this time. I am taking you home this minute." Joy and paternal panic warred on his face as he swept her off her feet.

"I can walk," she protested, laughing at the way this experienced father fell apart.

"Not now, *Liebling,* not while I have arms to hold you," he said with a tender concern that lifted her heart and braced her for the ordeal before her.

"The event is hours off."

"Nicholas can go for Sister Sarah. You can walk another day."

"There's no need for such heroics, husband. This is not a rescue." But it was, and she well knew it. For Jacob Blum had always rescued her, from the very first time they met. His steadfast love had seen her through her darkest fears and buried secrets, and he would always be her hero.

HISTORICAL NOTE

On July 4, 1783, in Salem, North Carolina, Moravians responded to Governor Alexander Martin's proclamation of a Day of Thanksgiving for Peace with an entire day and evening of music-making and feasting. It was arguably the first Fourth of July celebration in the new nation, for that first year the other states in the new union celebrated in December, and no one else in North Carolina seems to have bothered.

A wealth of detail about the Moravians survives in meticulous diaries kept by each settlement as well as by literate individuals. Many events in this novel happened: Sister Baumgarten's cow was troublesome, Brother Bonner's beating alarmed the town, the mill was repaired so that grain could be ground for the troops, and a thousand pairs of shoes were ordered and delivered.

Local militia, popularly called Liberty Men in North Carolina, acted fairly independently of the Continental Army. Fighting in the Carolinas had all the trappings of a bitter civil war. Tory neighbor engaged Whig neighbor, and brothers crossed swords. For all that the Liberty Men were patriotic and effective, at least one, William Lenoir, harassed Moravians, unconvinced by their claim of neutrality.

Lenoir inspired Sim Scaife's prejudices against the Moravians, but Scaife is otherwise wholly imaginary. Billeting of troops in Salem homes occurred mainly in February 1781, when both General Cornwallis's Redcoats and General Nathaniel Greene's Continentals came up from South Carolina. The latter stole cattle, coin, and laundry. Salem got off lightly compared to Bethania, one of the outlying Moravian settlements, which was virtually sacked.

Throughout the war, Moravians fostered good relationships with both armies, but particularly the Continentals. Their refusal to fight was tolerated largely, it is thought, because the armies needed their supplies more than they needed more men in arms. Though most Moravians paid the threefold tax required to avoid service, some were pressed into service. Jacob Blum's rescue of his cousin Andreas is based on my own great-great-great-great grandfather Adam Spach's rescue of his eldest son, Adam, who was drafted by local Surrey militia. Unlike the Quakers, Moravians were not true pacifists. By the time of the Civil War, Moravians could be found fighting on either side.

Moravians continued to arrange marriages by the drawing of the lot into the first quarter of the nineteenth century. In the love match of John Vogler, the clockmaker, and his wife Christina, seven lots were cast before their marriage was sanctioned. Their elegant home has been restored to its 1825 condition, and along with many other carefully restored homes and buildings, is open for tours at Old Salem in Winston-Salem, North Carolina.

During the Revolutionary War, a chandler named Jacob Blum practiced his craft in Salem. Apart from sharing my hero's name and his penchant for political trips that took him out of town, he bore no resemblance to Retha's Jacob.

JUDITH STANTON, formerly a university professor, now writes full time. She lives in North Carolina.